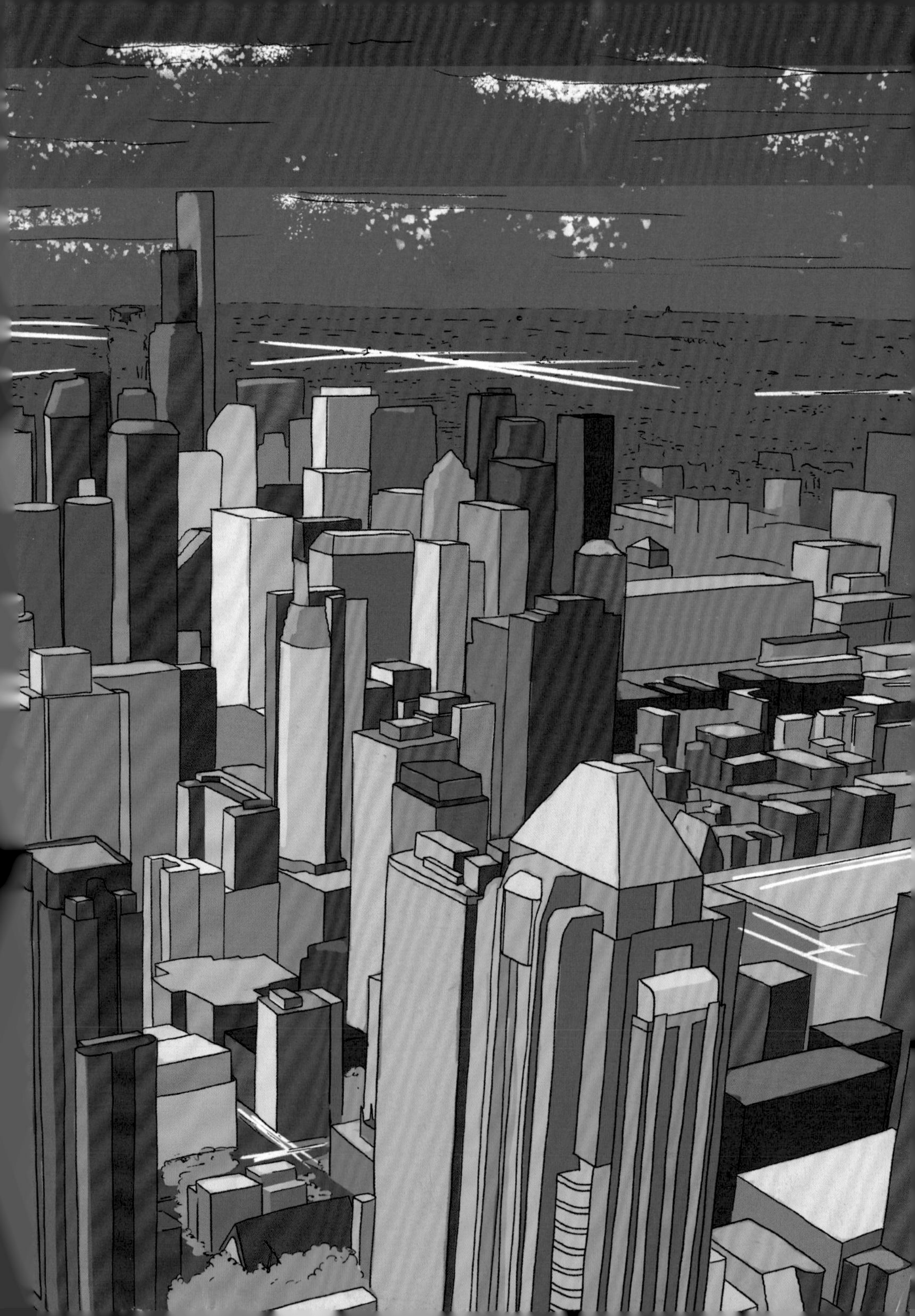

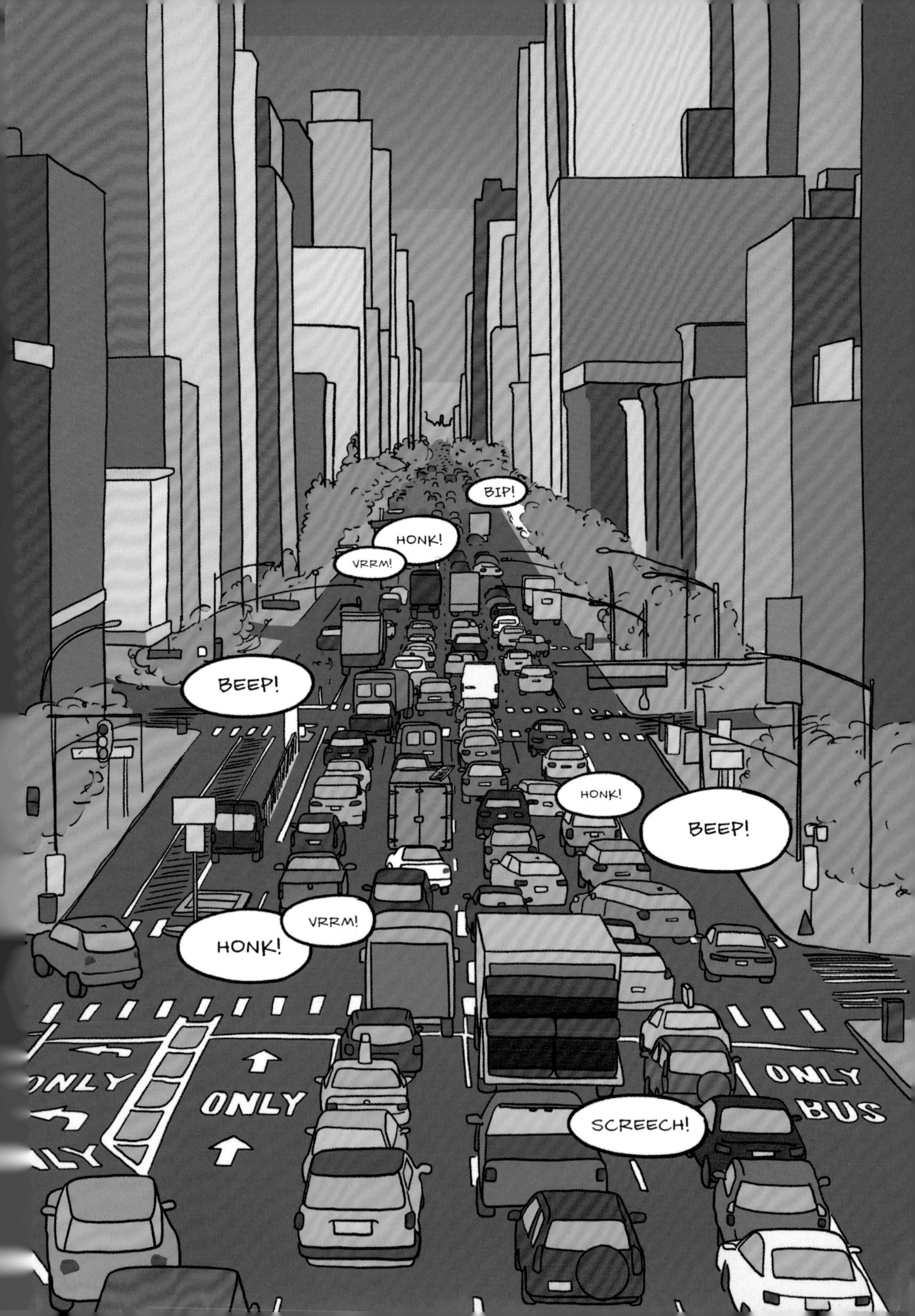
BIP!
HONK!
VRRM!
BEEP!
HONK!
BEEP!
VRRM!
HONK!
ONLY
ONLY
BUS
SCREECH!

For Bonnie, Boston,
Miller, and Sully

You are even more extraordinary
than I imagined.

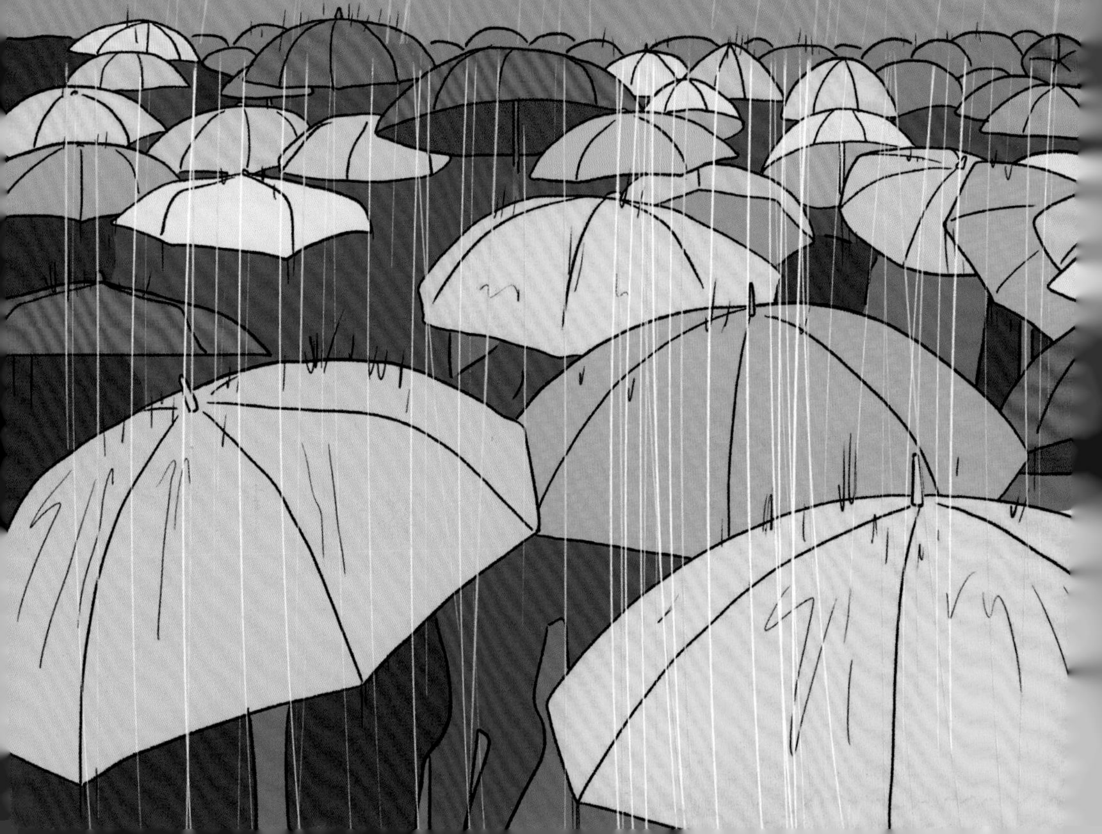

THE ODDS
RUN, ODDS, RUN

words and pictures by
Matt Stanton

An Imprint of HarperCollinsPublishers

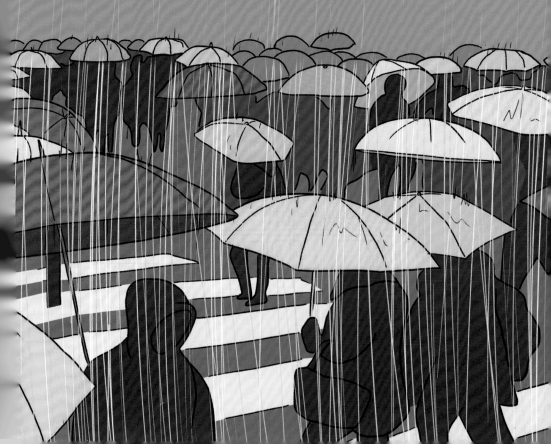

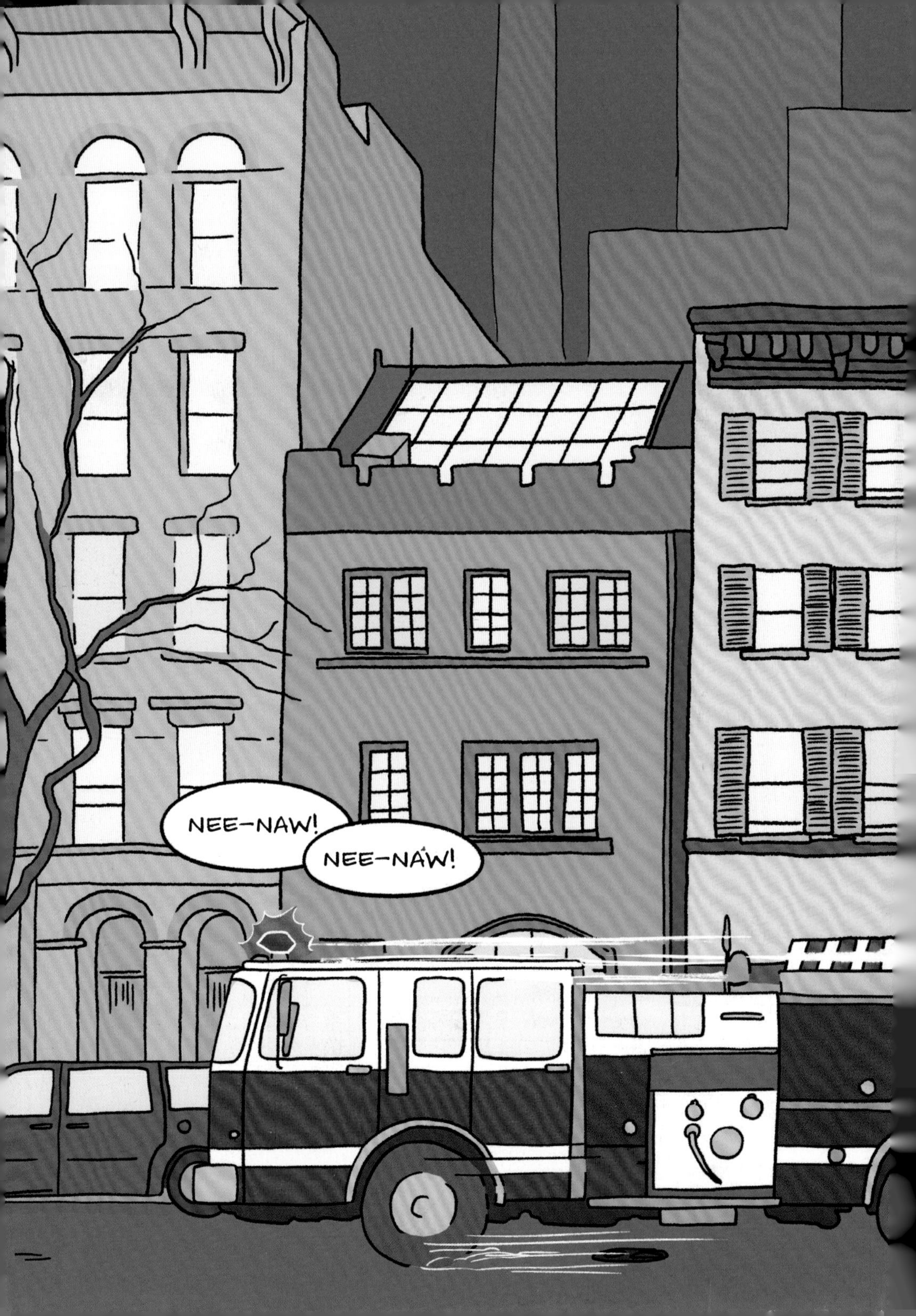
NEE-NAW!
NEE-NAW!

CHAPTER ONE
The Odds are a problem

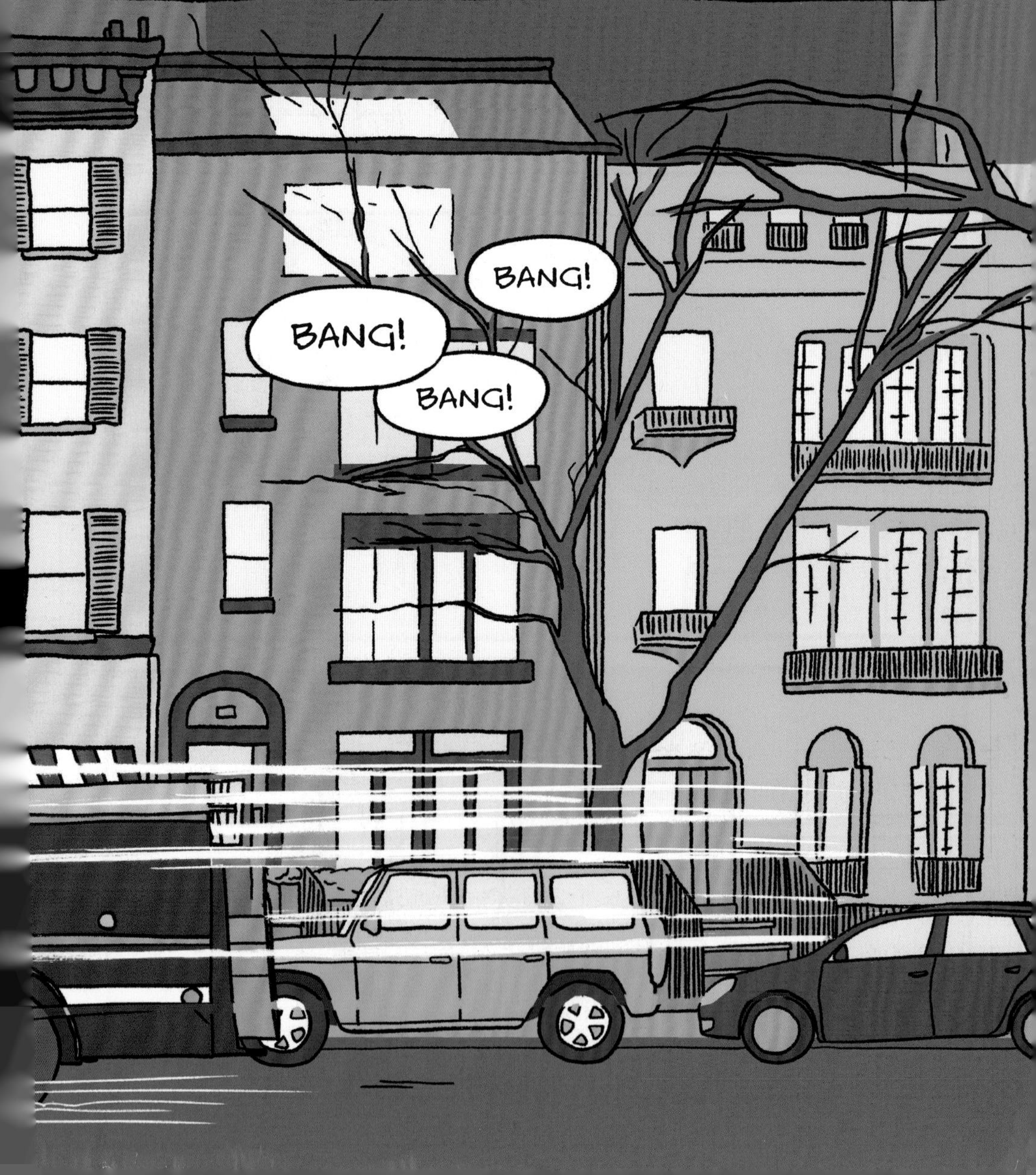
BANG!
BANG!
BANG!

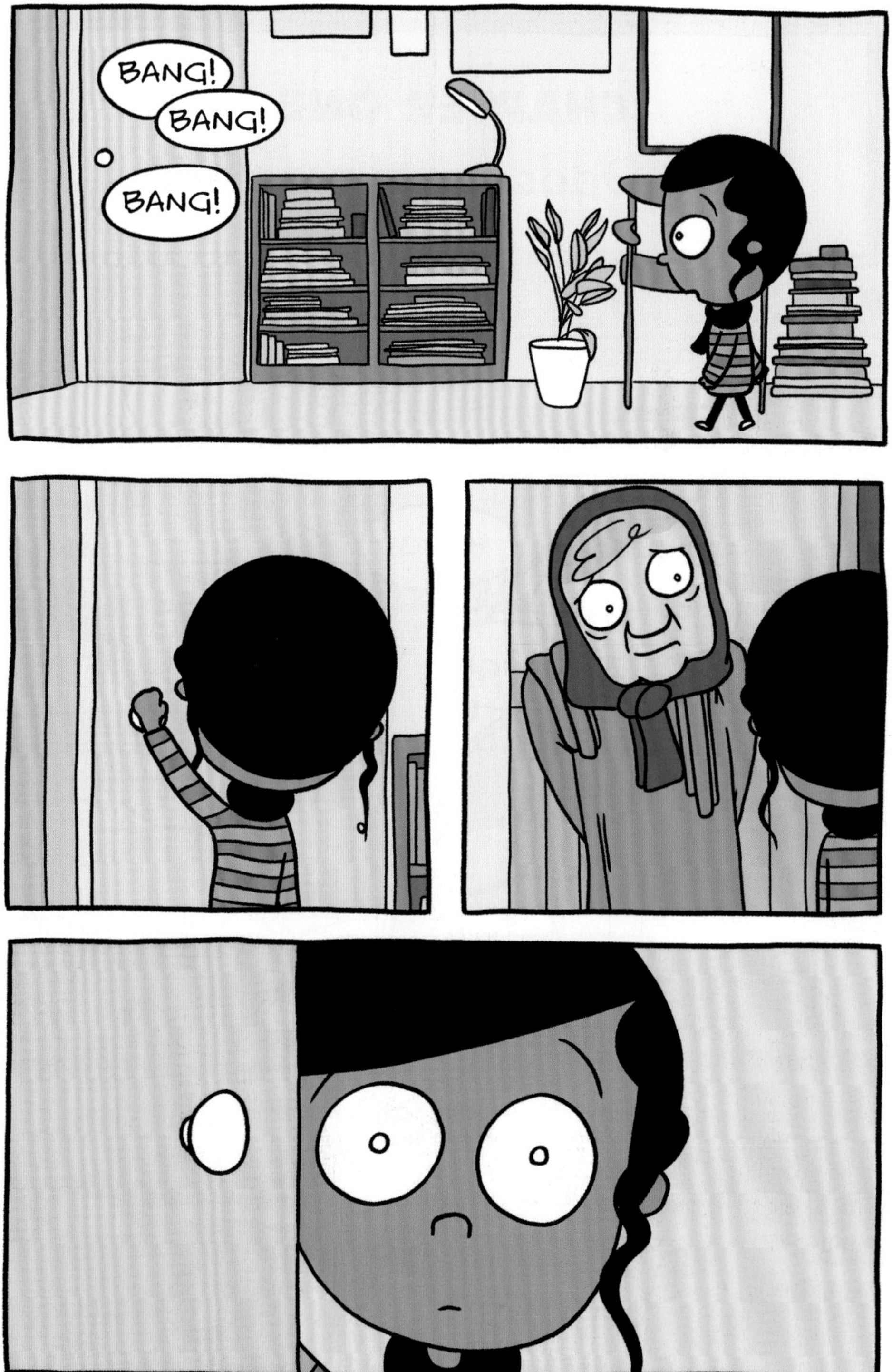
BANG!
BANG!
BANG!

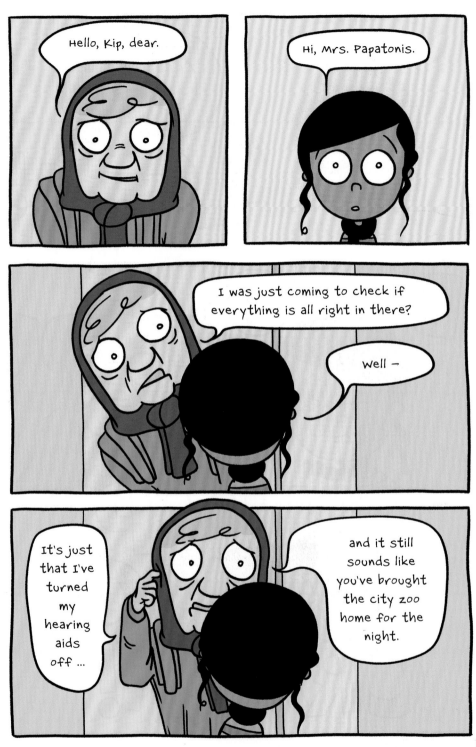

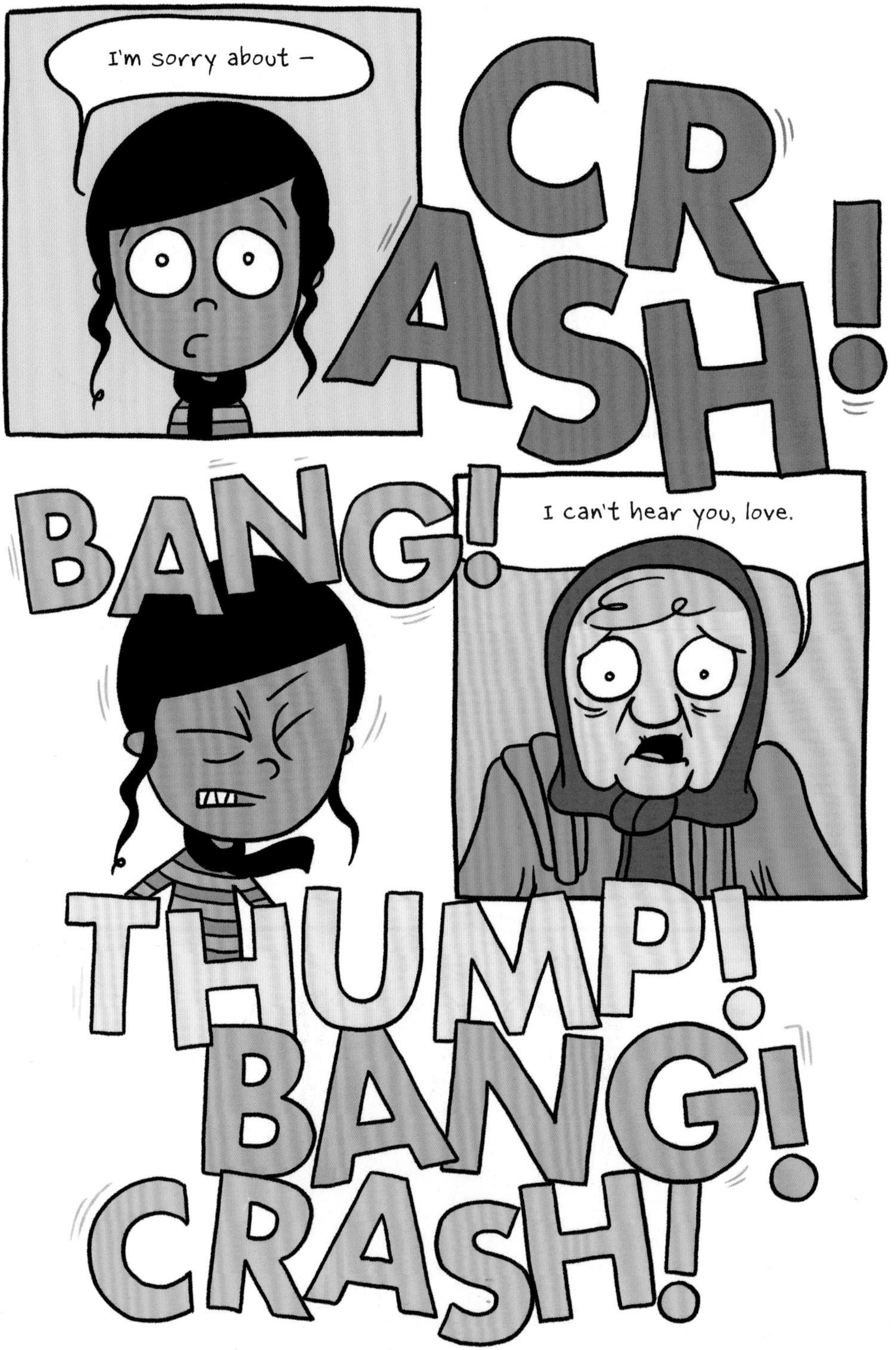

I'm sorry about –
CRASH!
BANG!
I can't hear you, love.
THUMP!
BANG!
CRASH!

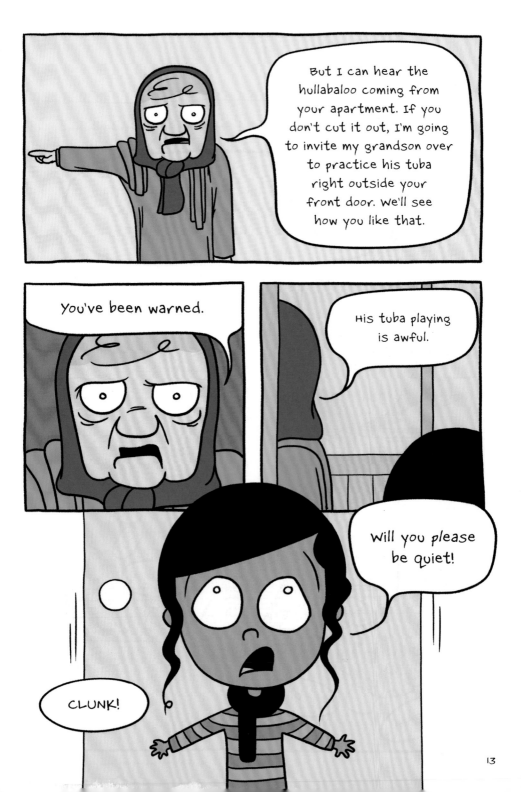

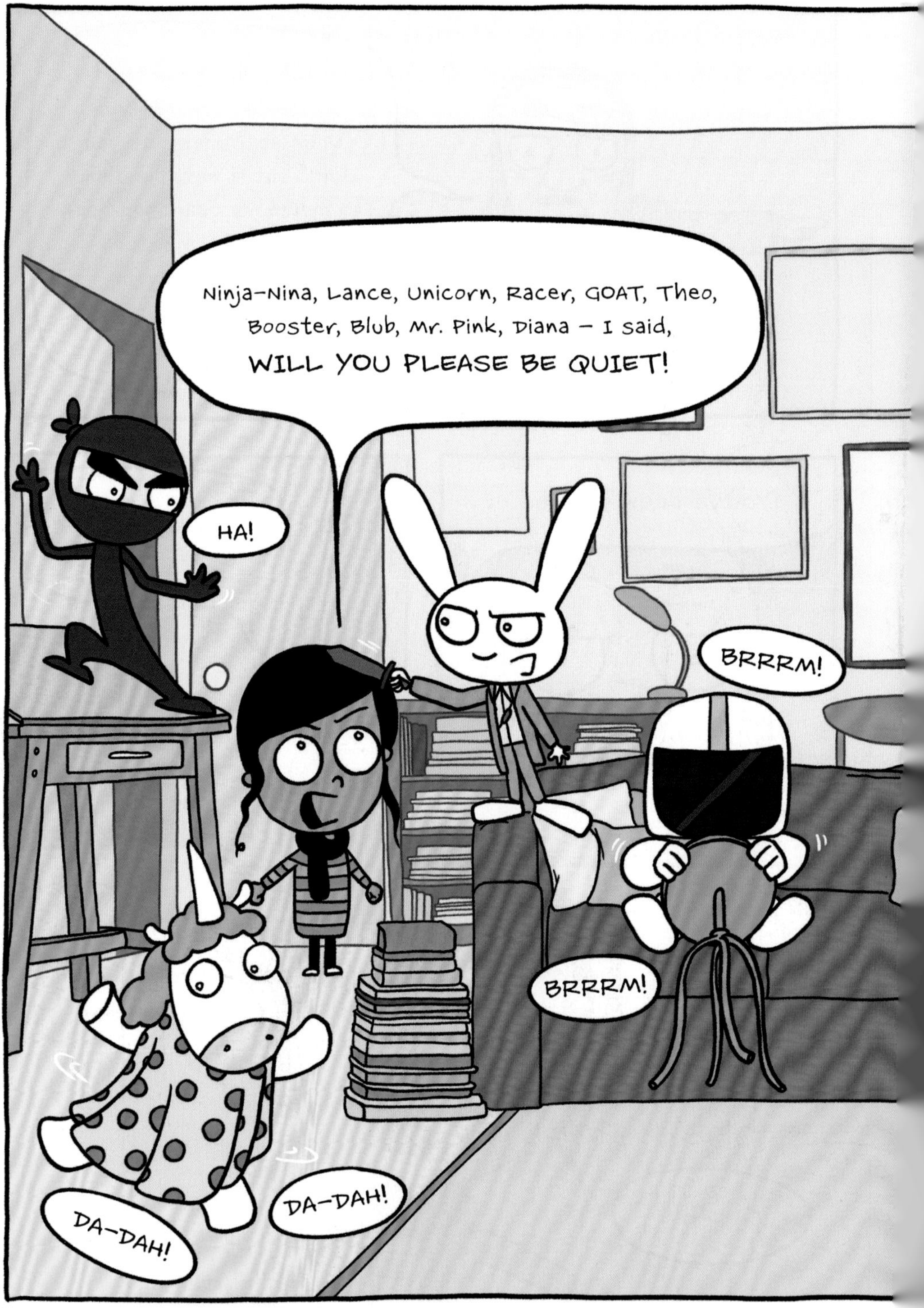
Ninja-Nina, Lance, Unicorn, Racer, GOAT, Theo, Booster, Blub, Mr. Pink, Diana – I said, WILL YOU PLEASE BE QUIET!
HA!
BRRRM!
BRRRM!
DA-DAH!
DA-DAH!

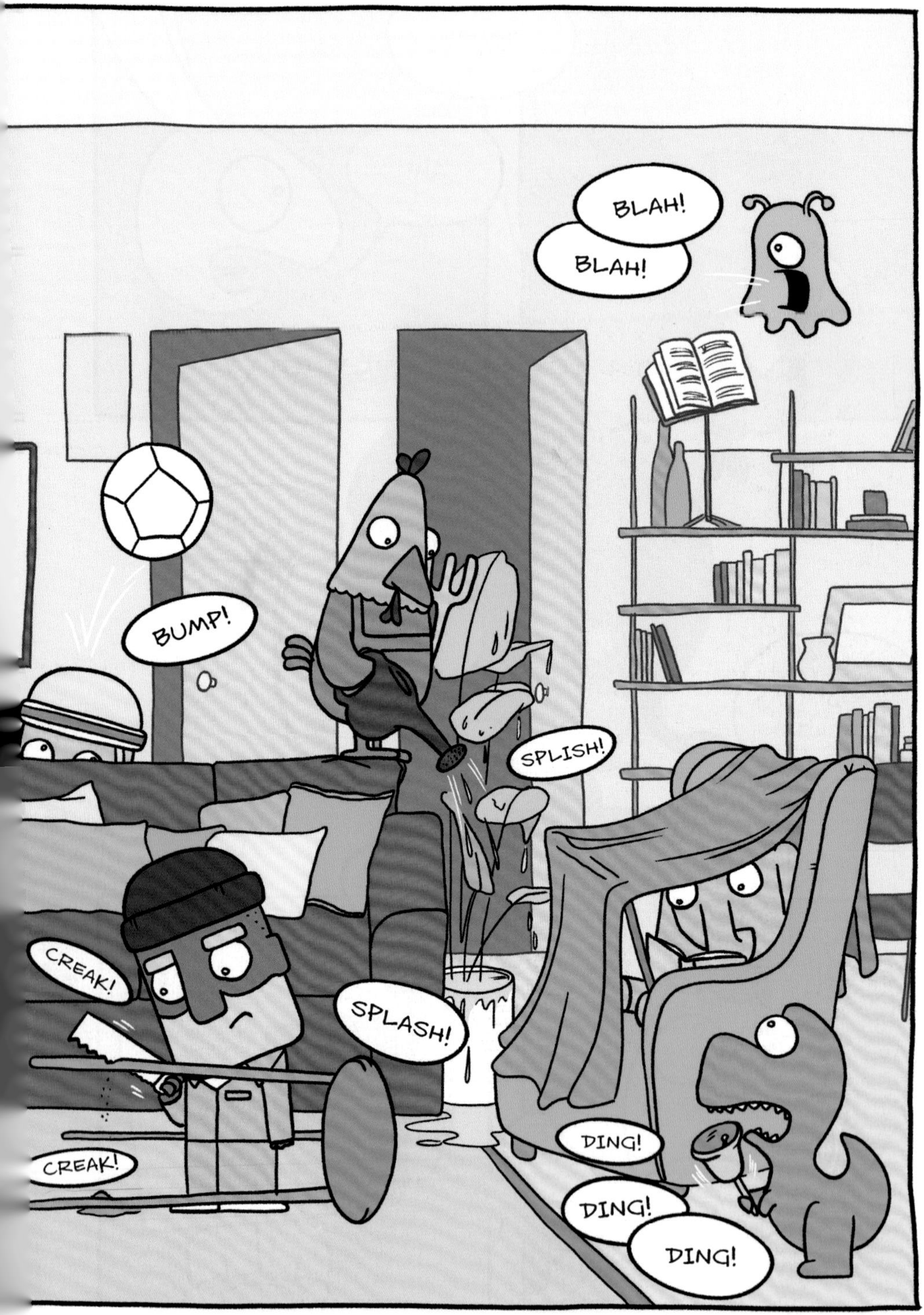
BLAH!
BLAH!
BUMP!
SPLISH!
CREAK!
SPLASH!
CREAK!
DING!
DING!
DING!

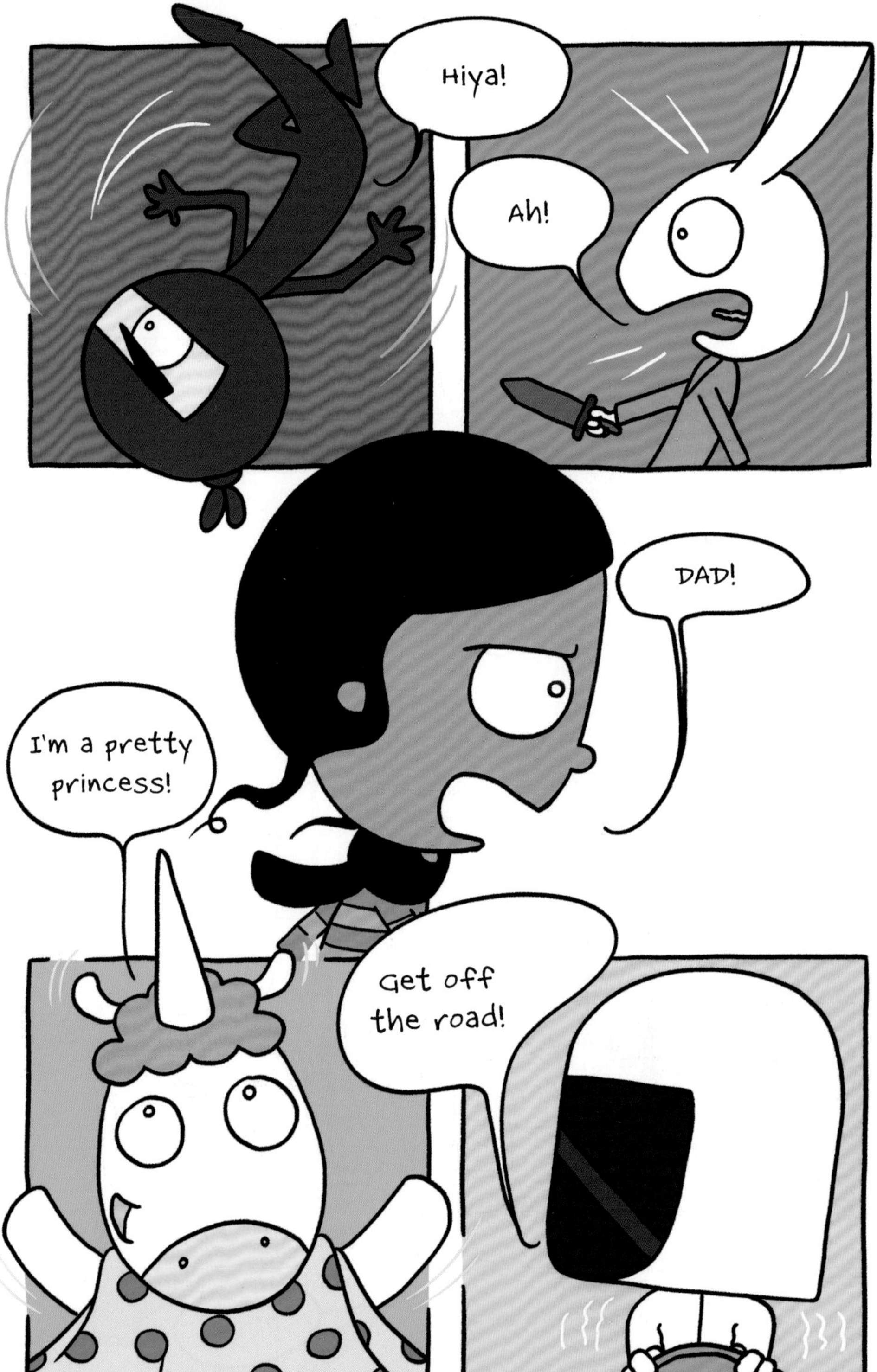
Hiya!
Ah!
DAD!
I'm a pretty princess!
Get off the road!

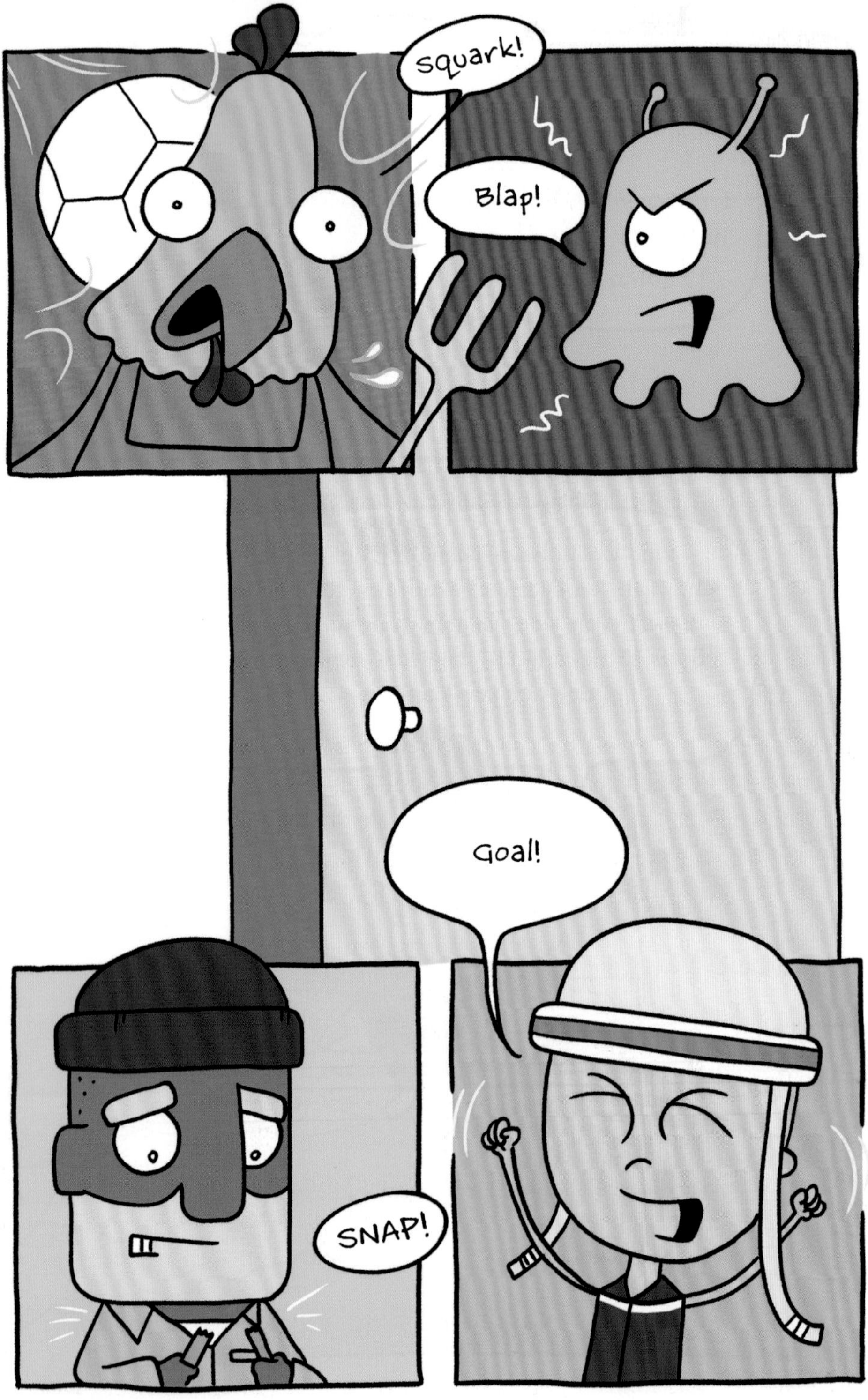
Squark!
Blap!
Goal!
SNAP!

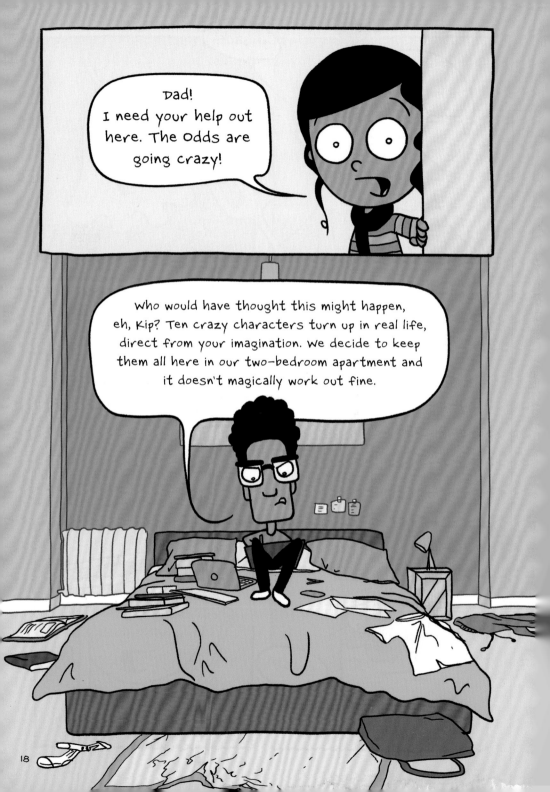

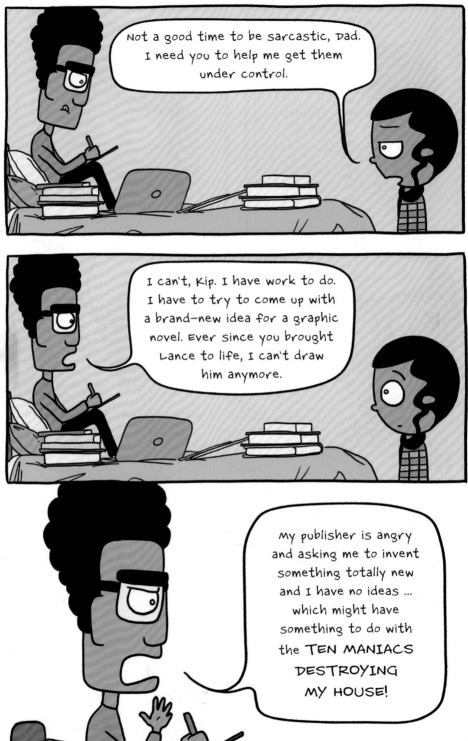

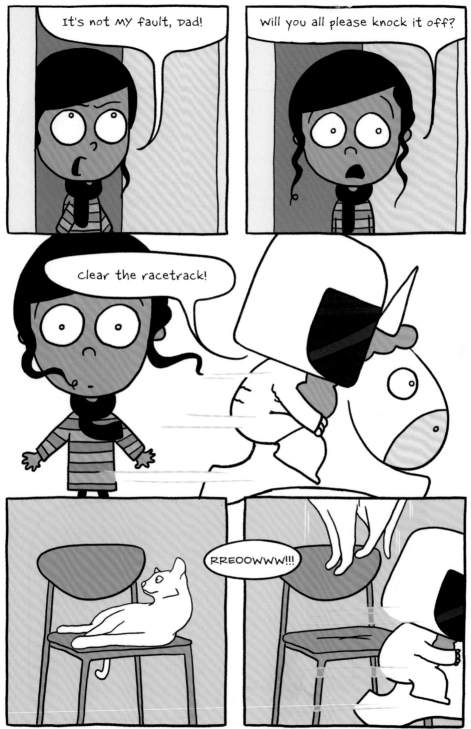

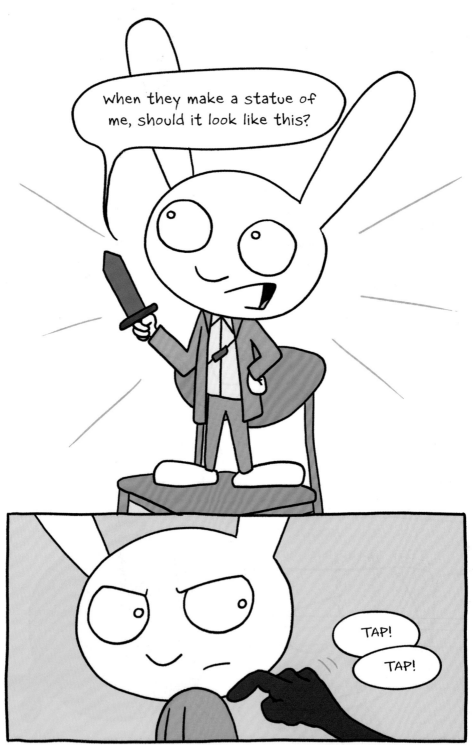

21

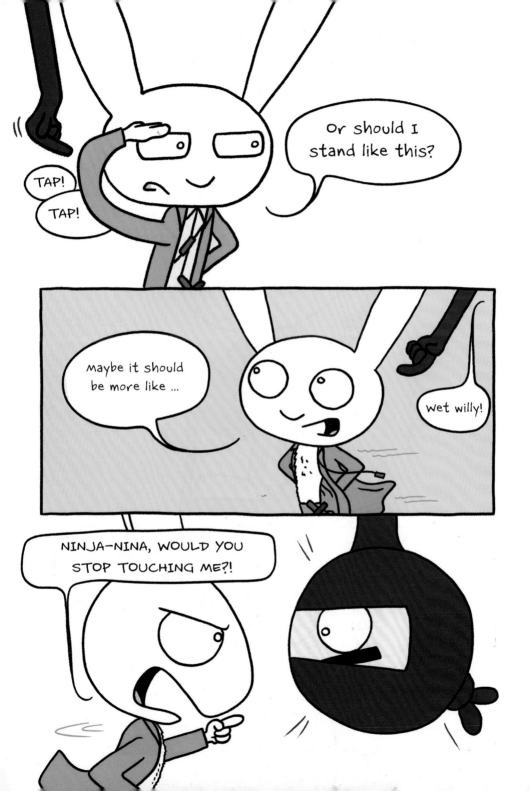

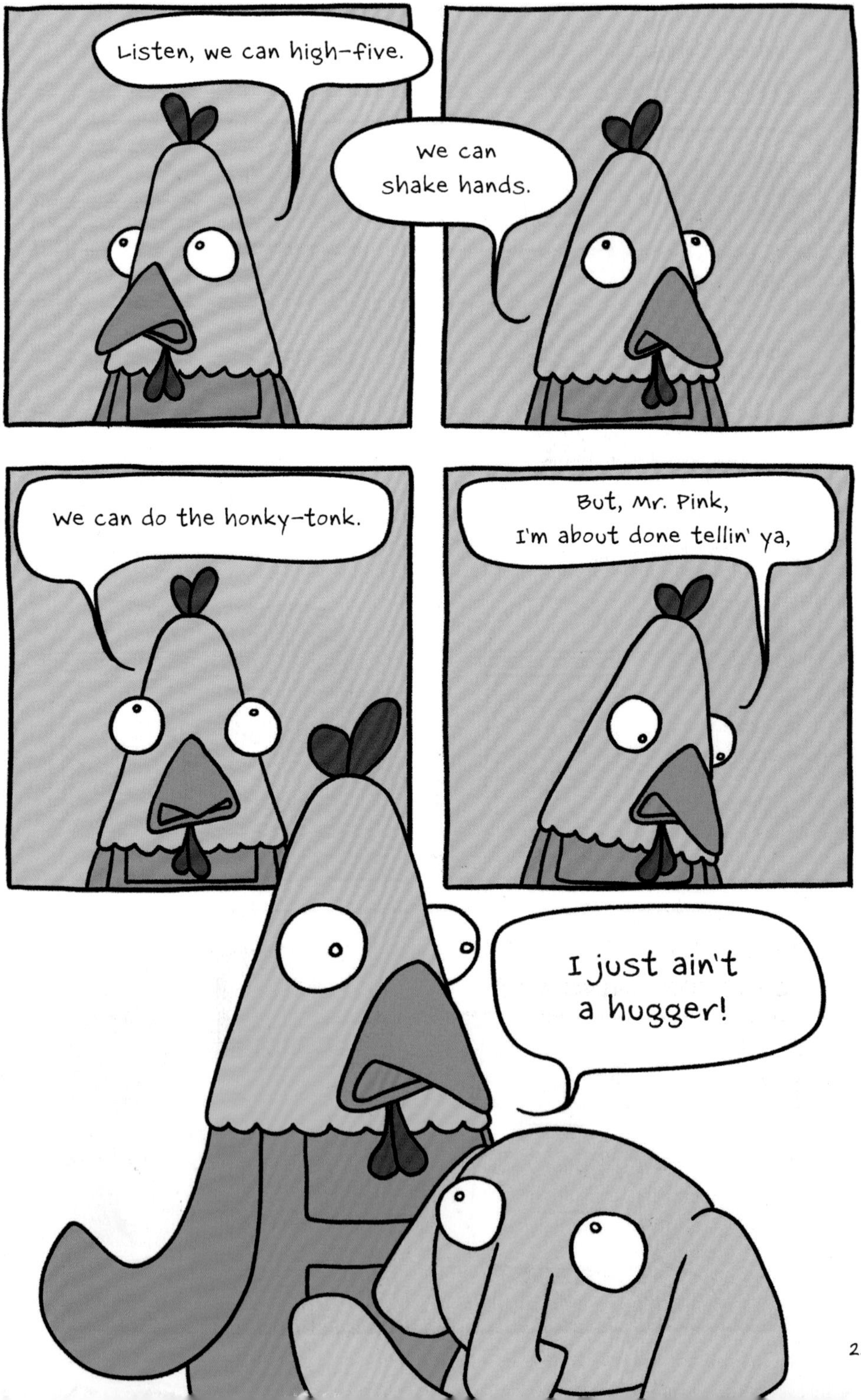
Listen, we can high-five.
We can shake hands.
We can do the honky-tonk.
But, Mr. Pink, I'm about done tellin' ya,
I just ain't a hugger!

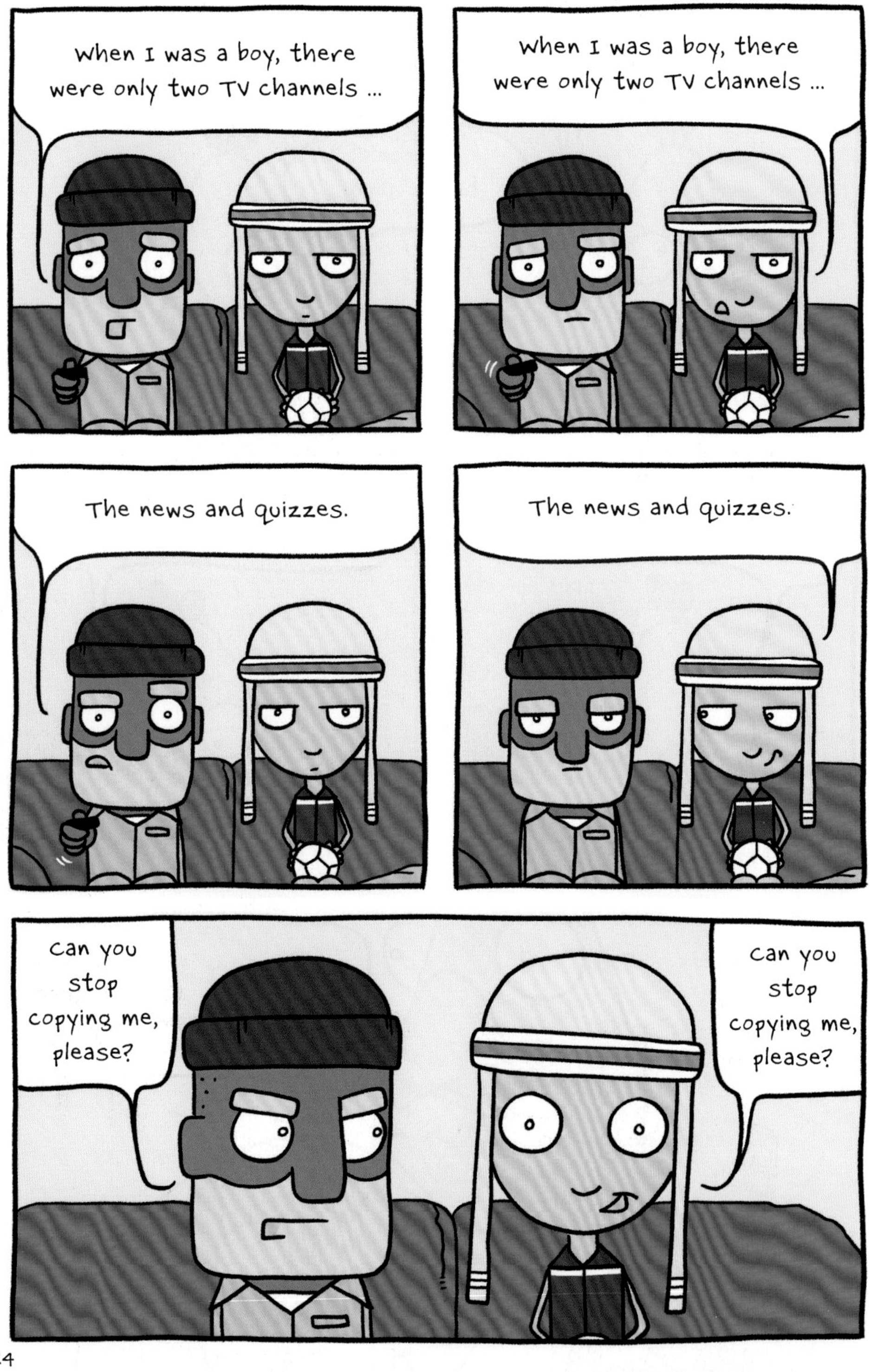
When I was a boy, there were only two TV channels ...
When I was a boy, there were only two TV channels ...
The news and quizzes.
The news and quizzes.
Can you stop copying me, please?
Can you stop copying me, please?

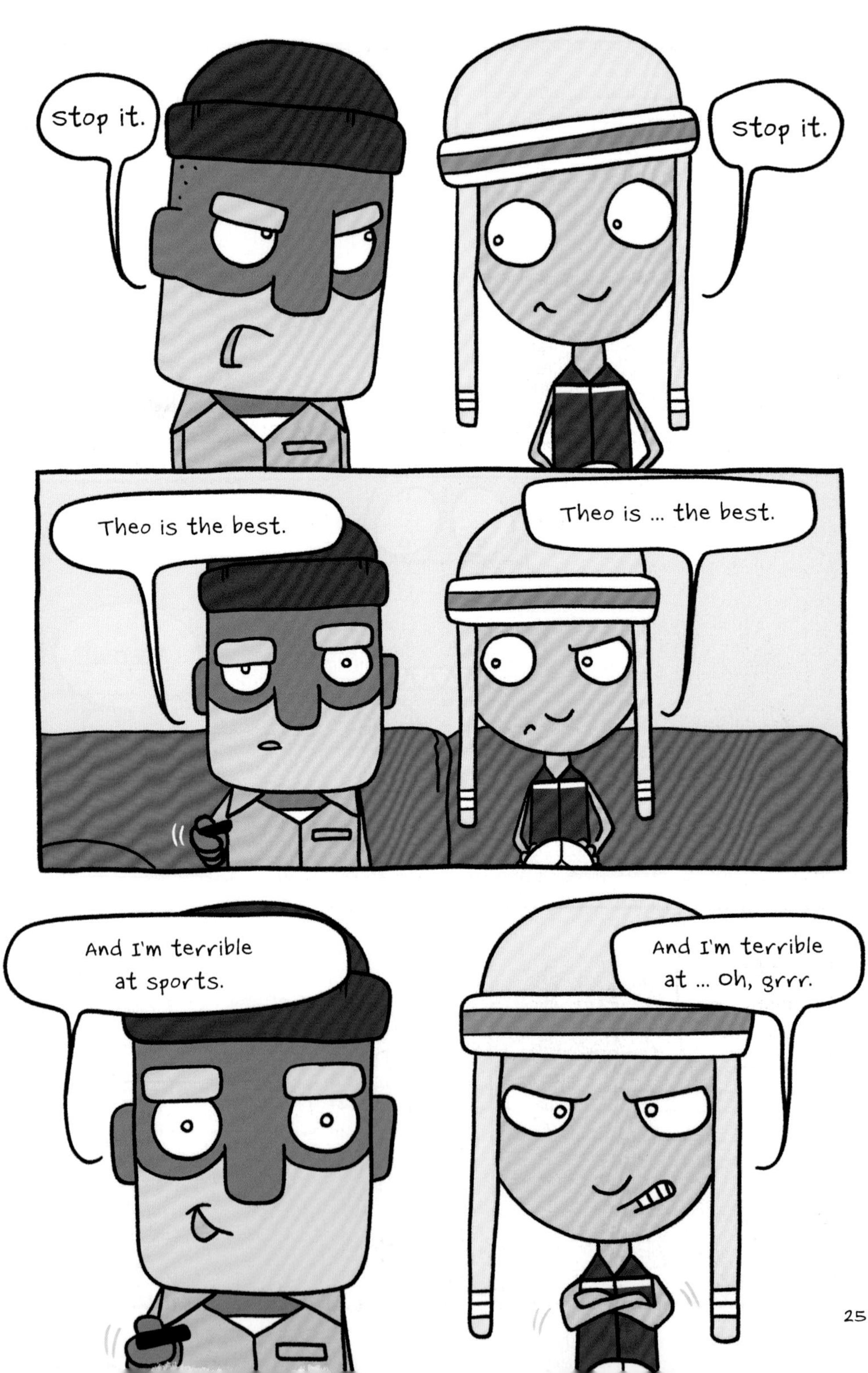
Stop it.
Stop it.
Theo is the best.
Theo is ... the best.
And I'm terrible at sports.
And I'm terrible at ... Oh, grrr.

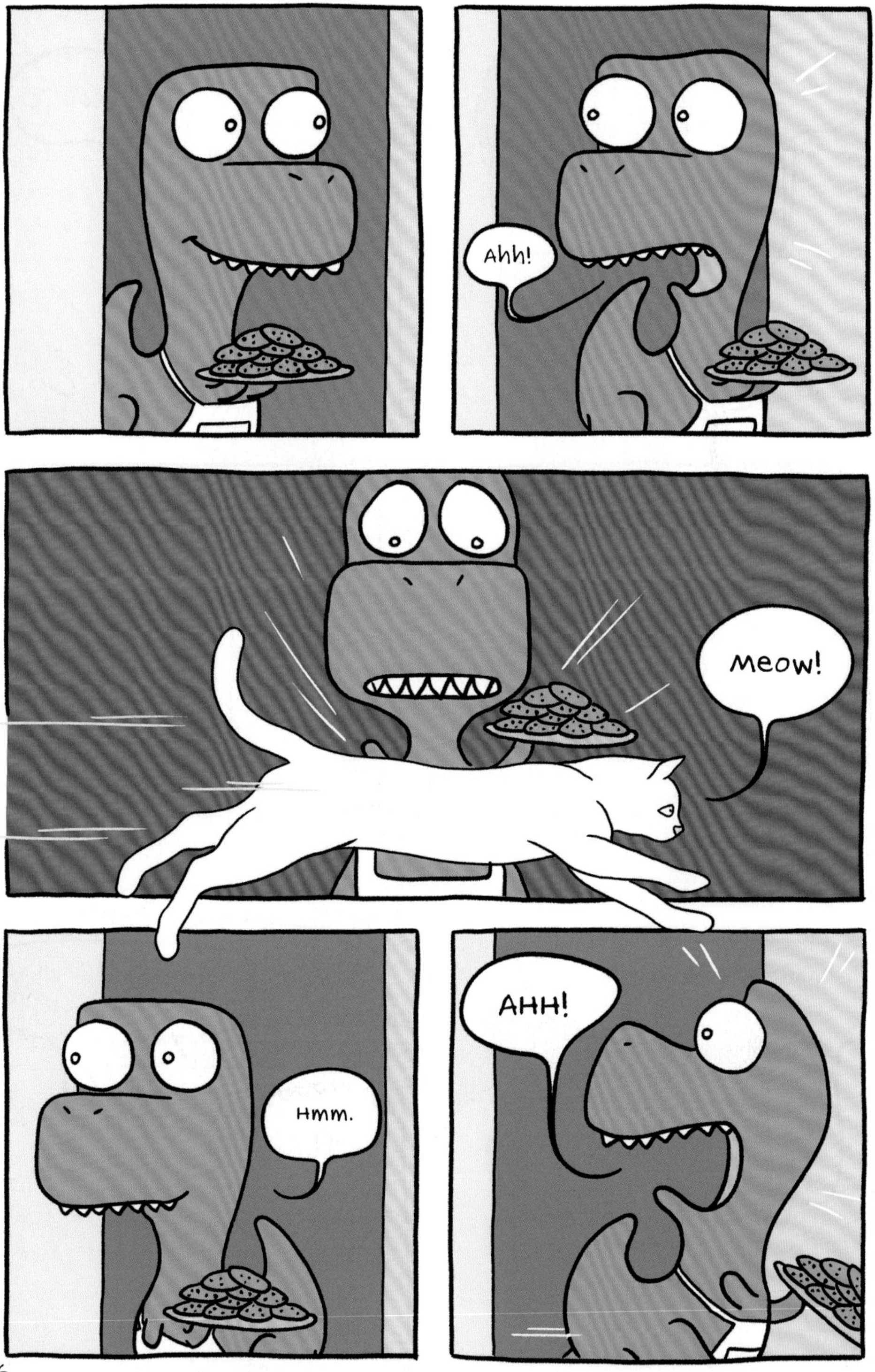
Ahh!
Meow!
Hmm.
AHH!

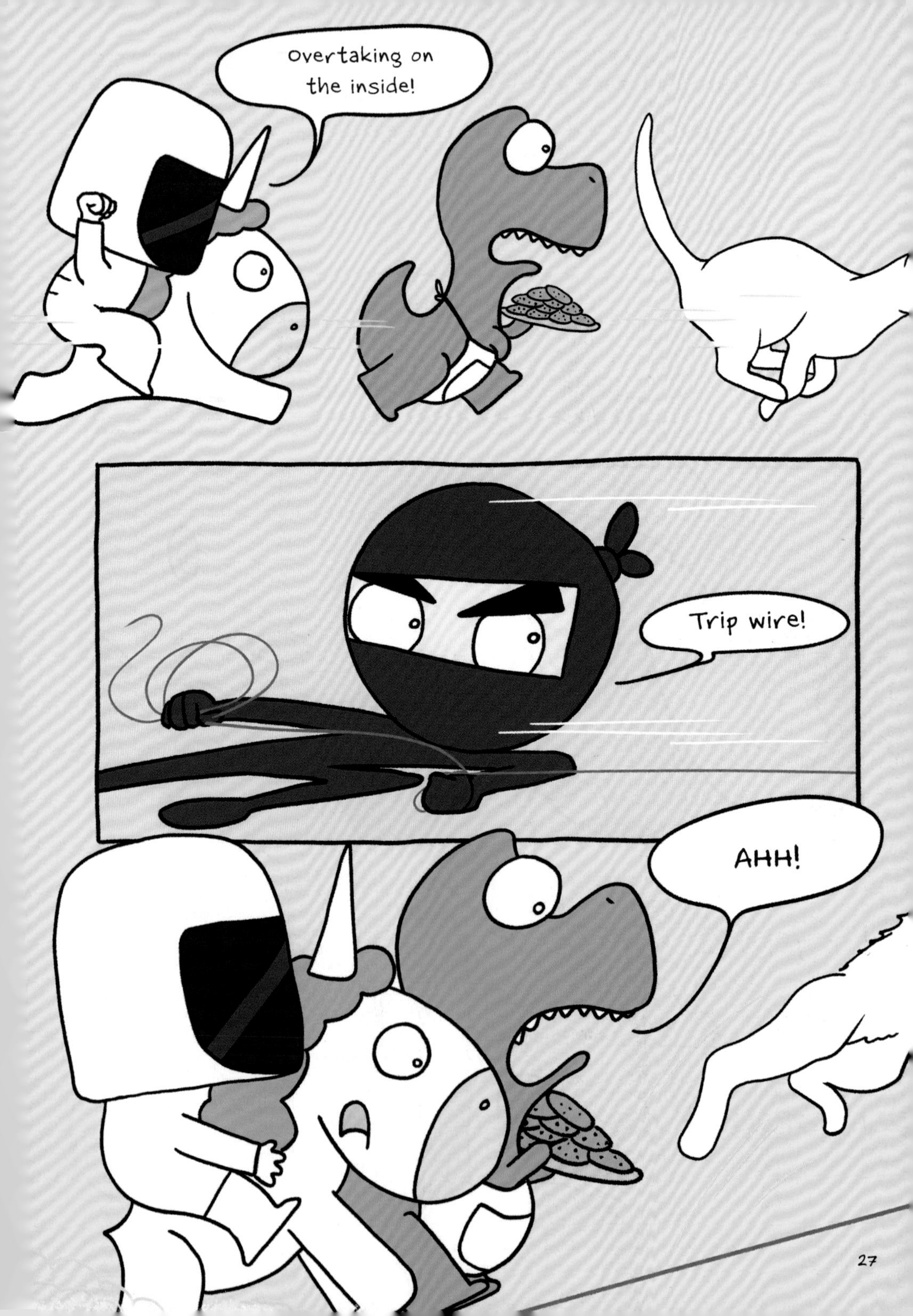

Overtaking on the inside!
Trip wire!
AHH!

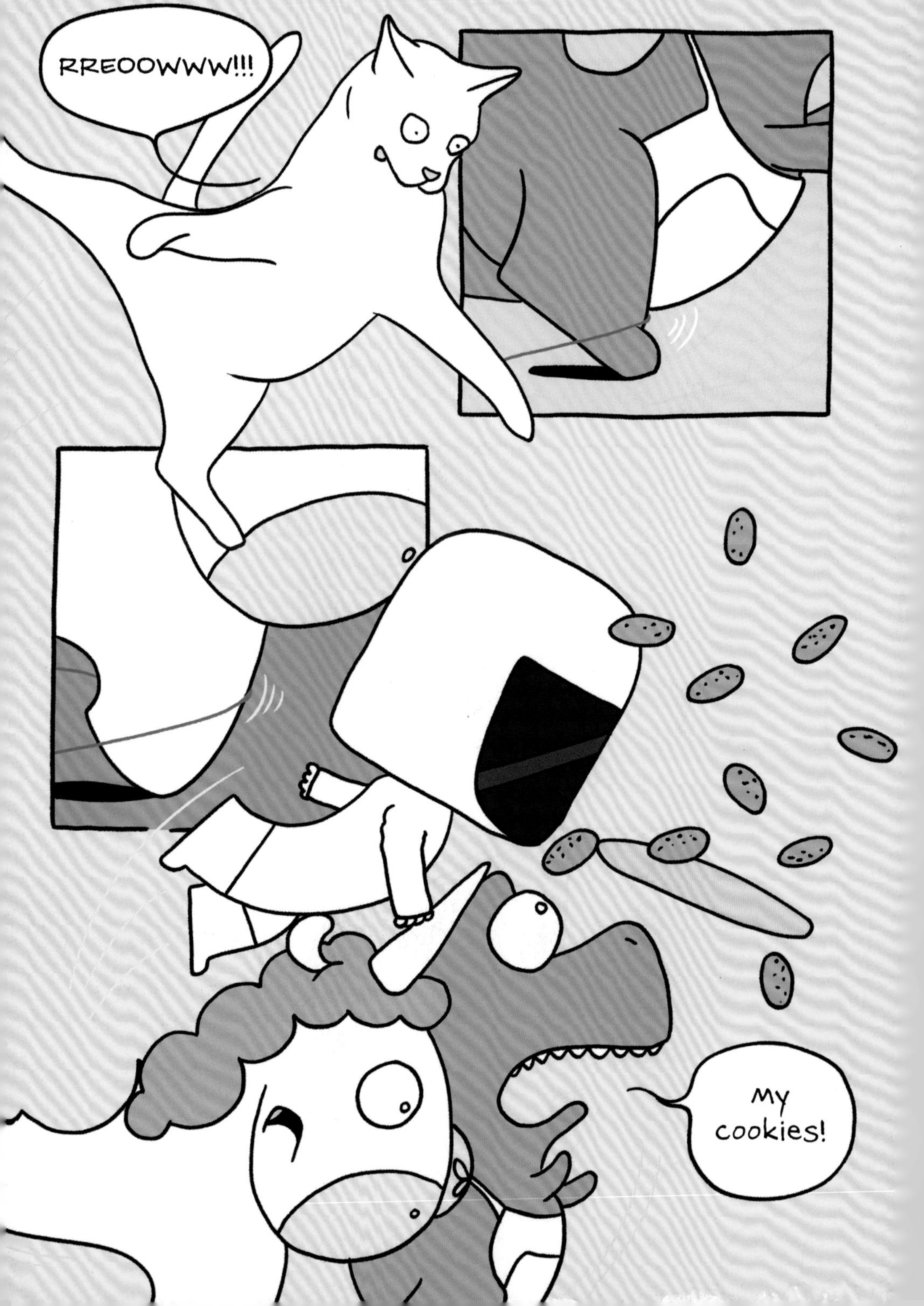
RREOOWWW!!!
My cookies!

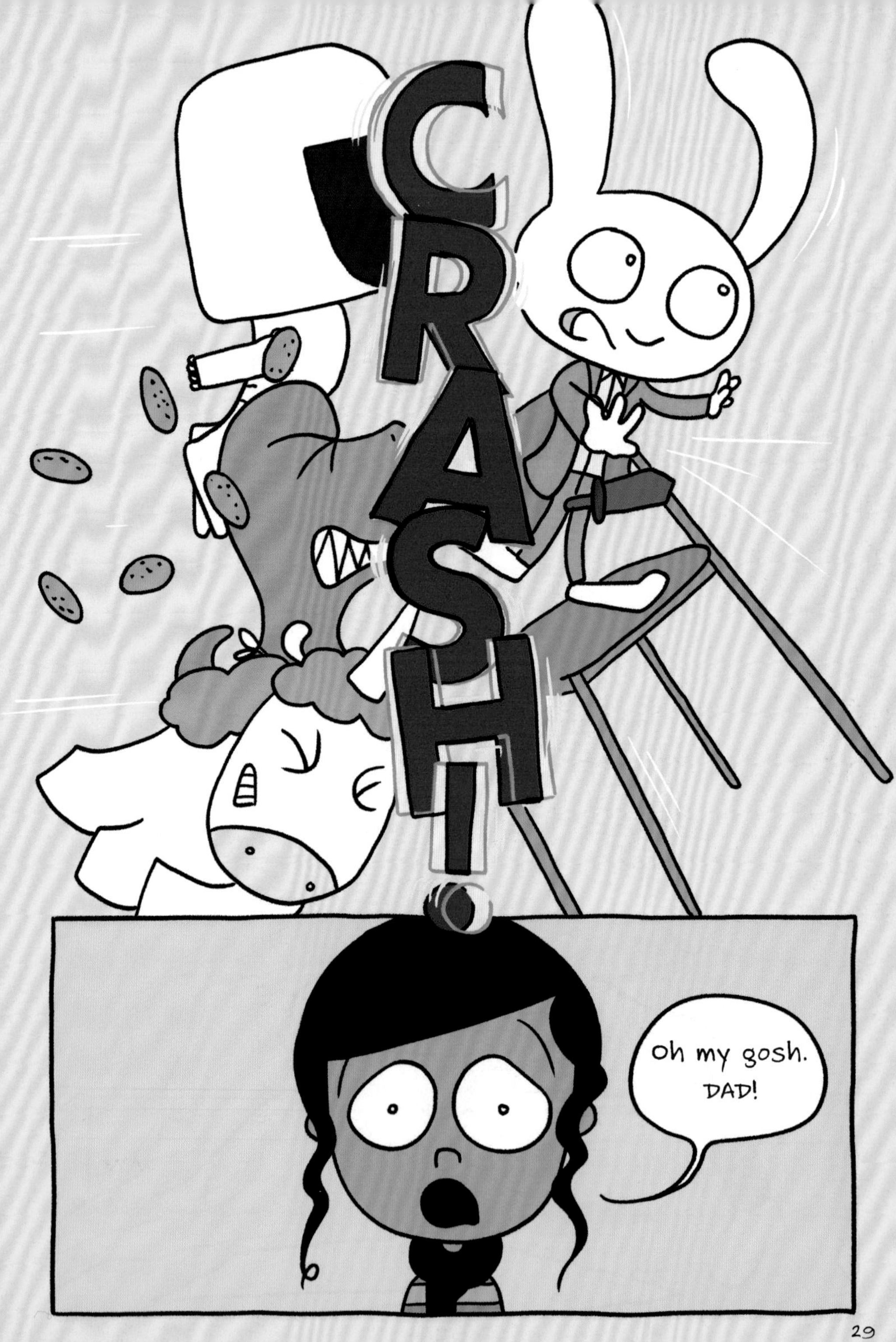
CRASH!
Oh my gosh.
DAD!

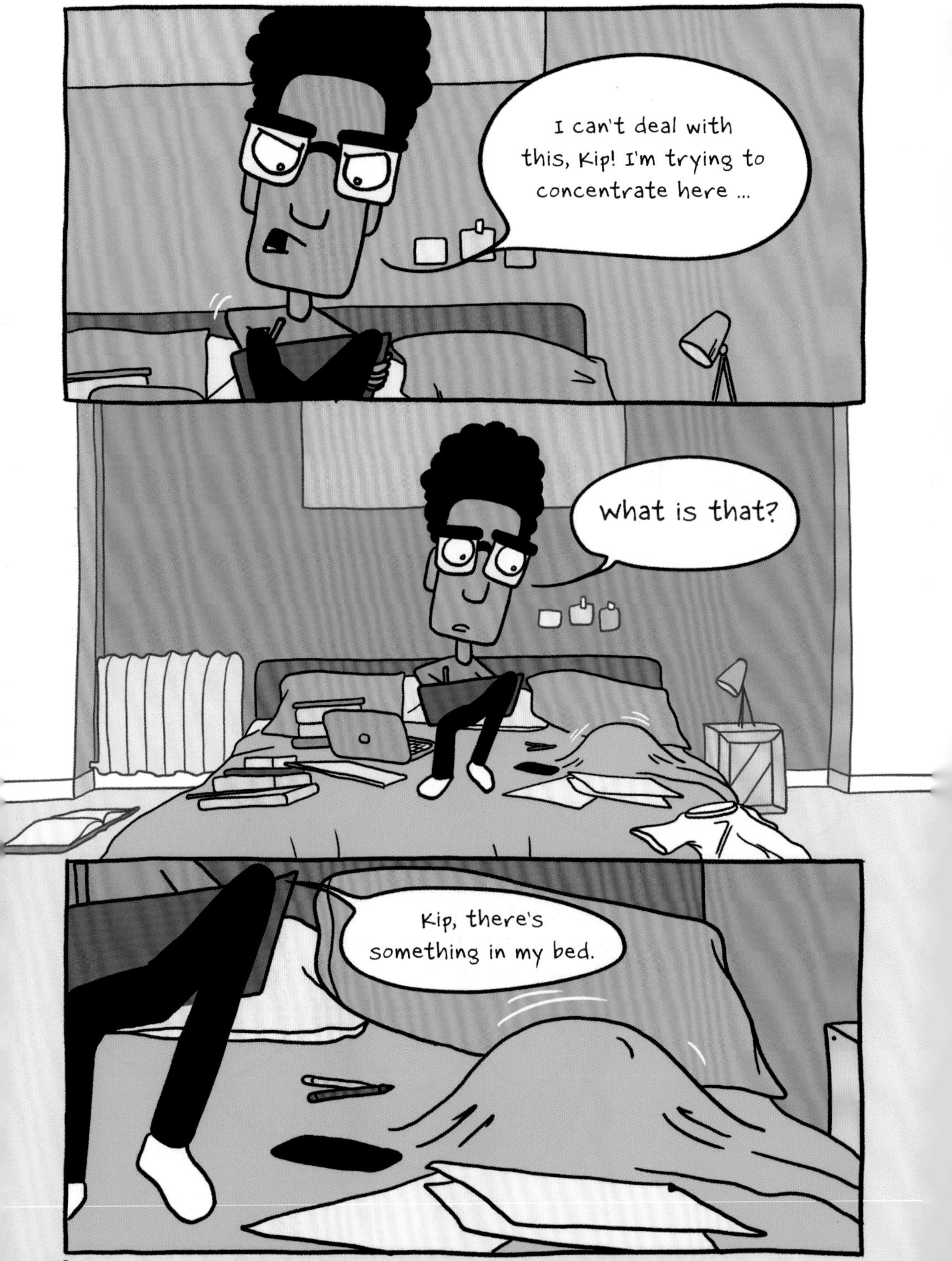
I can't deal with this, Kip! I'm trying to concentrate here ...
What is that?
Kip, there's something in my bed.

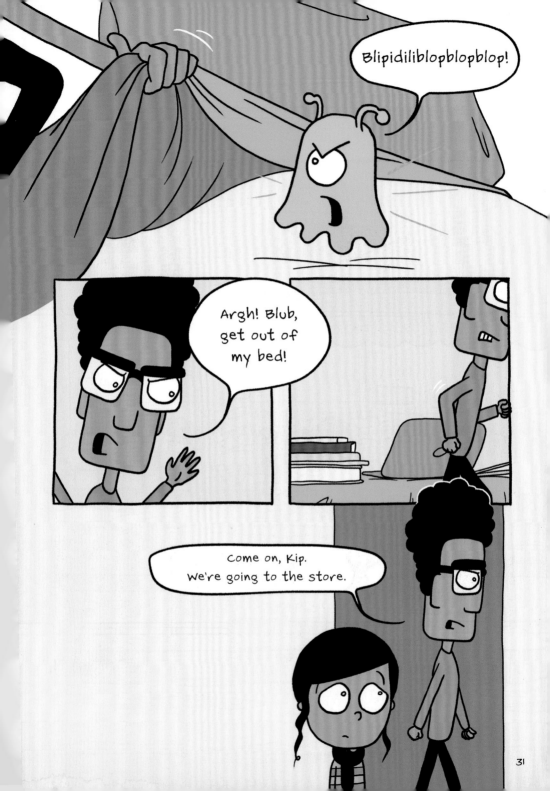

31

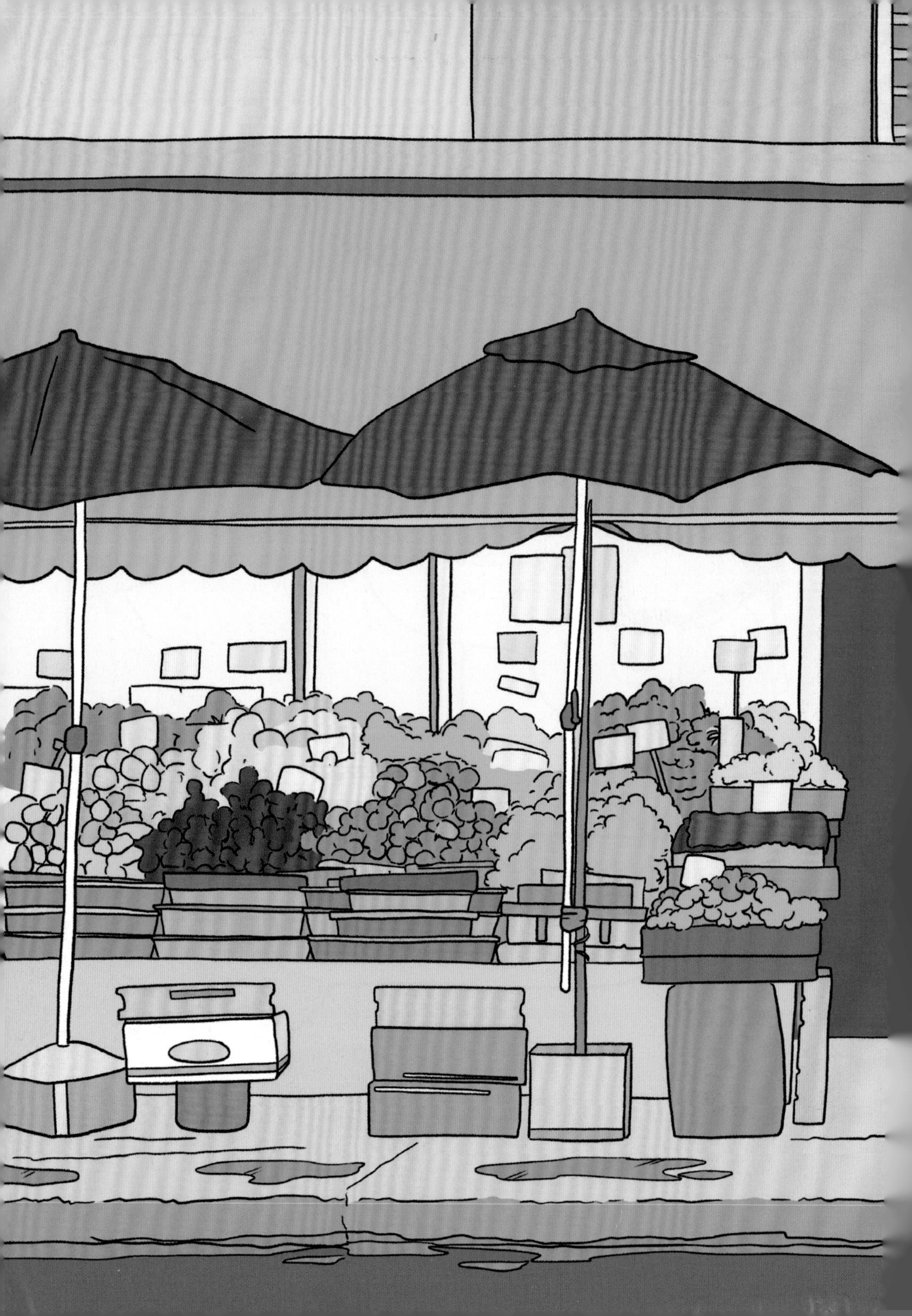

CHAPTER TWO
An odd visitor

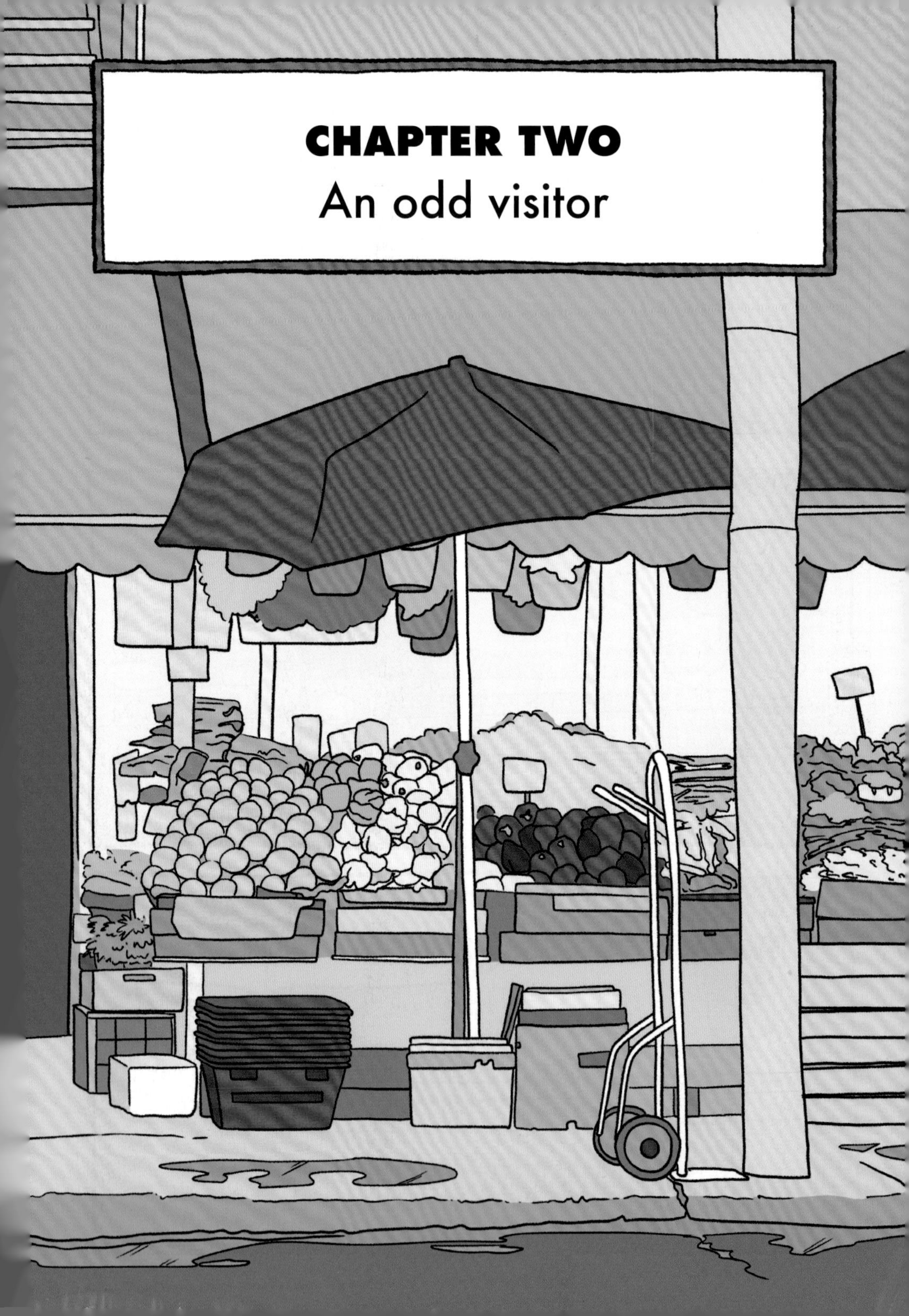

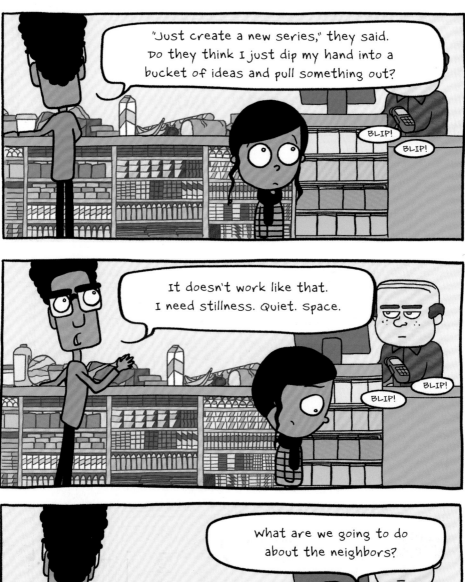
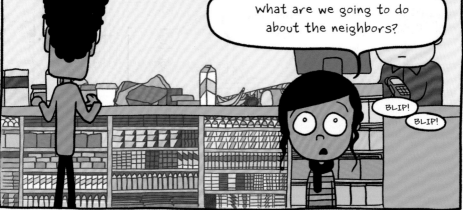

34

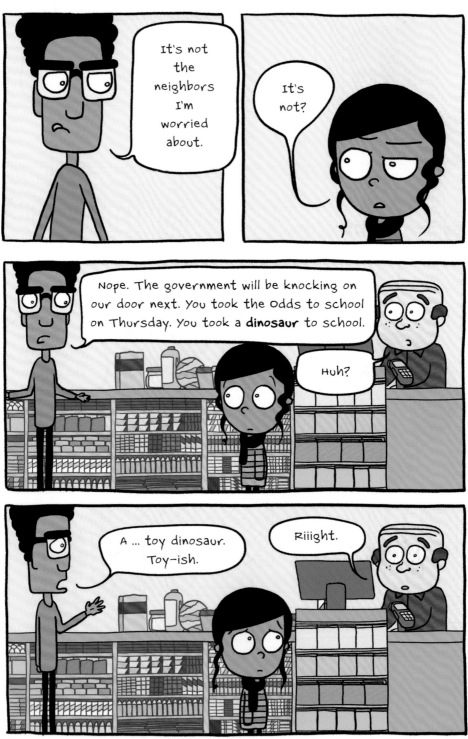

35

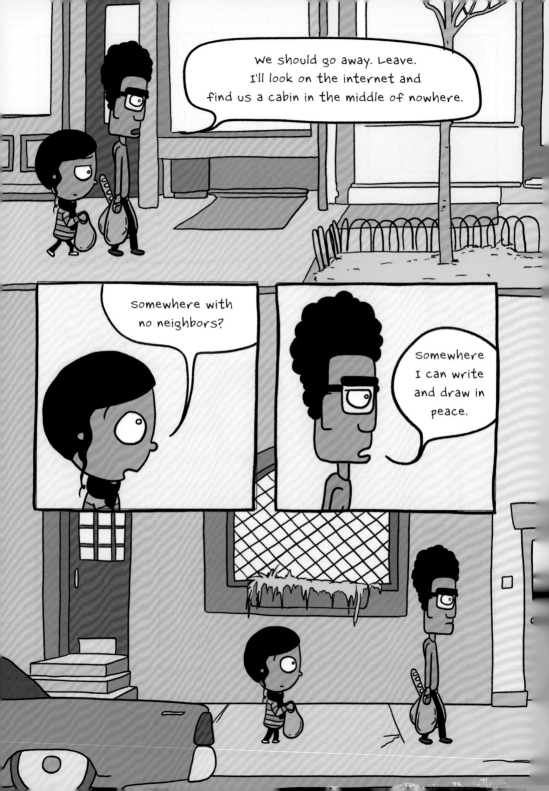

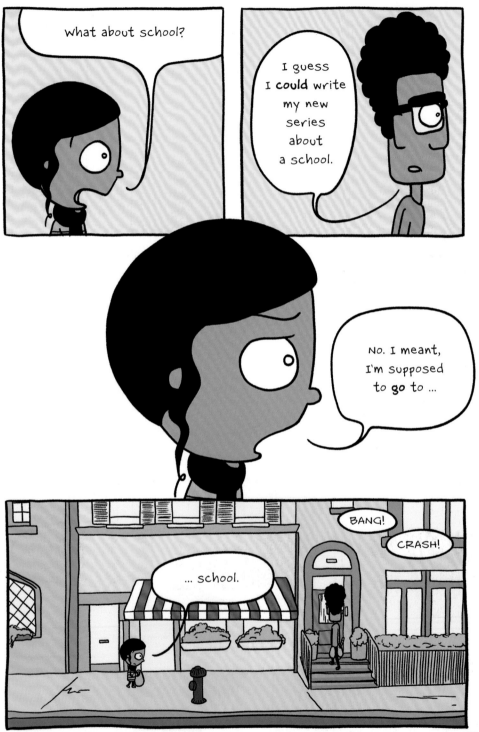

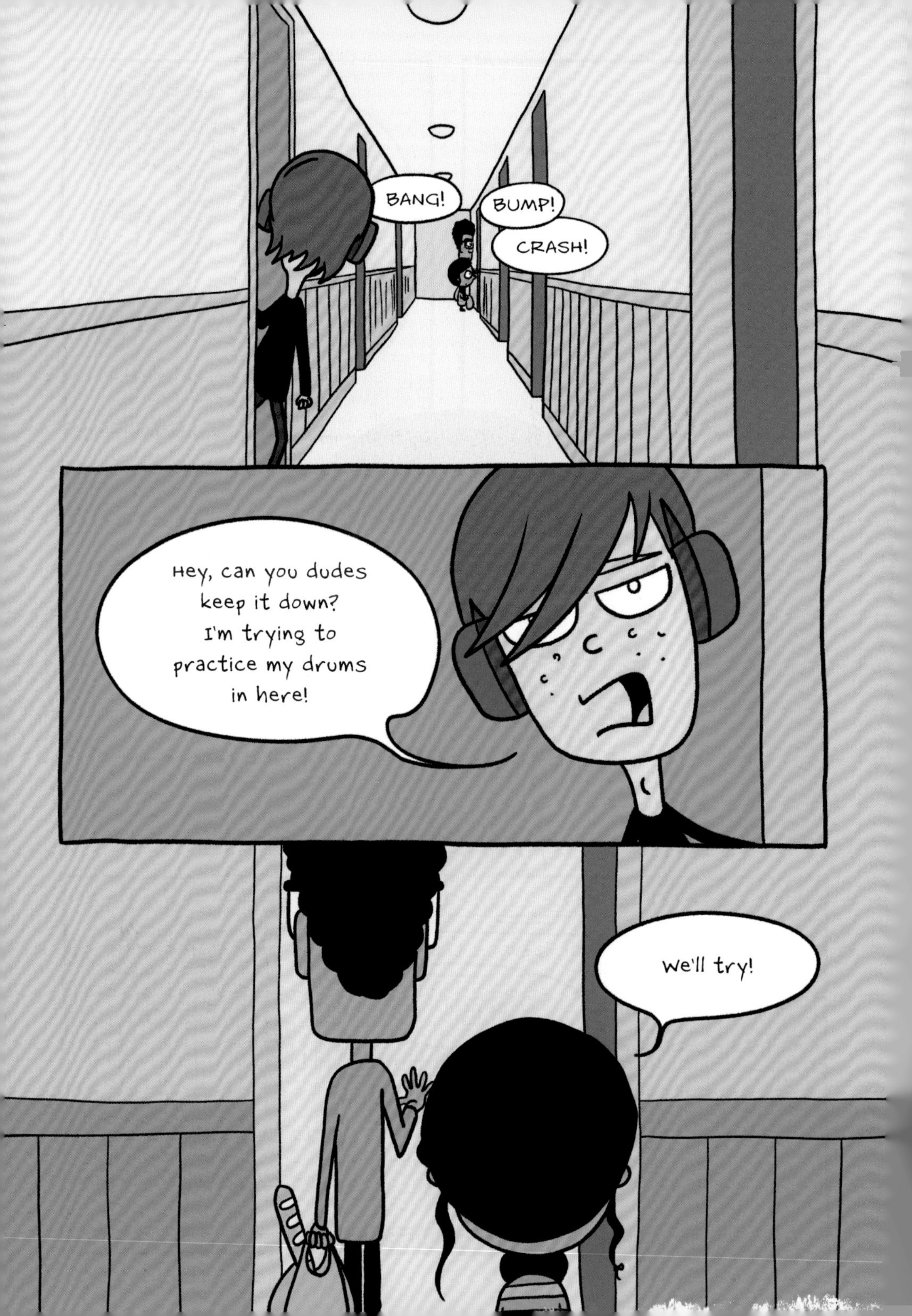
BANG!
BUMP!
CRASH!
Hey, can you dudes keep it down? I'm trying to practice my drums in here!
We'll try!

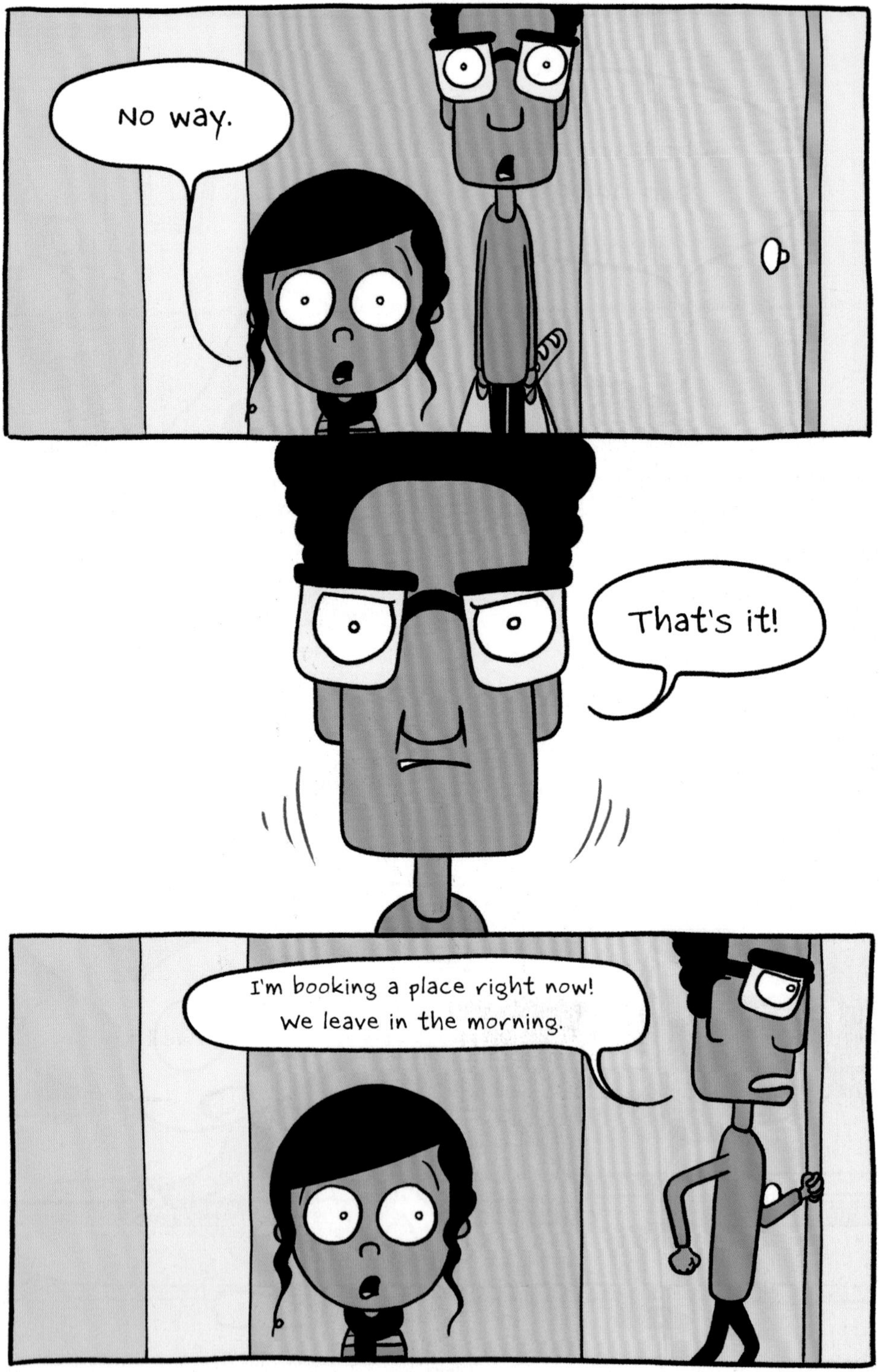
No way.
That's it!
I'm booking a place right now! We leave in the morning.

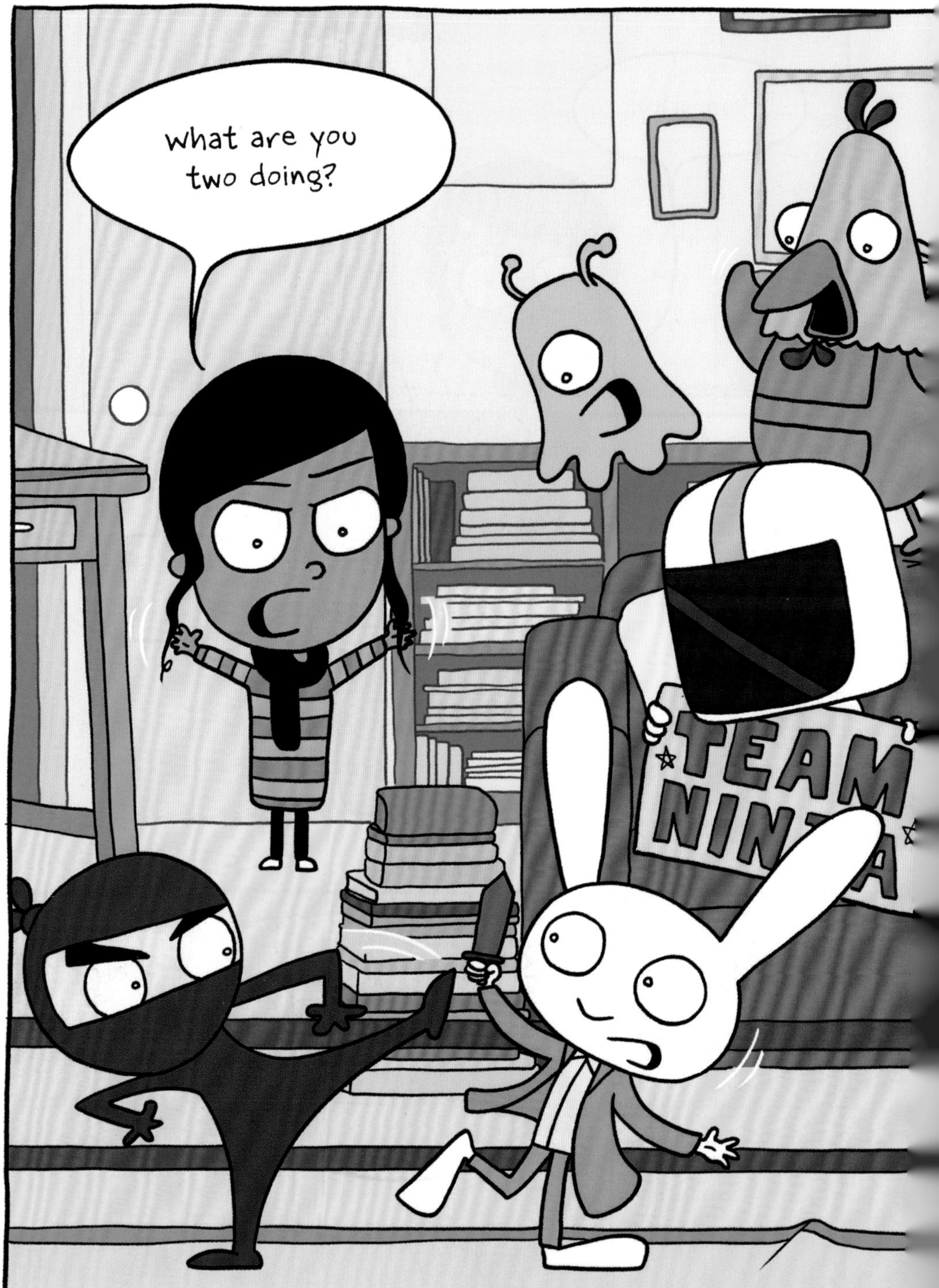
what are you two doing?
TEAM NINJA

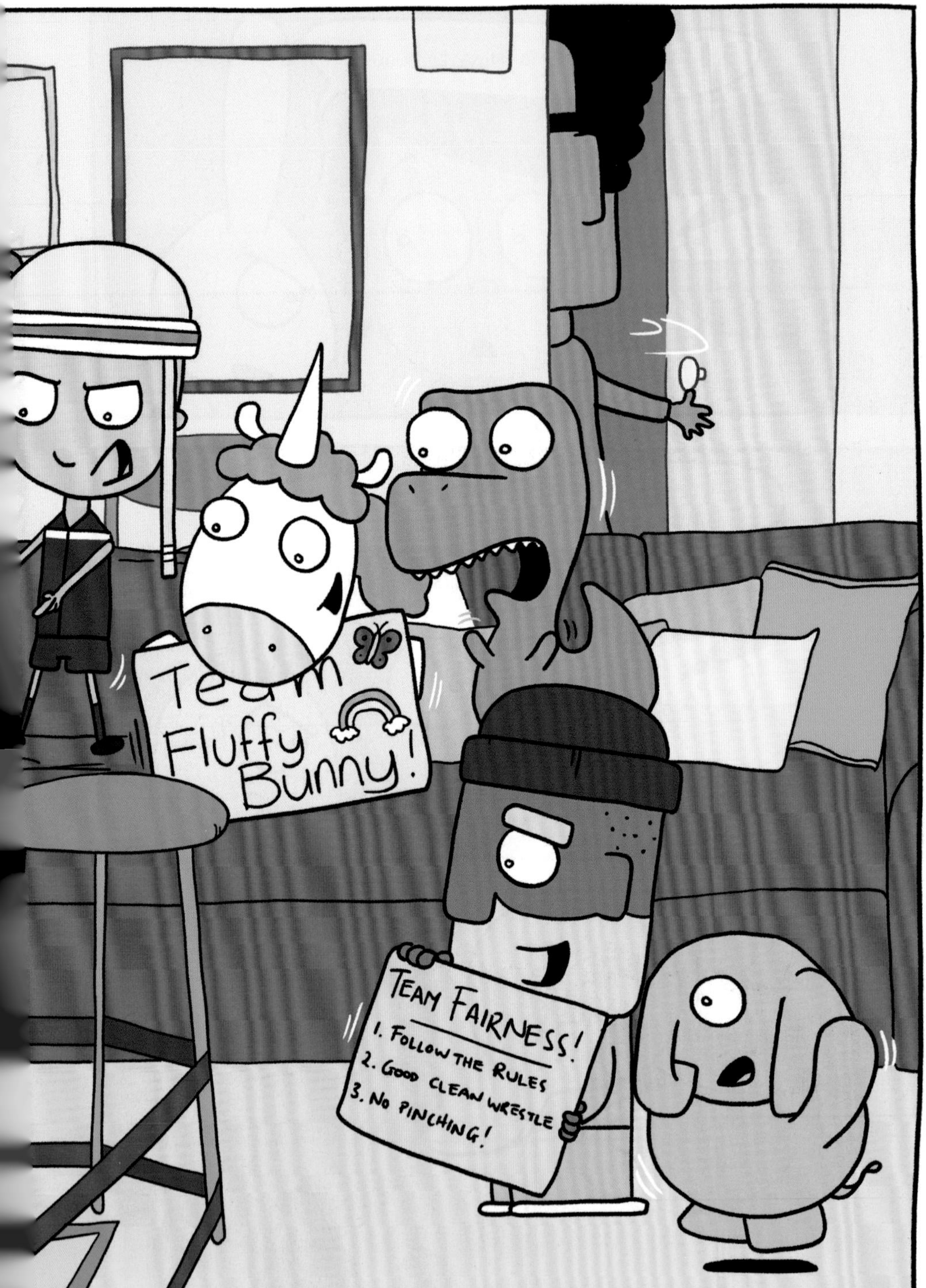
Team Fluffy Bunny!
TEAM FAIRNESS!
1. FOLLOW THE RULES
2. GOOD CLEAN WRESTLE
3. NO PINCHING!

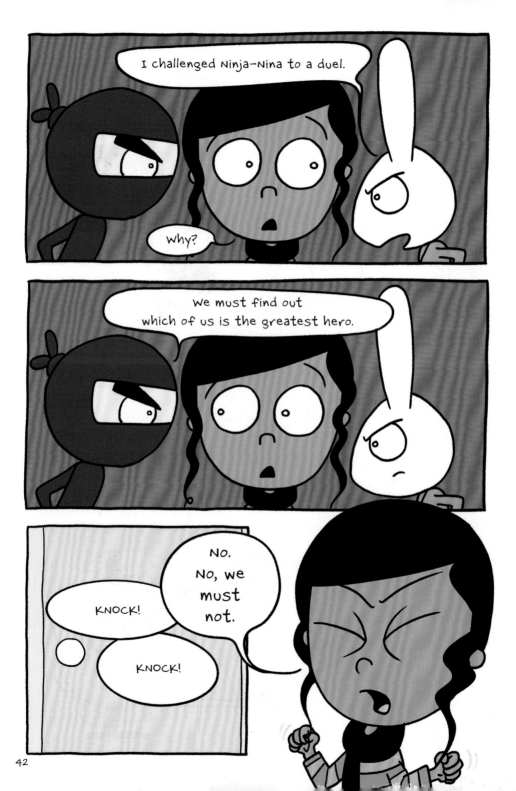

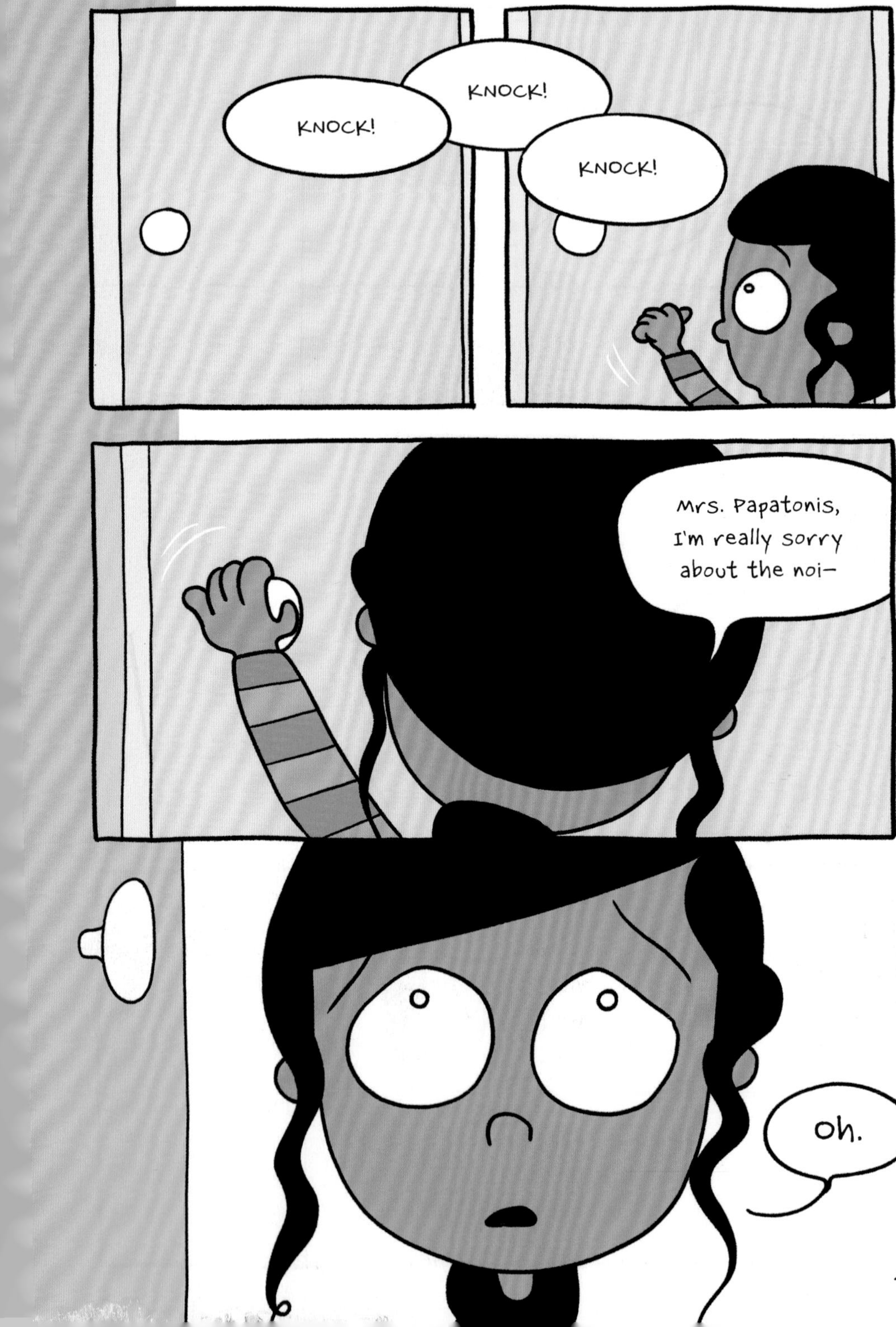
KNOCK!
KNOCK!
KNOCK!
Mrs. Papatonis, I'm really sorry about the noi—
Oh.

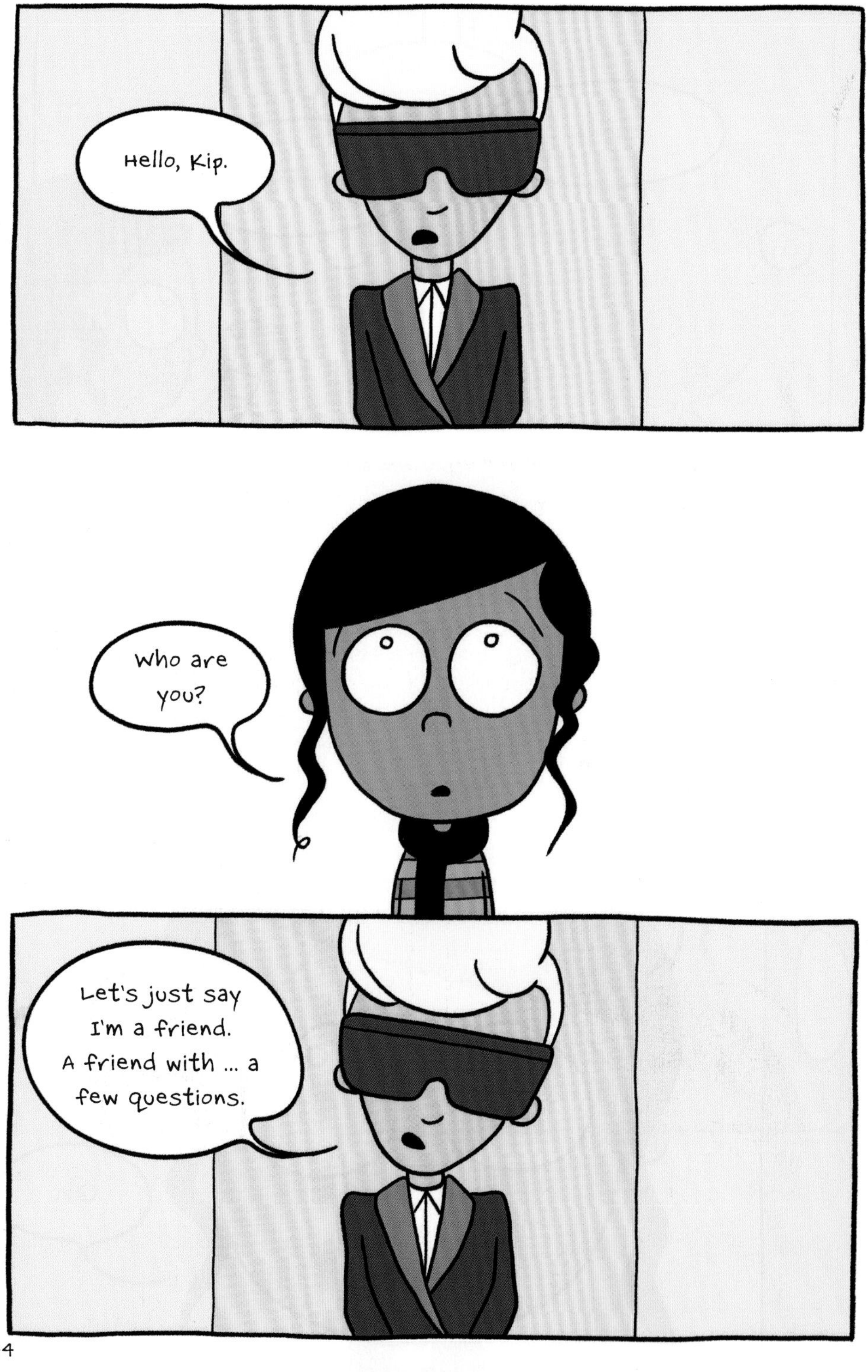
Hello, Kip.
Who are you?
Let's just say I'm a friend. A friend with ... a few questions.

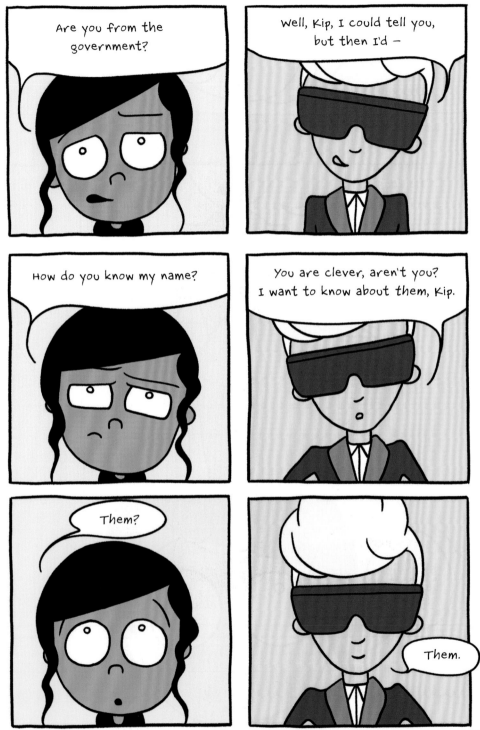

45

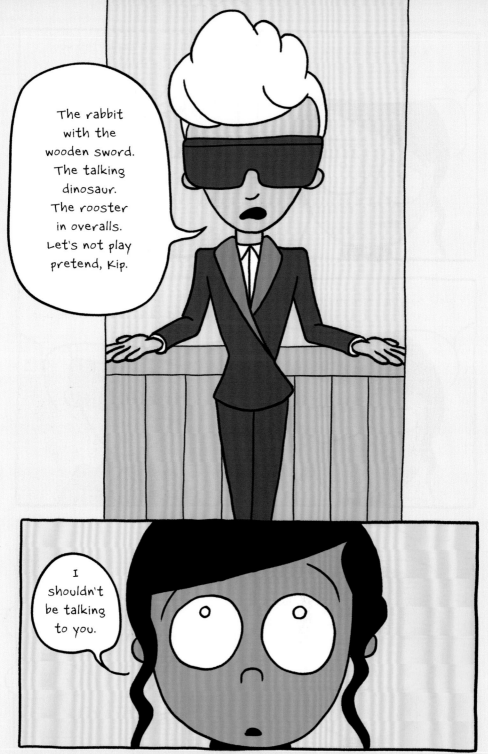

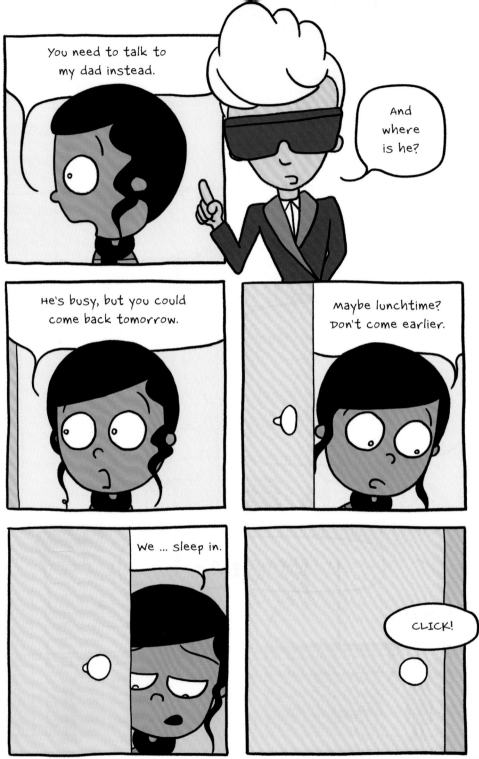

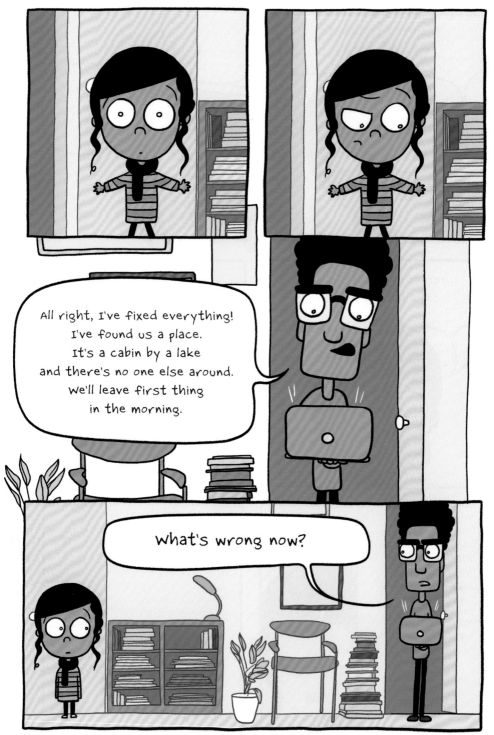

48

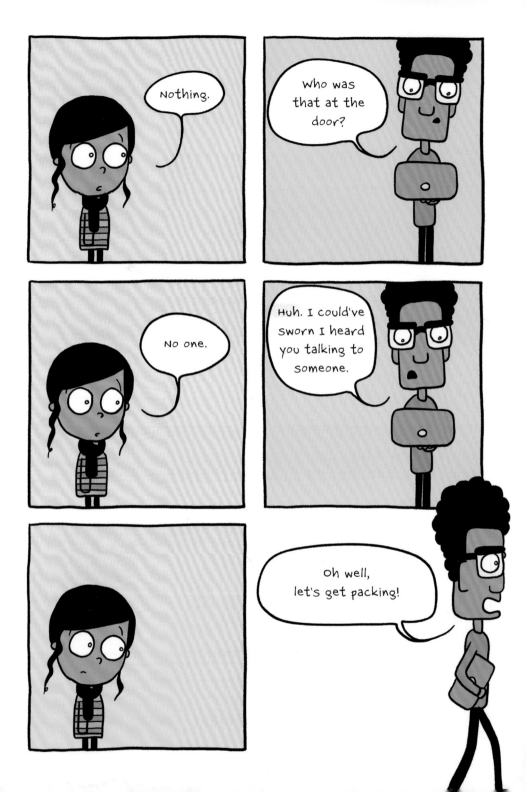

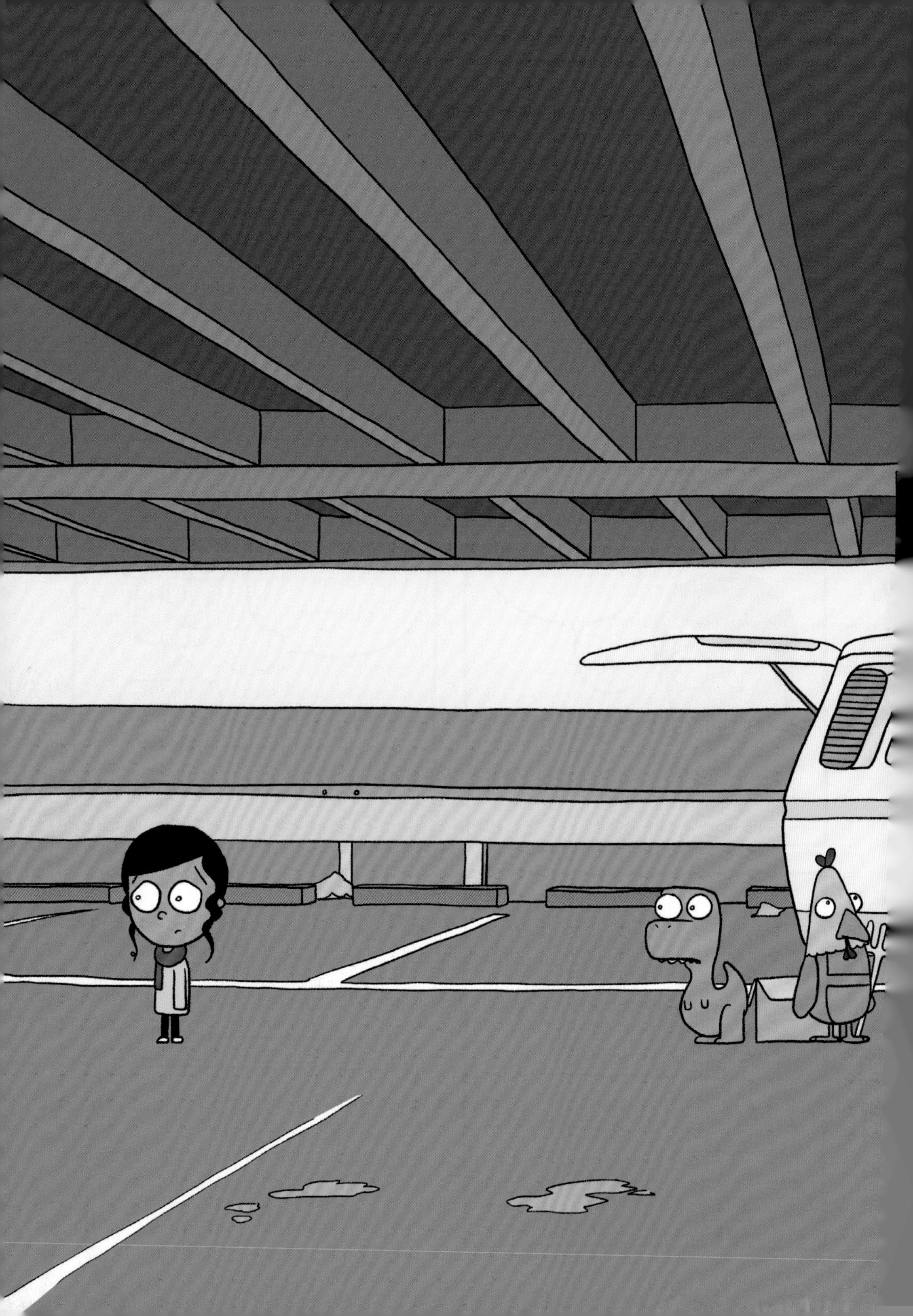

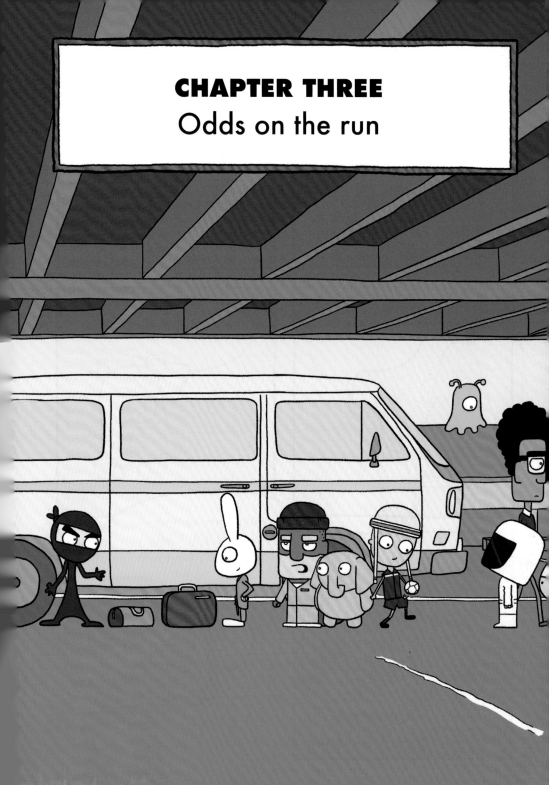

CHAPTER THREE
Odds on the run

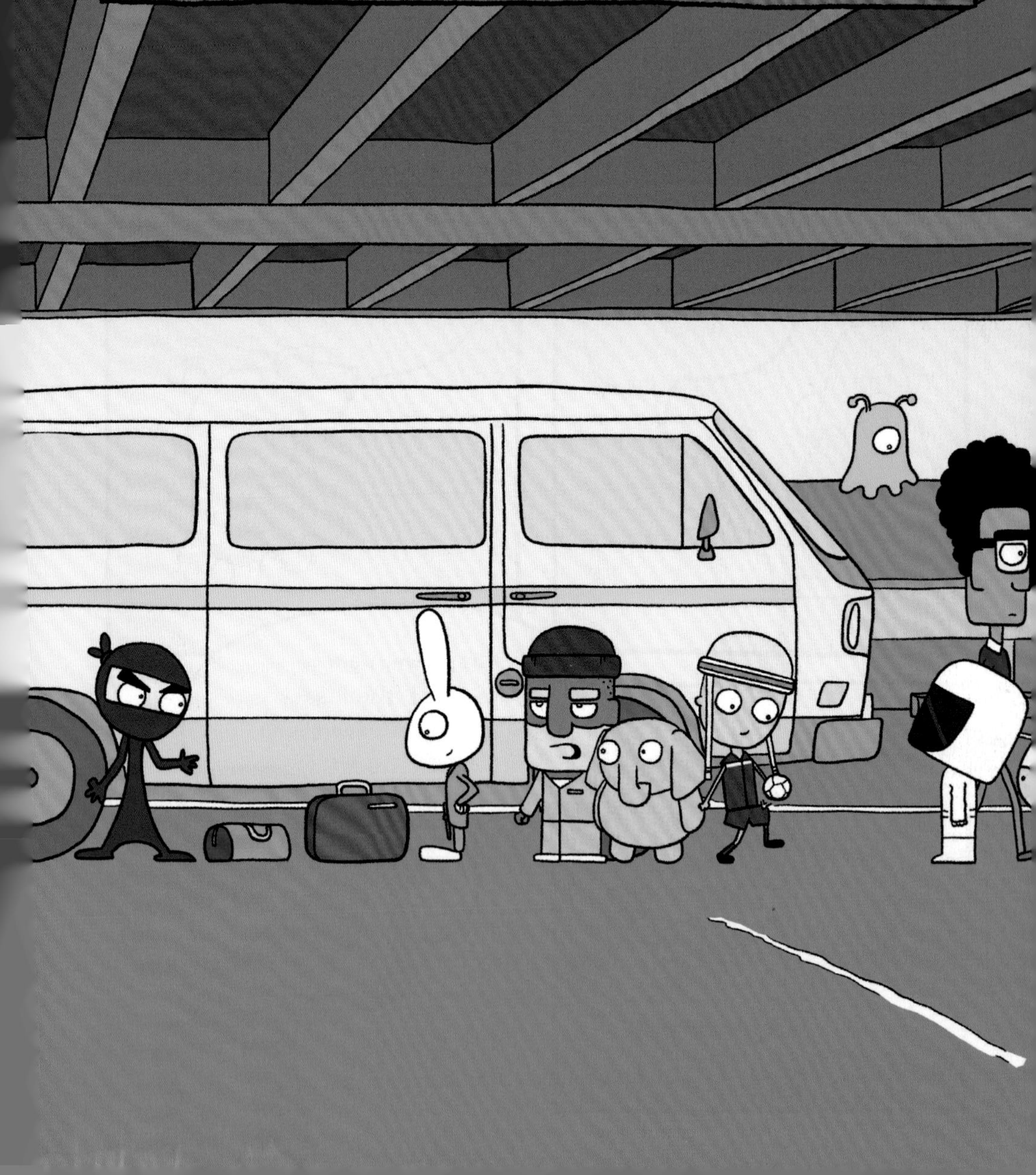

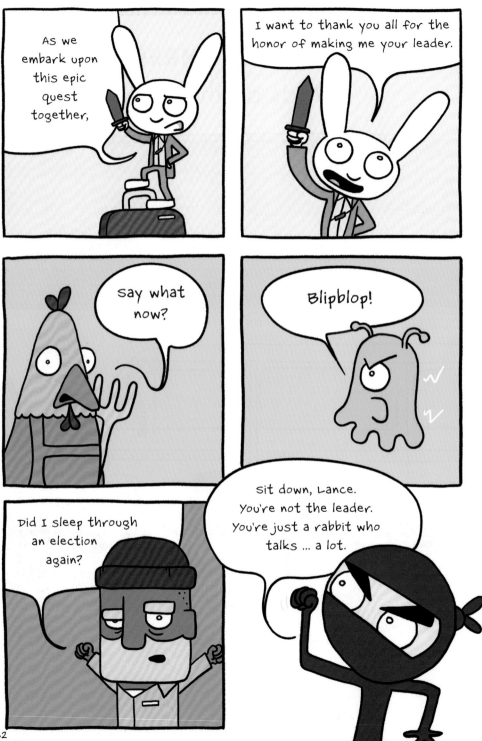

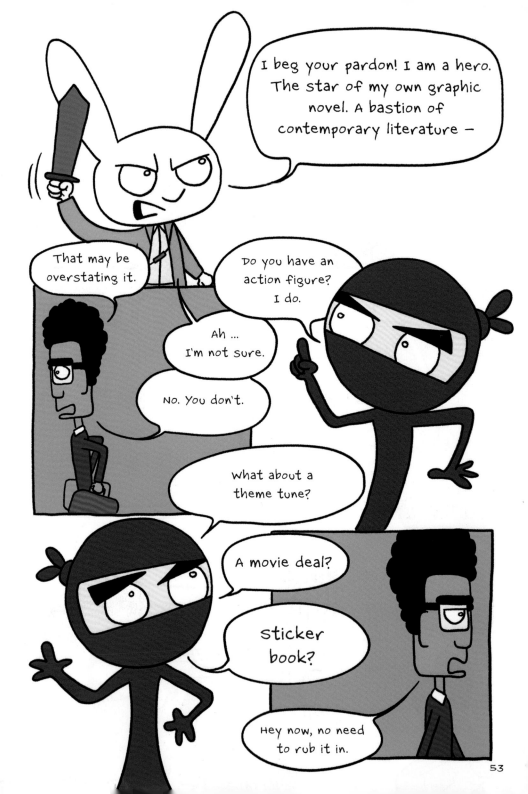

53

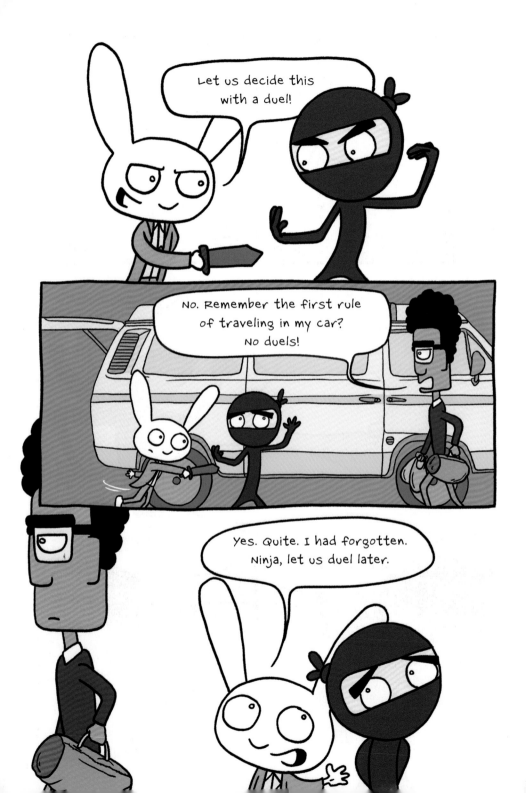

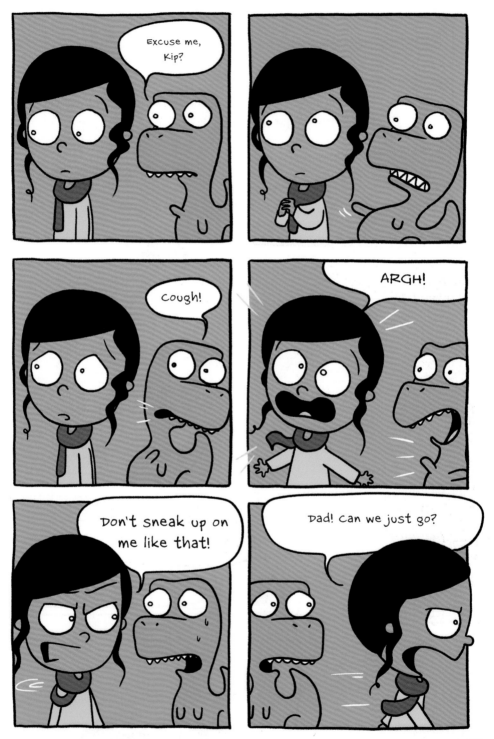

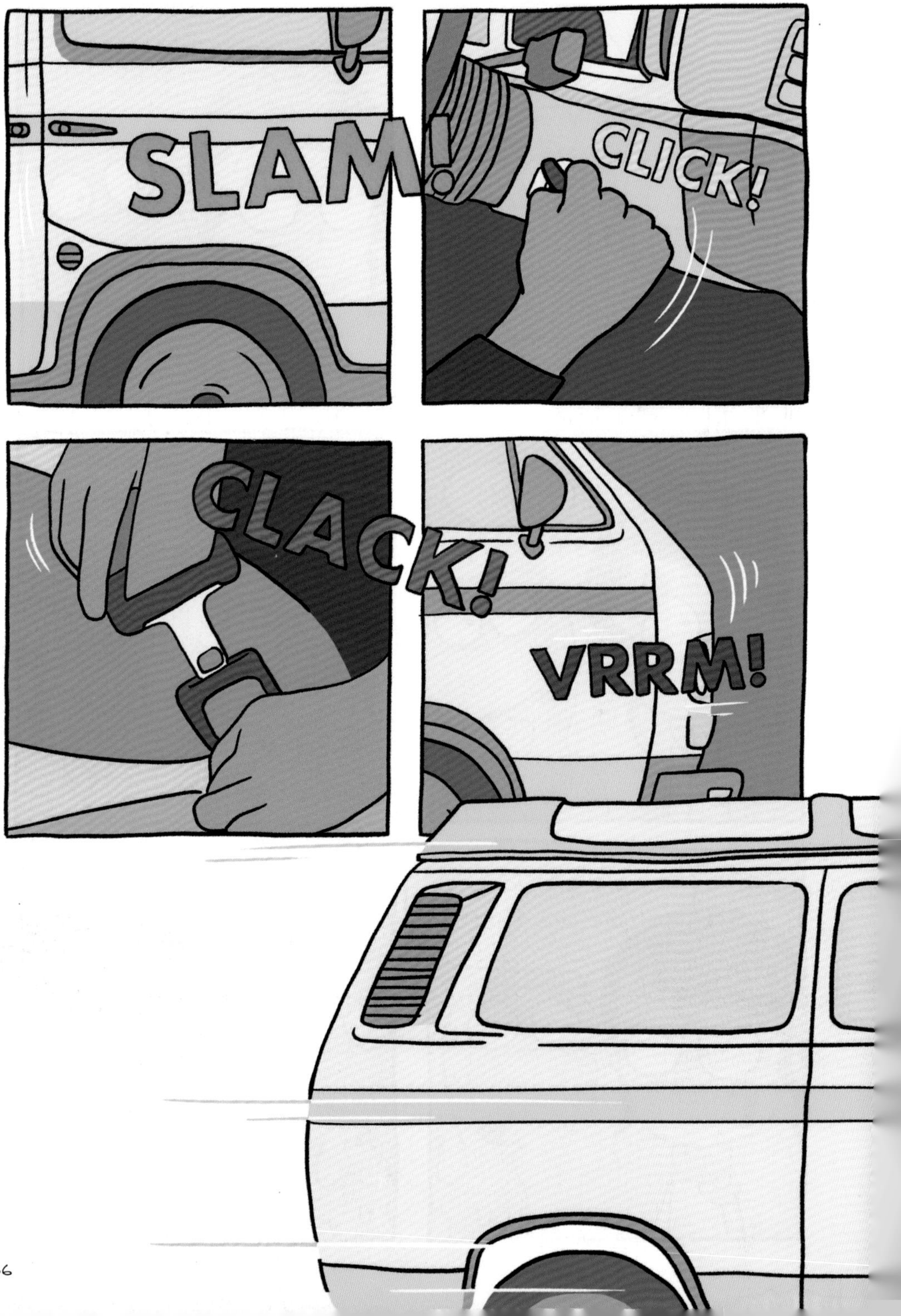
SLAM!
CLICK!
CLACK!
VRRM!

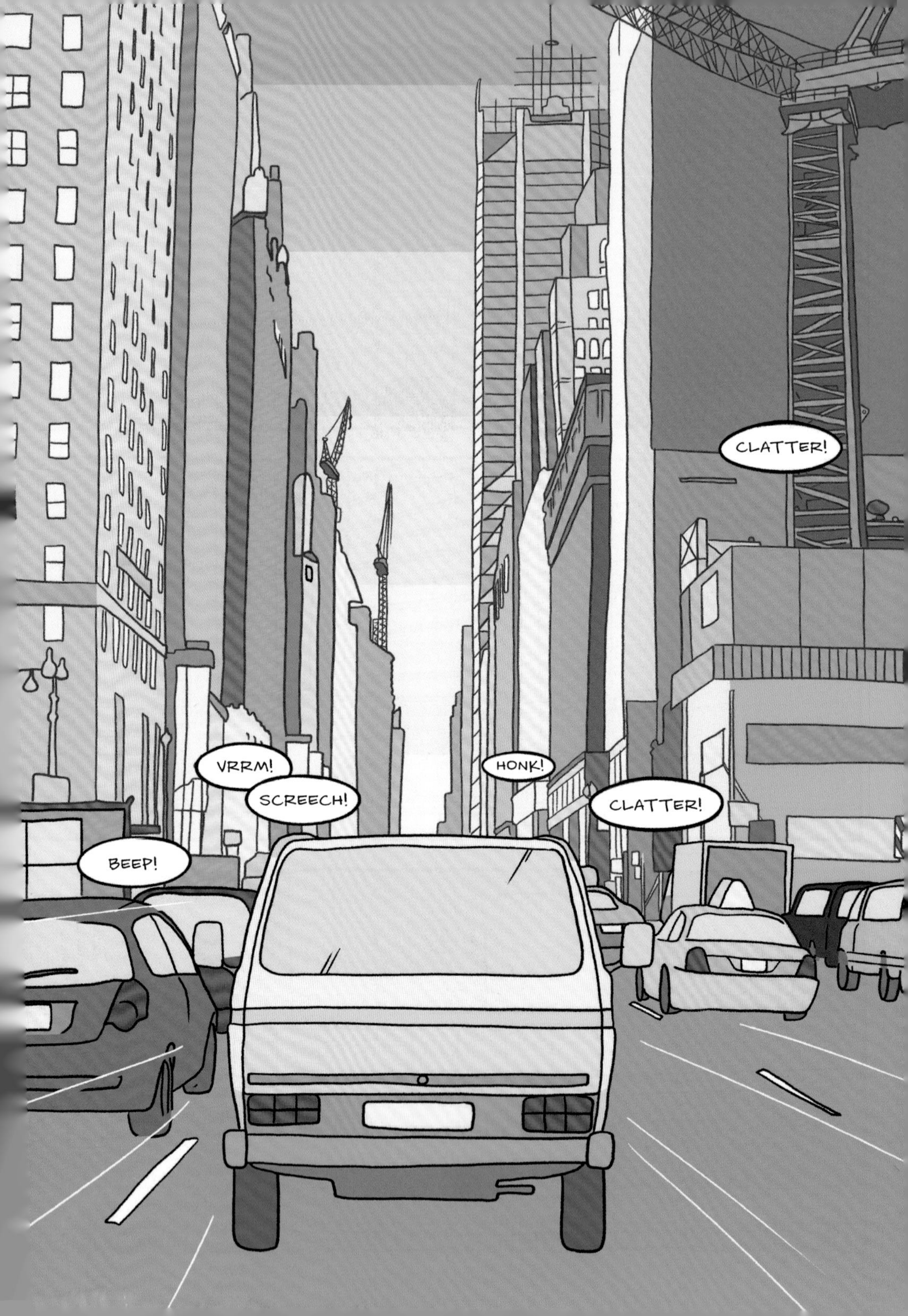
CLATTER!
VRRM!
SCREECH!
HONK!
CLATTER!
BEEP!

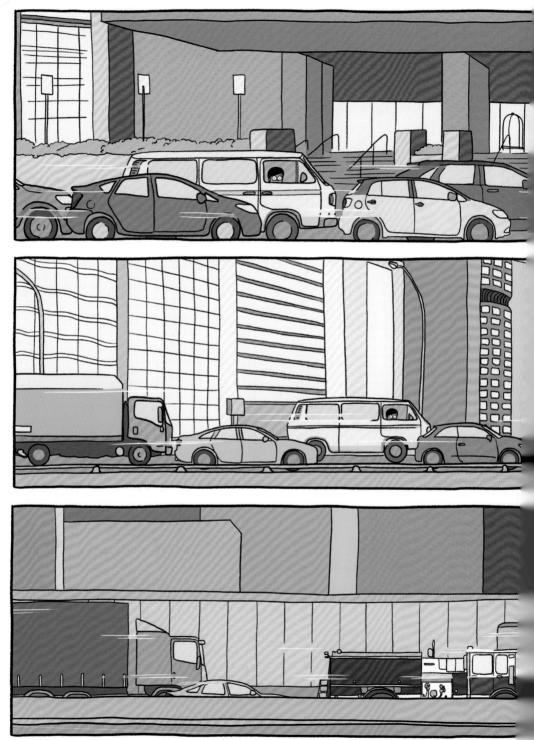

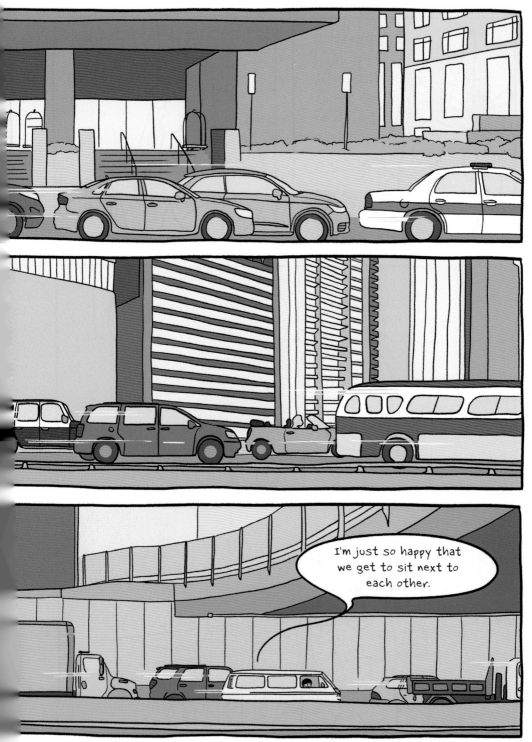

59

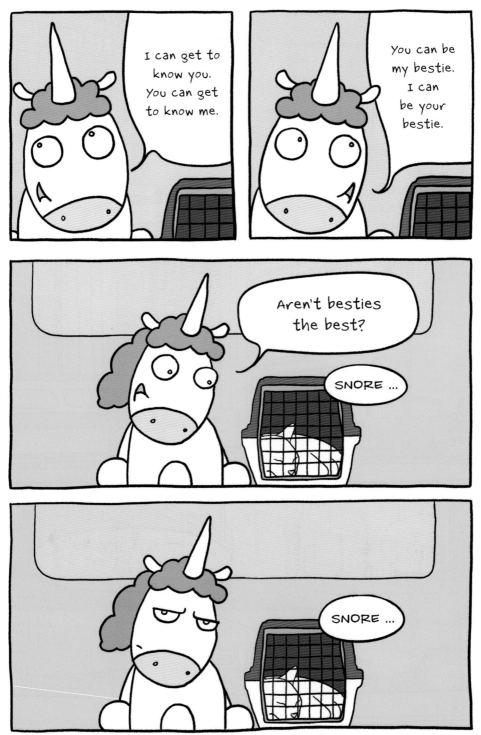

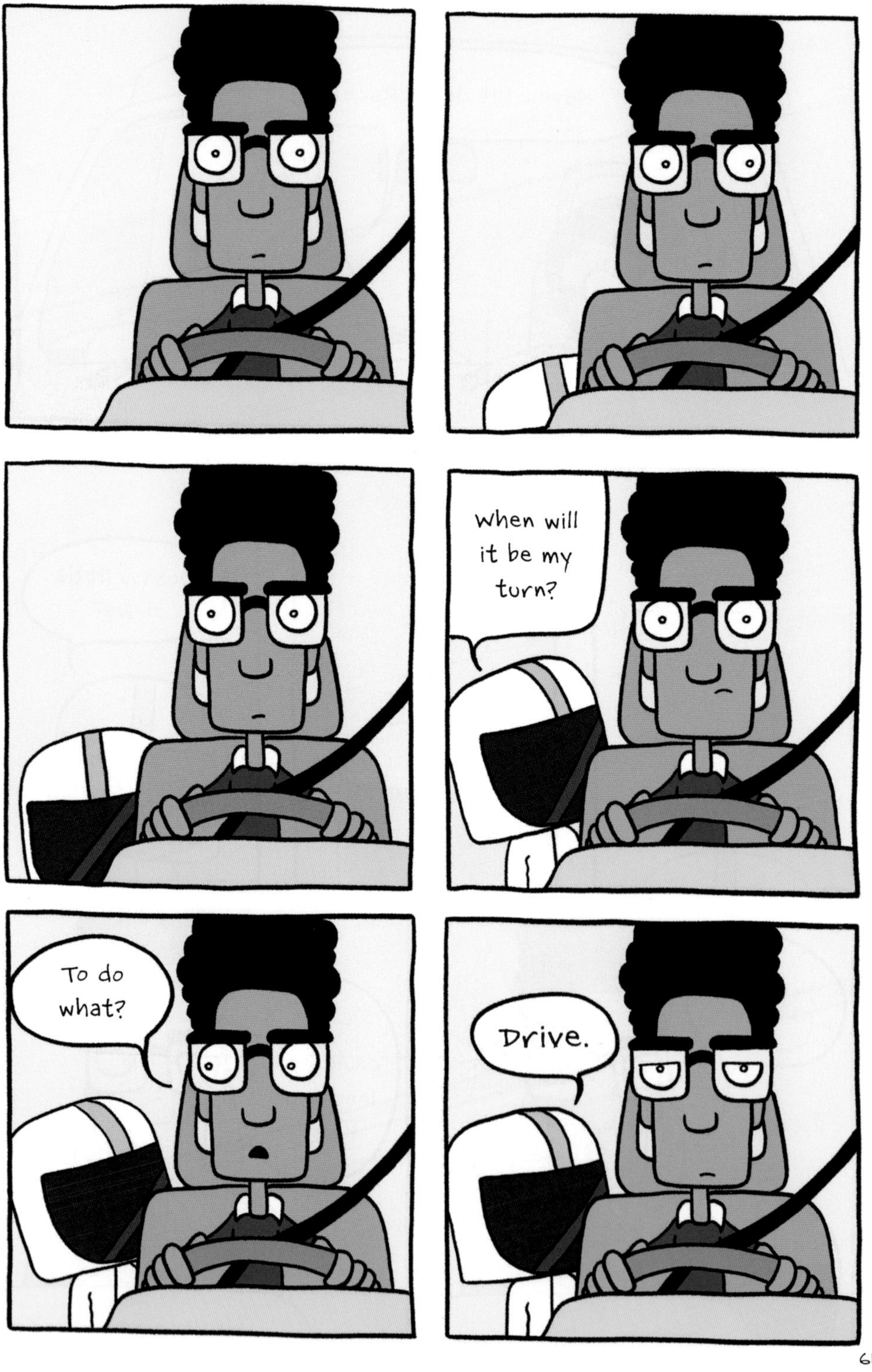
When will
it be my
turn?
To do
what?
Drive.

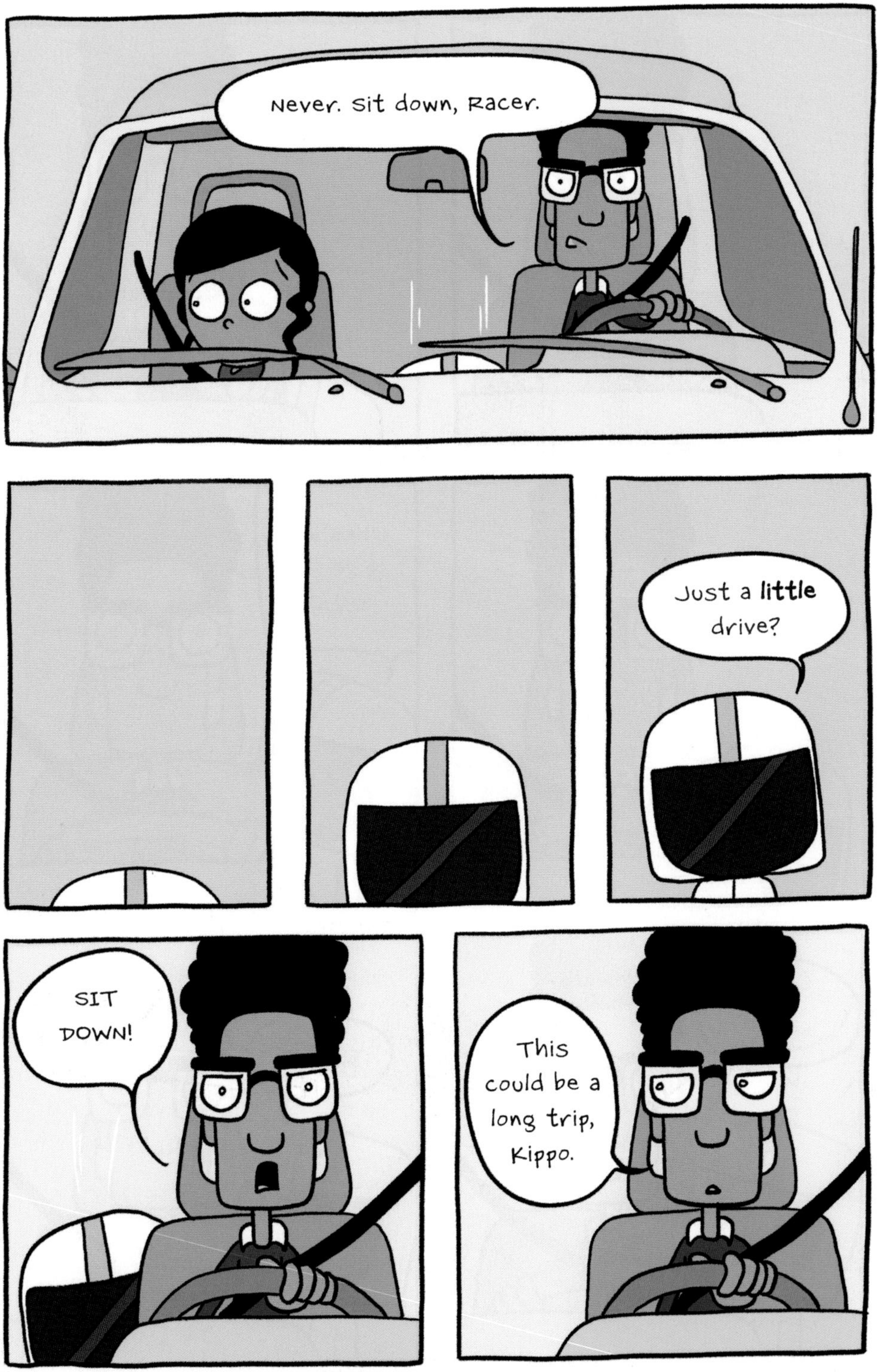
Never. Sit down, Racer.
Just a little drive?
SIT DOWN!
This could be a long trip, Kippo.

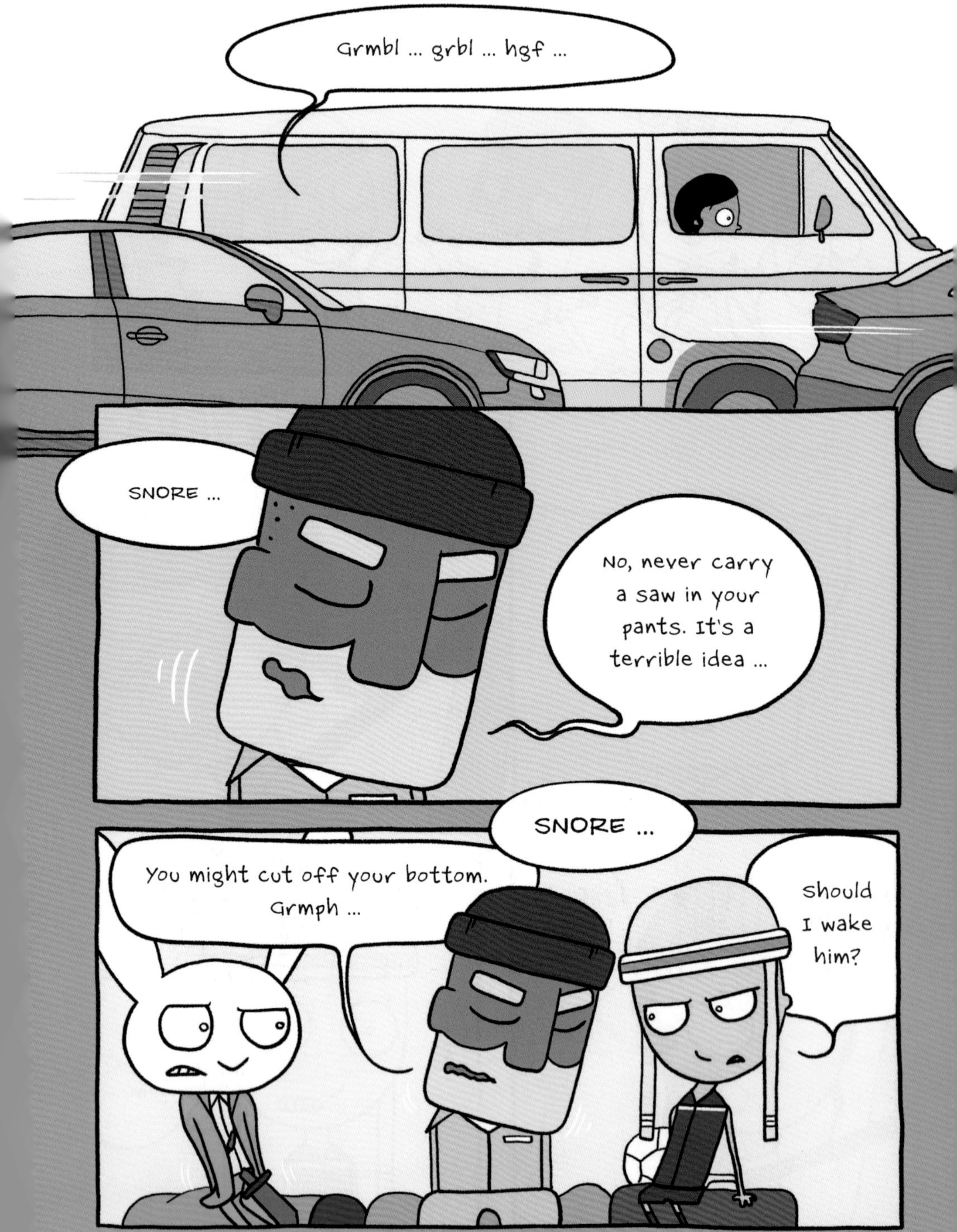
Grmbl ... grbl ... hgf ...
SNORE ...
No, never carry a saw in your pants. It's a terrible idea ...
You might cut off your bottom. Grmph ...
SNORE ...
Should I wake him?

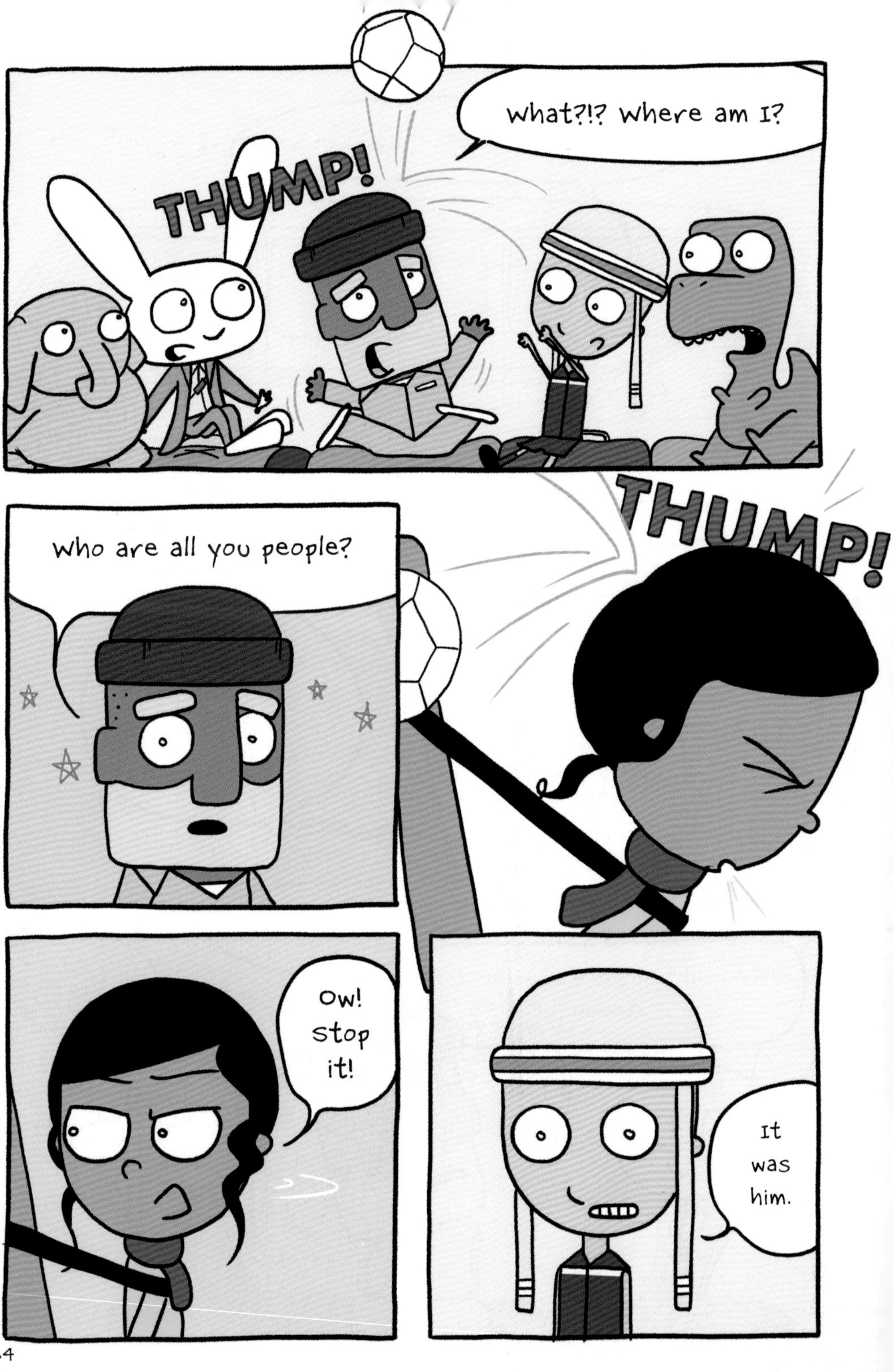
THUMP!
What?!? Where am I?
Who are all you people?
THUMP!
Ow! Stop it!
It was him.

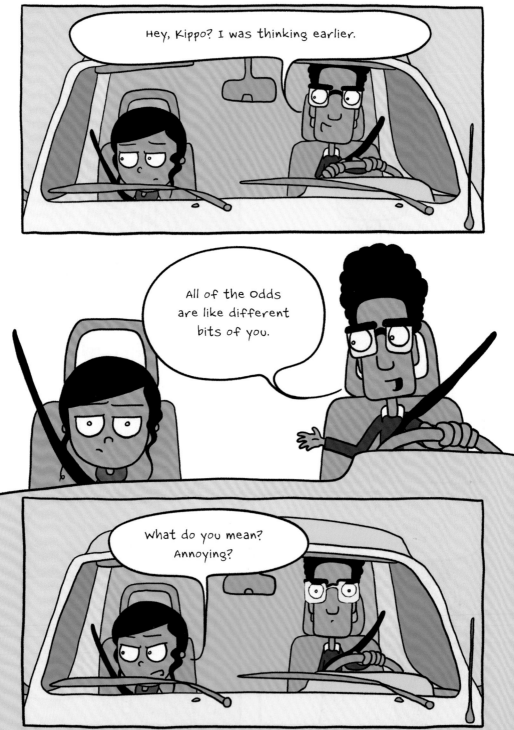

65

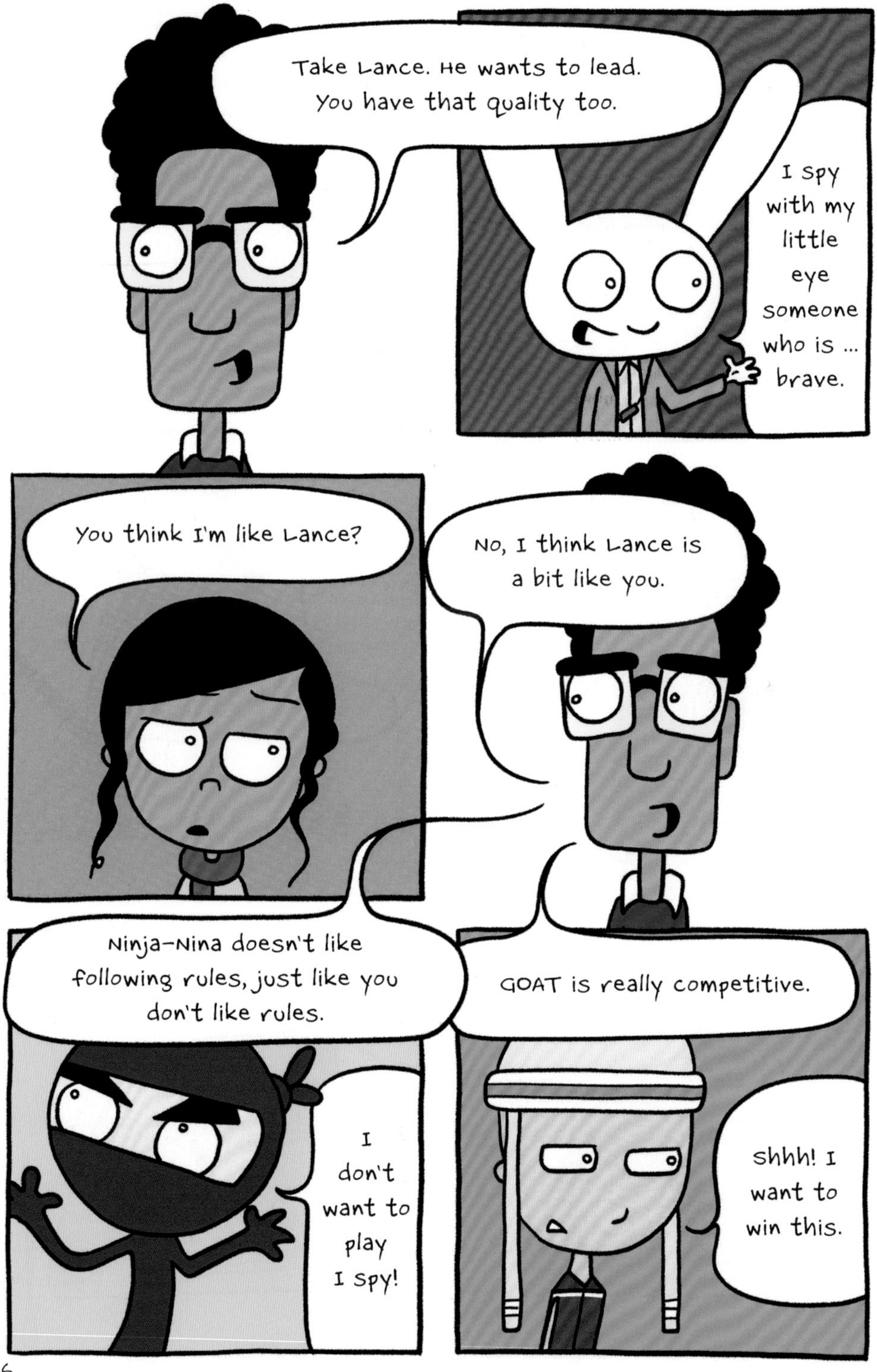
Take Lance. He wants to lead. You have that quality too.
I spy with my little eye someone who is ... brave.
You think I'm like Lance?
No, I think Lance is a bit like you.
Ninja-Nina doesn't like following rules, just like you don't like rules.
I don't want to play I spy!
GOAT is really competitive.
Shhh! I want to win this.

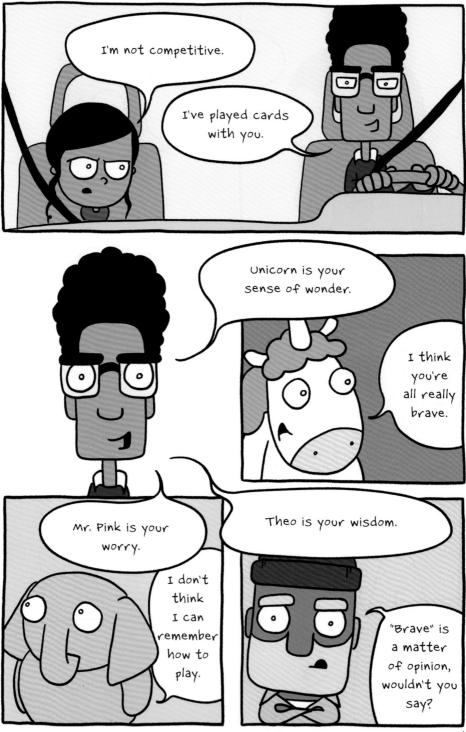

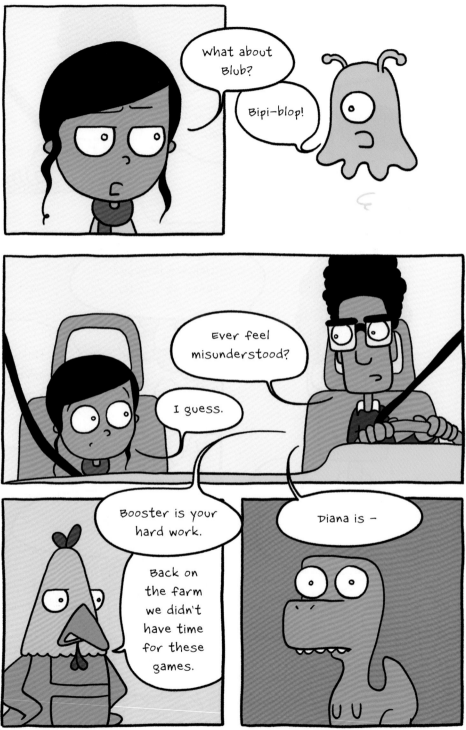

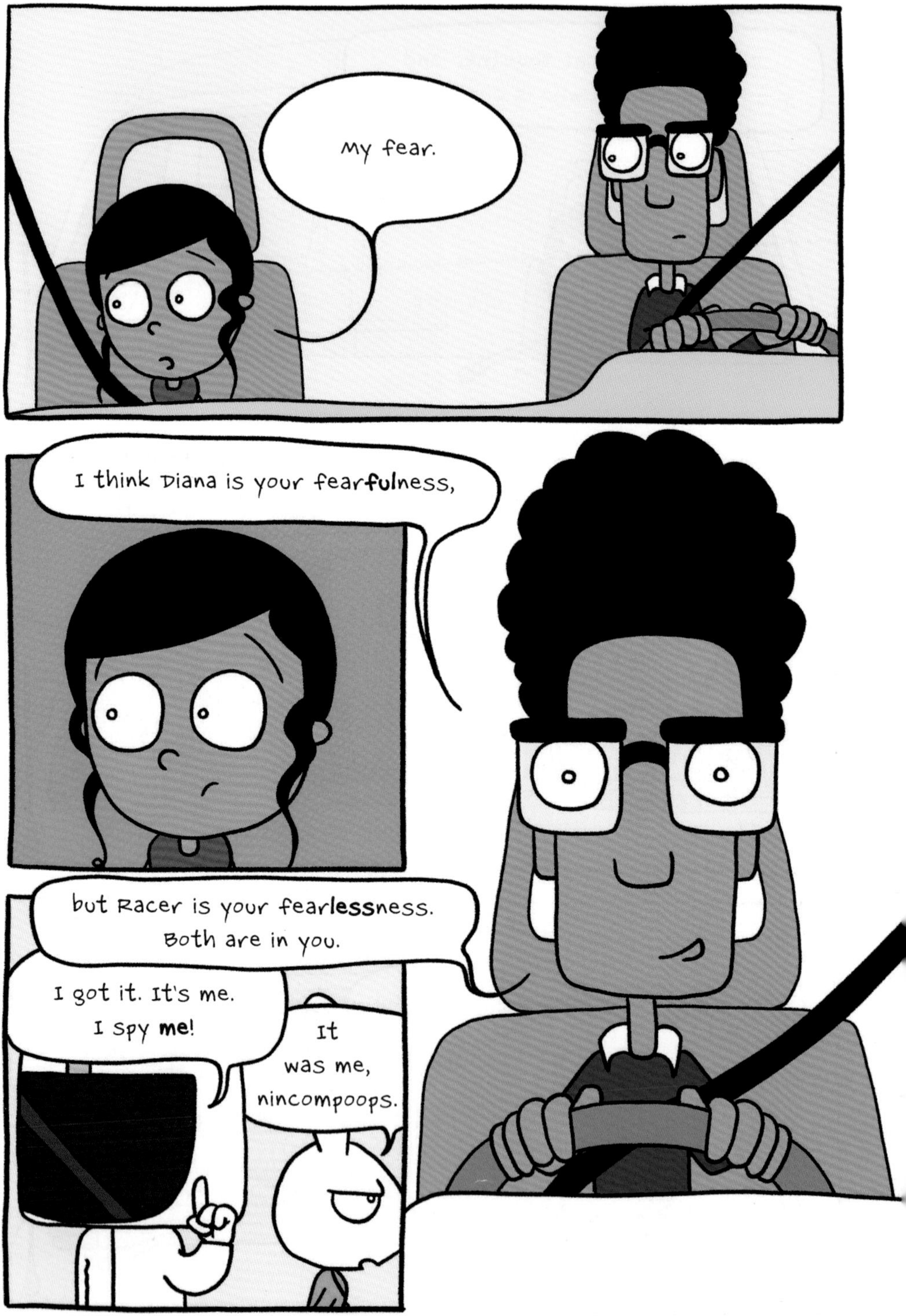
My fear.
I think Diana is your fear**ful**ness,
but Racer is your fear**less**ness. Both are in you.
I got it. It's me. I spy **me**!
It was me, nincompoops.

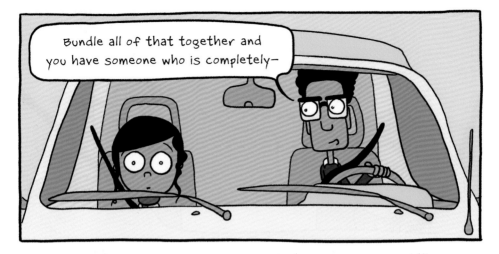

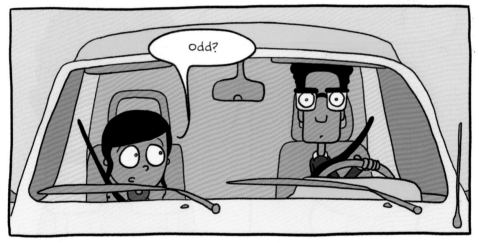

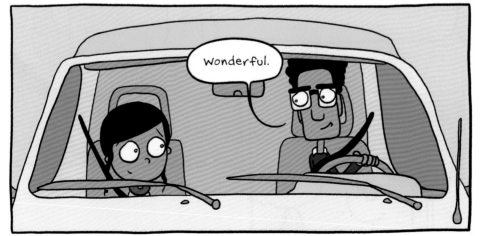

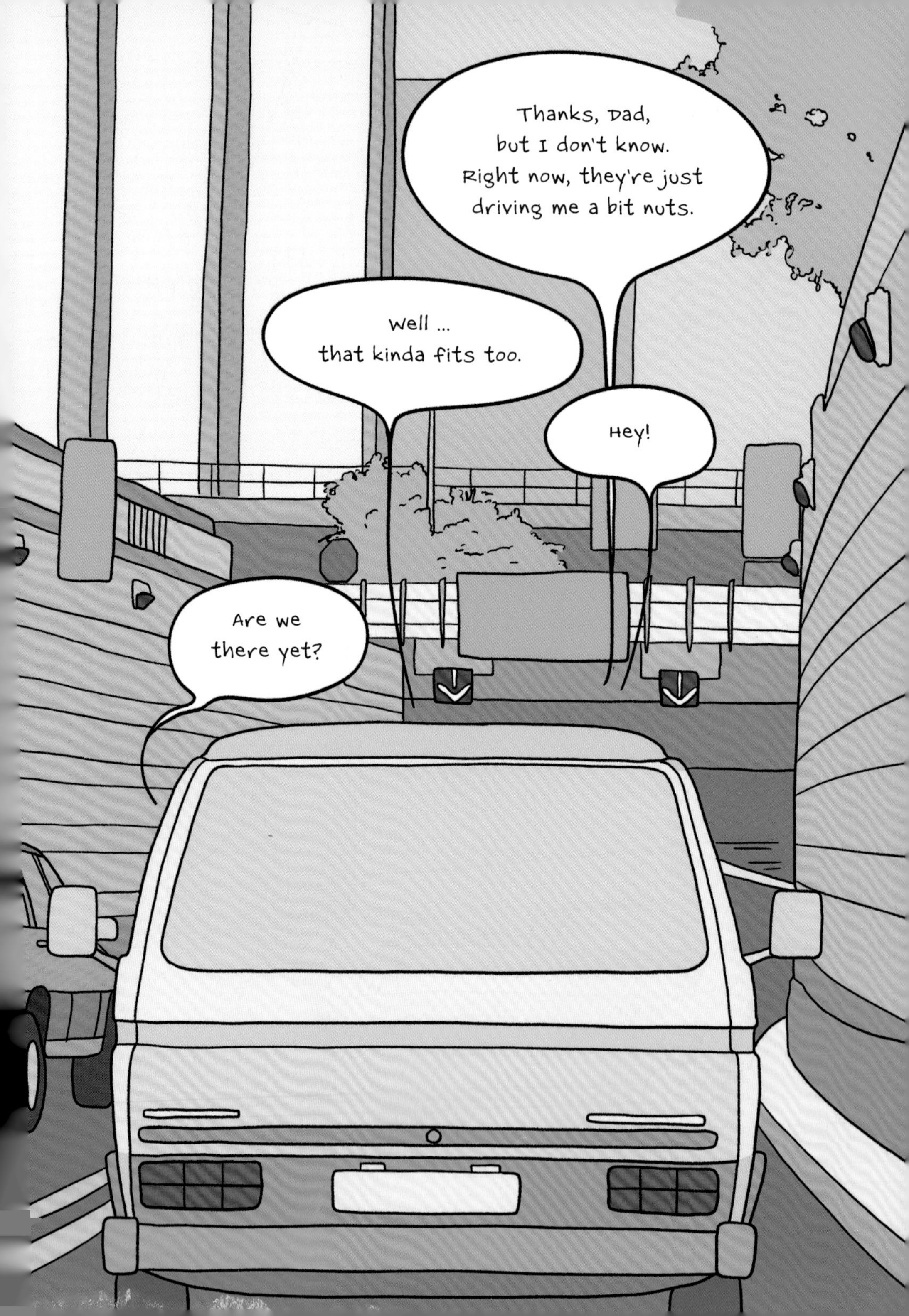
Thanks, Dad,
but I don't know.
Right now, they're just
driving me a bit nuts.
Well ...
that kinda fits too.
Hey!
Are we
there yet?

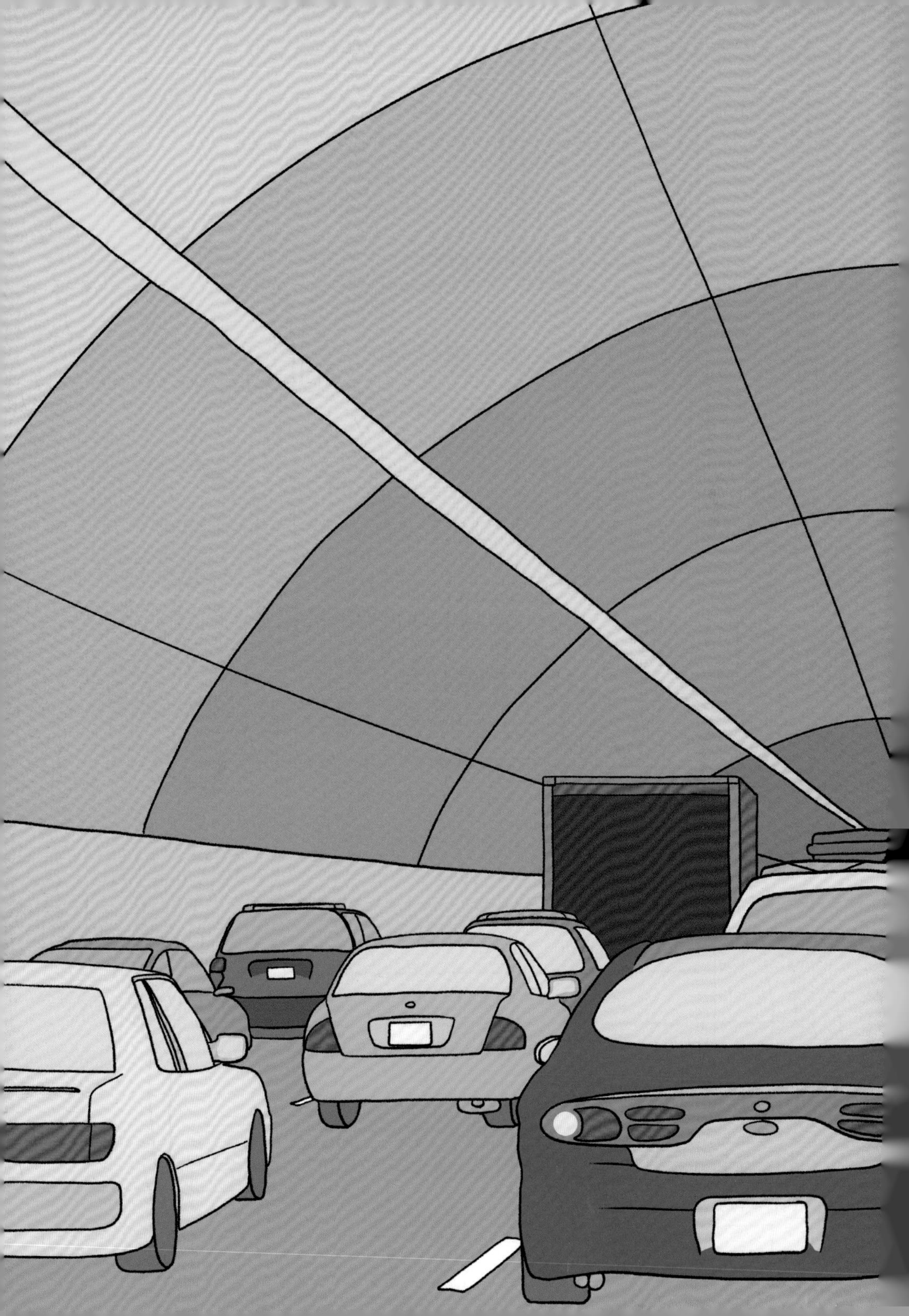

CHAPTER FOUR
An odd sort of road trip

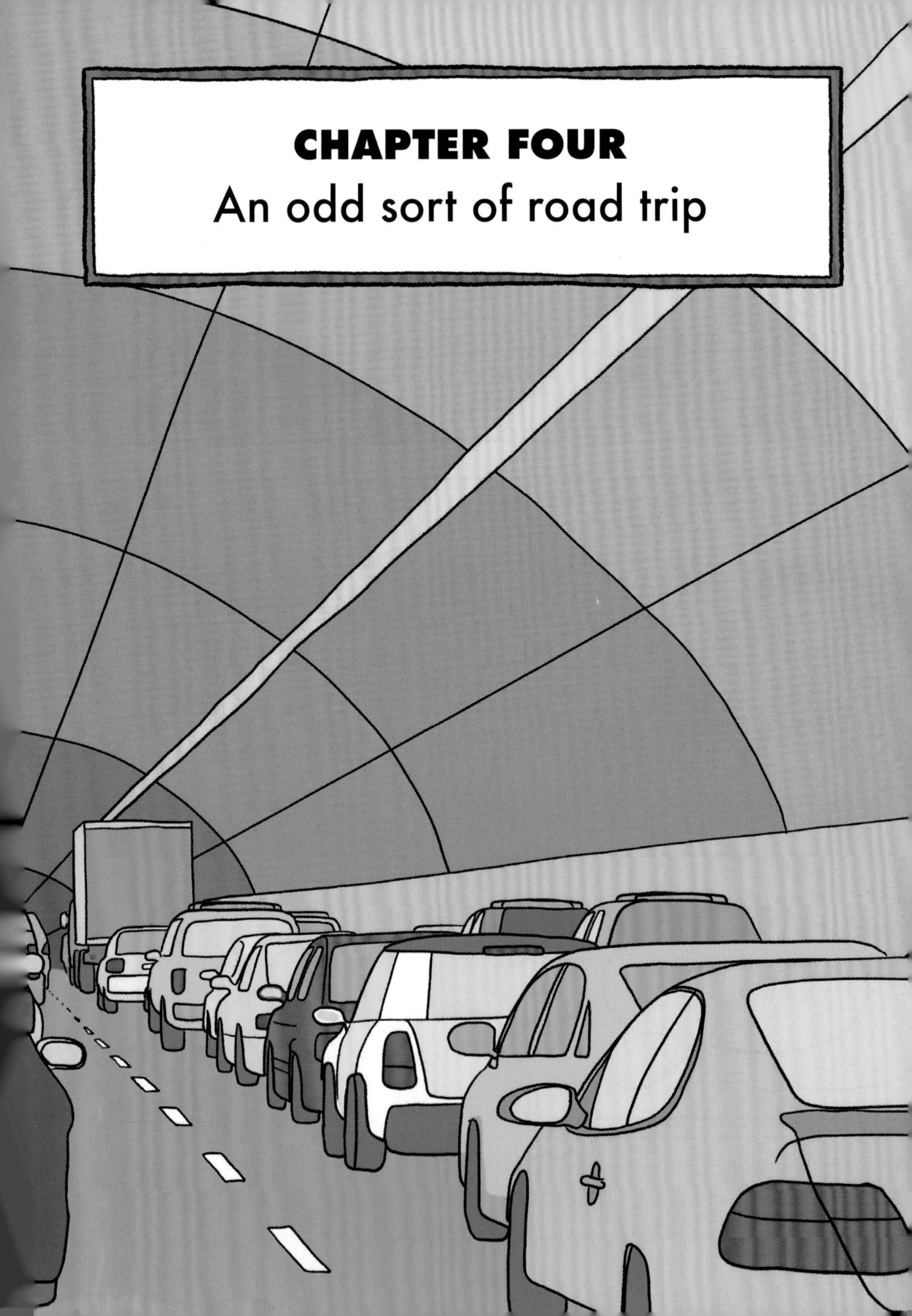

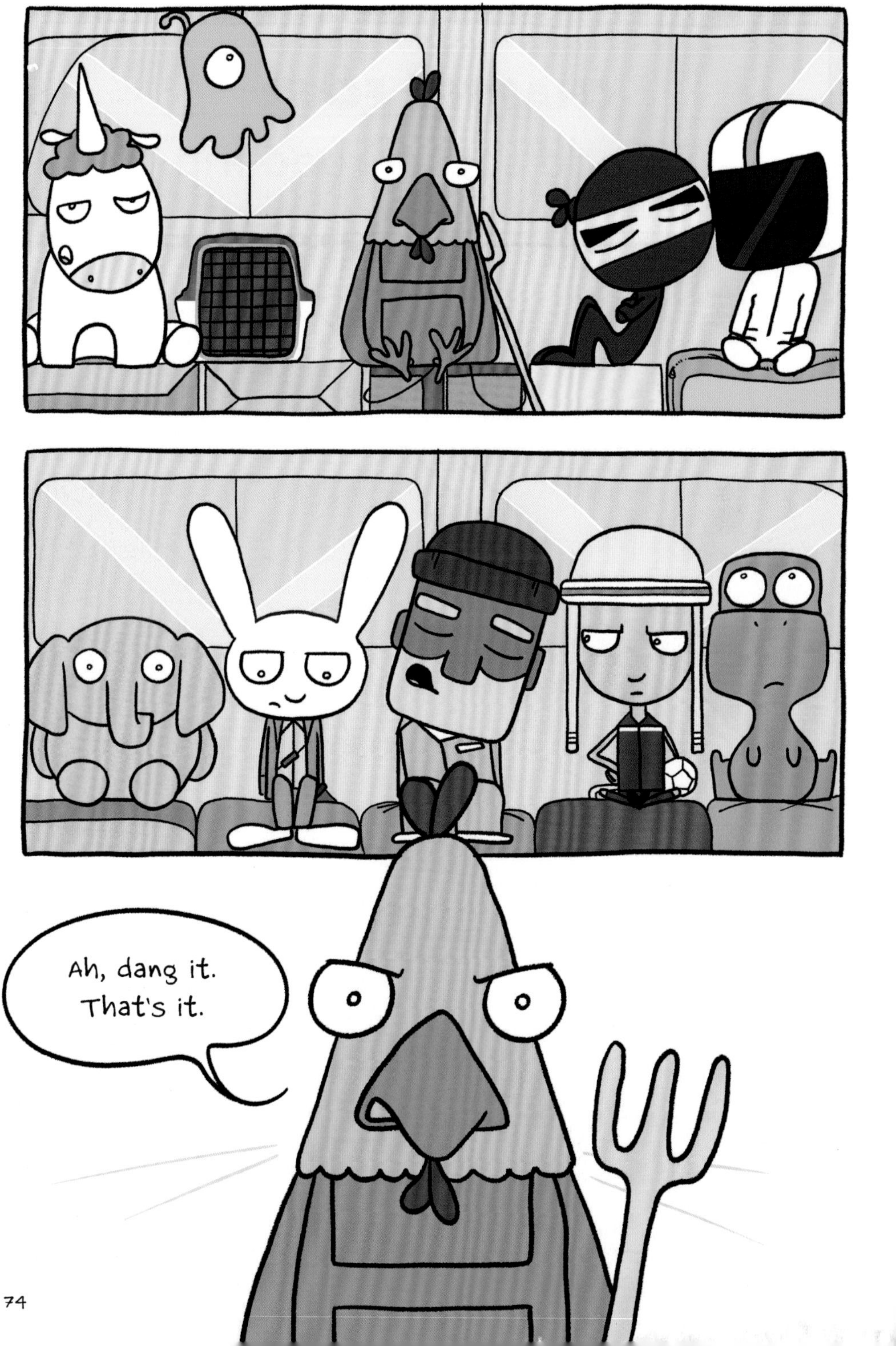
Ah, dang it.
That's it.

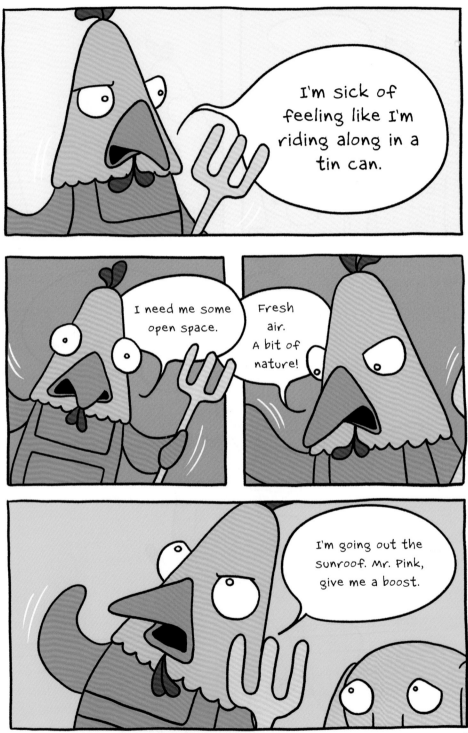

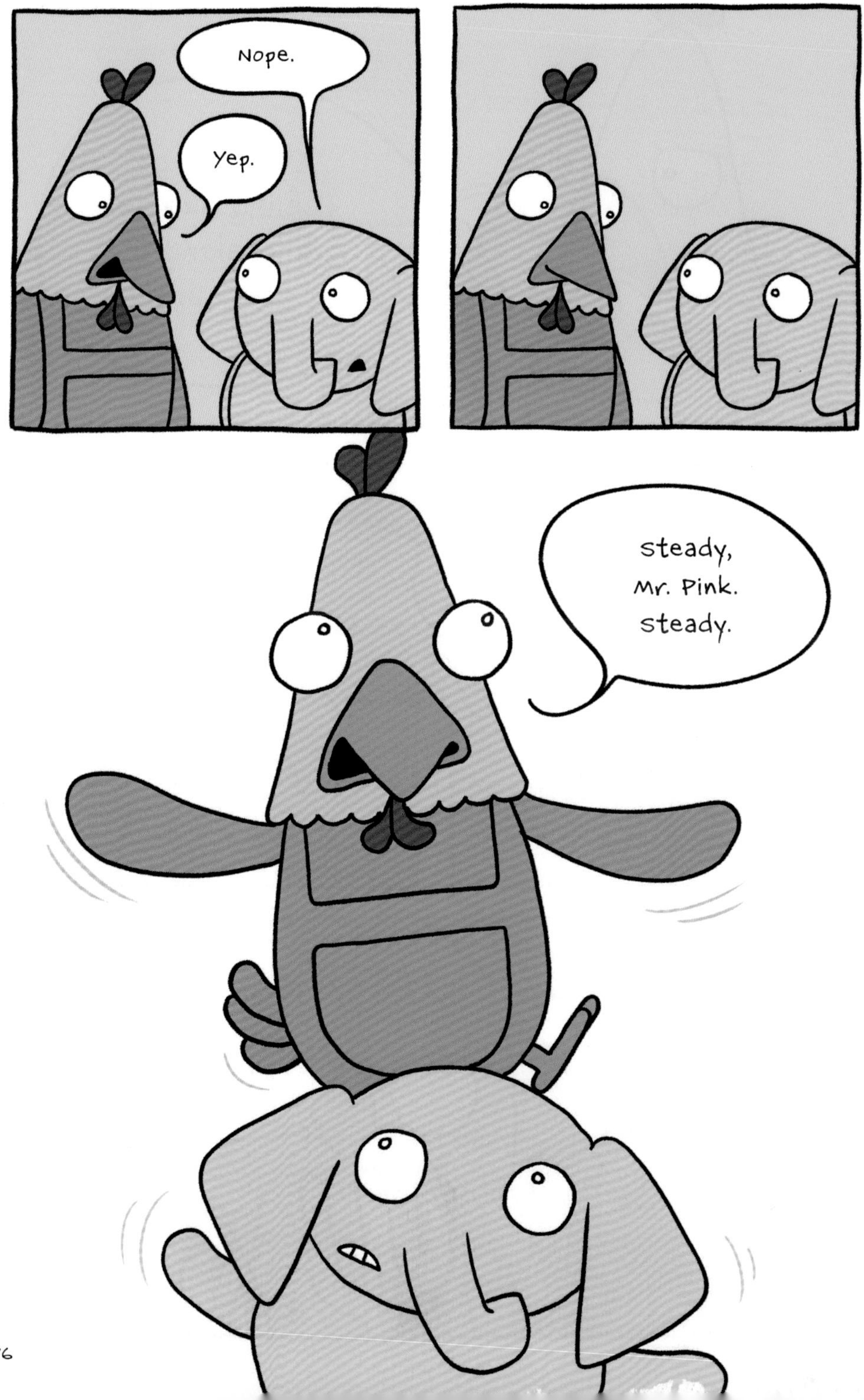
Yep.
Nope.
Steady,
Mr. Pink.
Steady.

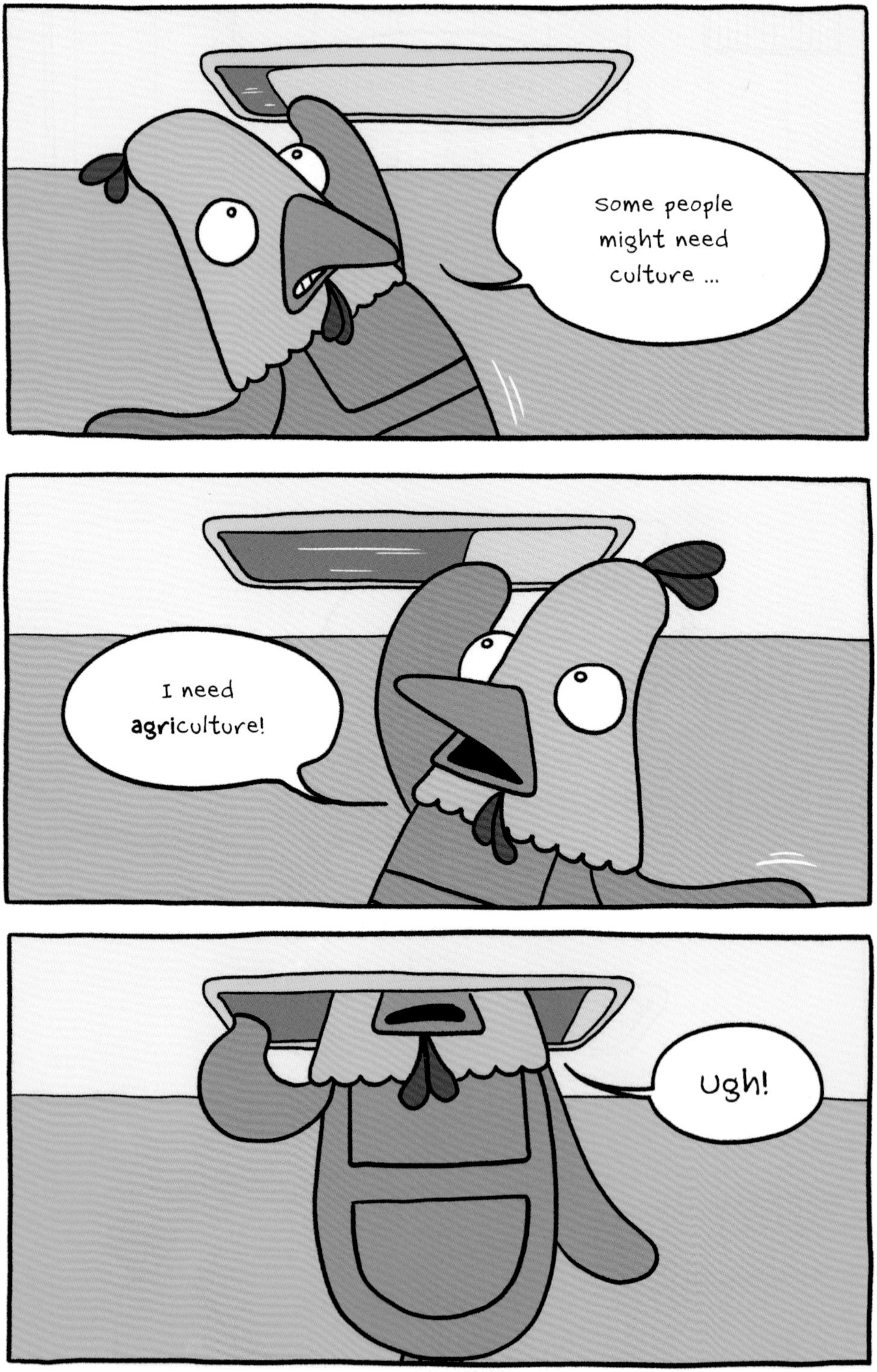
Some people might need culture ...
I need **agri**culture!
Ugh!

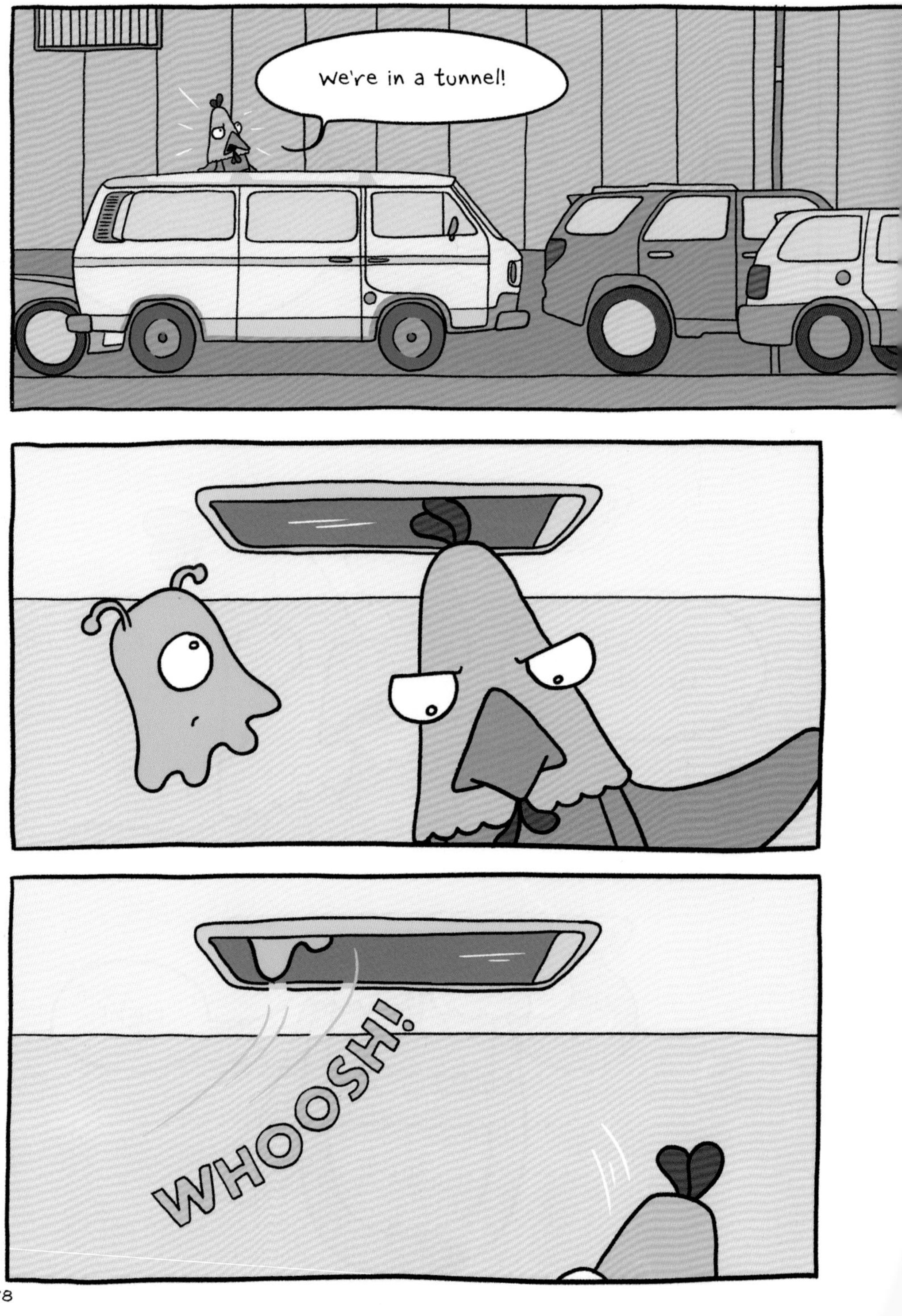
We're in a tunnel!
WHOOSH!

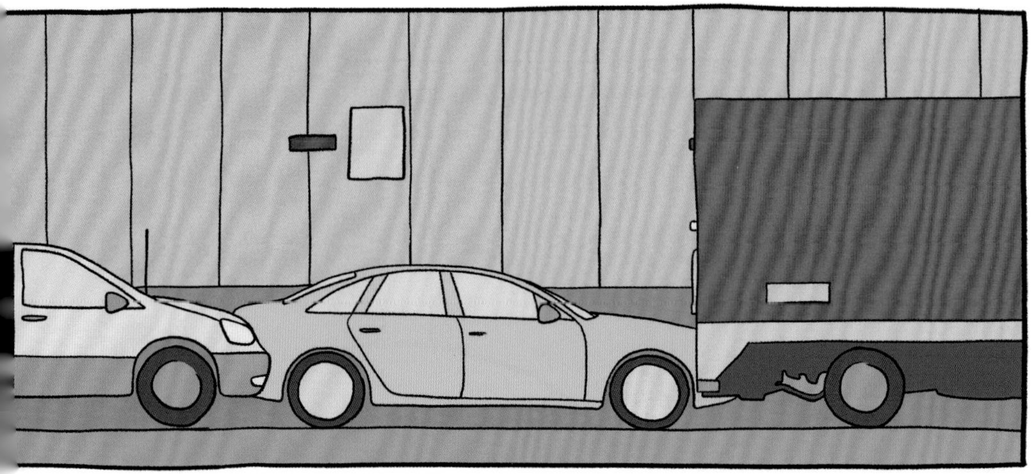

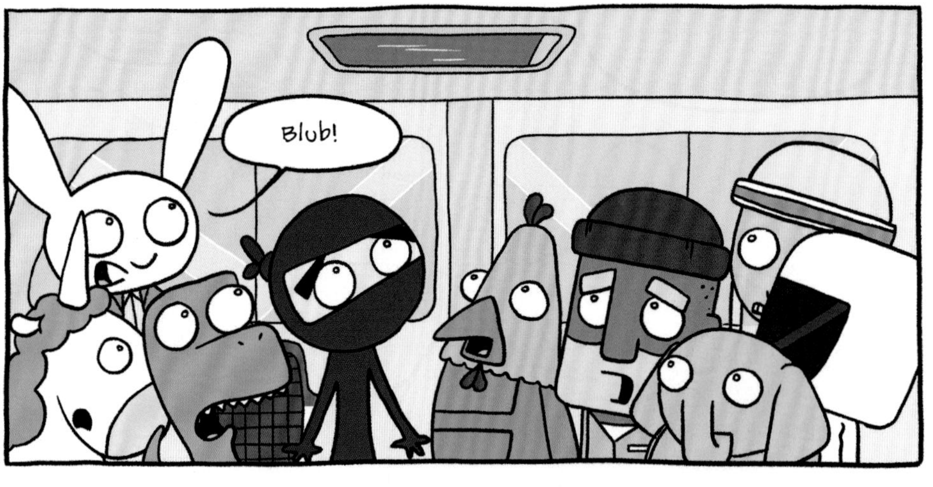
Blub!

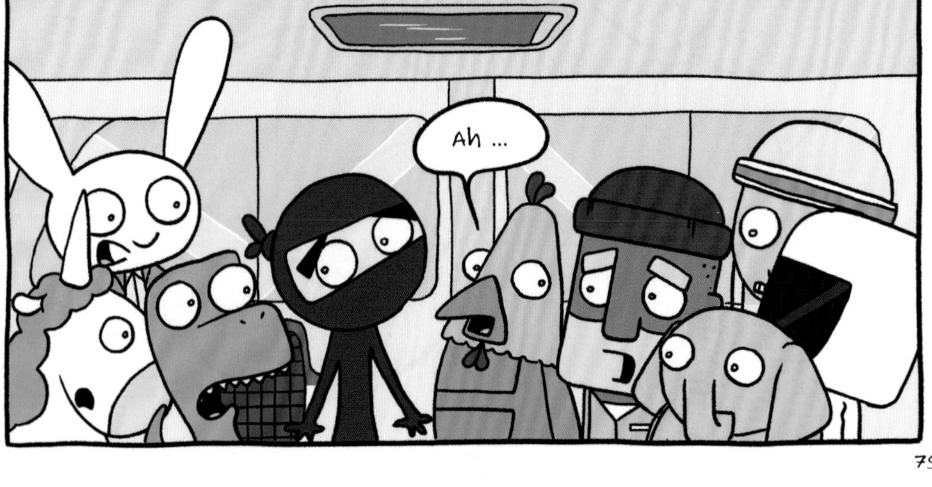
Ah ...

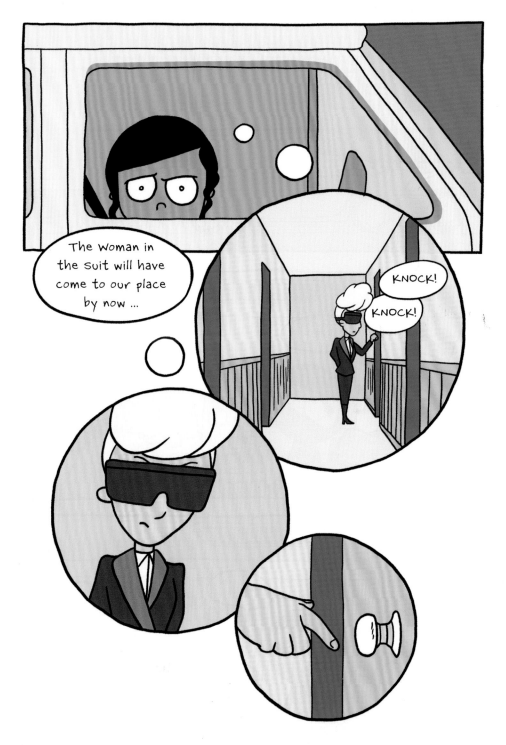

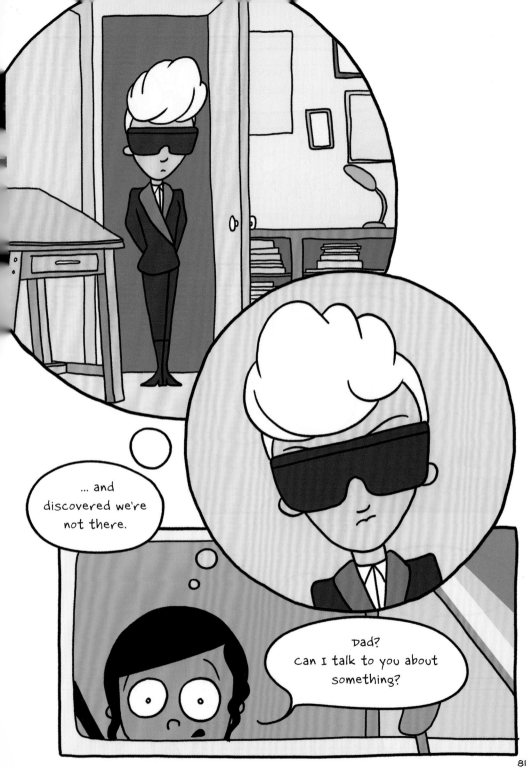

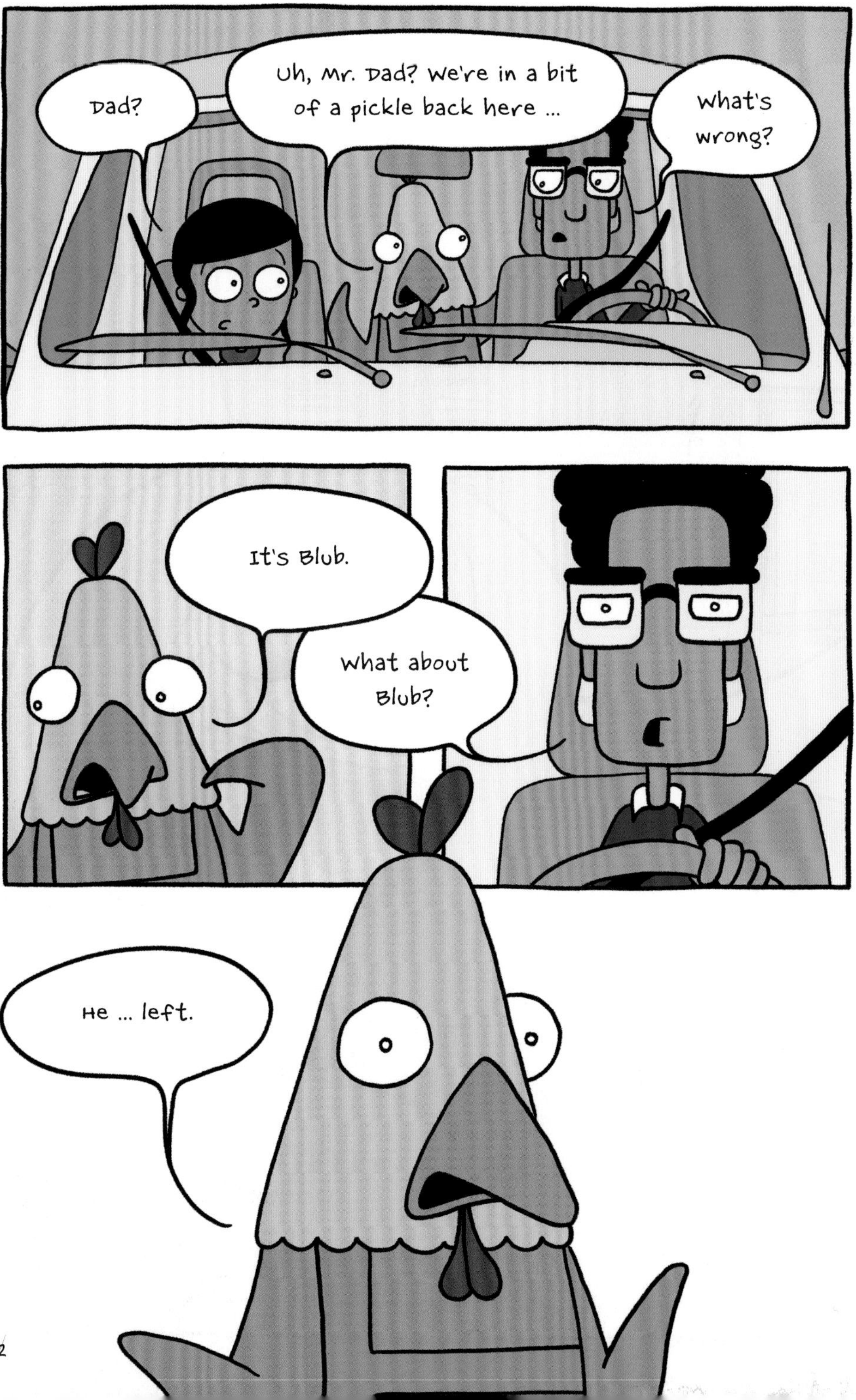
Dad?
Uh, Mr. Dad? We're in a bit of a pickle back here ...
What's wrong?
It's Blub.
What about Blub?
He ... left.

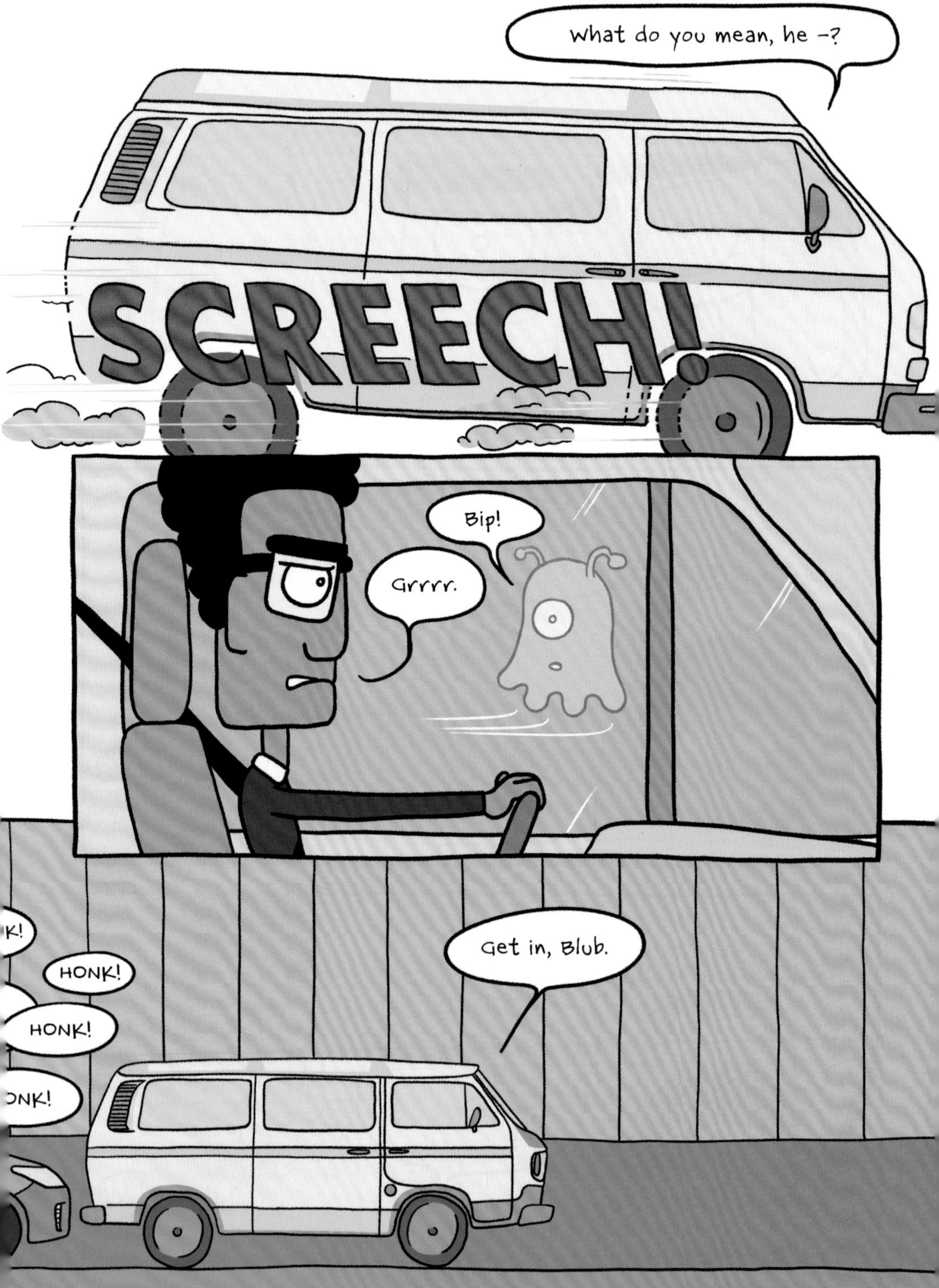
What do you mean, he -?
SCREECH!
Bip!
Grrrr.
HONK!
HONK!
Get in, Blub.

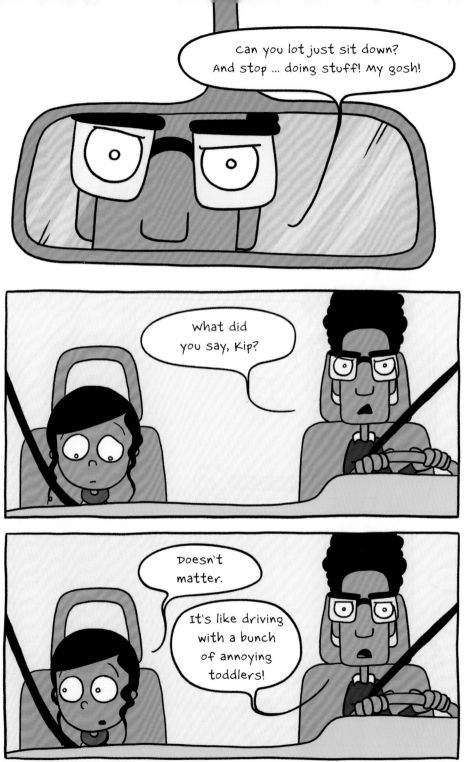

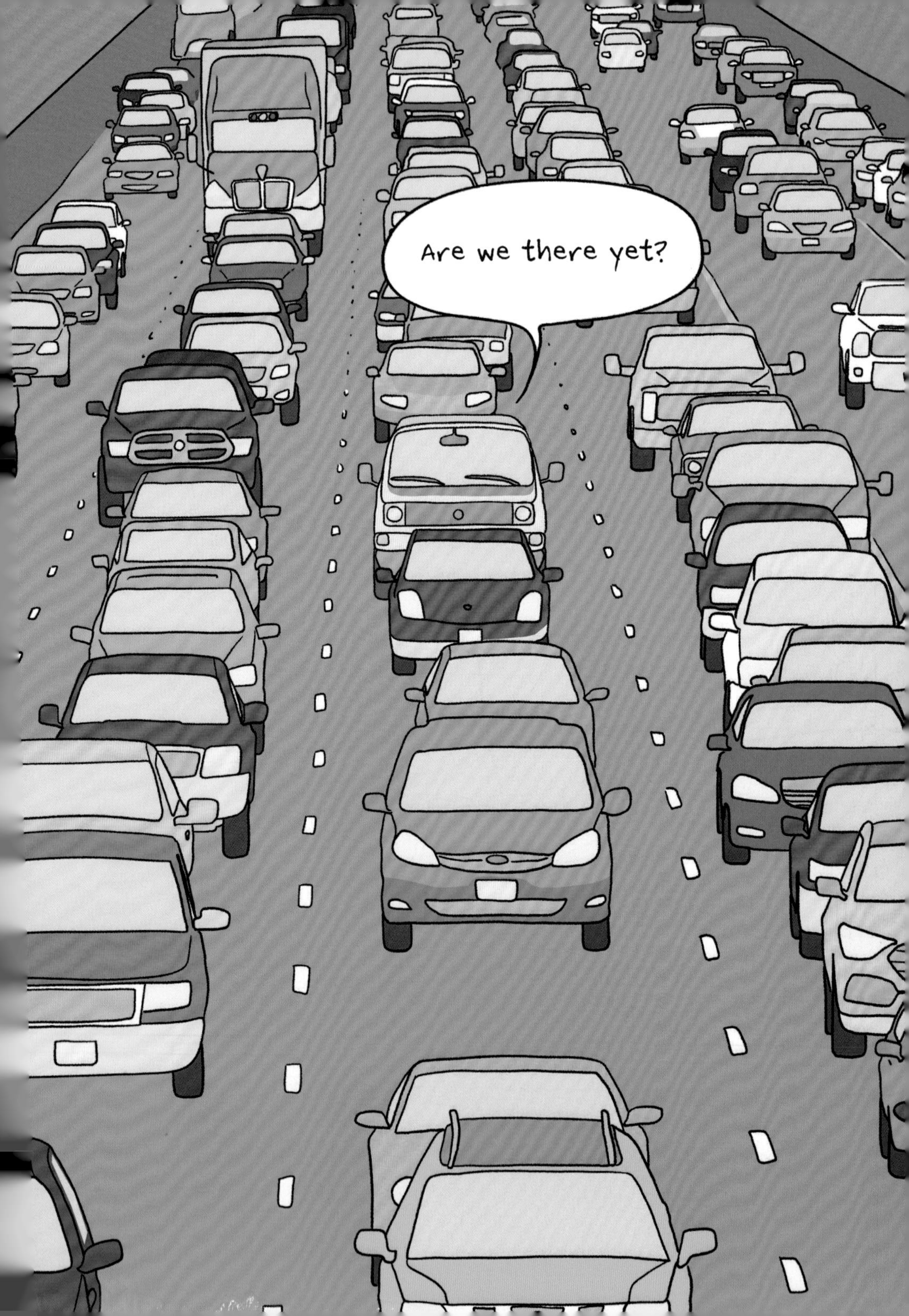
Are we there yet?

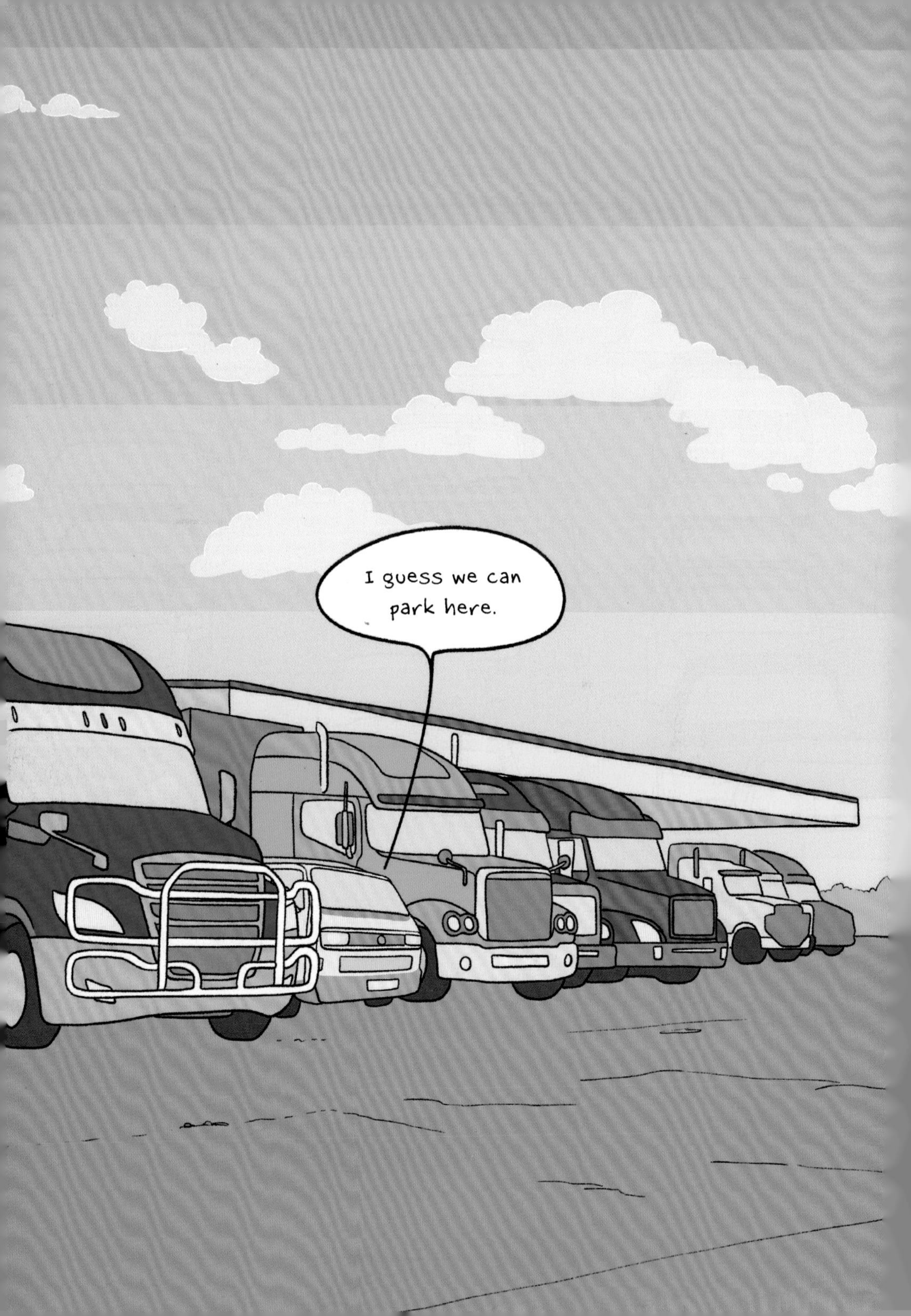
I guess we can park here.

CHAPTER FIVE
Odds in, Odds out

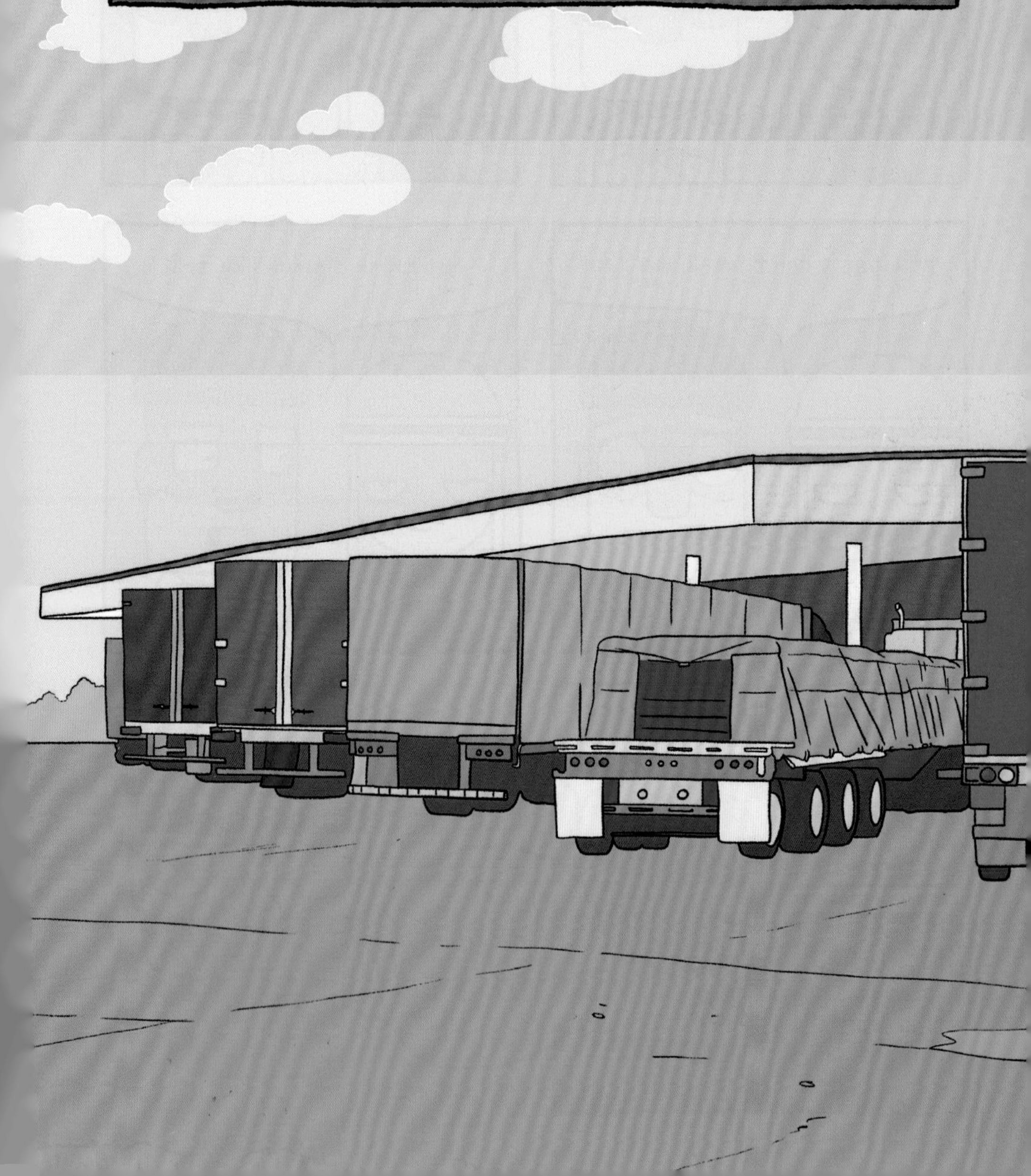

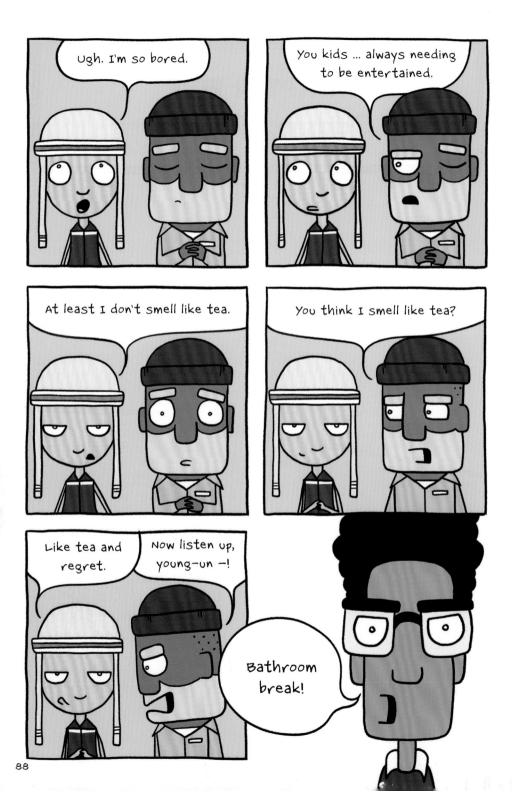

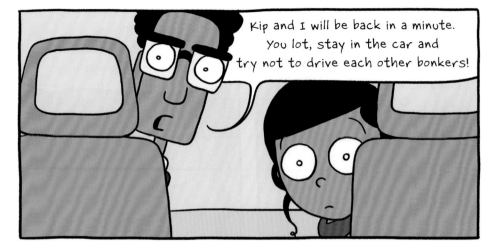

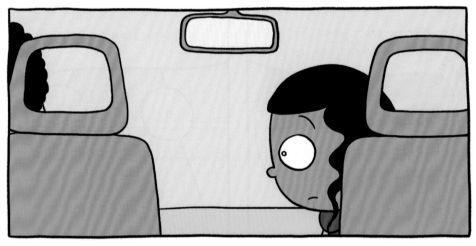

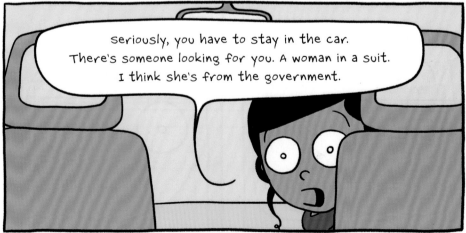

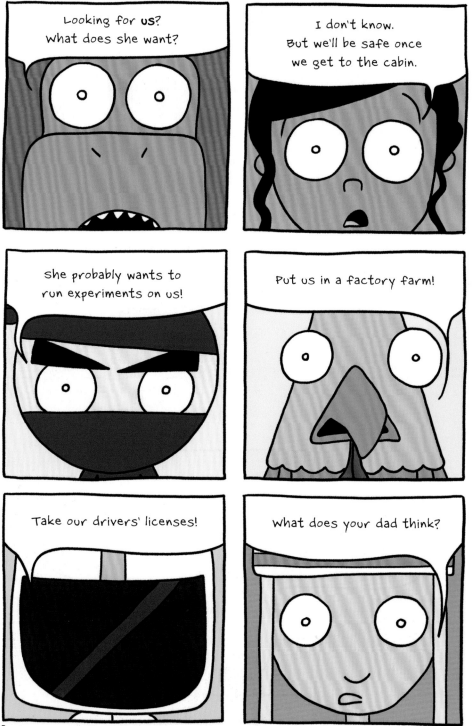

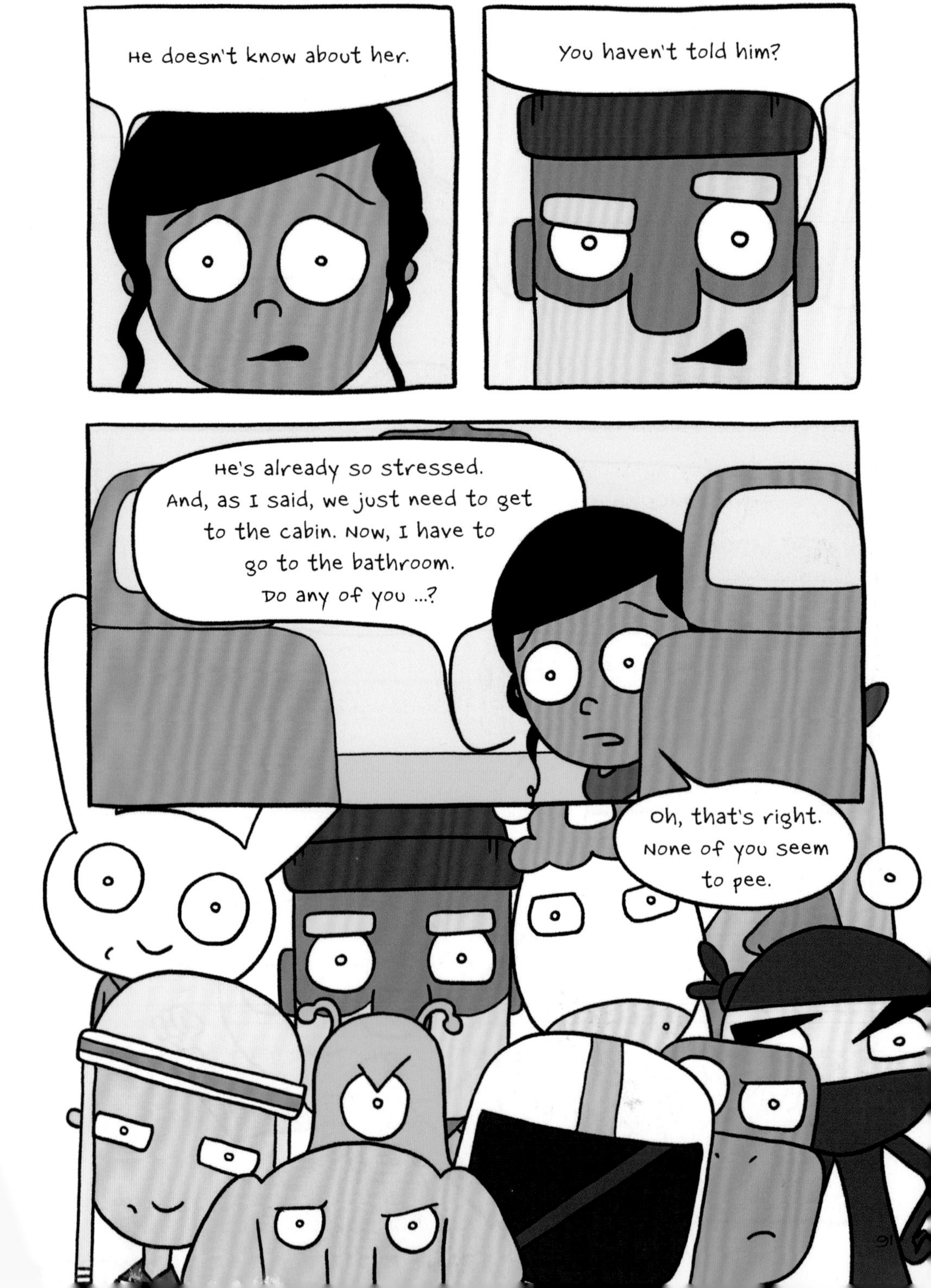
He doesn't know about her.
You haven't told him?
He's already so stressed. And, as I said, we just need to get to the cabin. Now, I have to go to the bathroom. Do any of you ...?
Oh, that's right. None of you seem to pee.

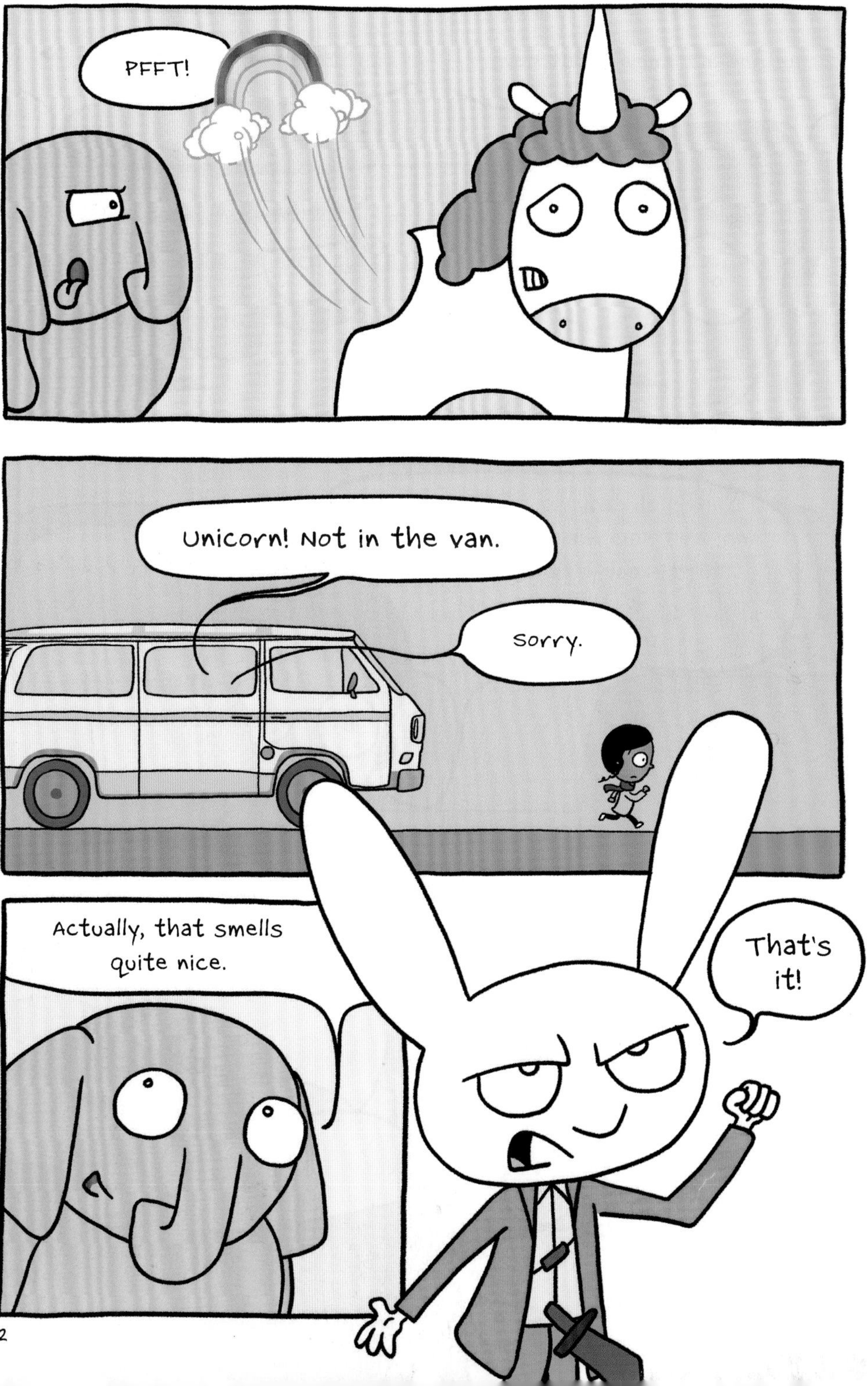
PFFT!
Unicorn! Not in the van.
Sorry.
Actually, that smells quite nice.
That's it!

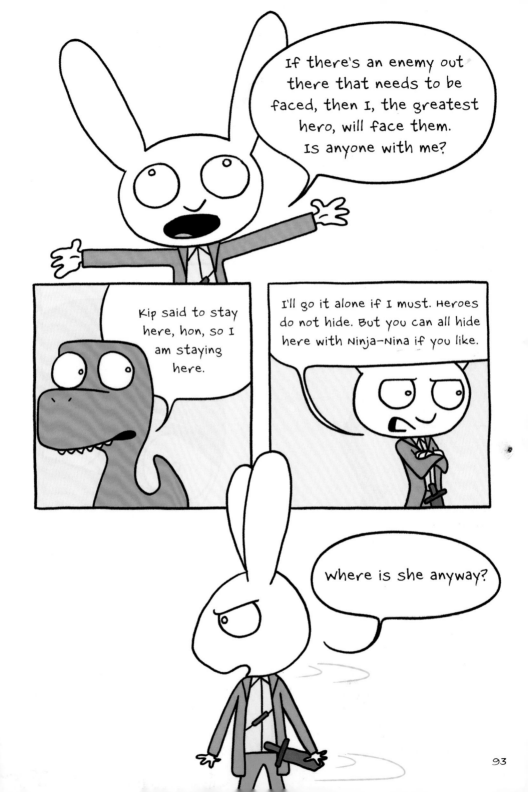

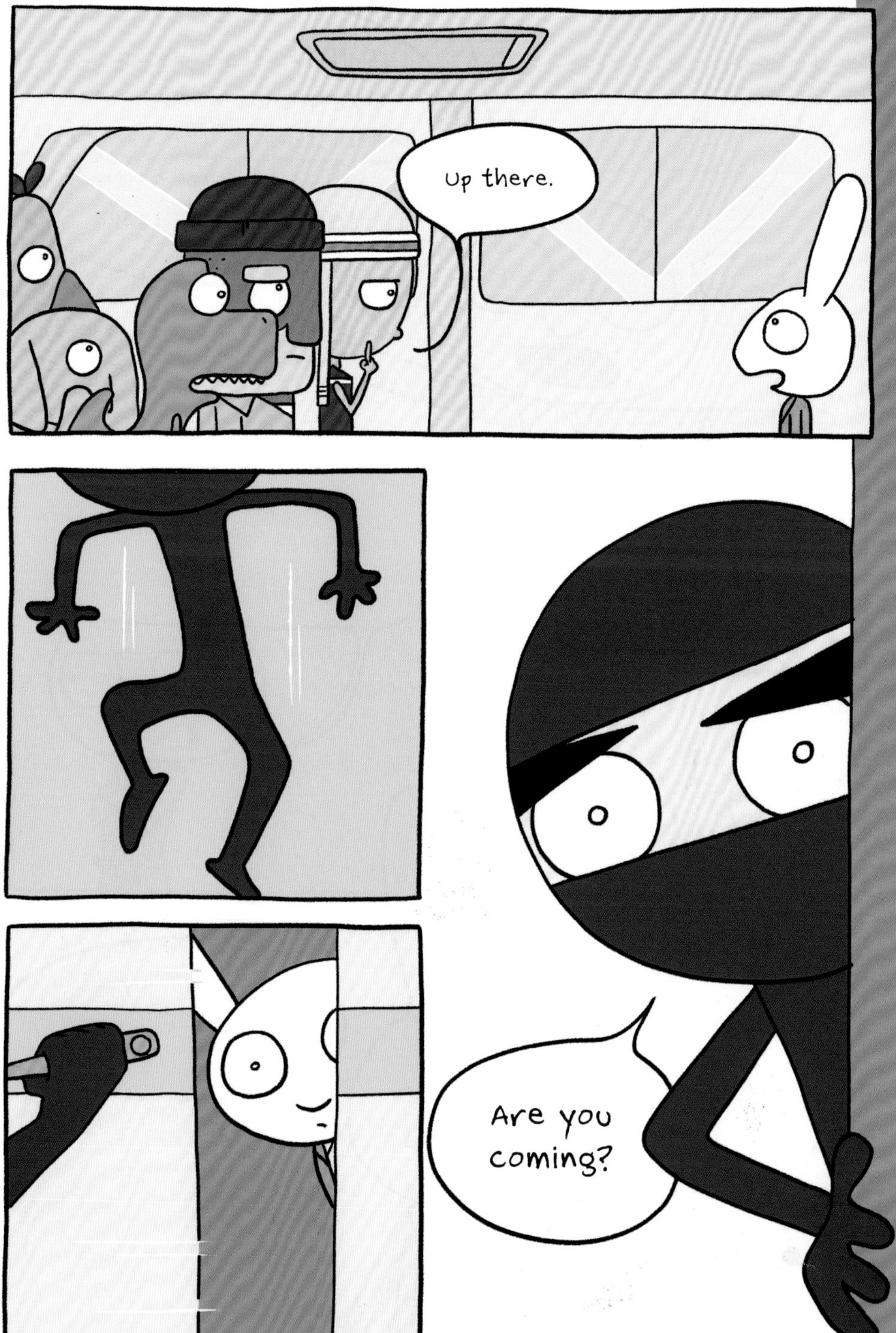
Up there.
Are you coming?

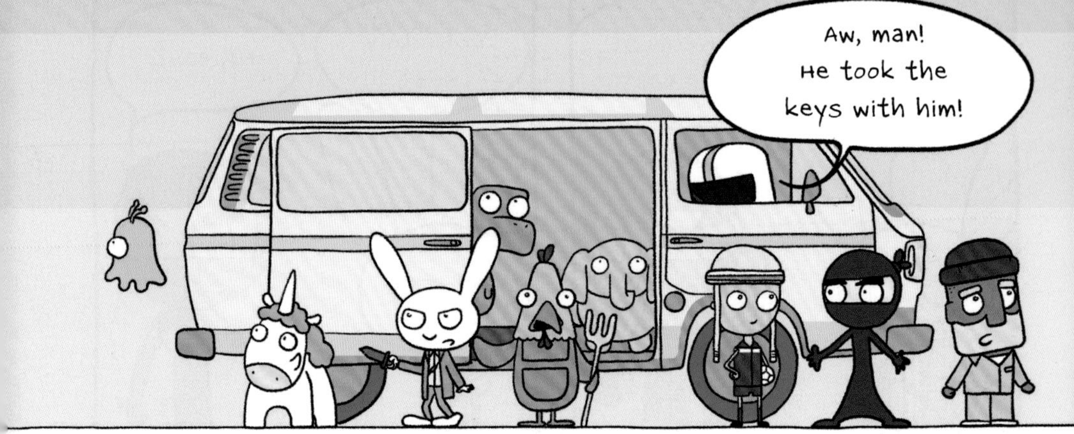
Aw, man!
He took the
keys with him!

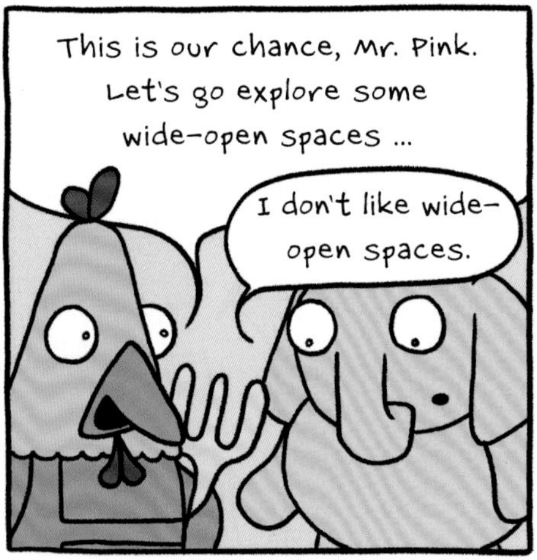
This is our chance, Mr. Pink.
Let's go explore some
wide-open spaces ...
I don't like wide-
open spaces.

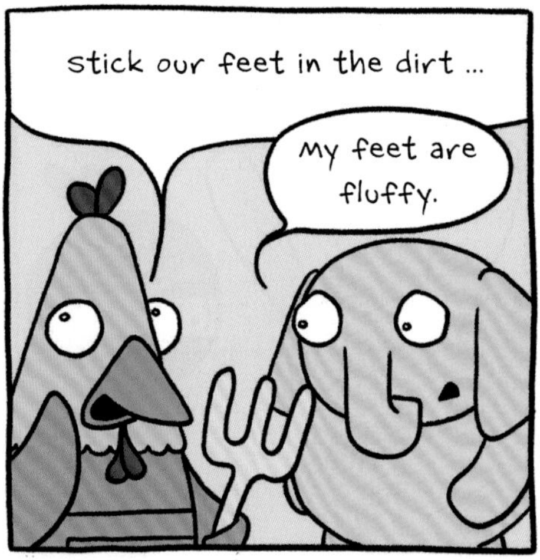
Stick our feet in the dirt ...
My feet are
fluffy.

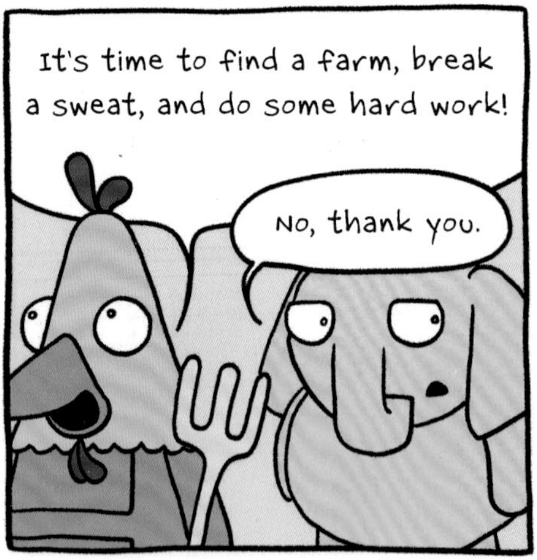
It's time to find a farm, break
a sweat, and do some hard work!
No, thank you.

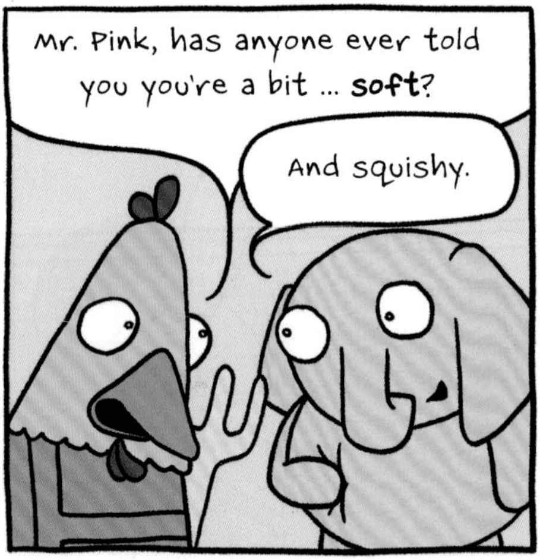
Mr. Pink, has anyone ever told
you you're a bit ... **soft**?
And squishy.

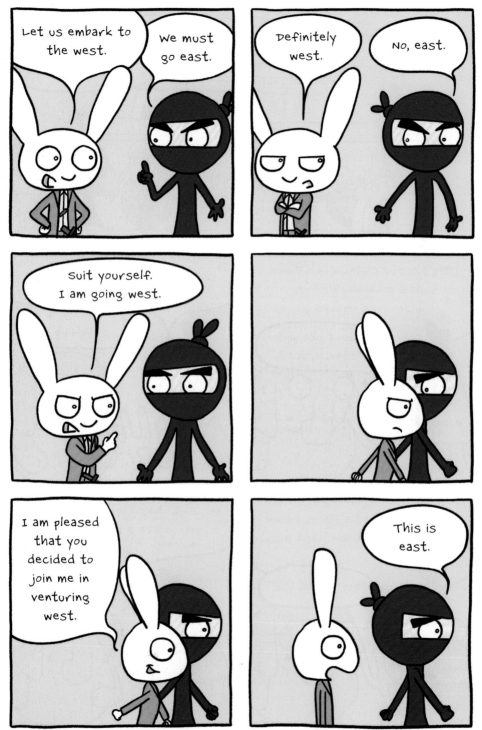

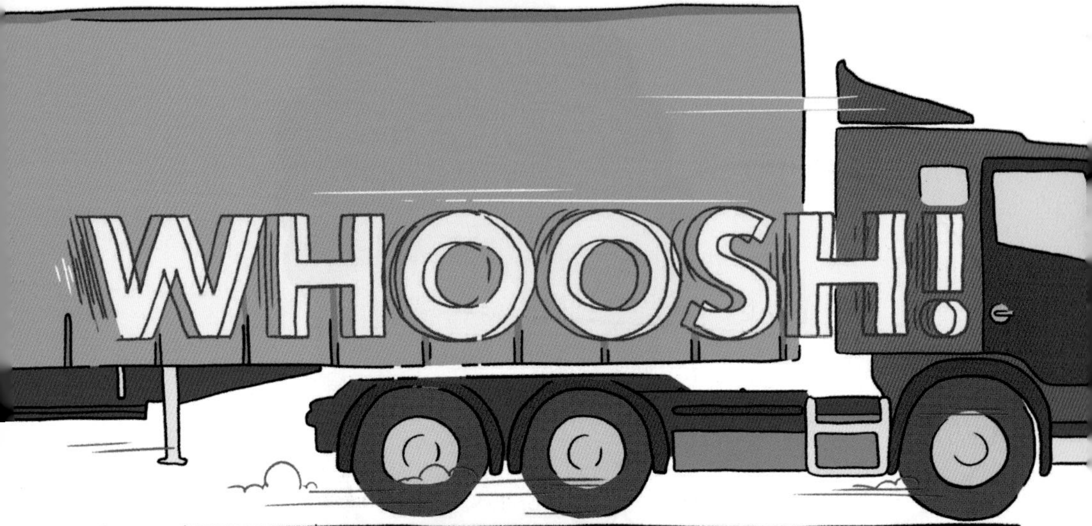
WHOOSH!
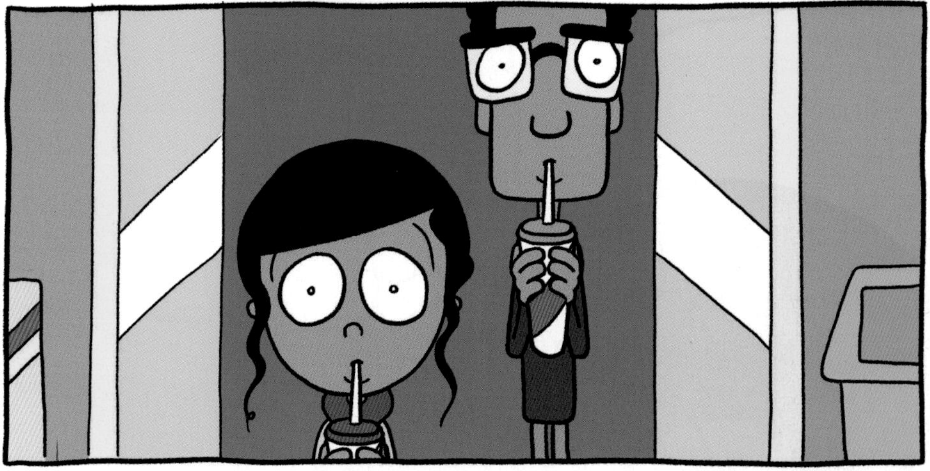
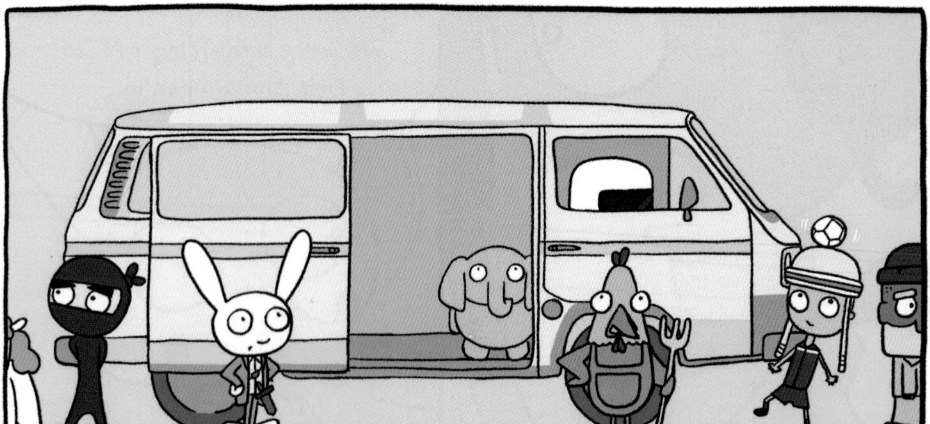

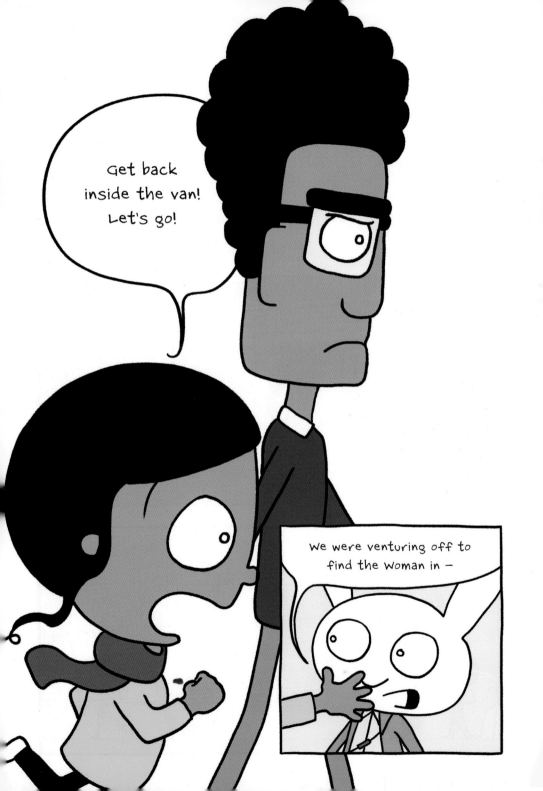

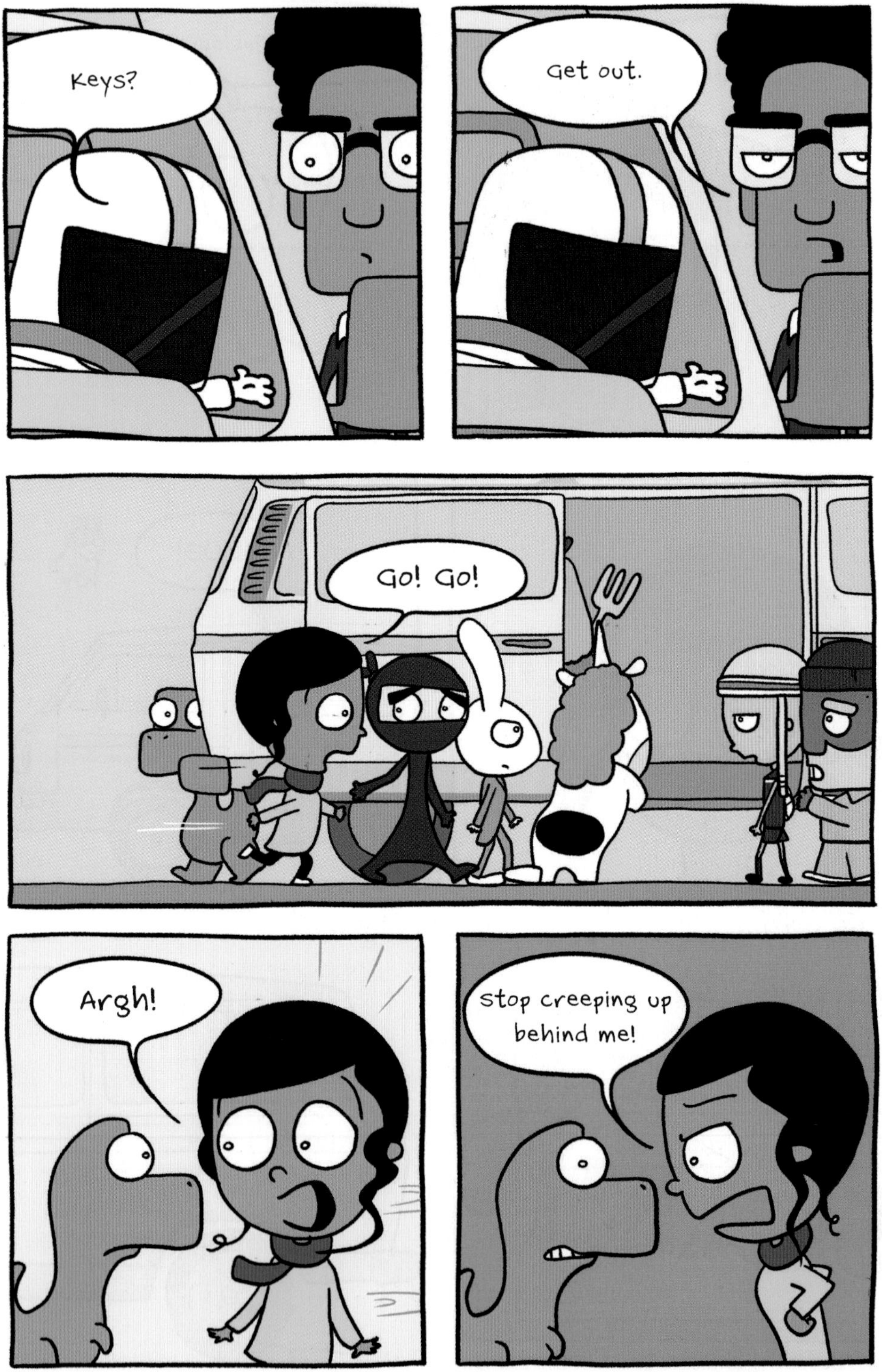
Keys?
Get out.
Go! Go!
Argh!
Stop creeping up behind me!

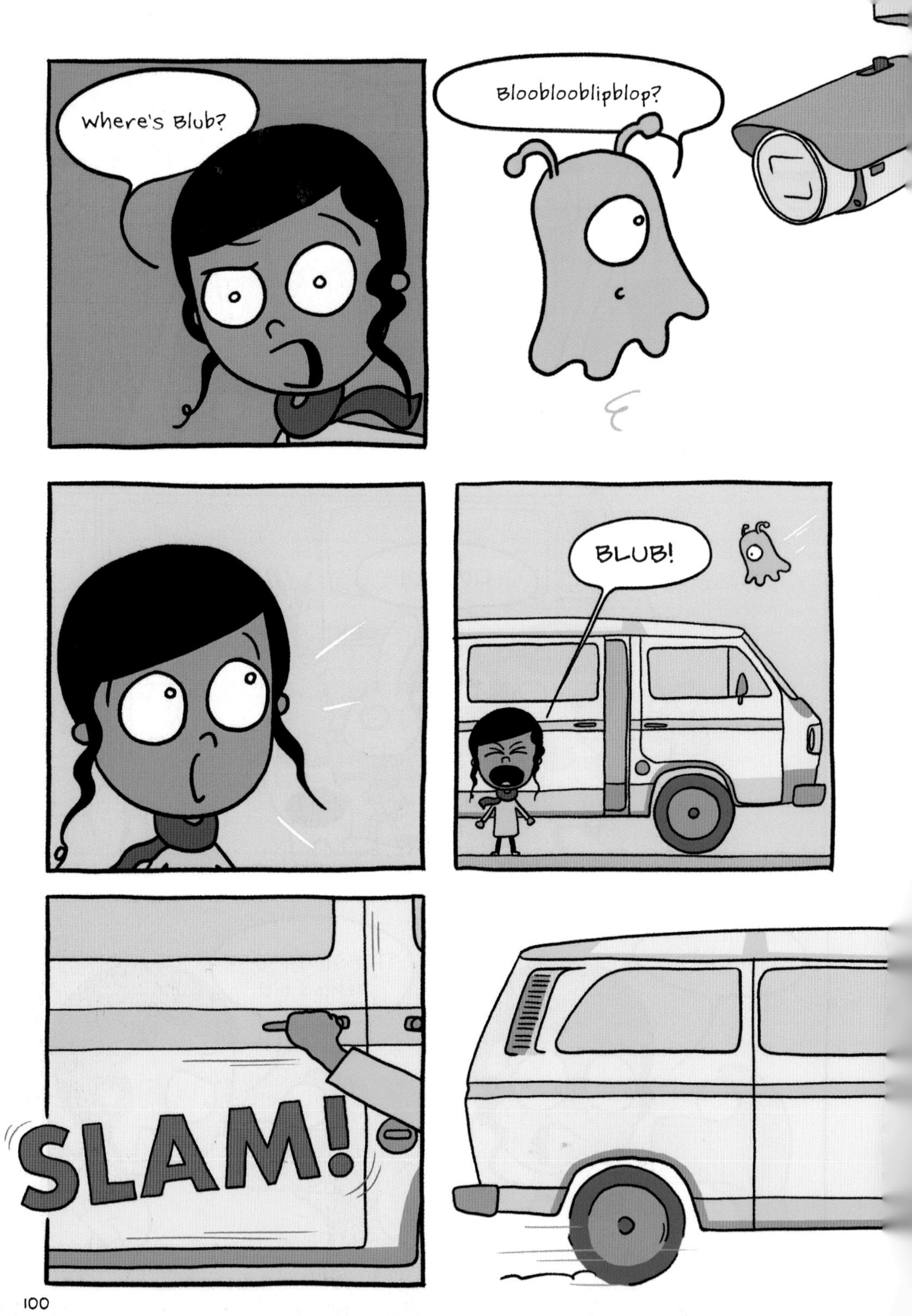
Where's Blub?
Blooblooblipblop?
BLUB!
SLAM!

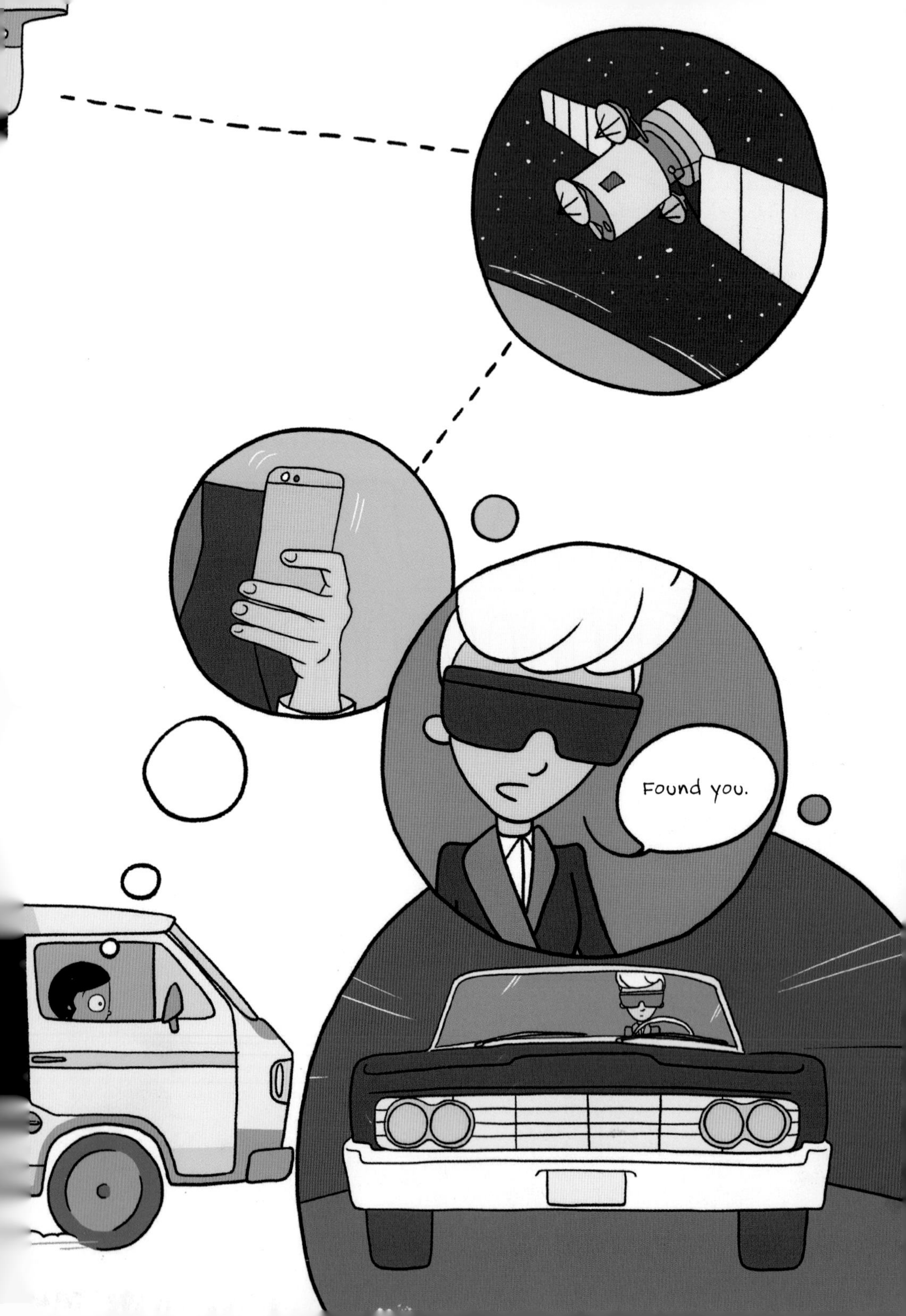
Found you.

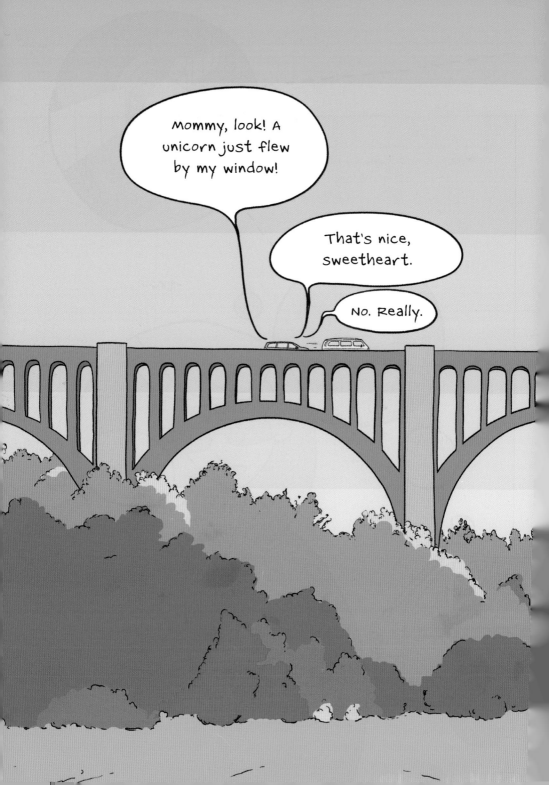

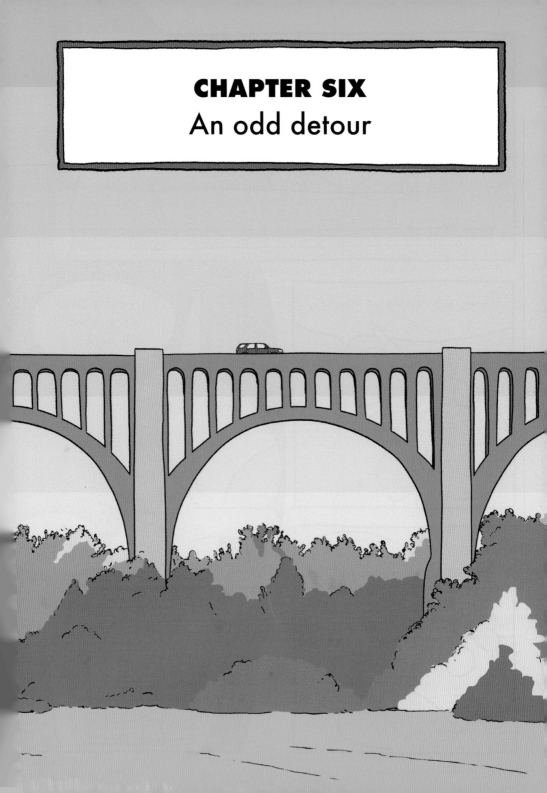

CHAPTER SIX
An odd detour

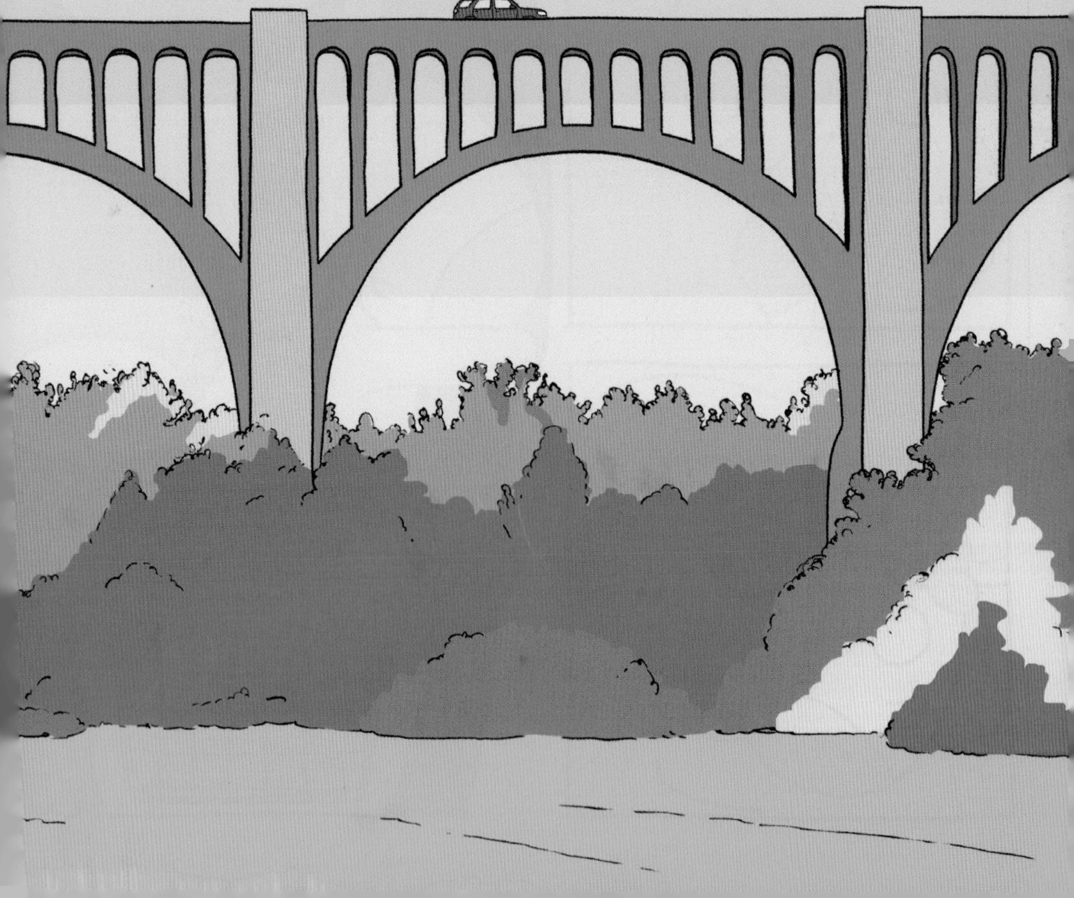

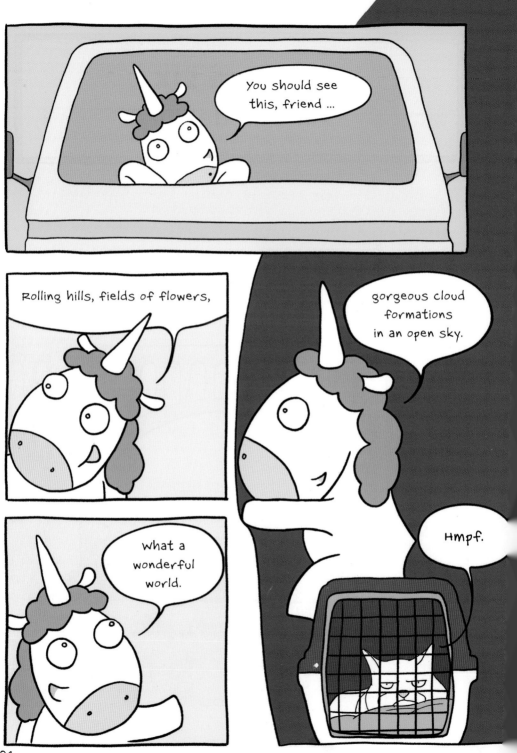

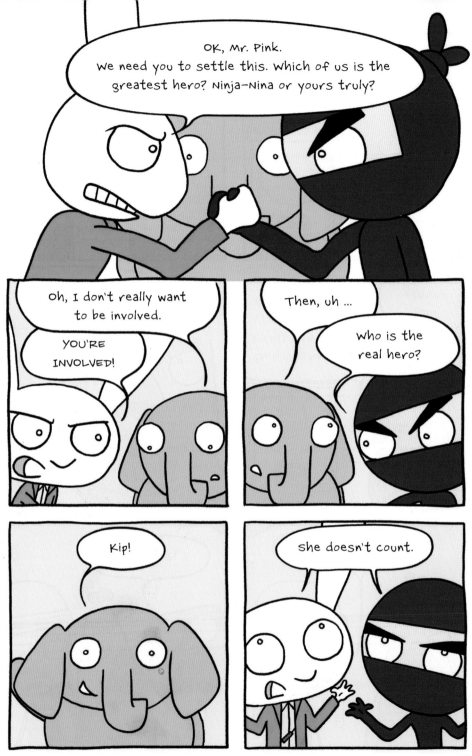

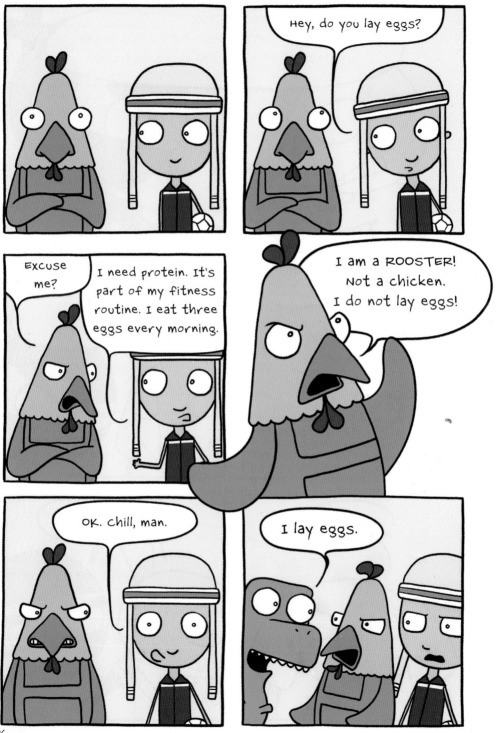

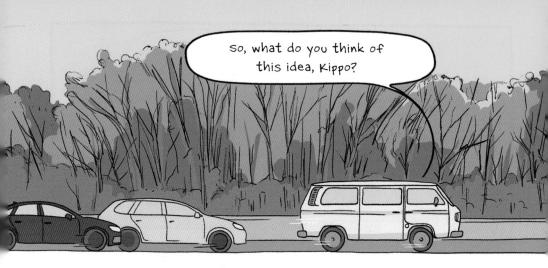

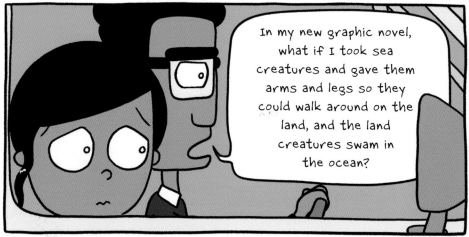

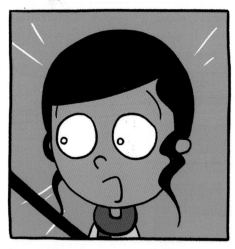

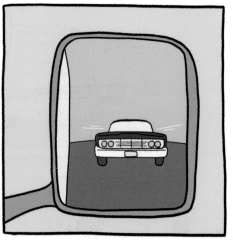

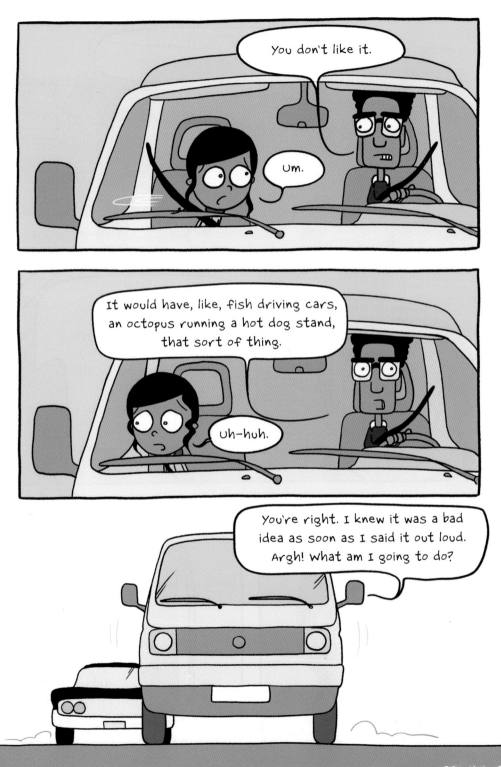

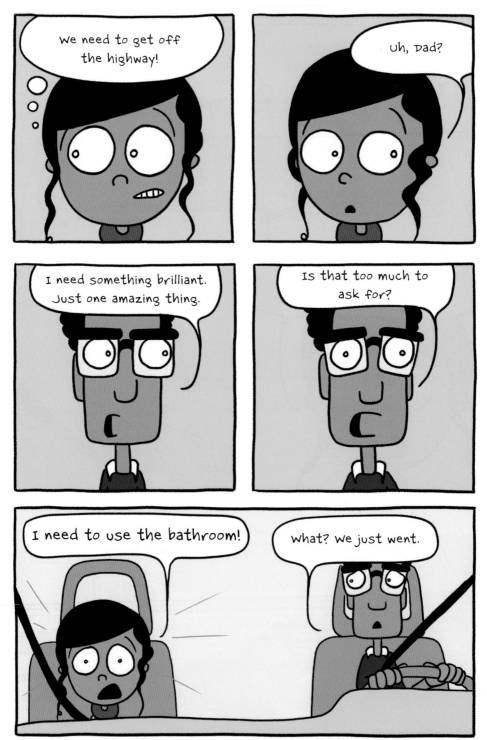

109

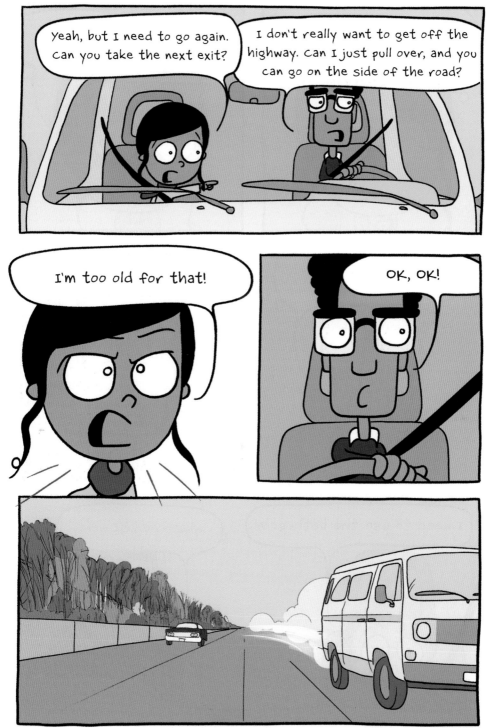

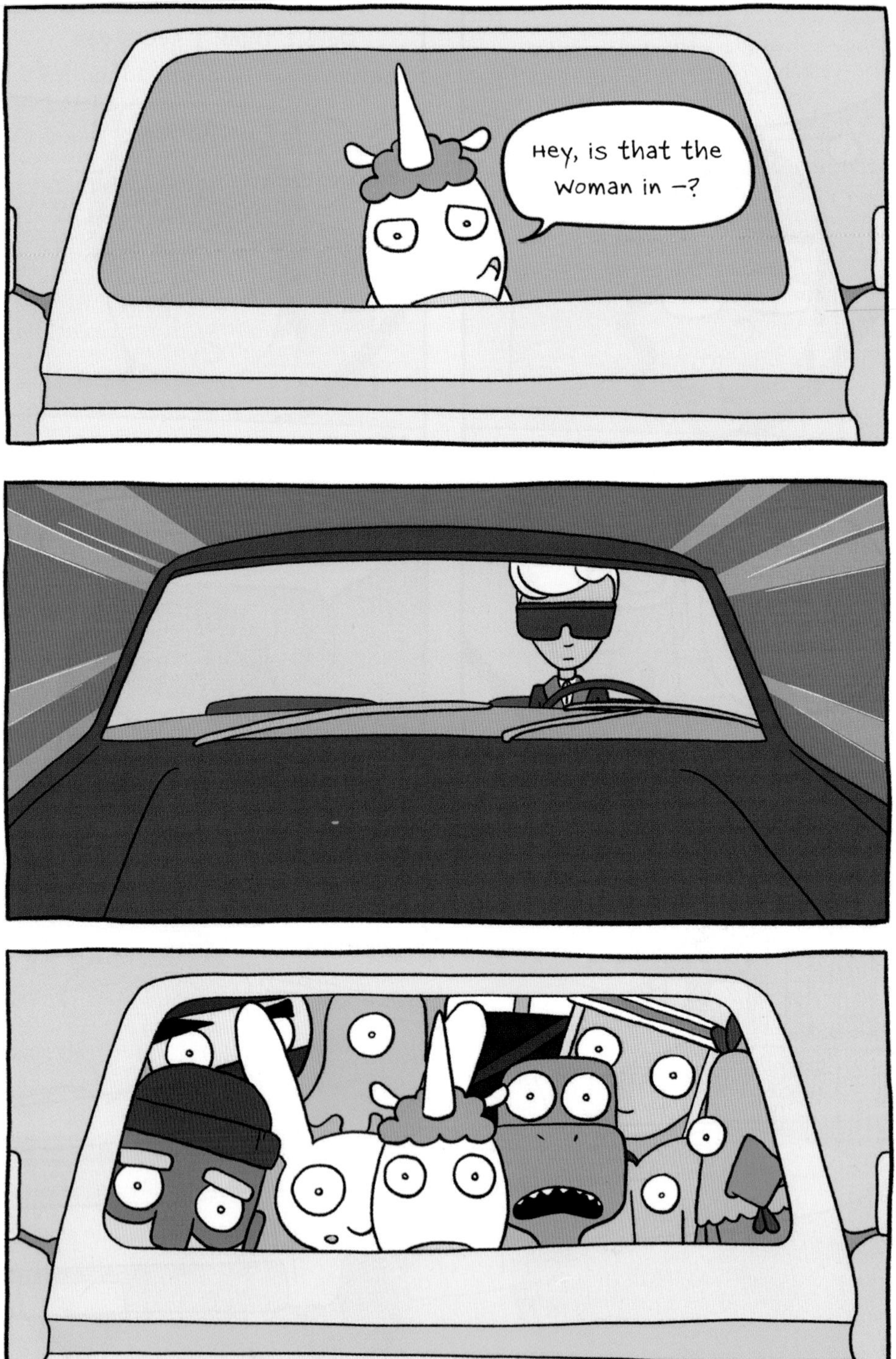
Hey, is that the woman in –?

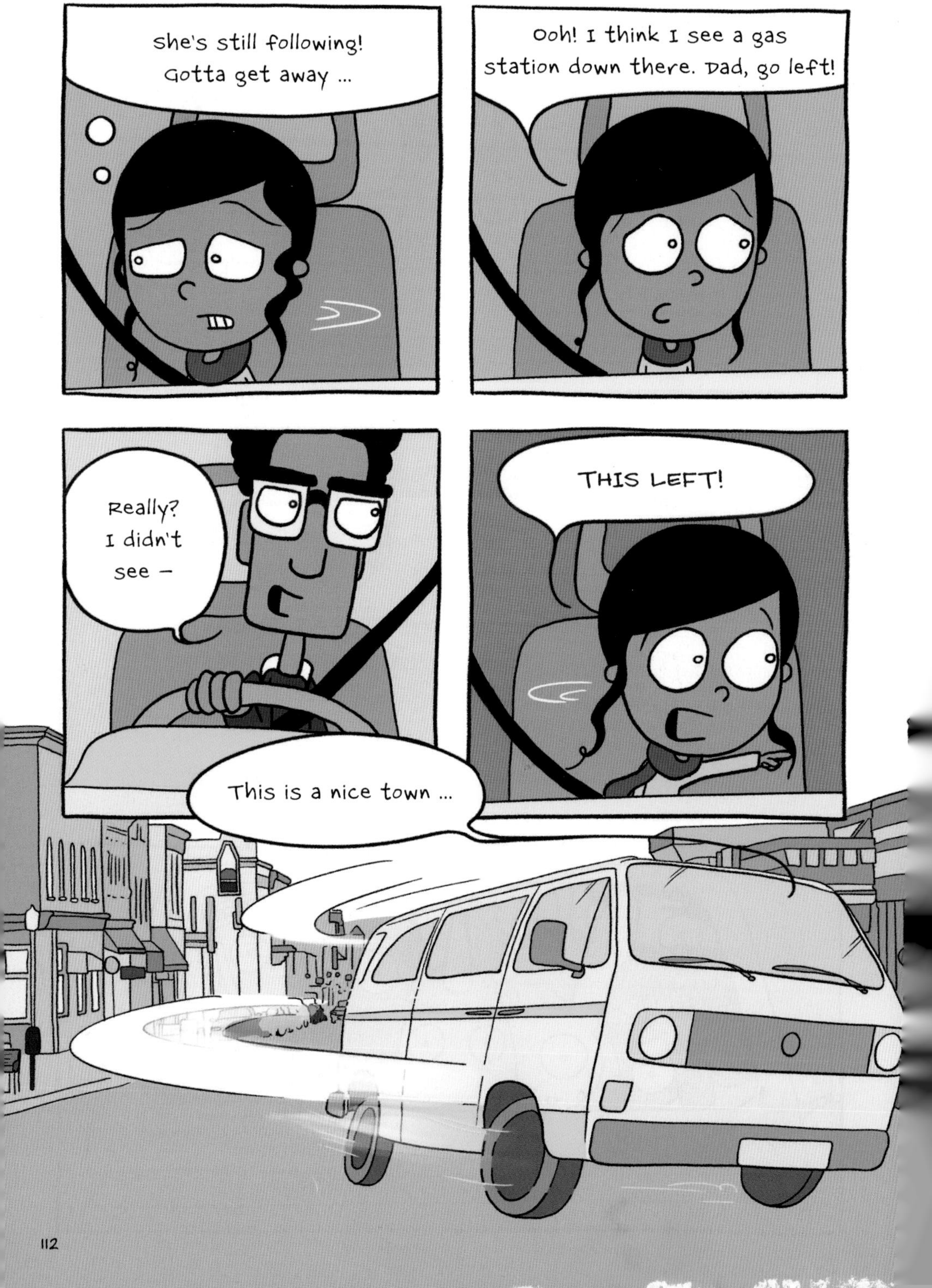
She's still following! Gotta get away ...
Ooh! I think I see a gas station down there. Dad, go left!
Really? I didn't see –
THIS LEFT!
This is a nice town ...

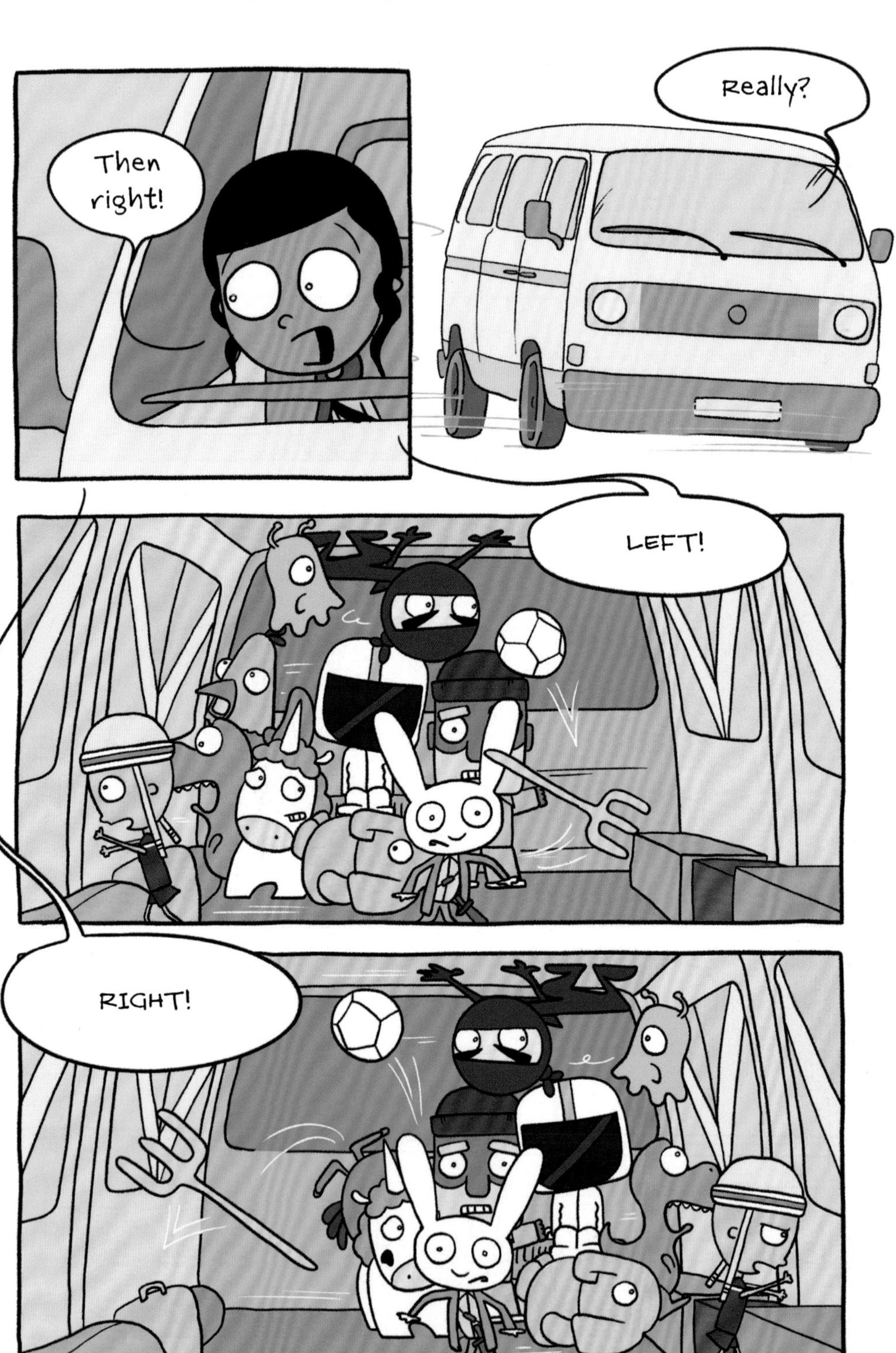
Then right!
Really?
LEFT!
RIGHT!

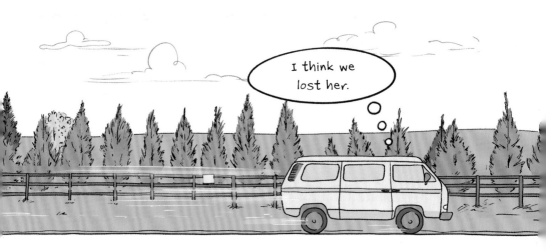

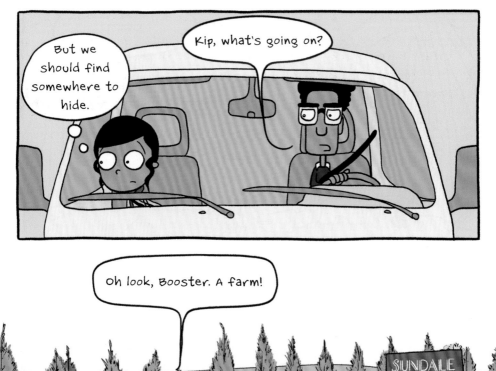

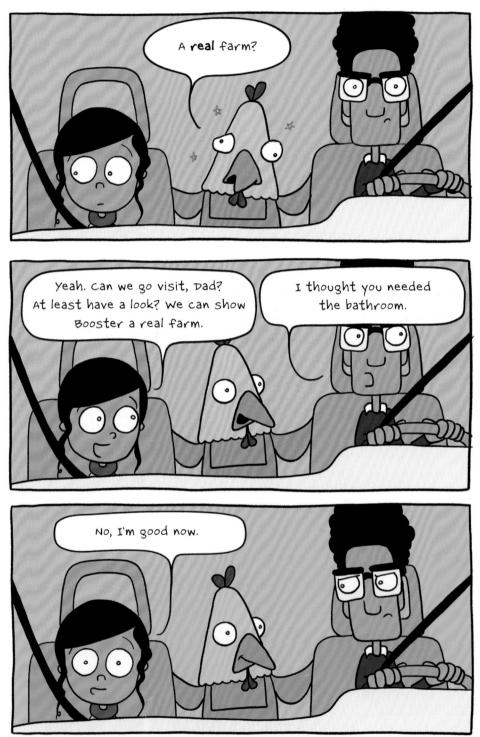

115

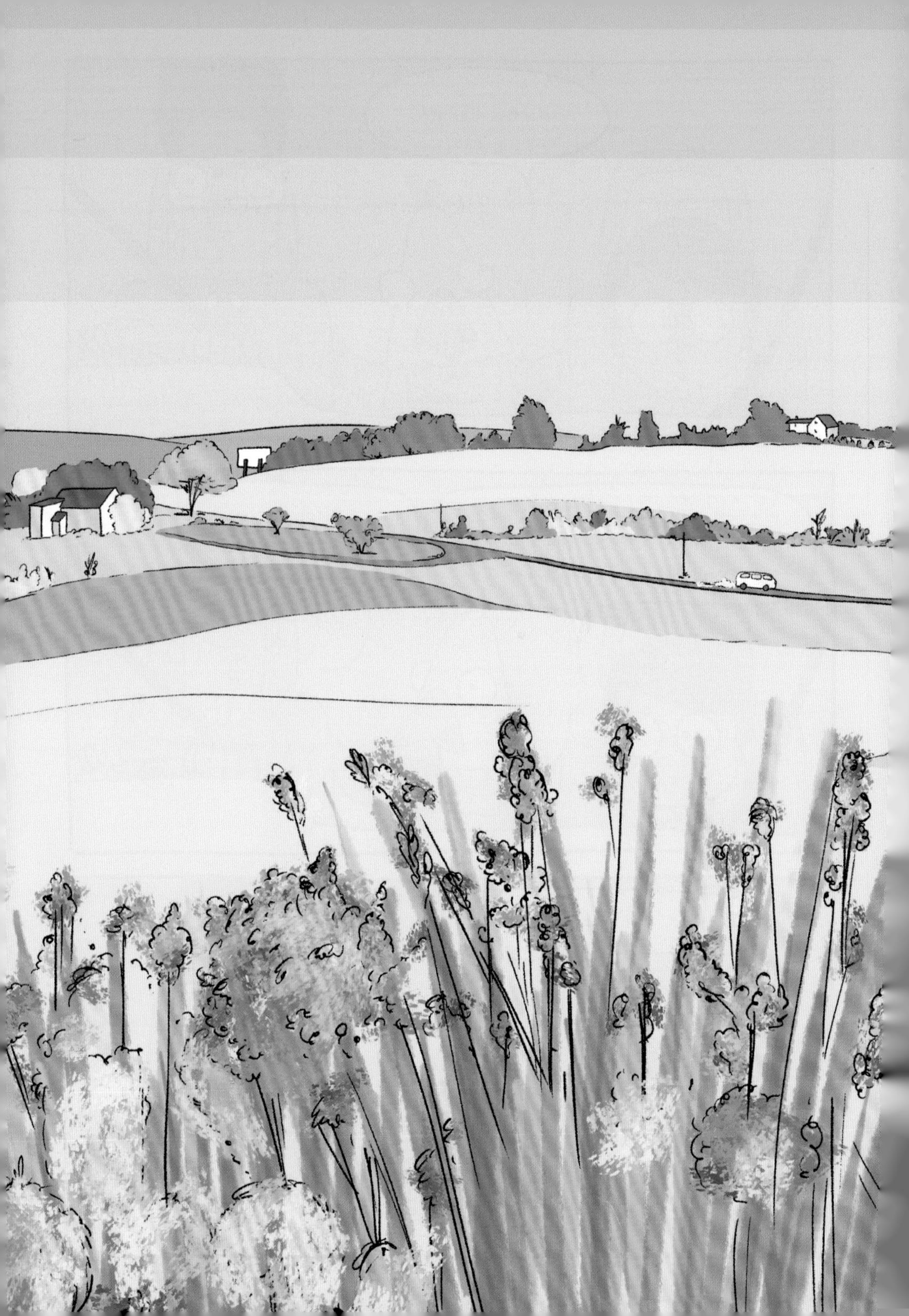

CHAPTER SEVEN
The Odds take a farm tour

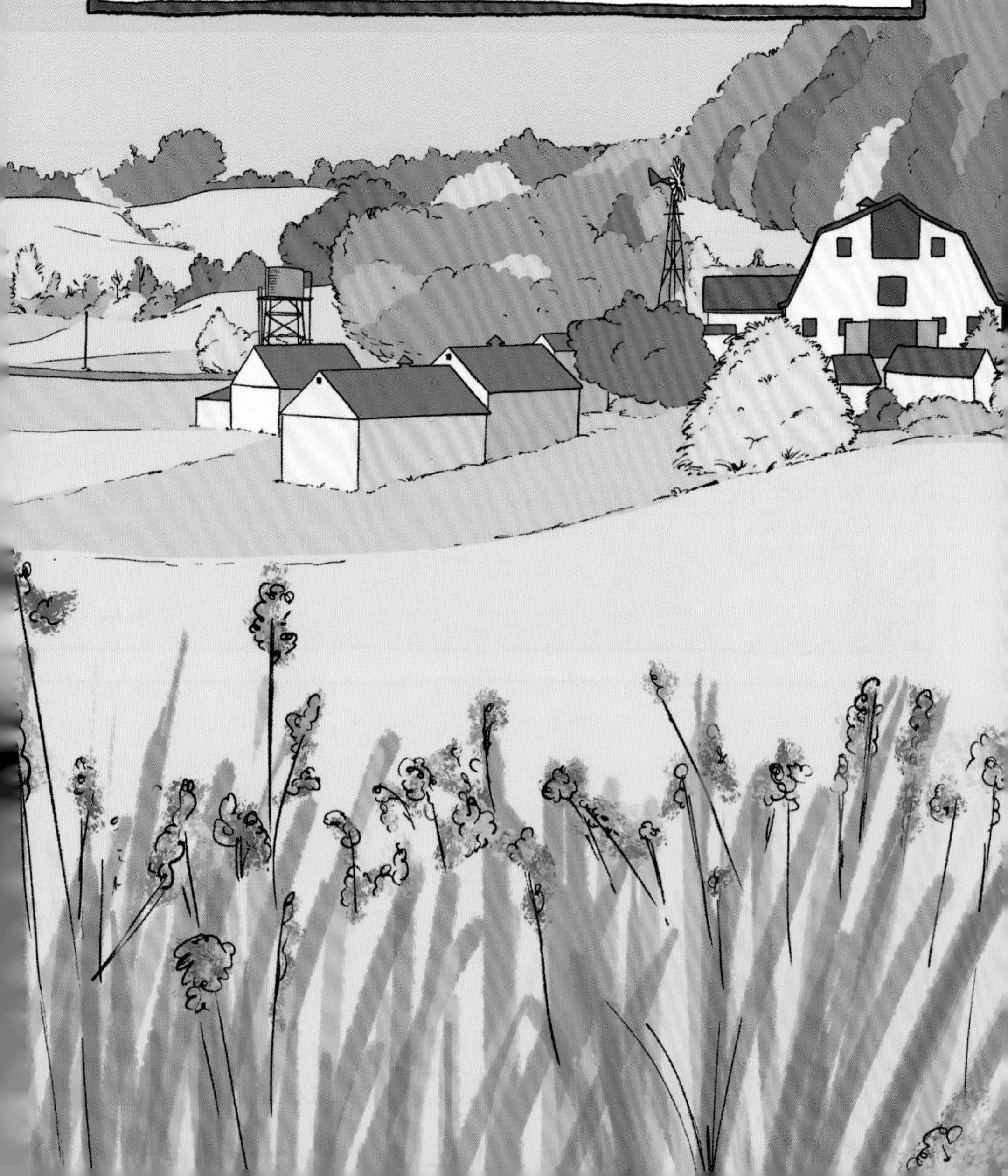

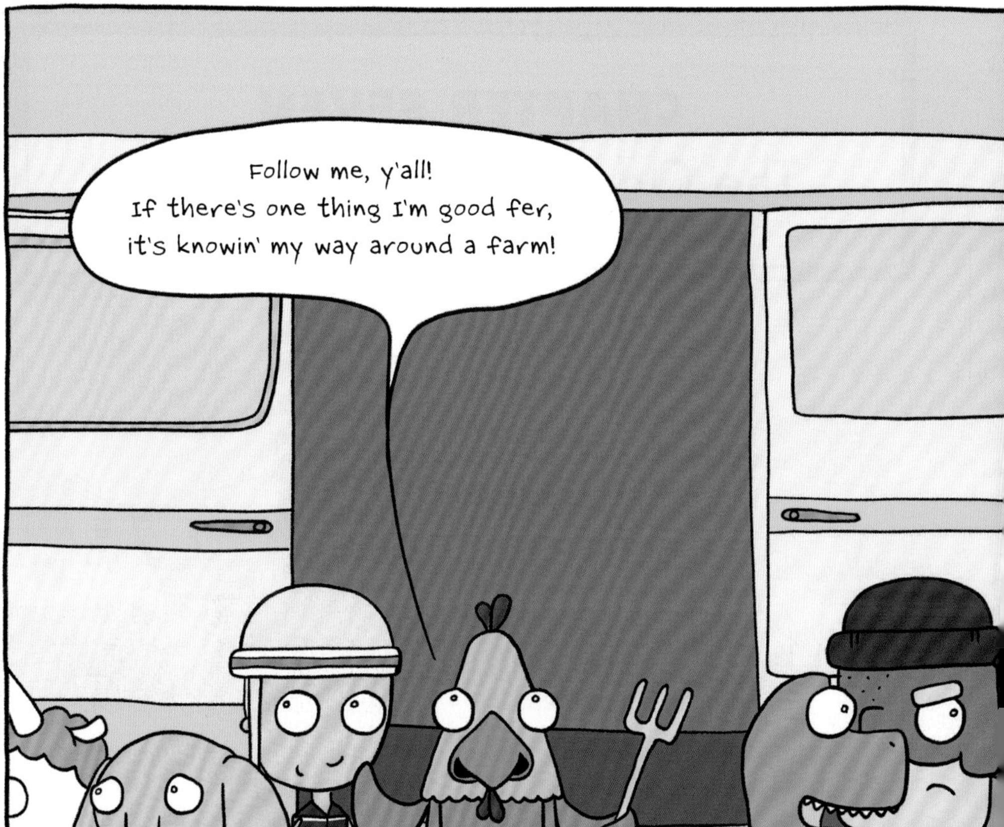
Follow me, y'all!
If there's one thing I'm good fer,
it's knowin' my way around a farm!

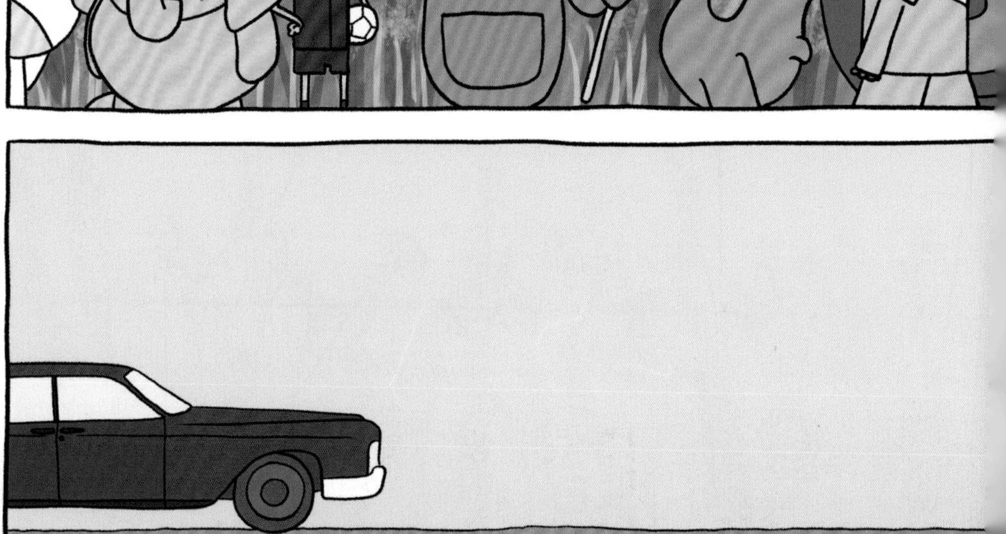

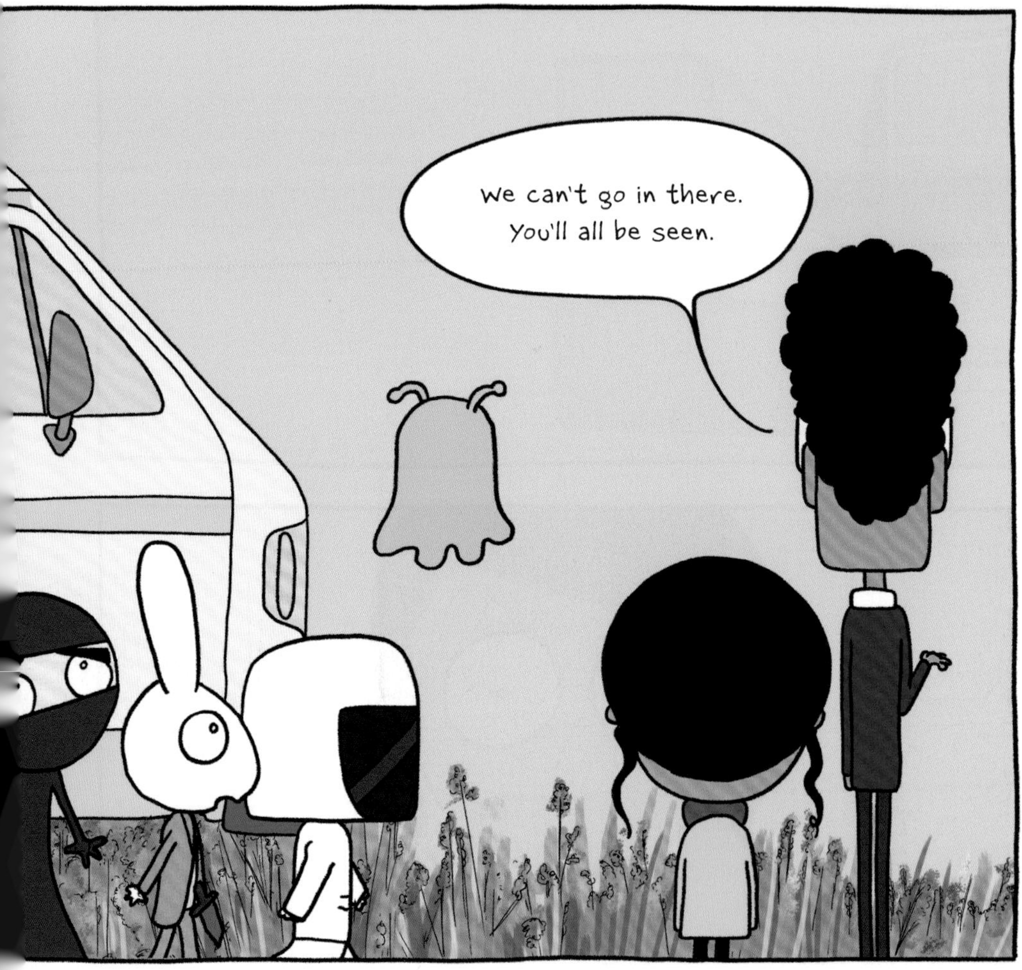

We can't go in there.
You'll all be seen.

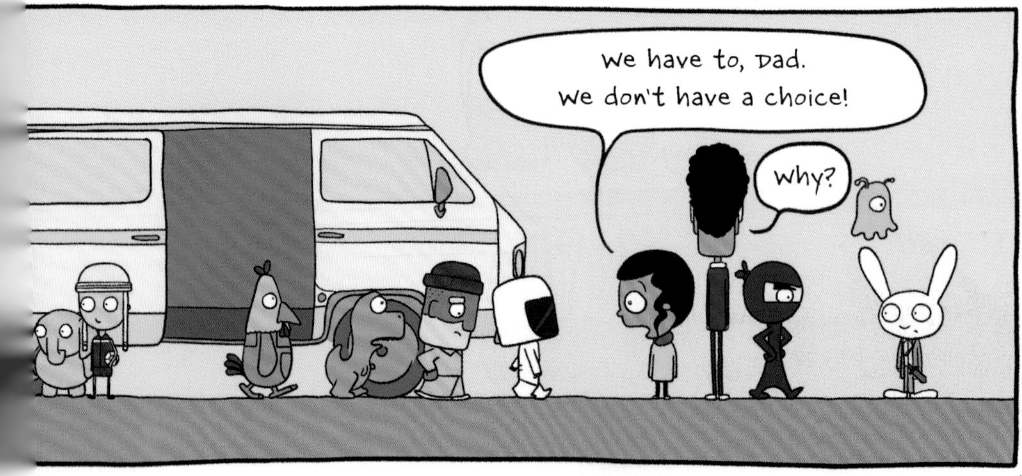

We have to, Dad.
We don't have a choice!
Why?

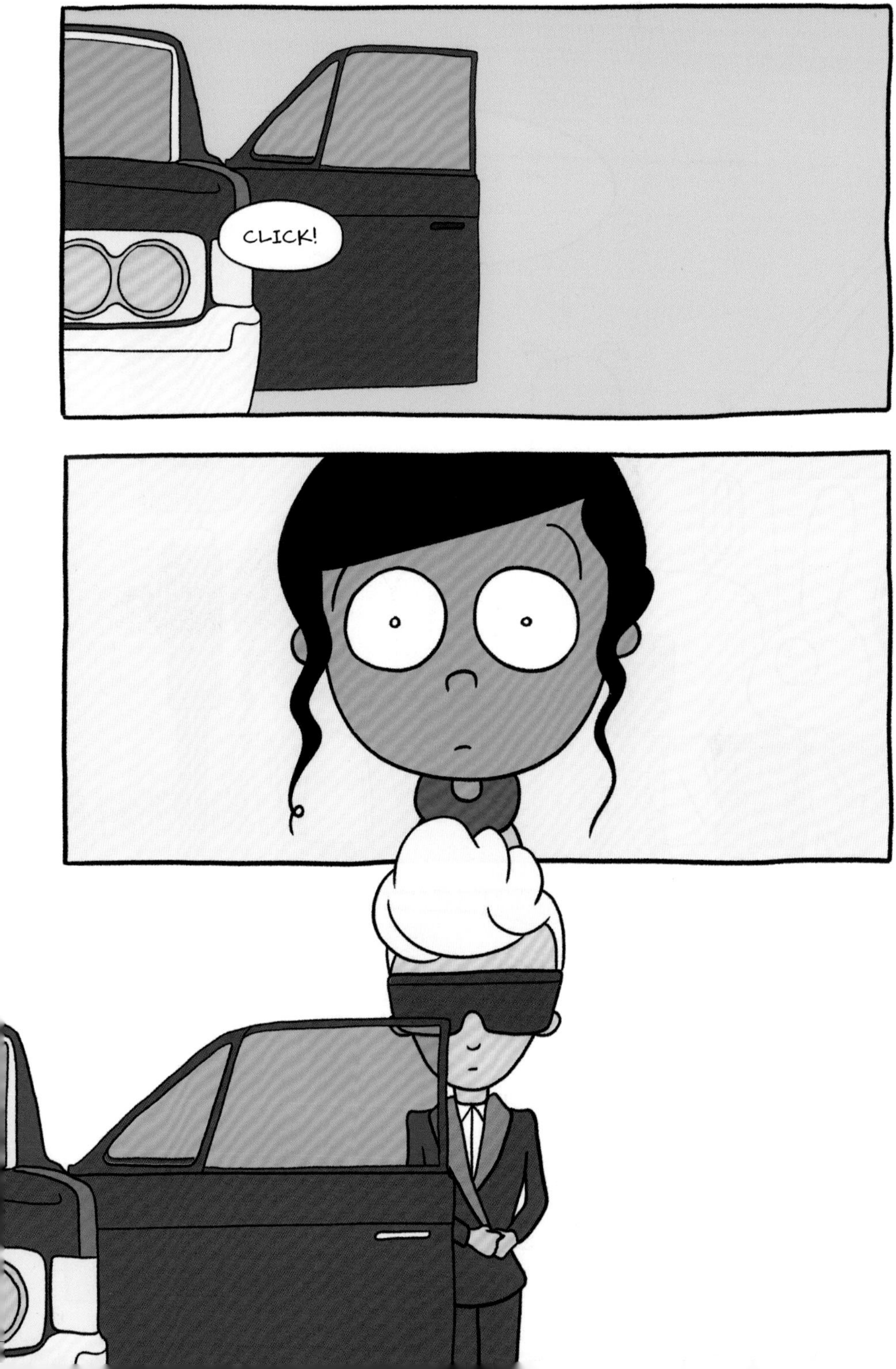
CLICK!

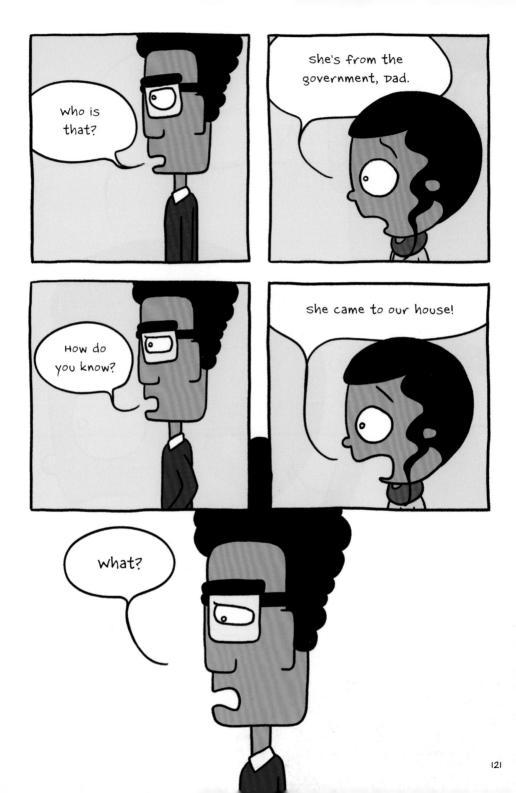

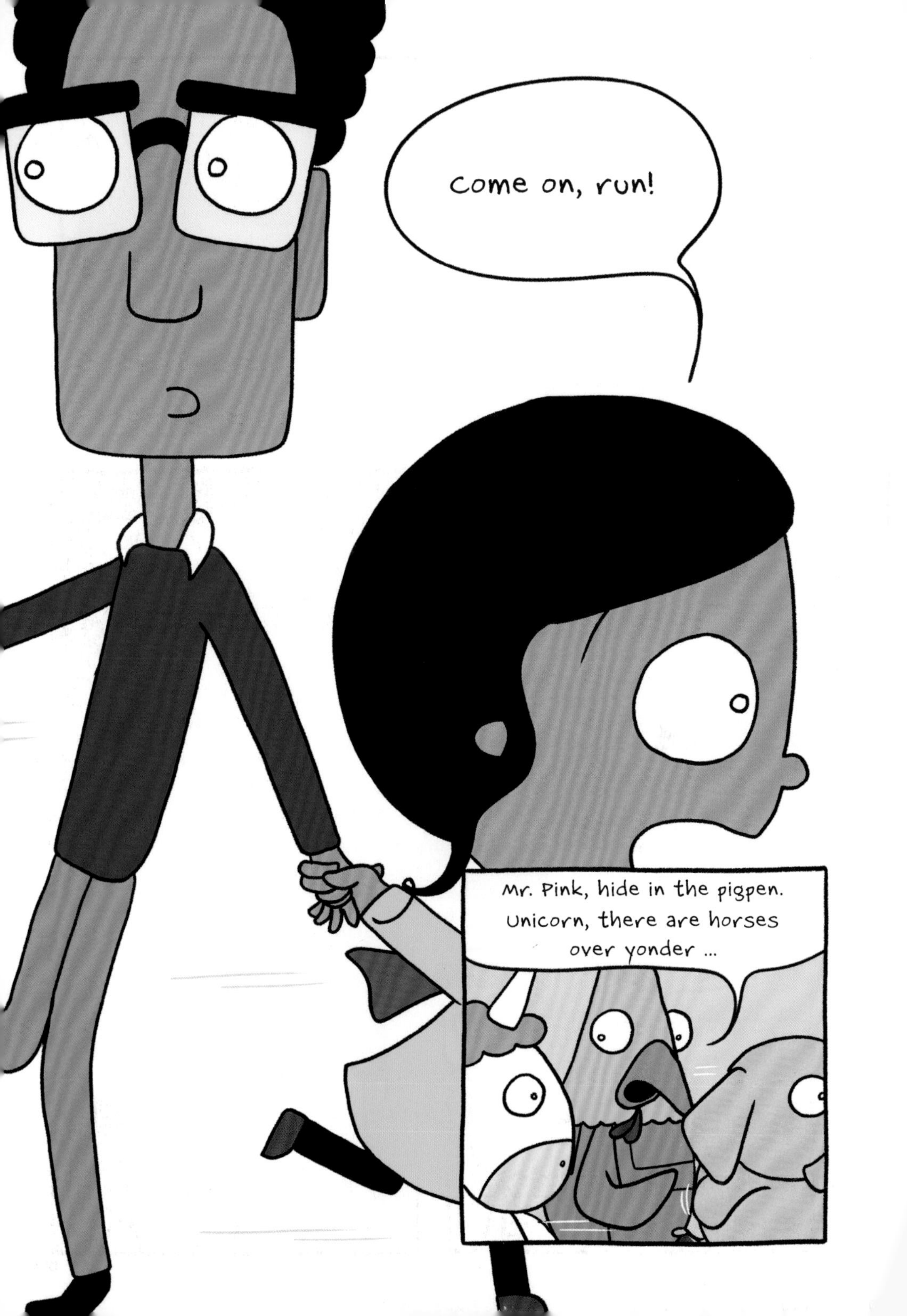
Come on, run!
Mr. Pink, hide in the pigpen. Unicorn, there are horses over yonder ...

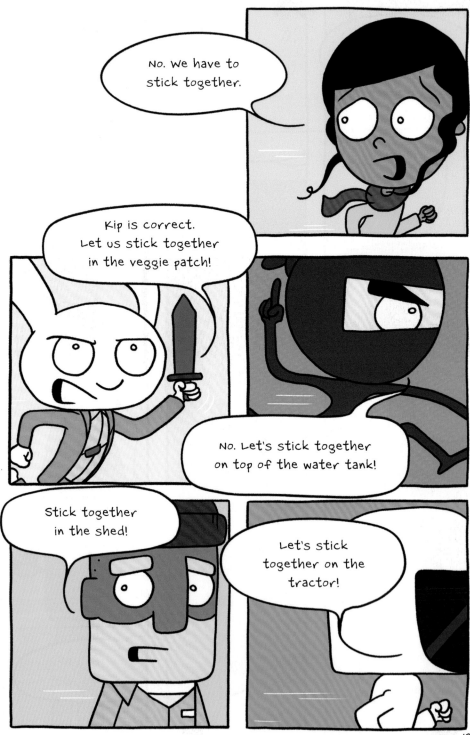

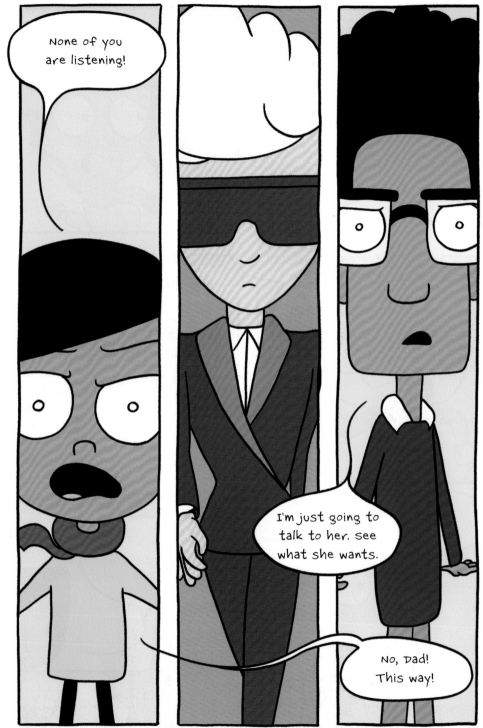

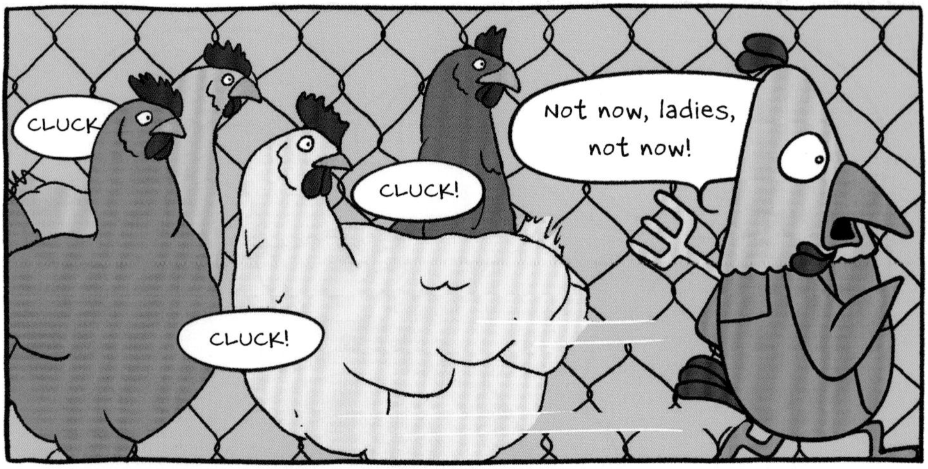
CLUCK
CLUCK!
CLUCK!
Not now, ladies, not now!

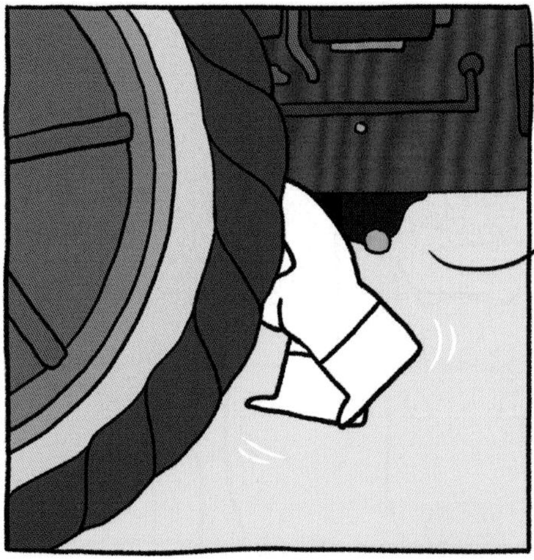

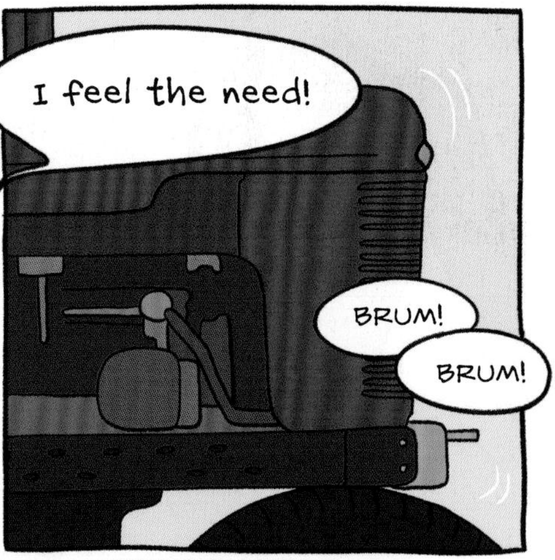
I feel the need!
BRUM!
BRUM!

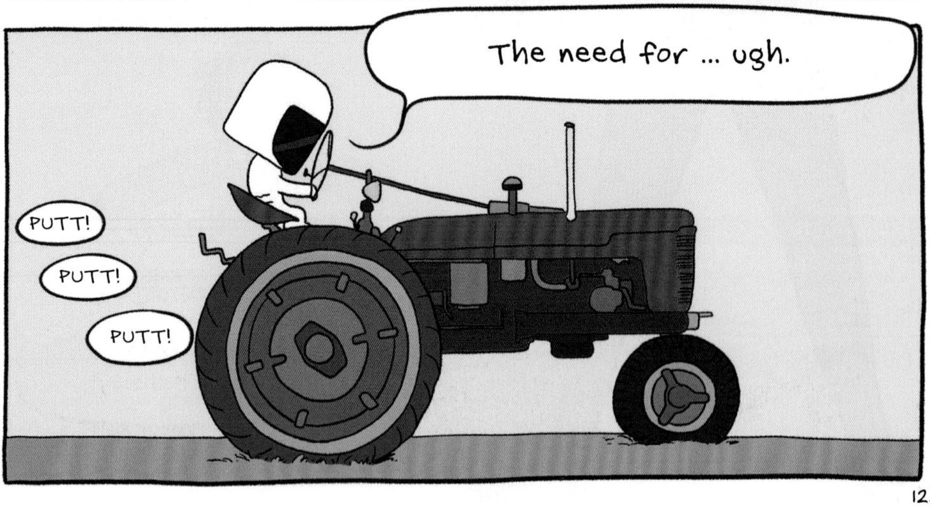
The need for ... ugh.
PUTT!
PUTT!
PUTT!

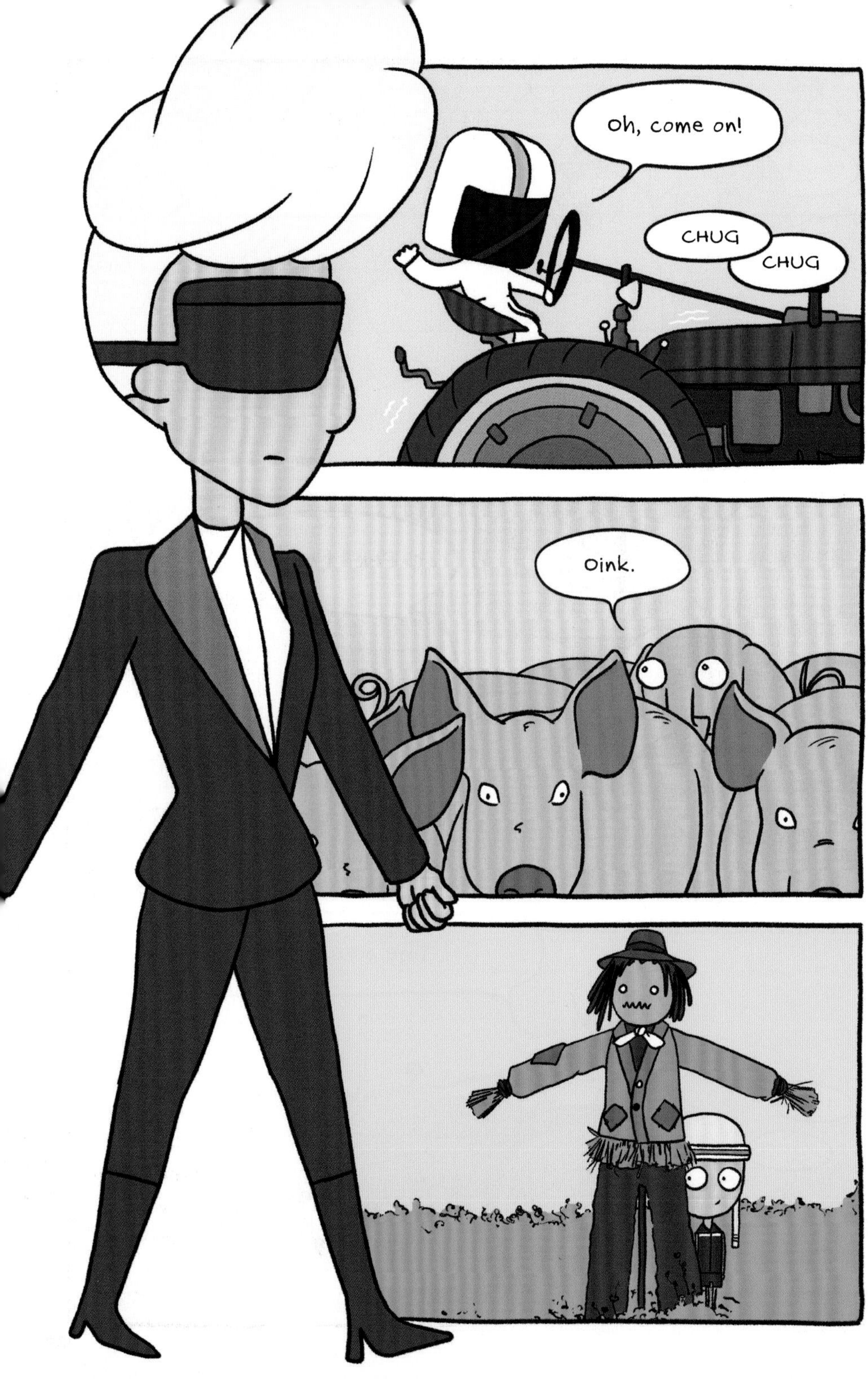
Oh, come on!
CHUG
CHUG
Oink.

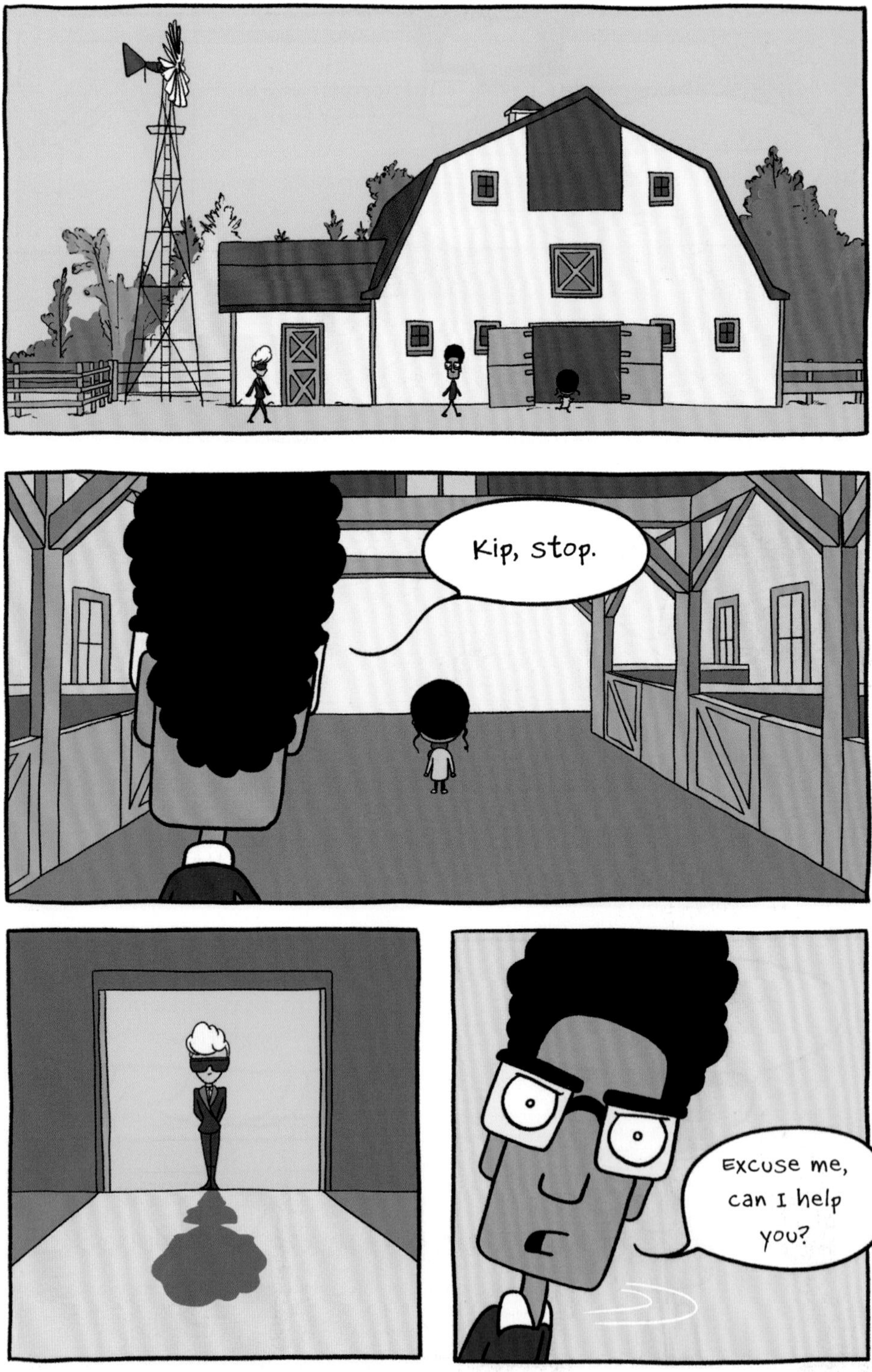
Kip, stop.
Excuse me, can I help you?

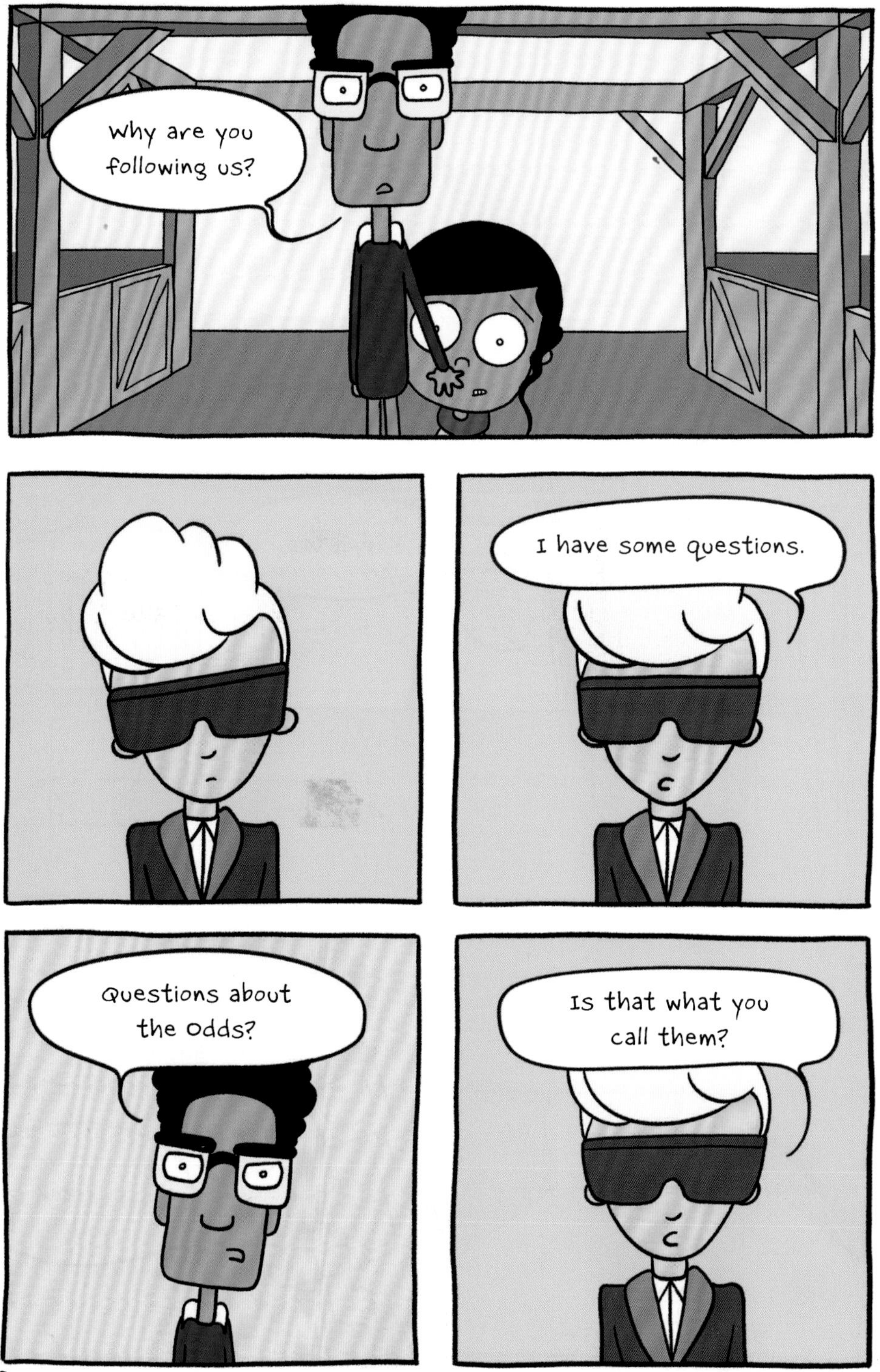
Why are you following us?
I have some questions.
Questions about the Odds?
Is that what you call them?

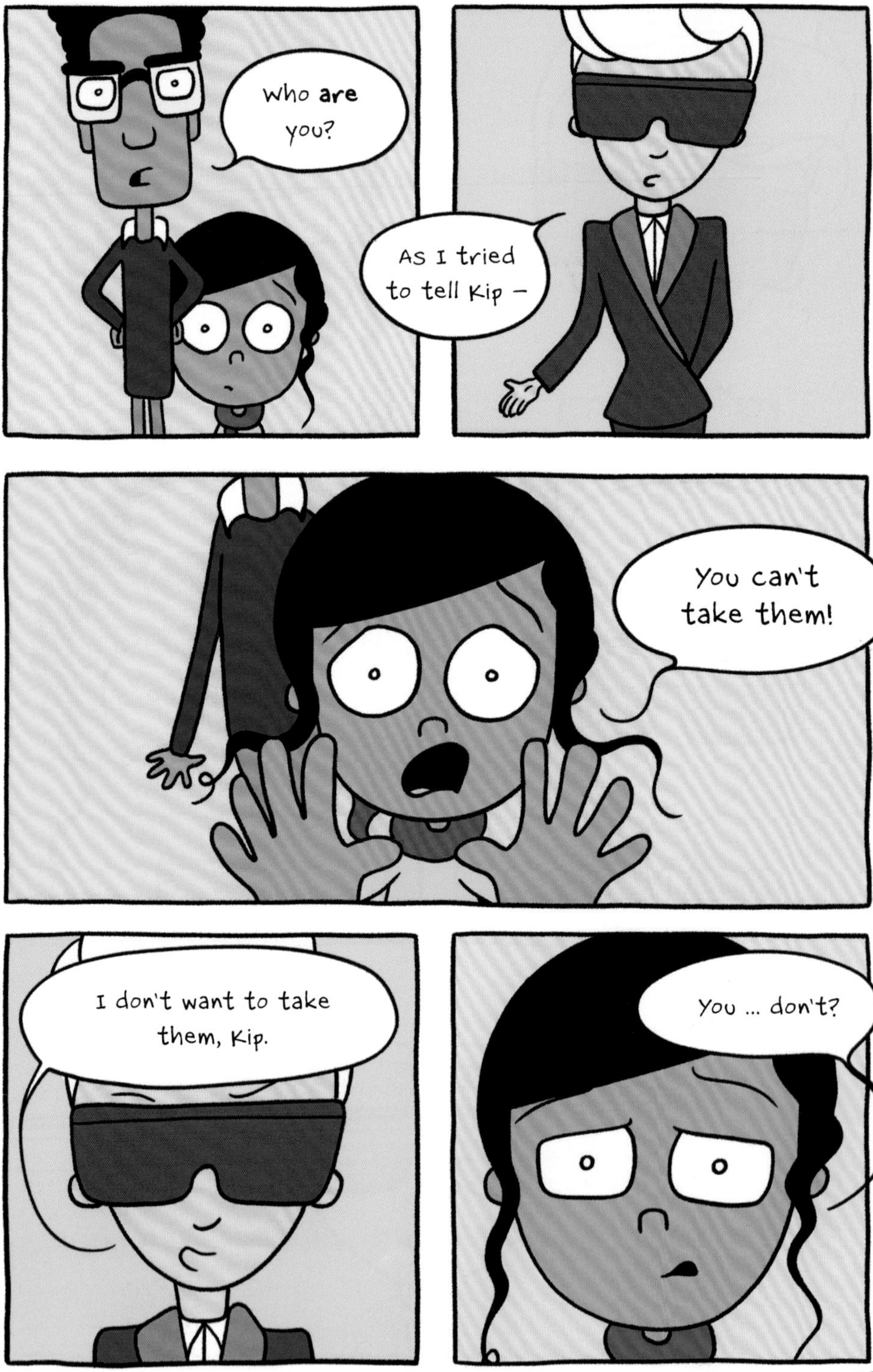
Who **are** you?
As I tried to tell Kip –
You can't take them!
I don't want to take them, Kip.
You ... don't?

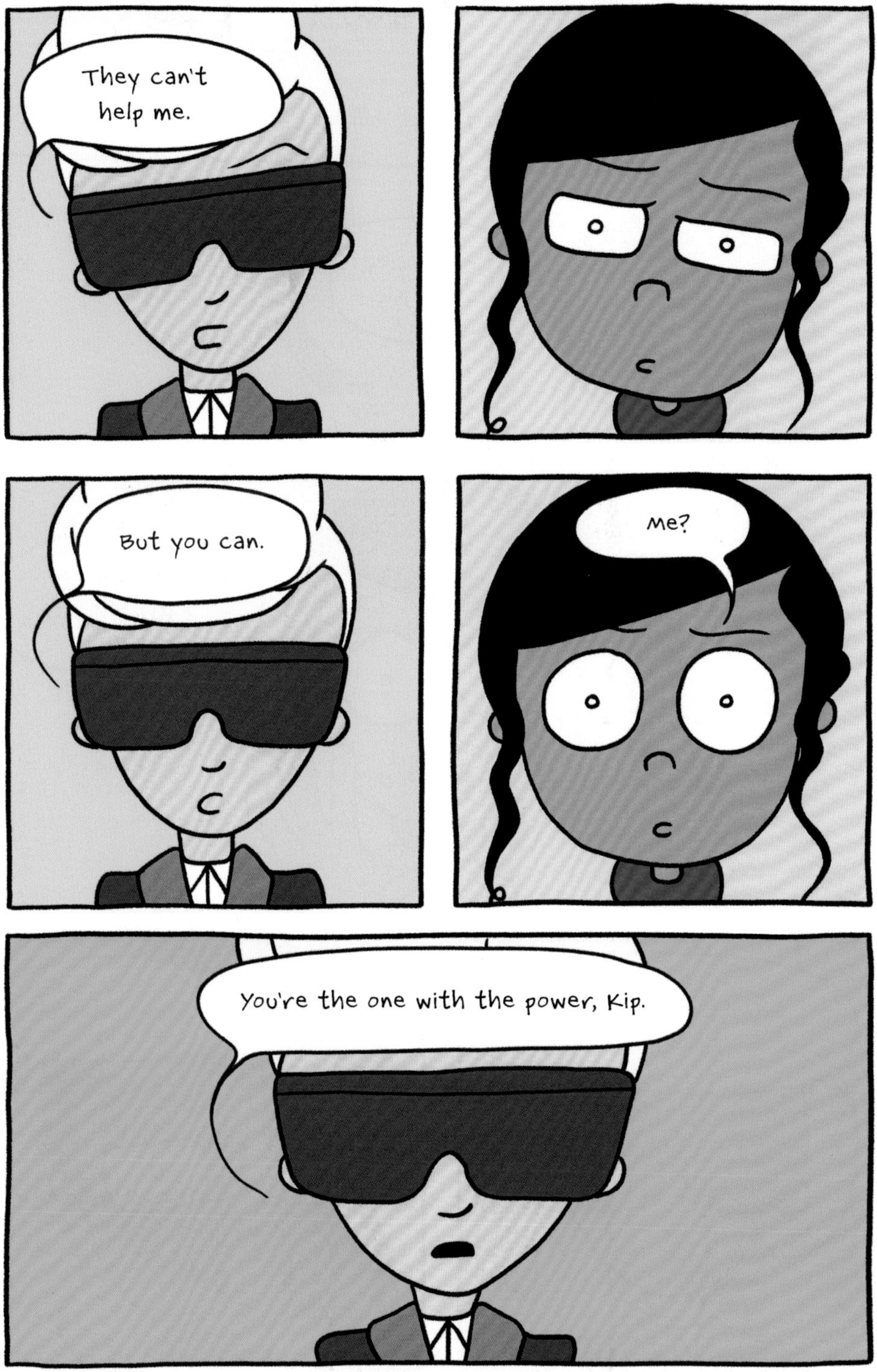
They can't help me.
But you can.
Me?
You're the one with the power, Kip.

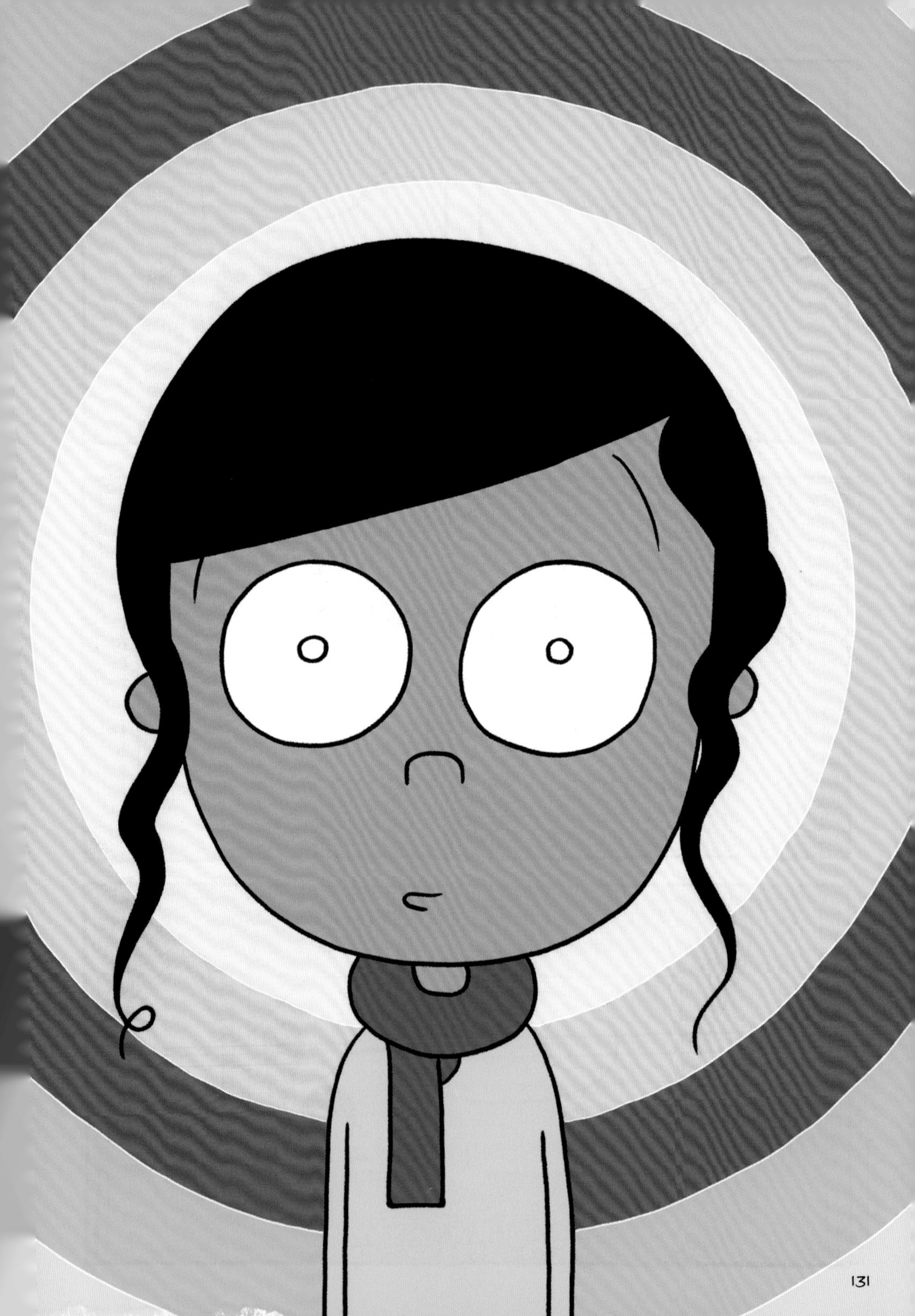

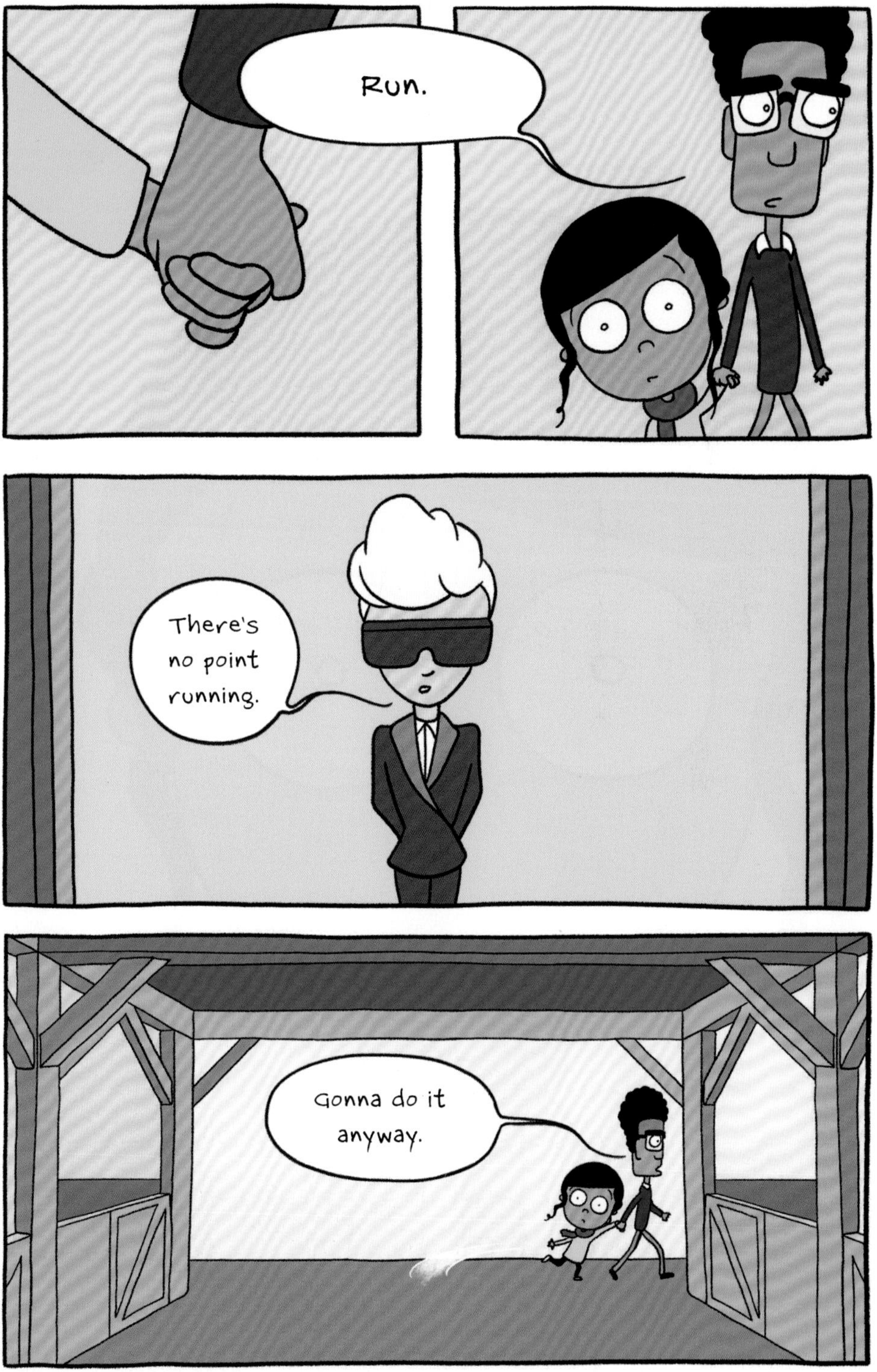
Run.
There's no point running.
Gonna do it anyway.

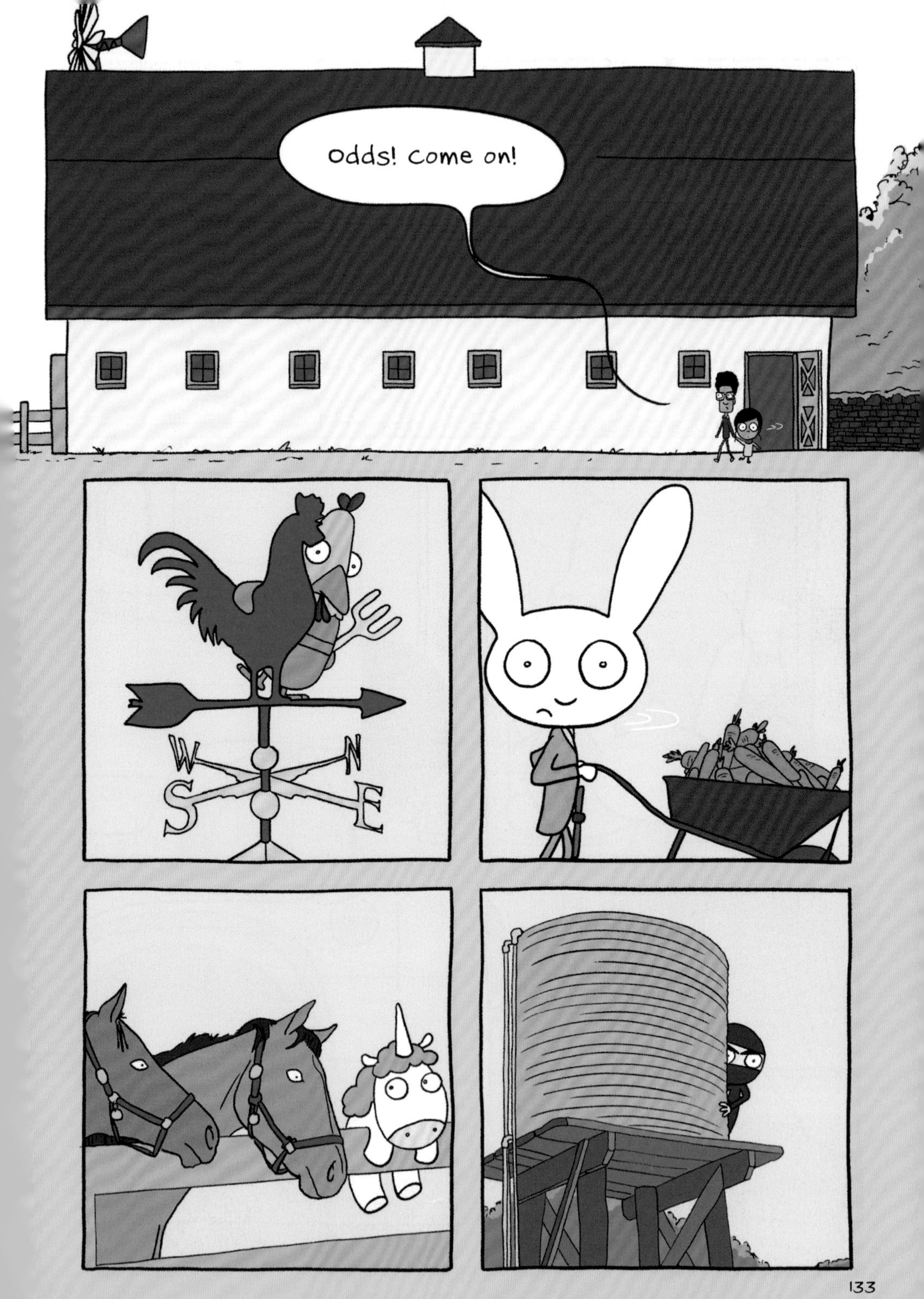
Odds! Come on!

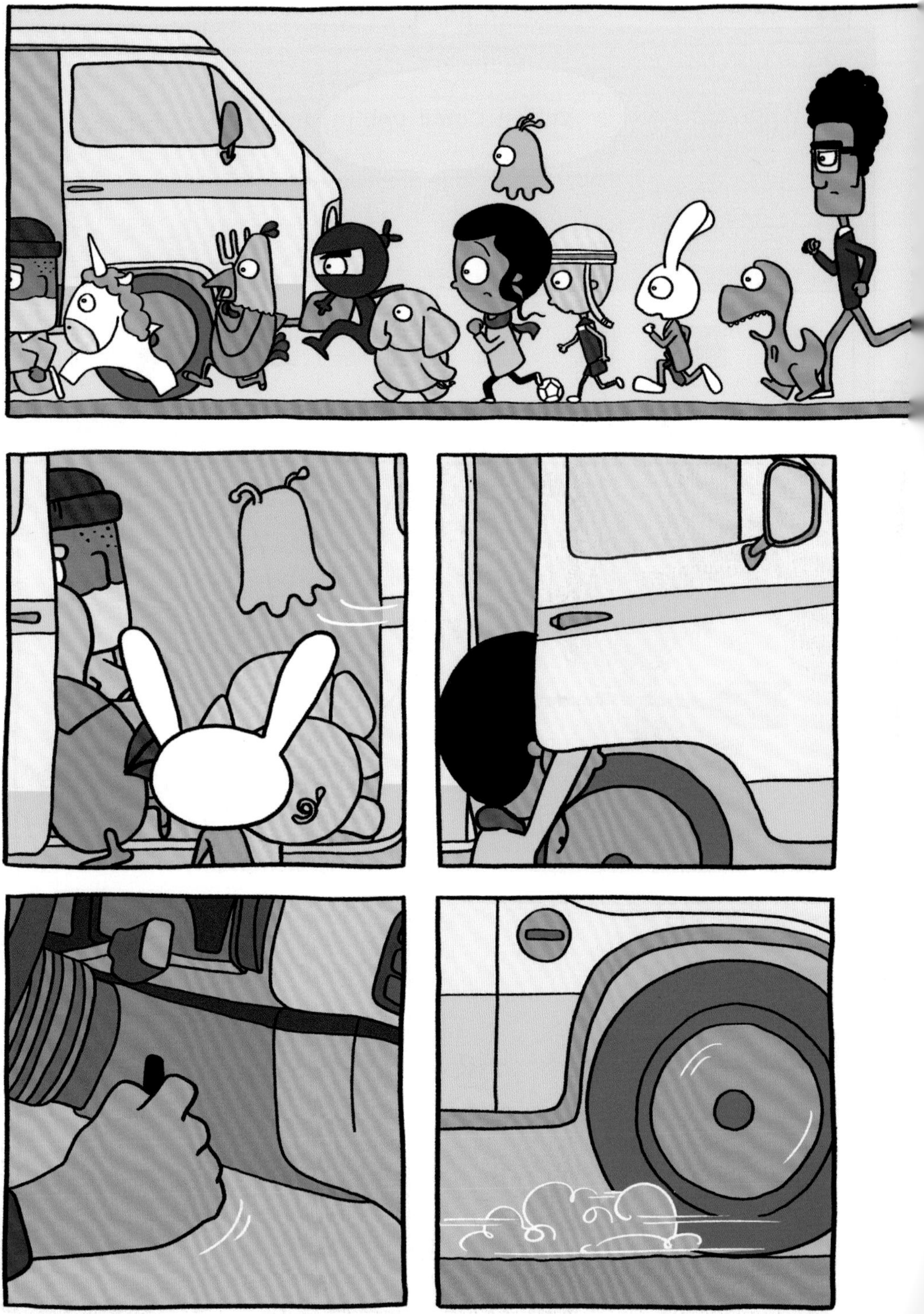

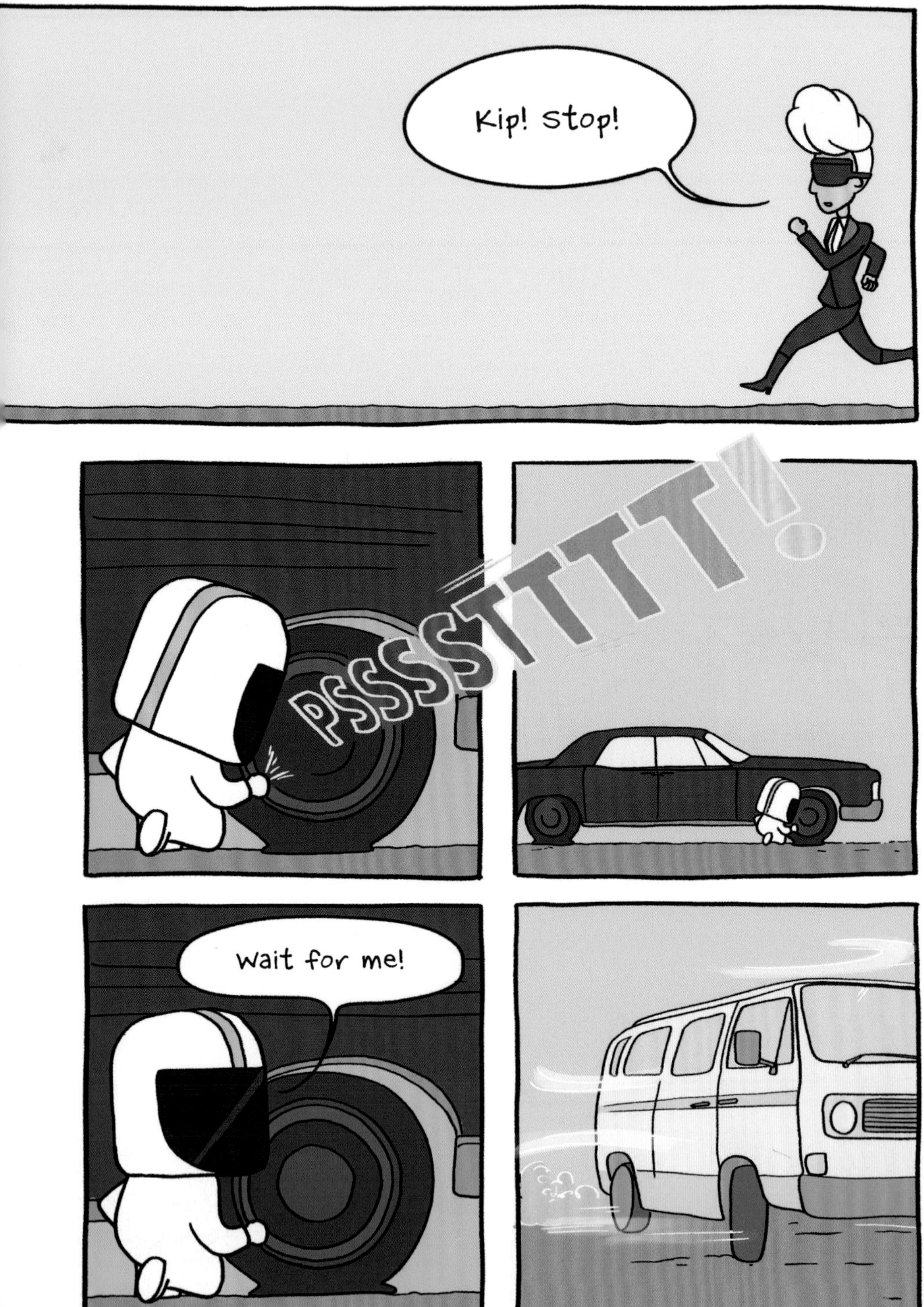
Kip! Stop!
PSSSSTTTT!
Wait for me!

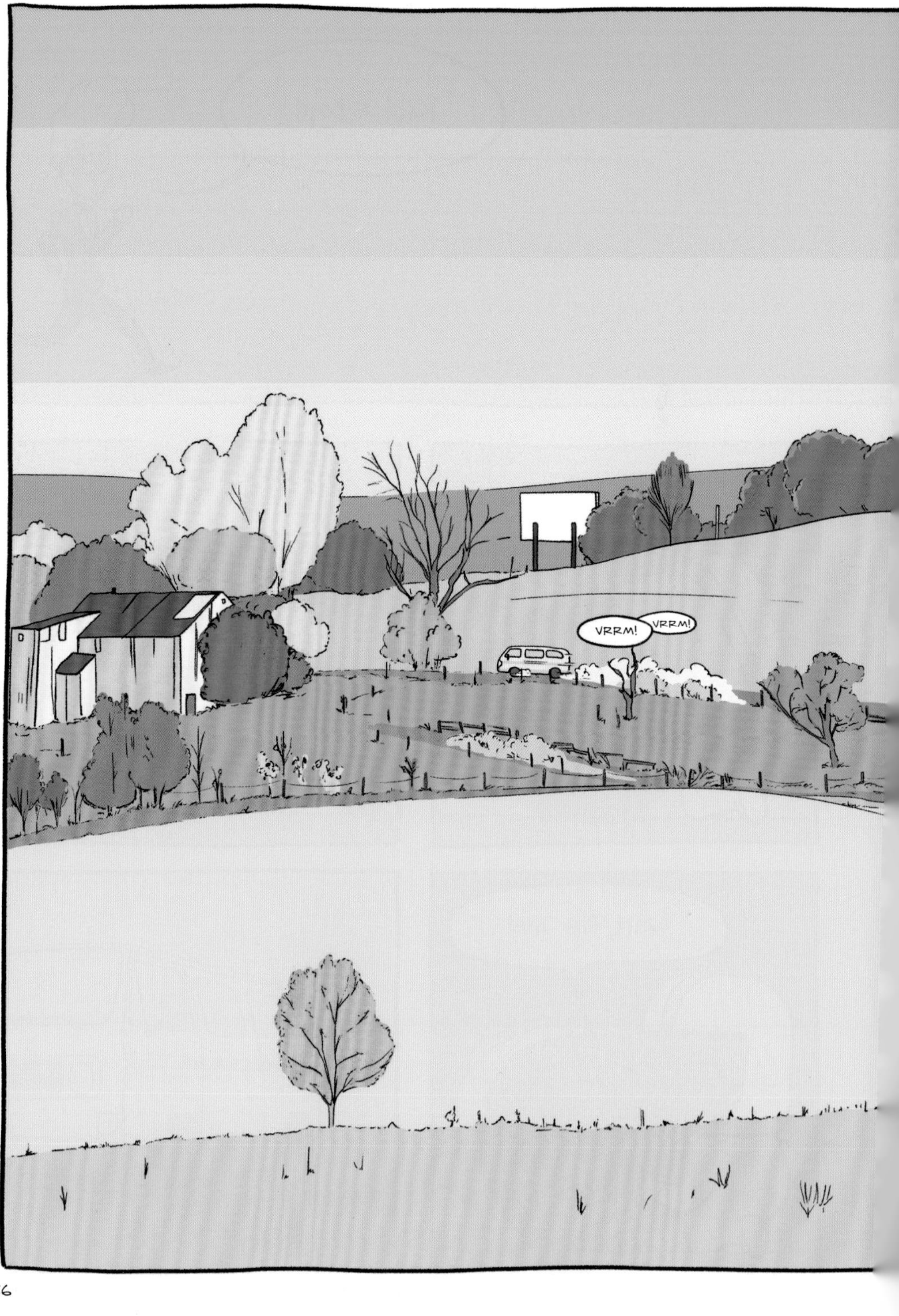
VRRM!
VRRM!

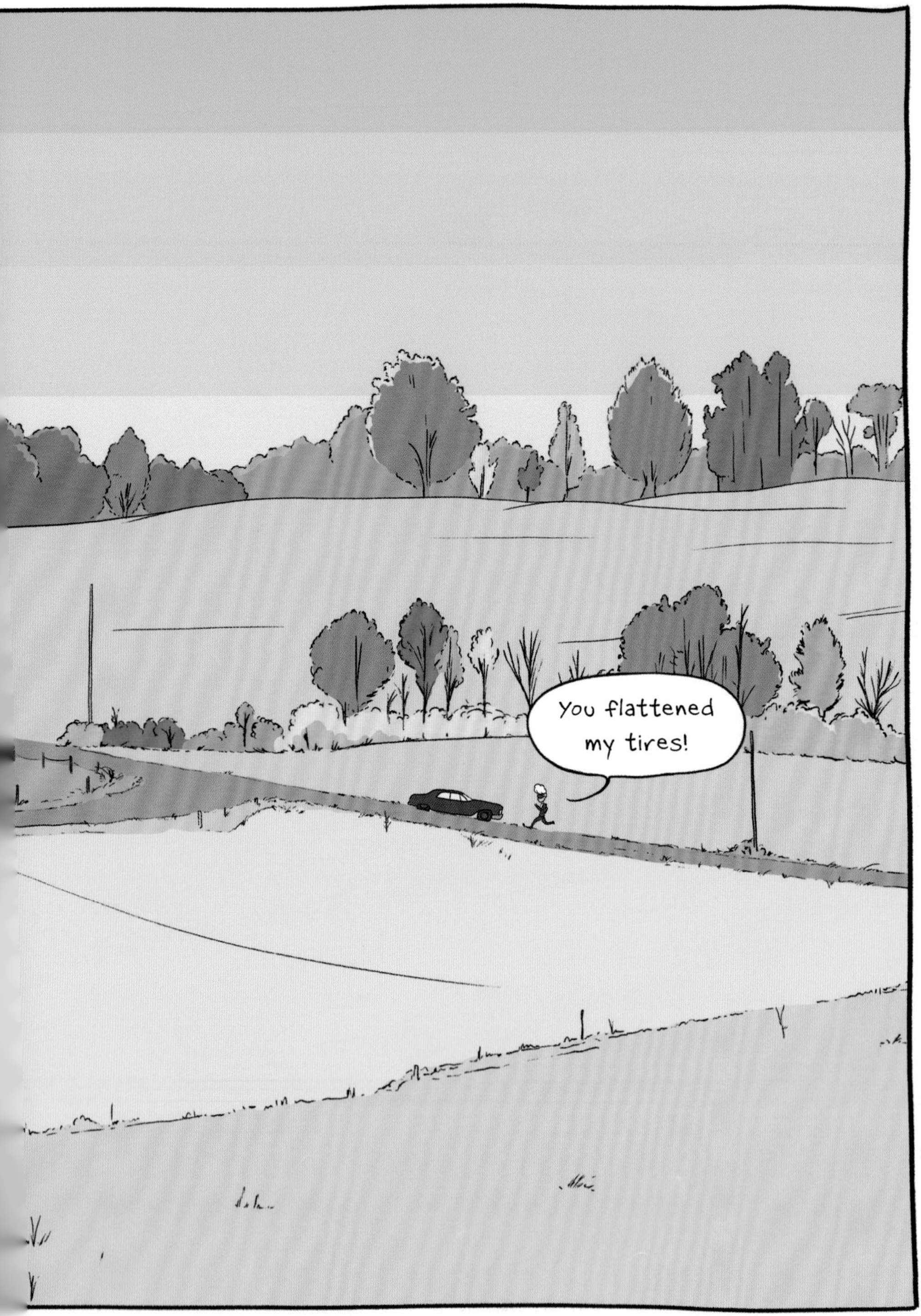
You flattened my tires!

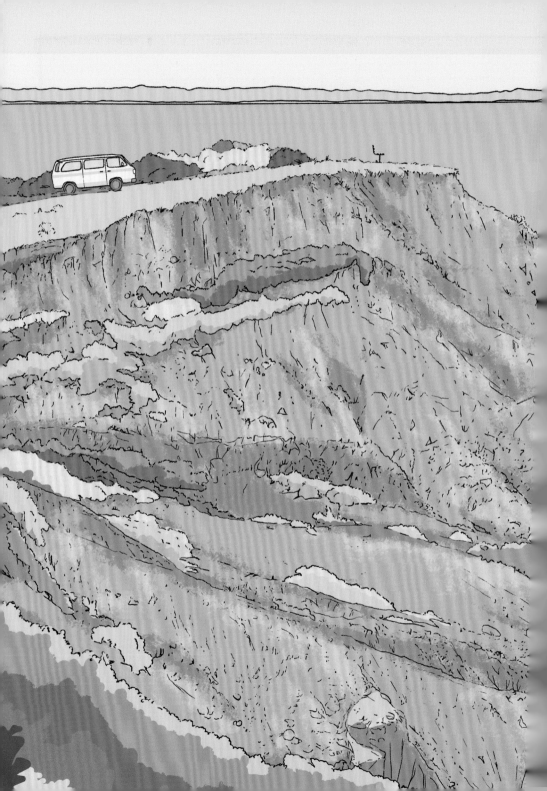

CHAPTER EIGHT
An odd moment of peace

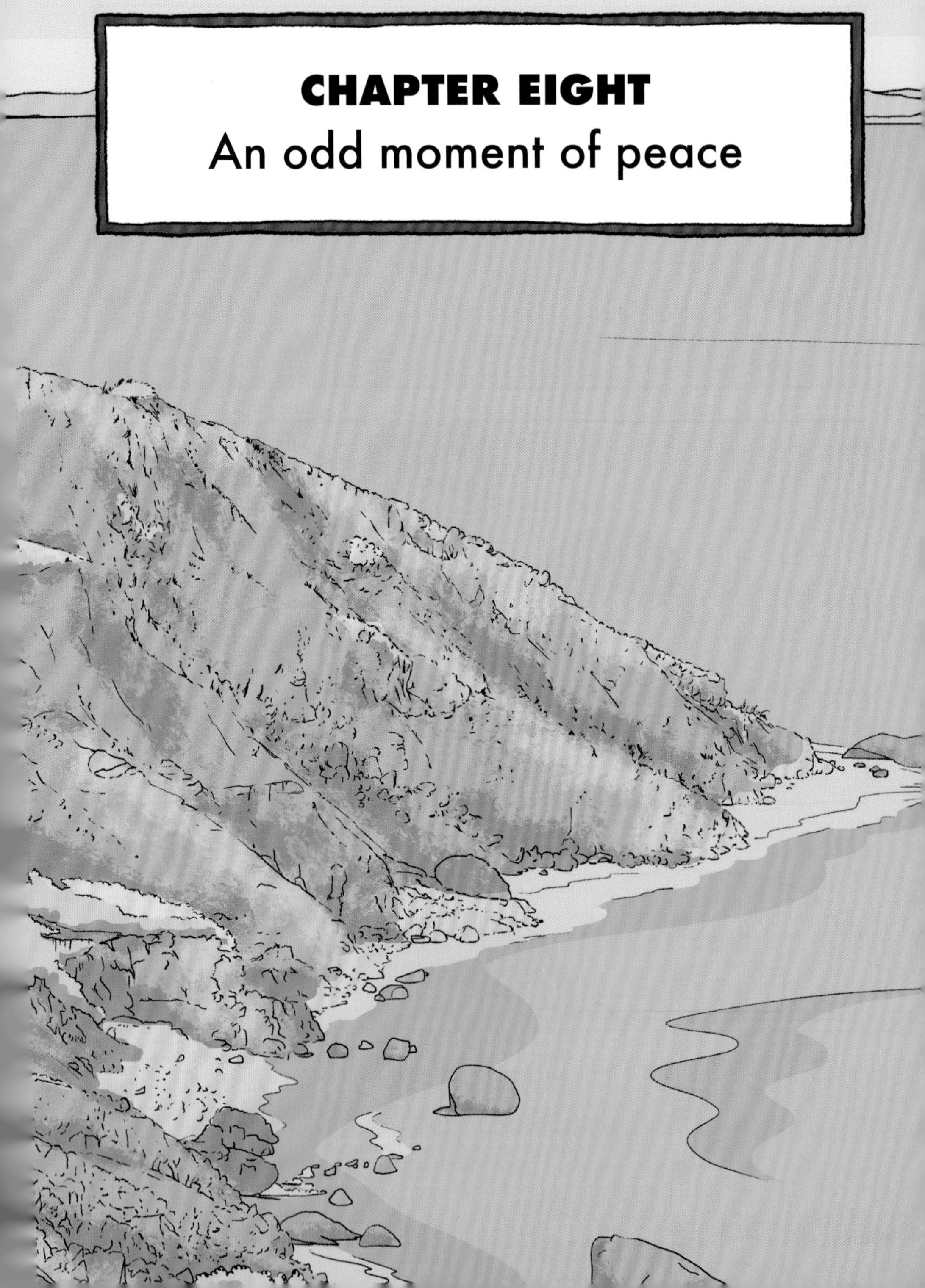

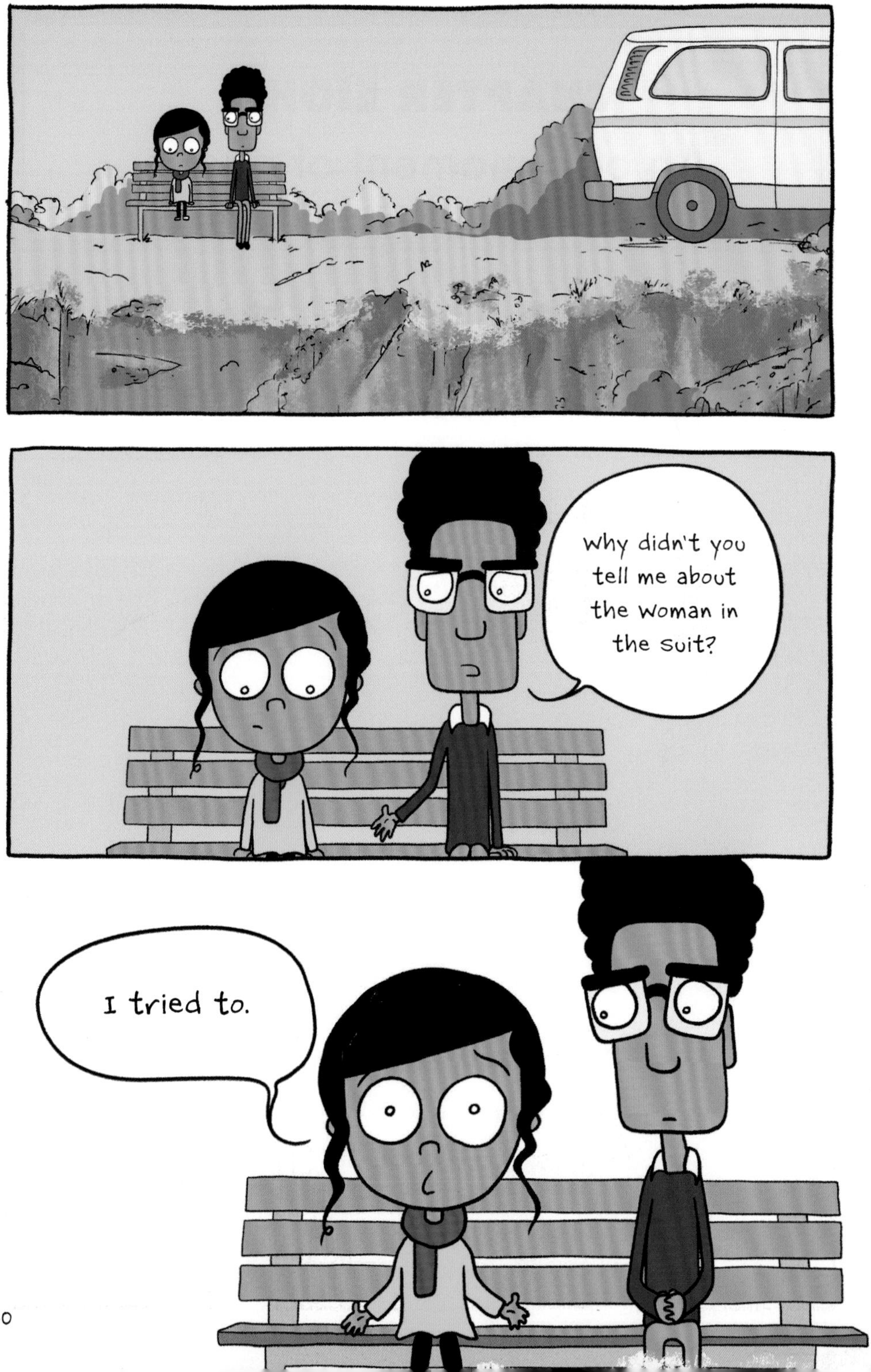
Why didn't you tell me about the woman in the suit?
I tried to.

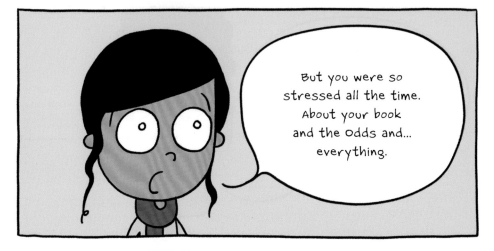

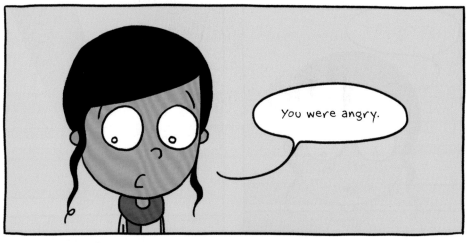

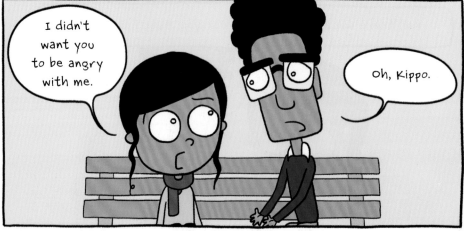

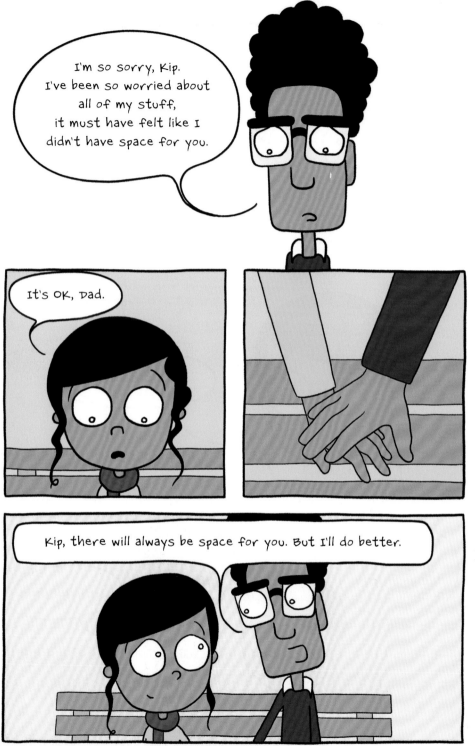

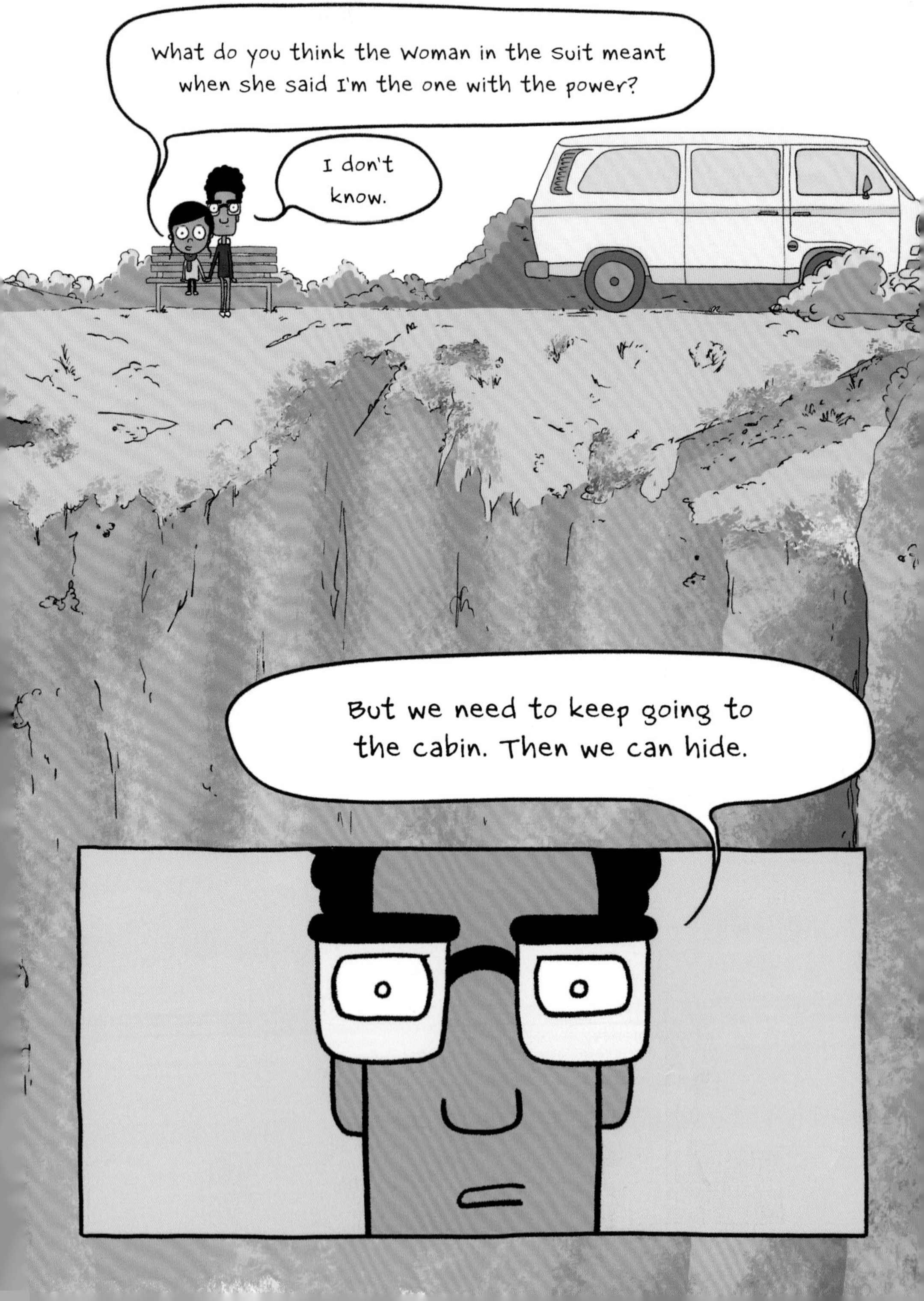
What do you think the woman in the suit meant when she said I'm the one with the power?
I don't know.
But we need to keep going to the cabin. Then we can hide.

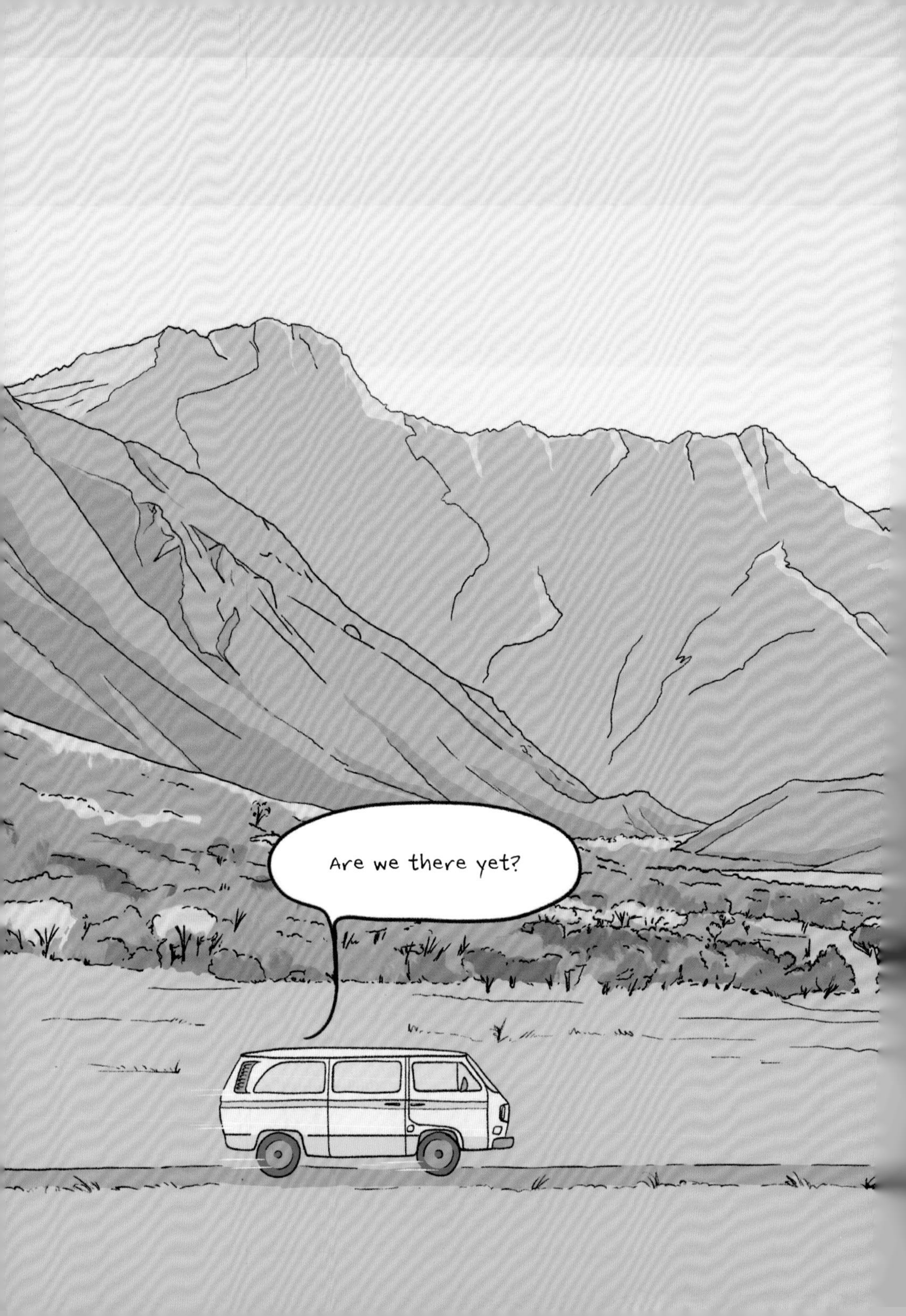
Are we there yet?

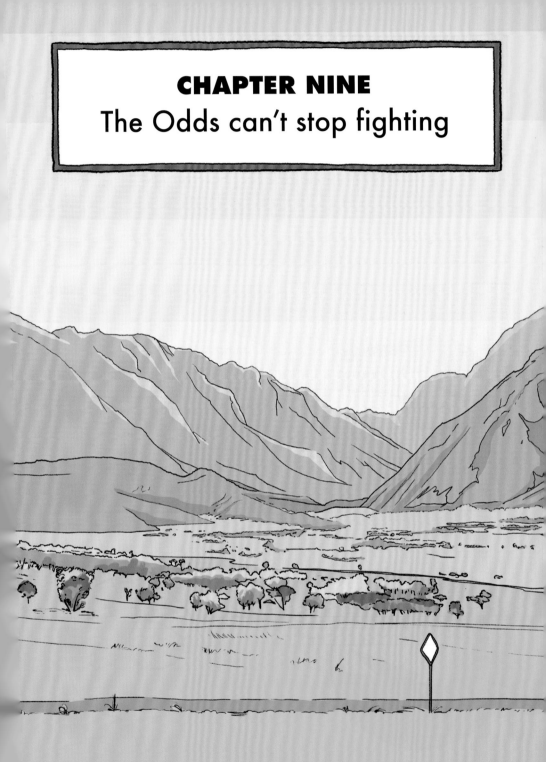

CHAPTER NINE
The Odds can't stop fighting

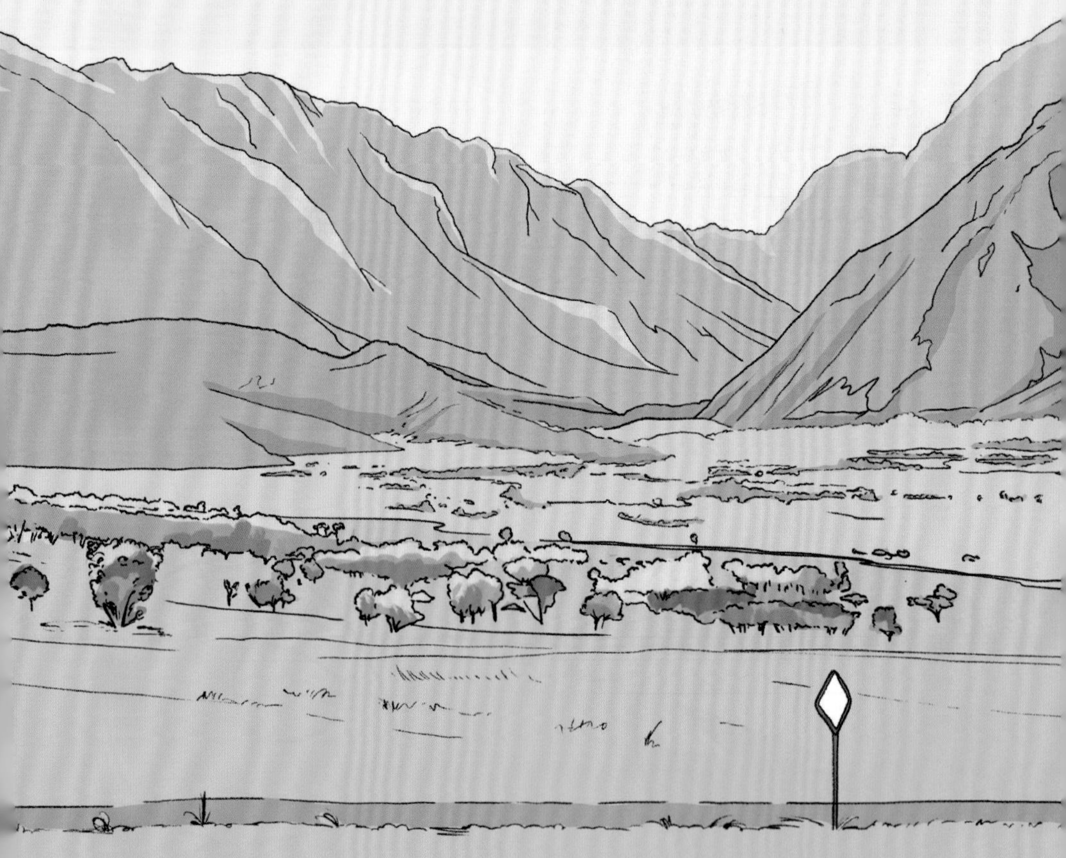

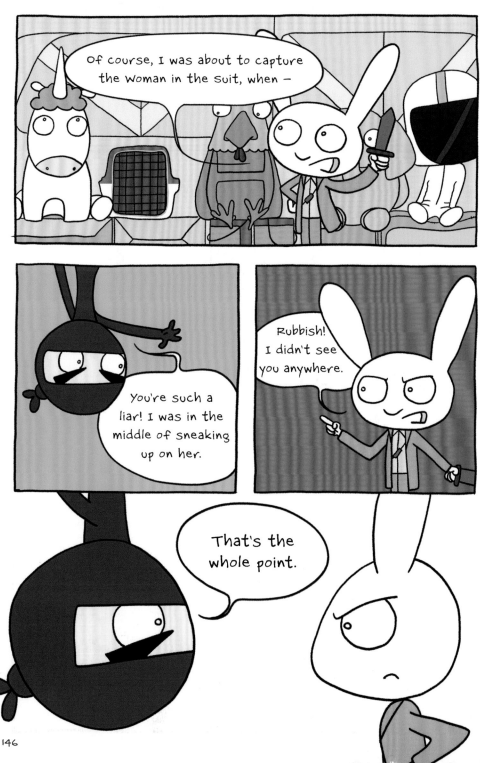

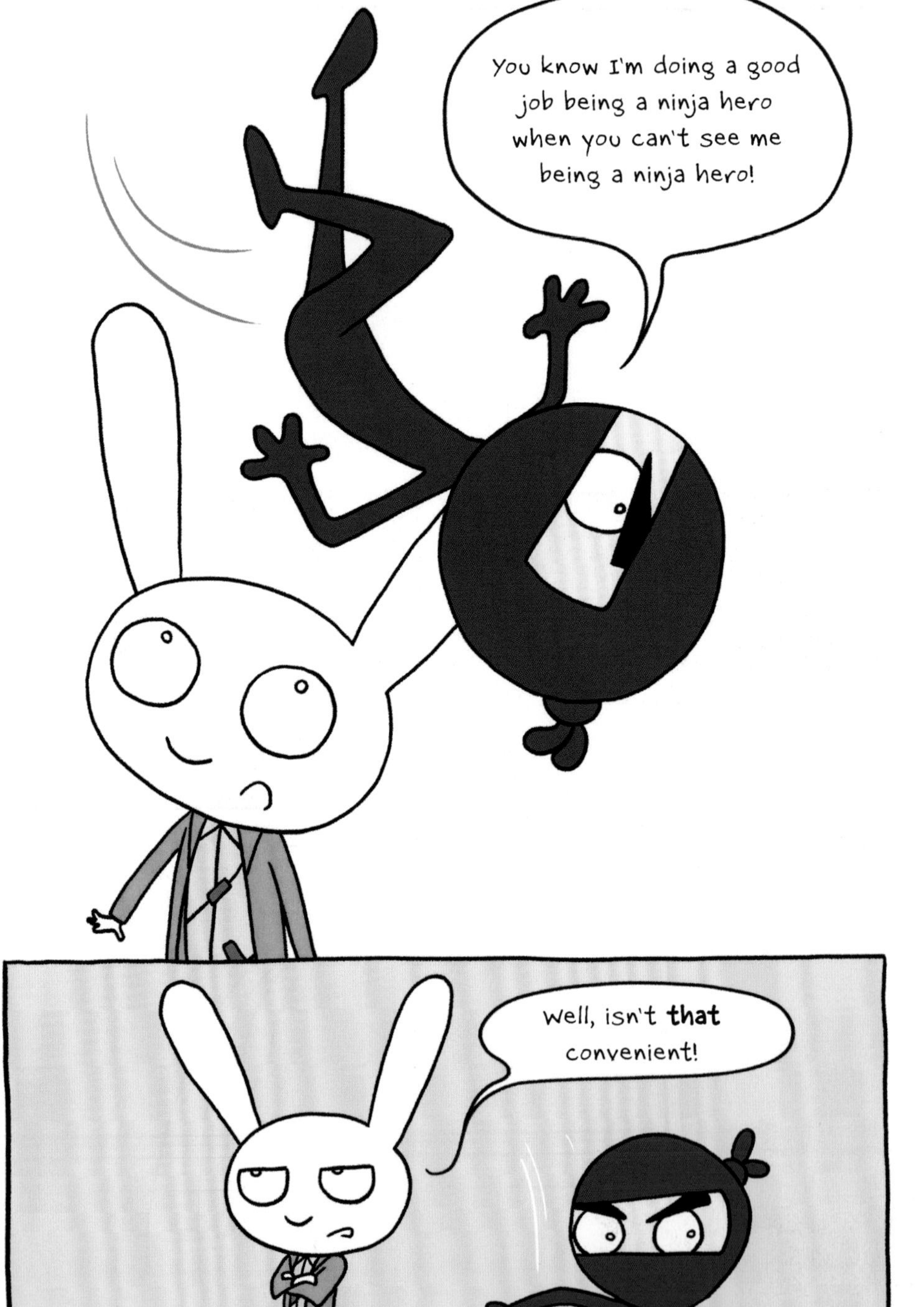
You know I'm doing a good job being a ninja hero when you can't see me being a ninja hero!
Well, isn't **that** convenient!

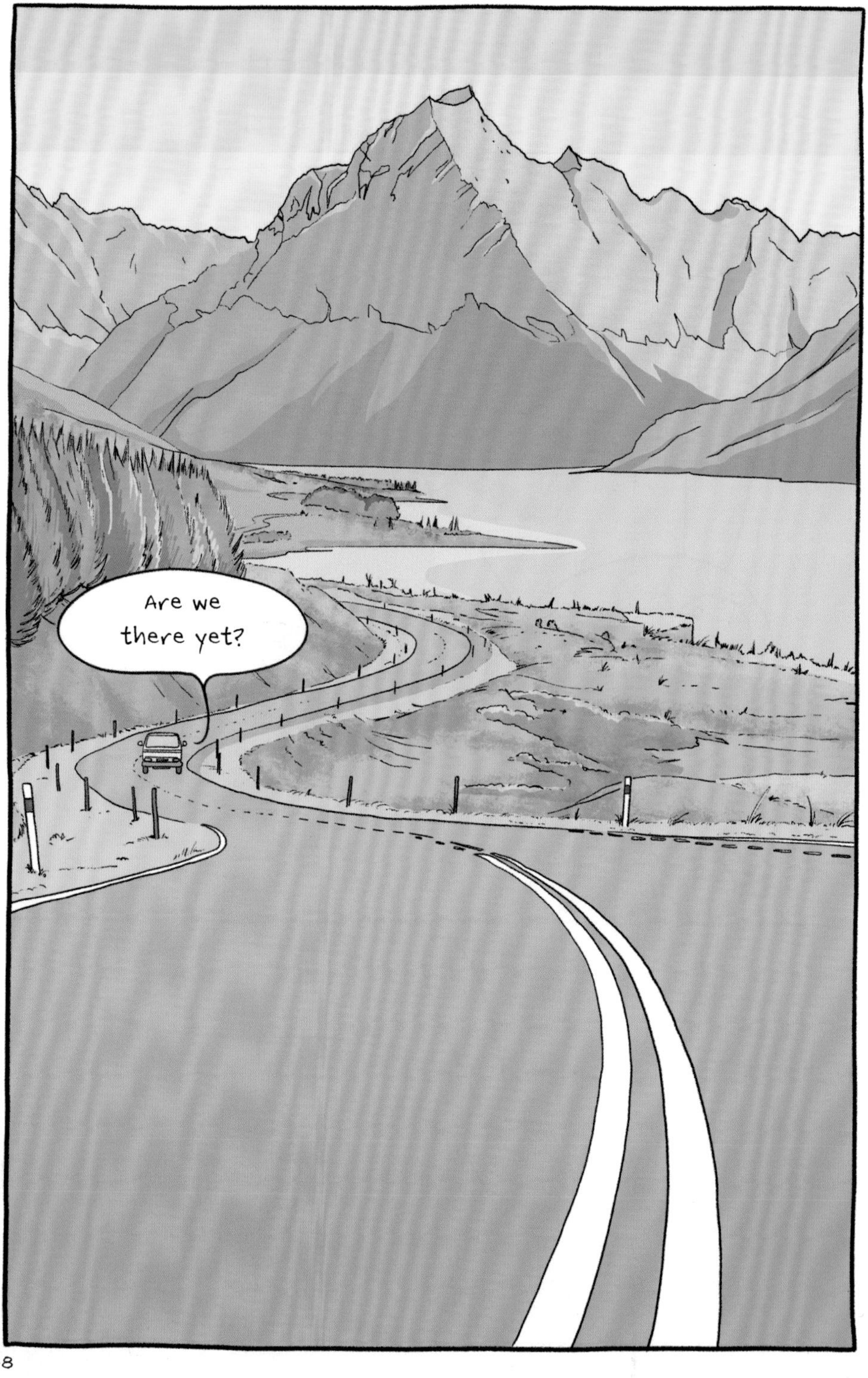
Are we there yet?

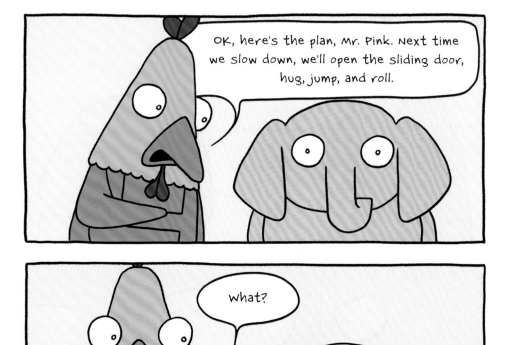

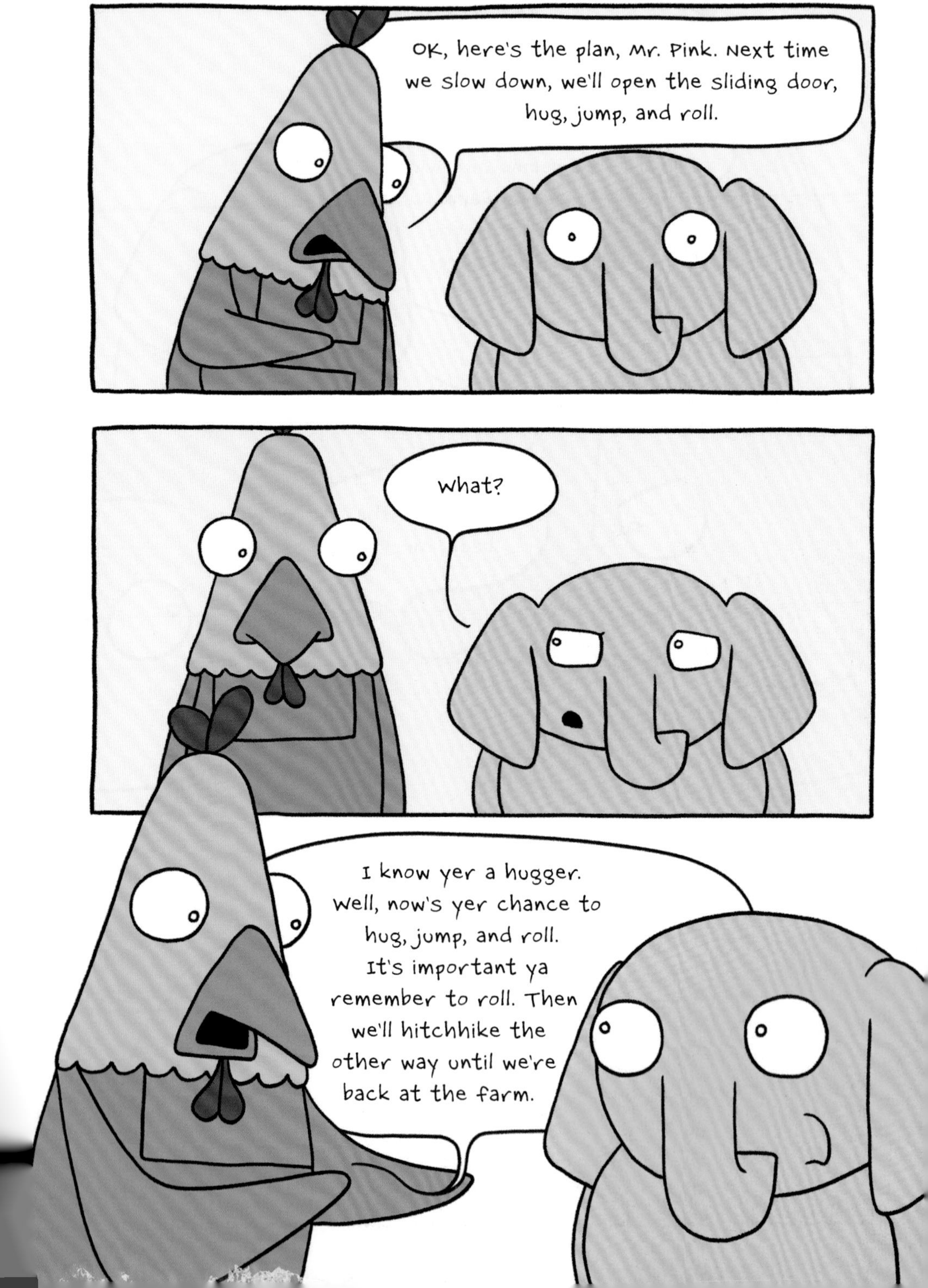

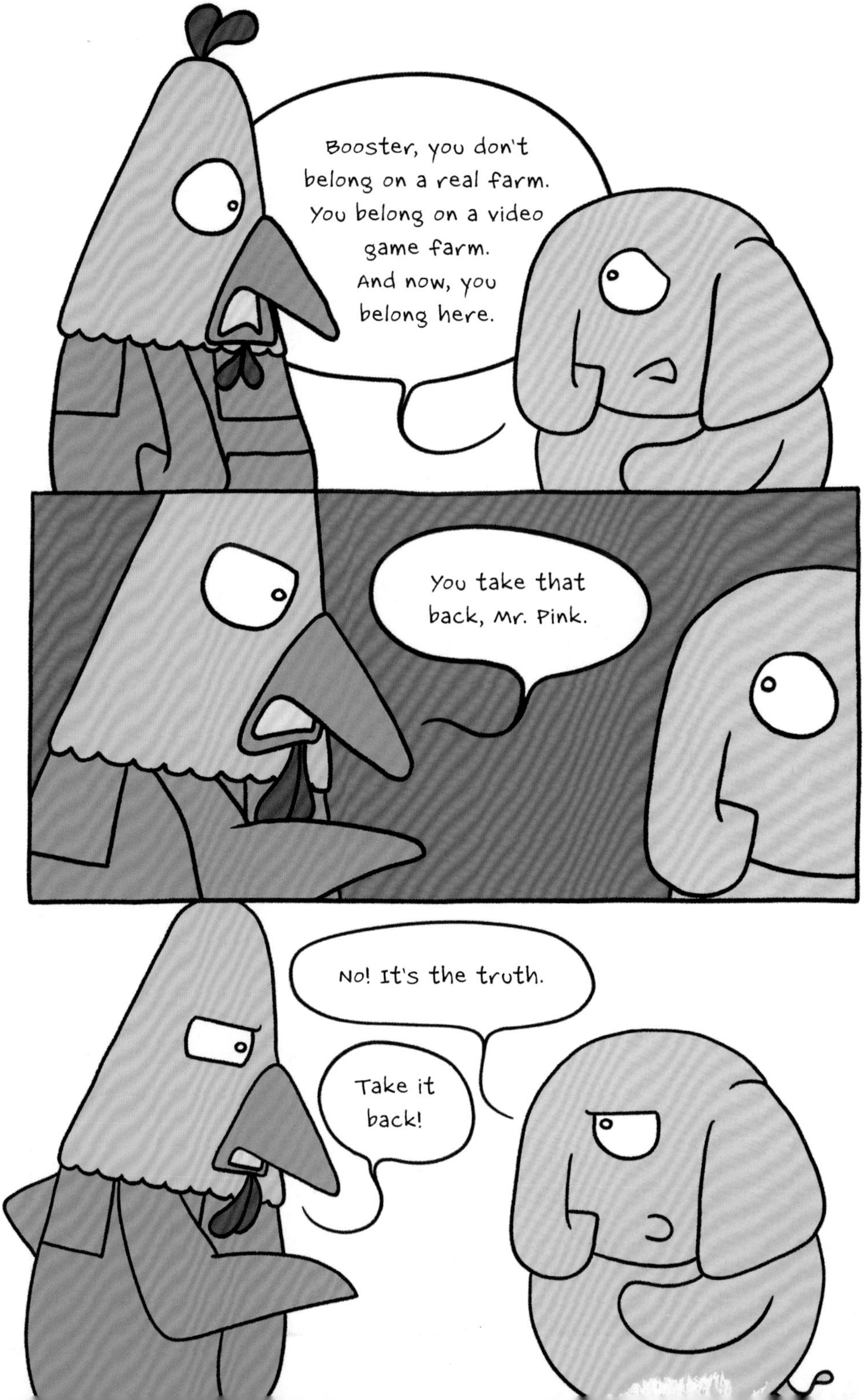
Booster, you don't belong on a real farm. You belong on a video game farm. And now, you belong here.
You take that back, Mr. Pink.
No! It's the truth.
Take it back!

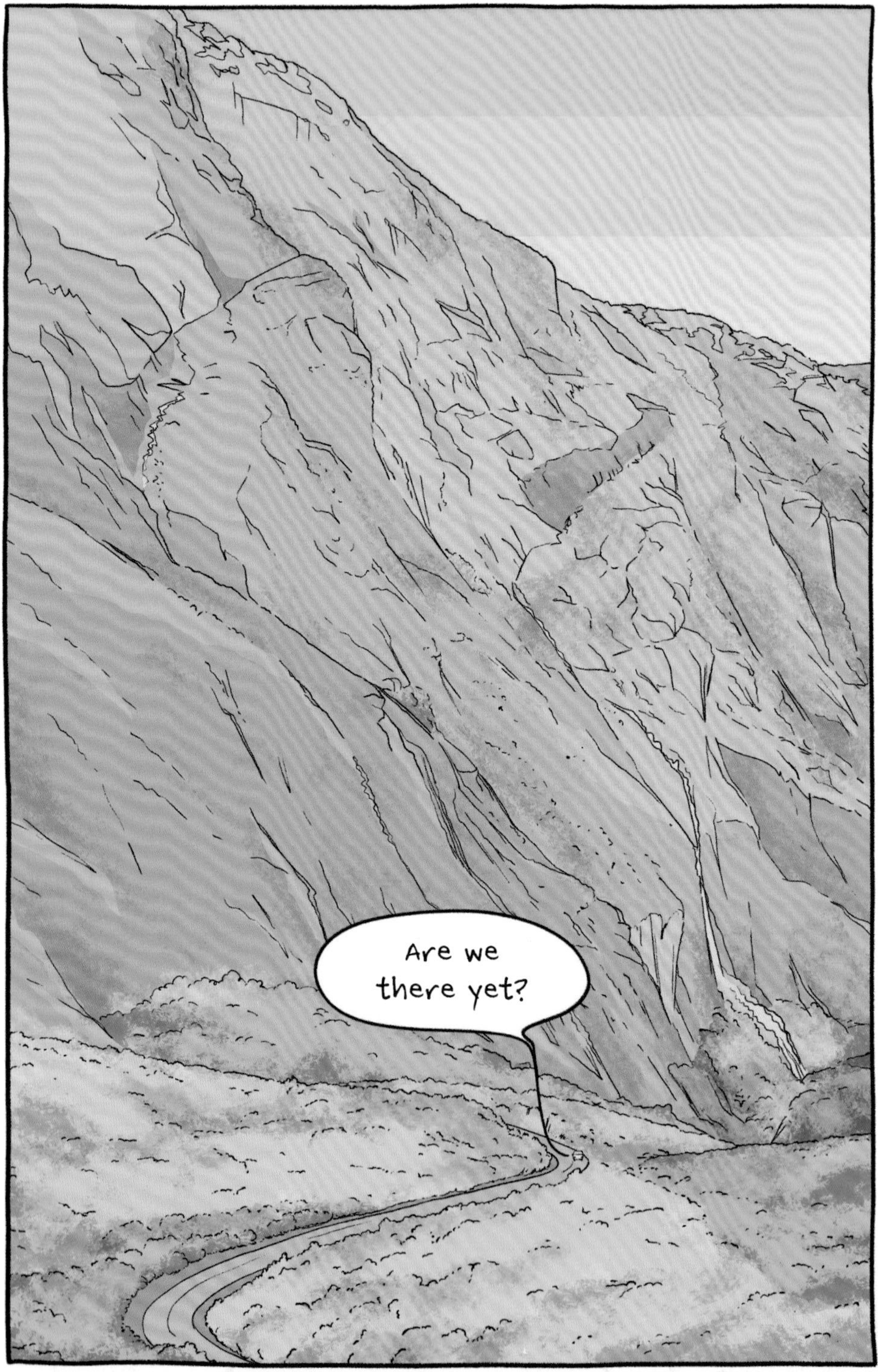
Are we there yet?

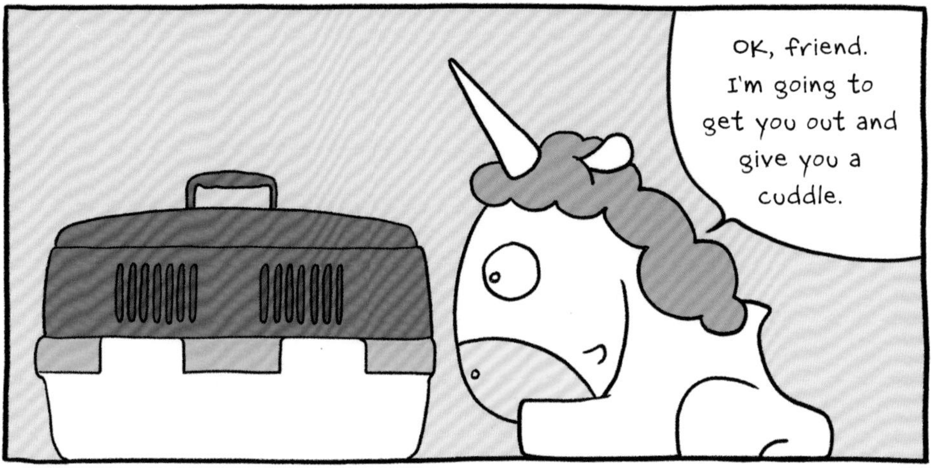
OK, friend. I'm going to get you out and give you a cuddle.

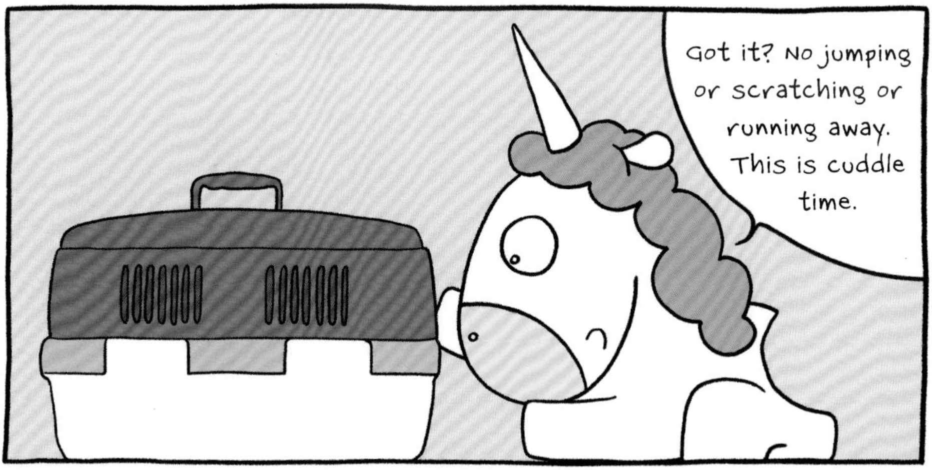
Got it? No jumping or scratching or running away. This is cuddle time.

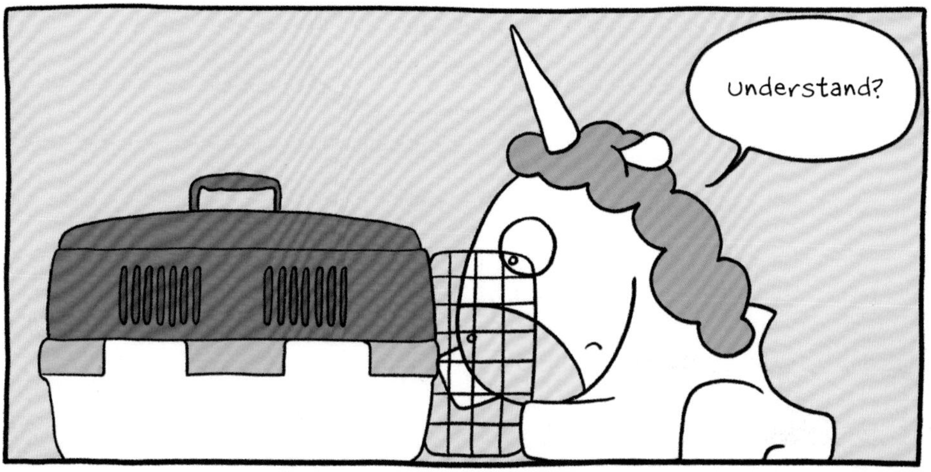
Understand?

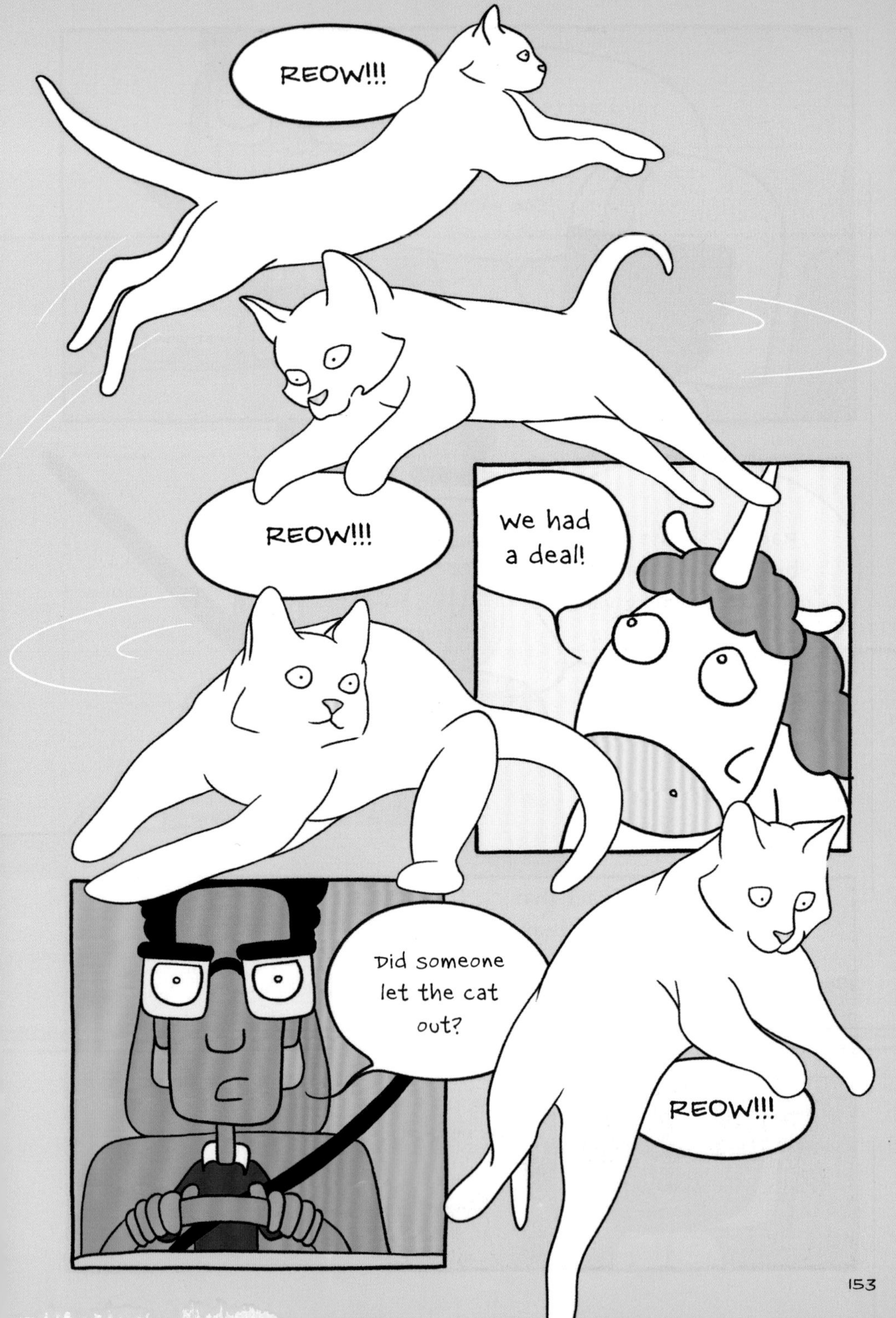
REOW!!!
REOW!!!
We had a deal!
Did someone let the cat out?
REOW!!!

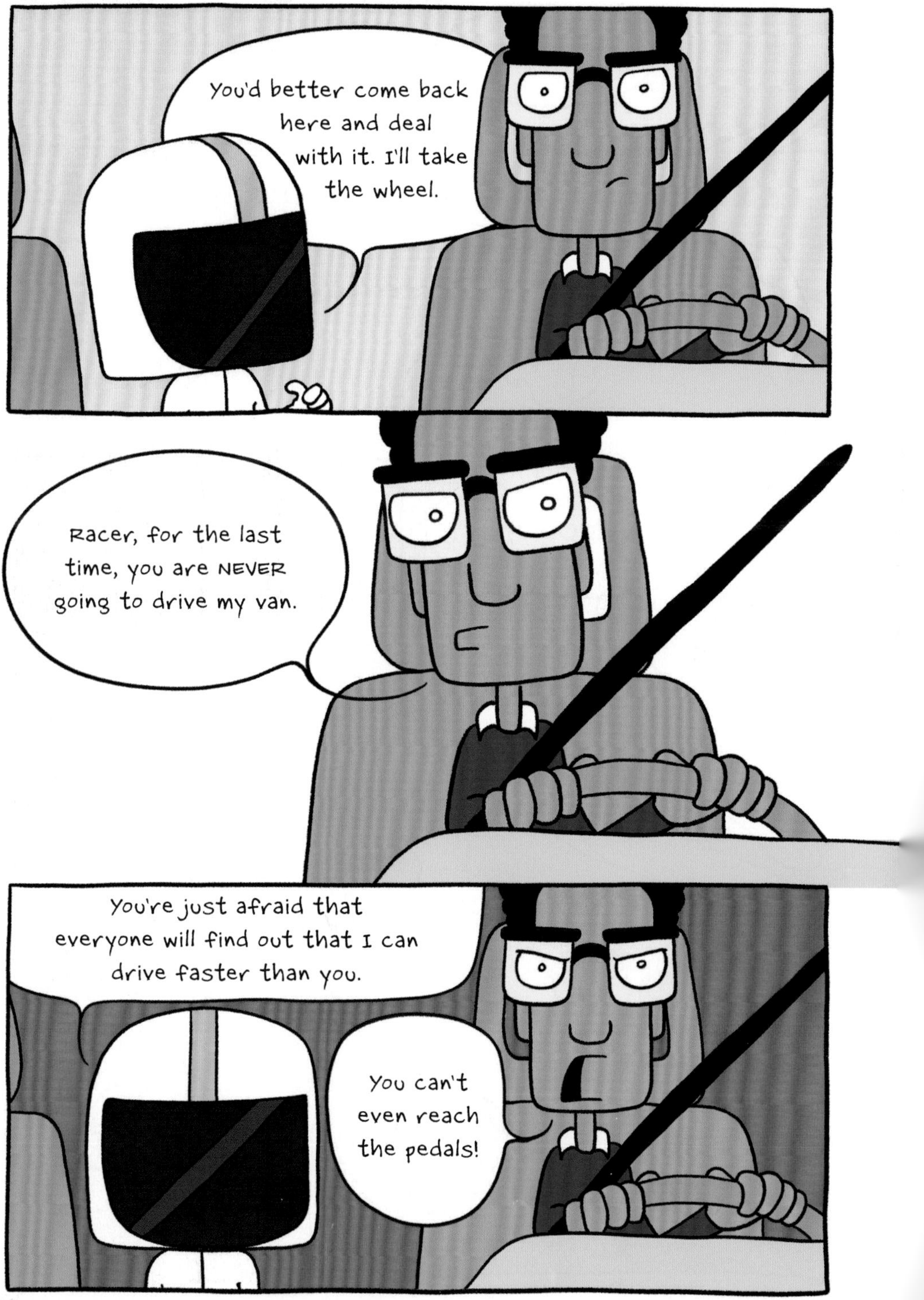
You'd better come back here and deal with it. I'll take the wheel.
Racer, for the last time, you are NEVER going to drive my van.
You're just afraid that everyone will find out that I can drive faster than you.
You can't even reach the pedals!

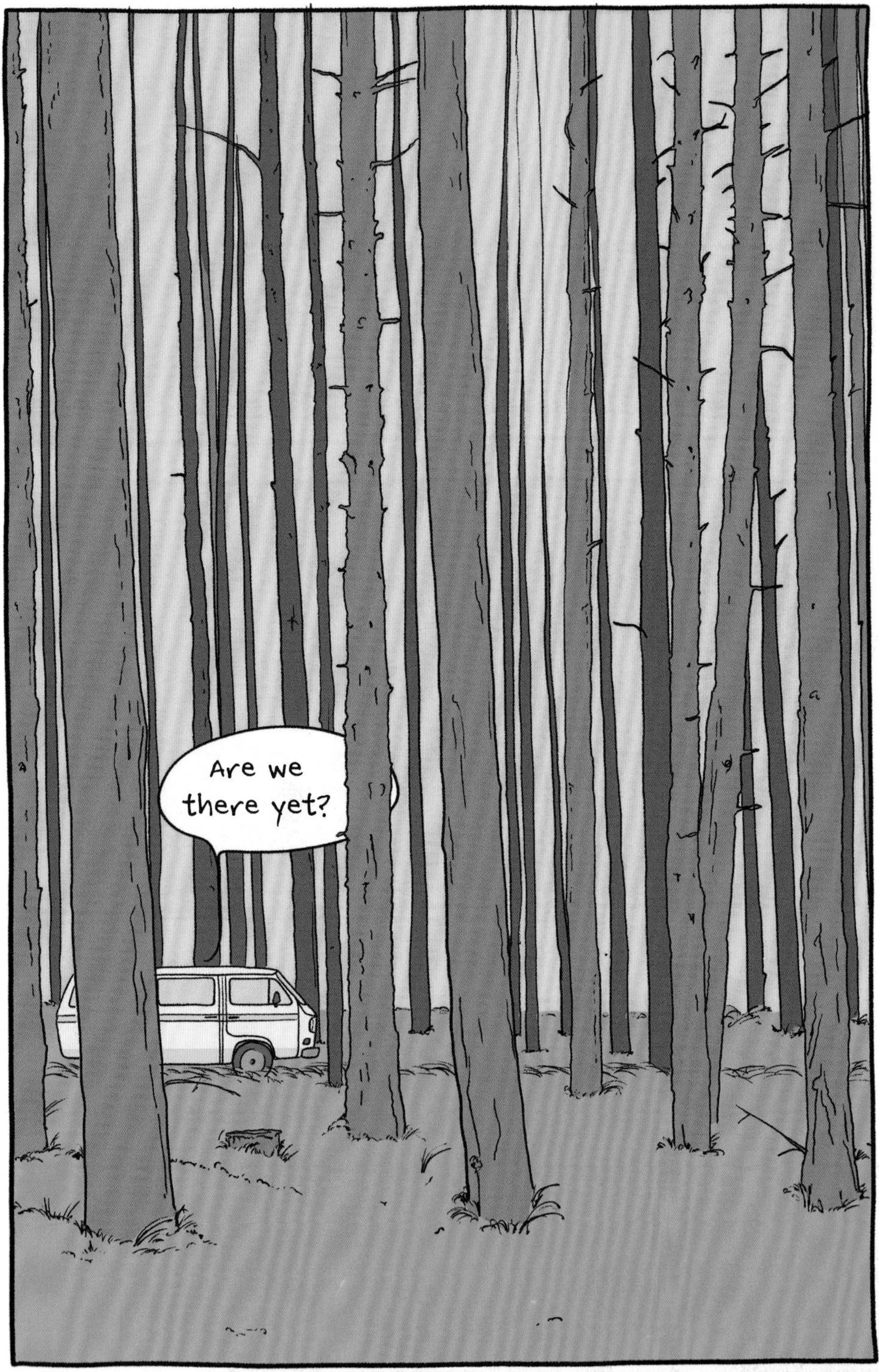
Are we there yet?

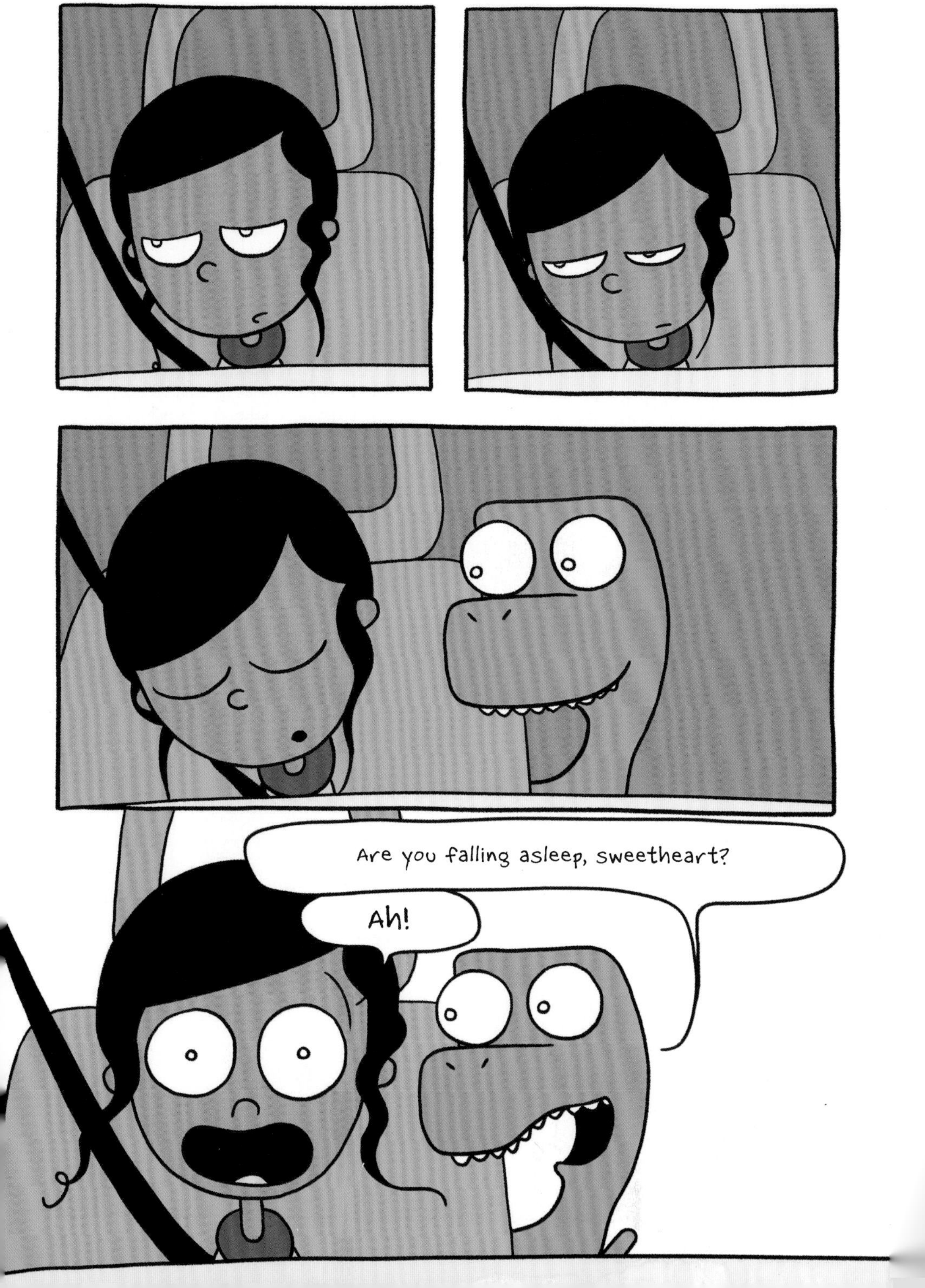
Are you falling asleep, sweetheart?
Ah!

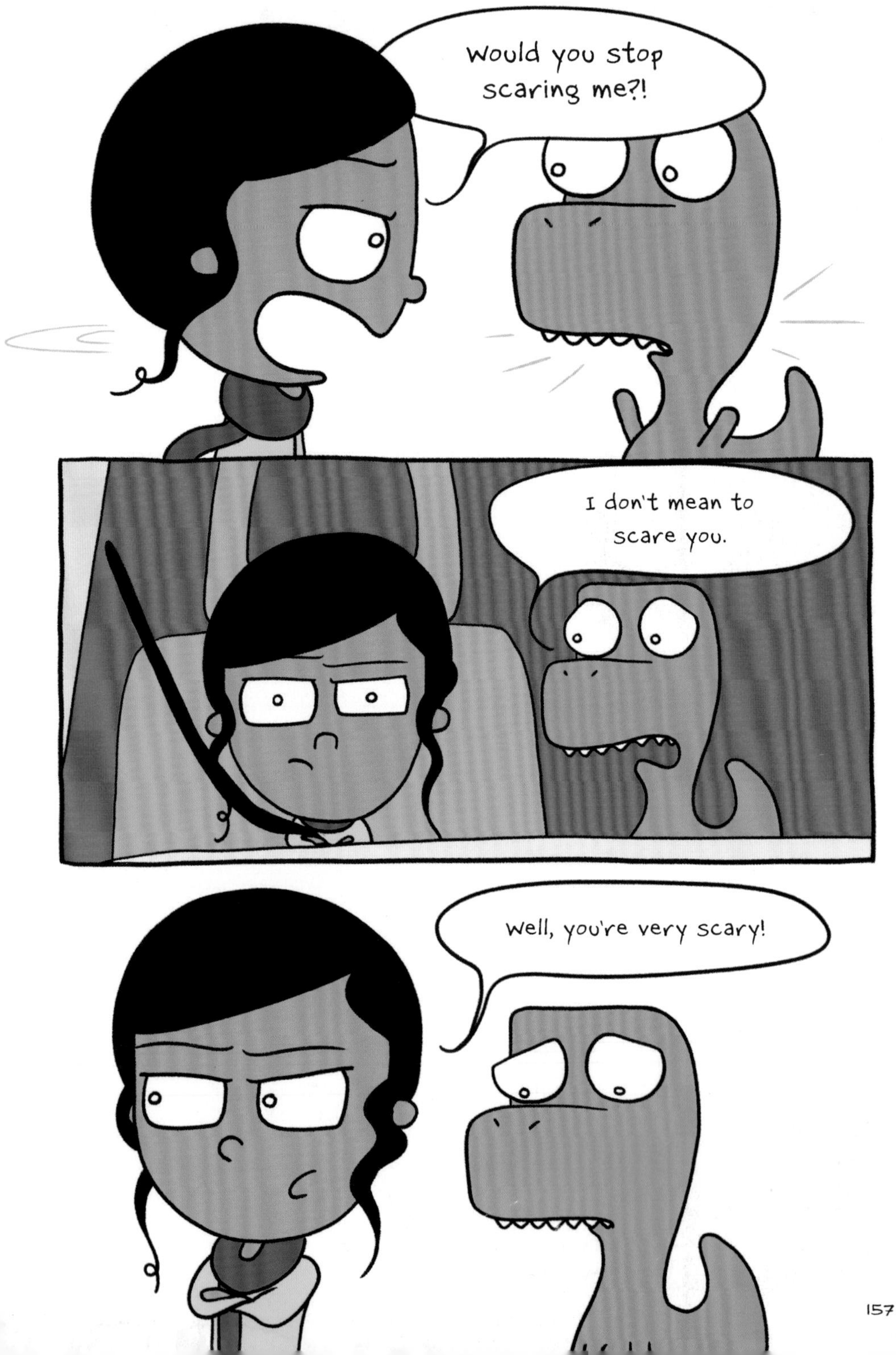
Would you stop scaring me?!
I don't mean to scare you.
Well, you're very scary!

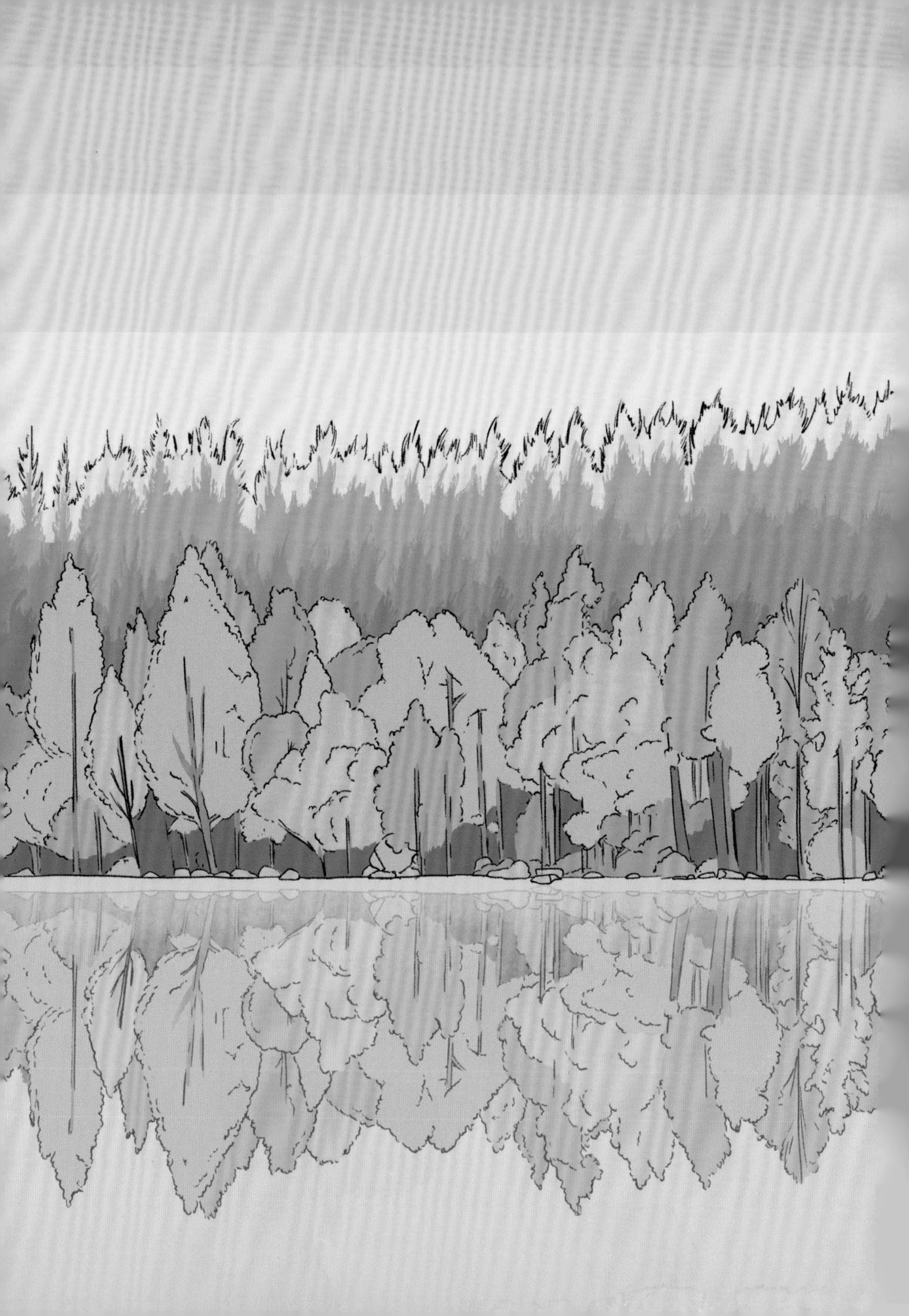

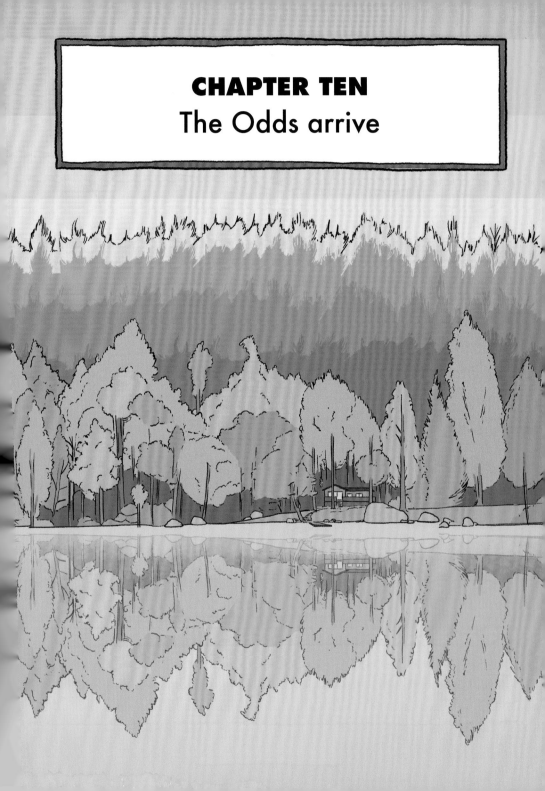

CHAPTER TEN
The Odds arrive

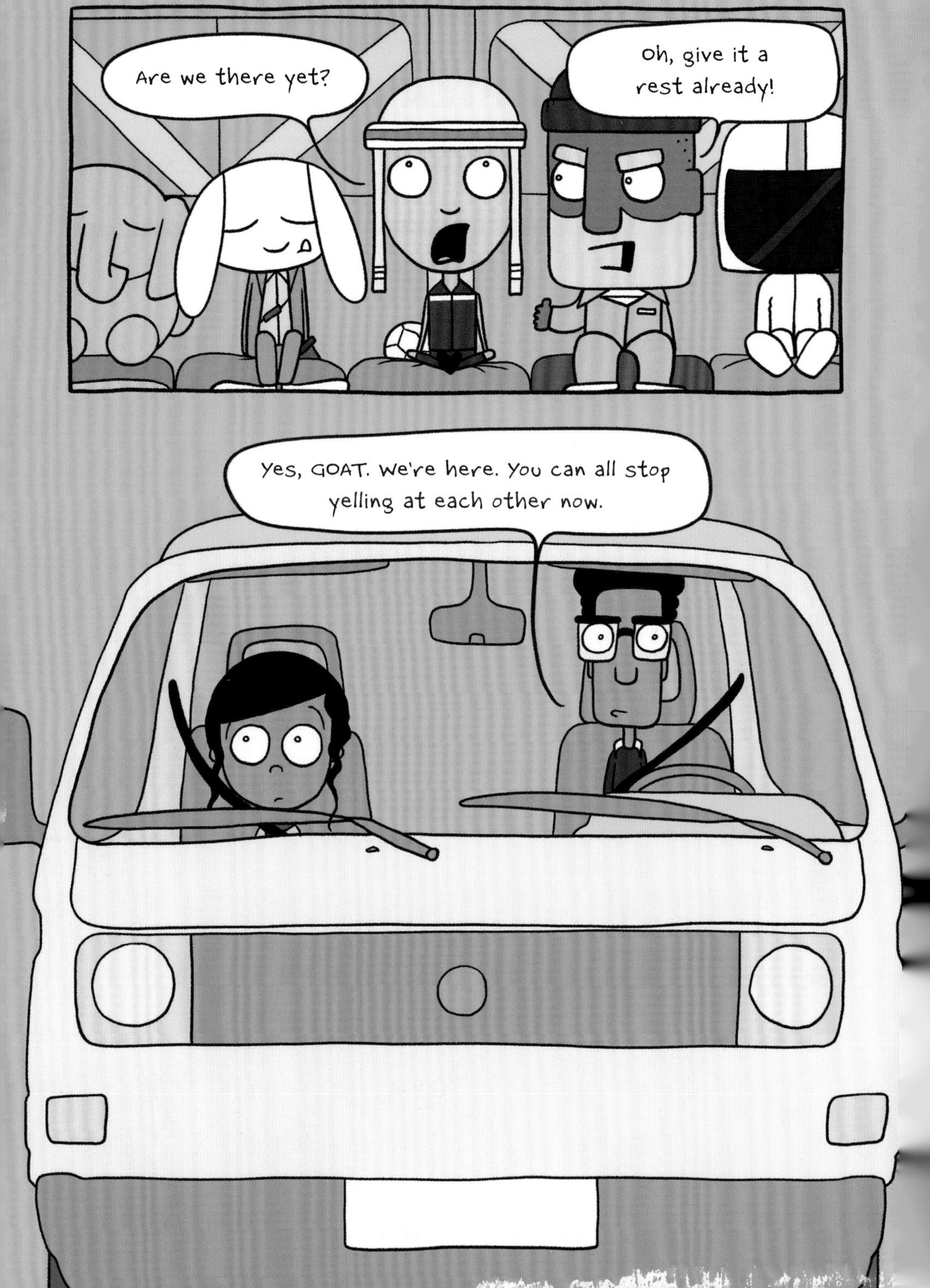
Are we there yet?
Oh, give it a rest already!
Yes, GOAT. We're here. You can all stop yelling at each other now.

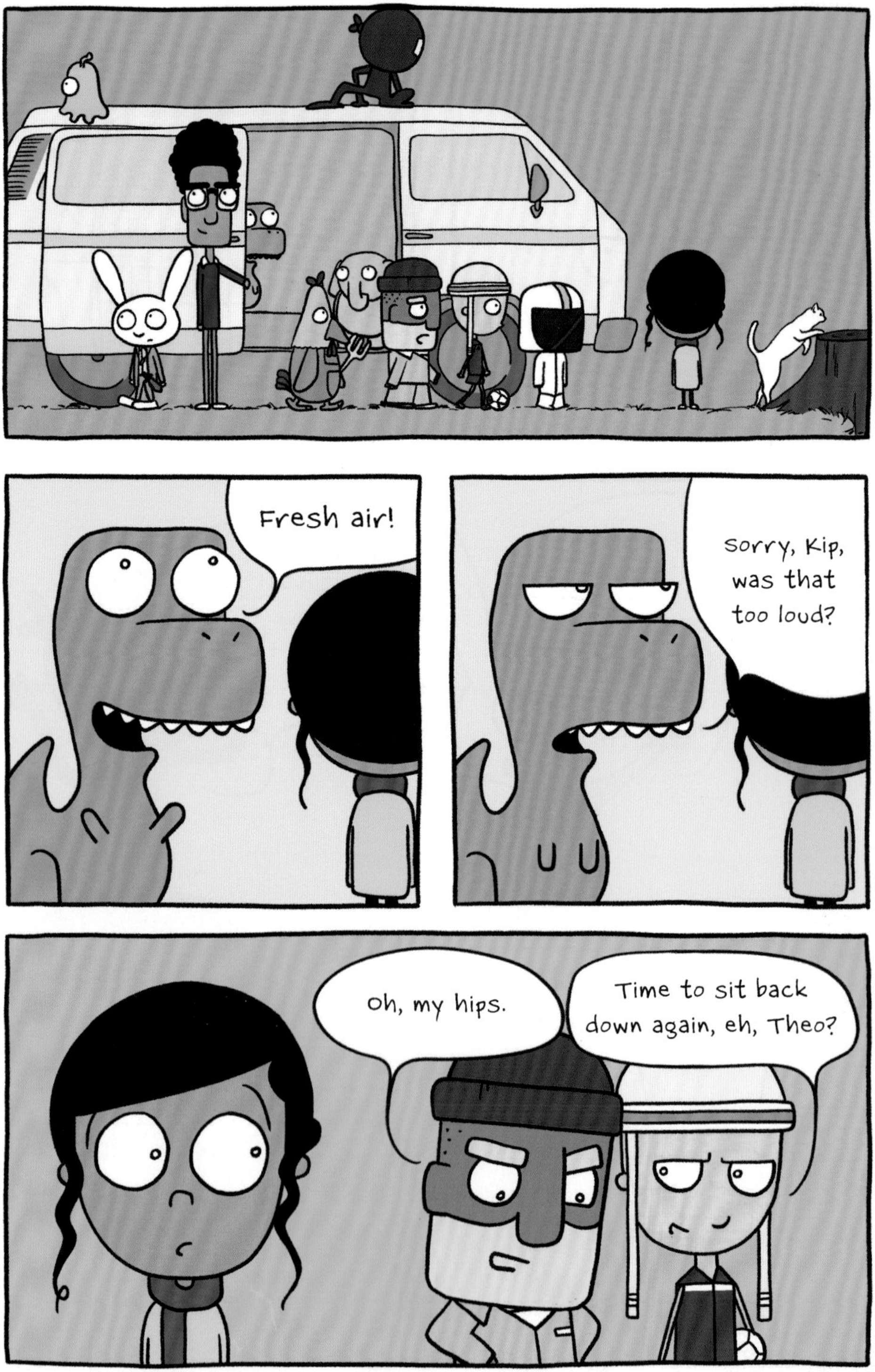
Fresh air!
Sorry, Kip, was that too loud?
Oh, my hips.
Time to sit back down again, eh, Theo?

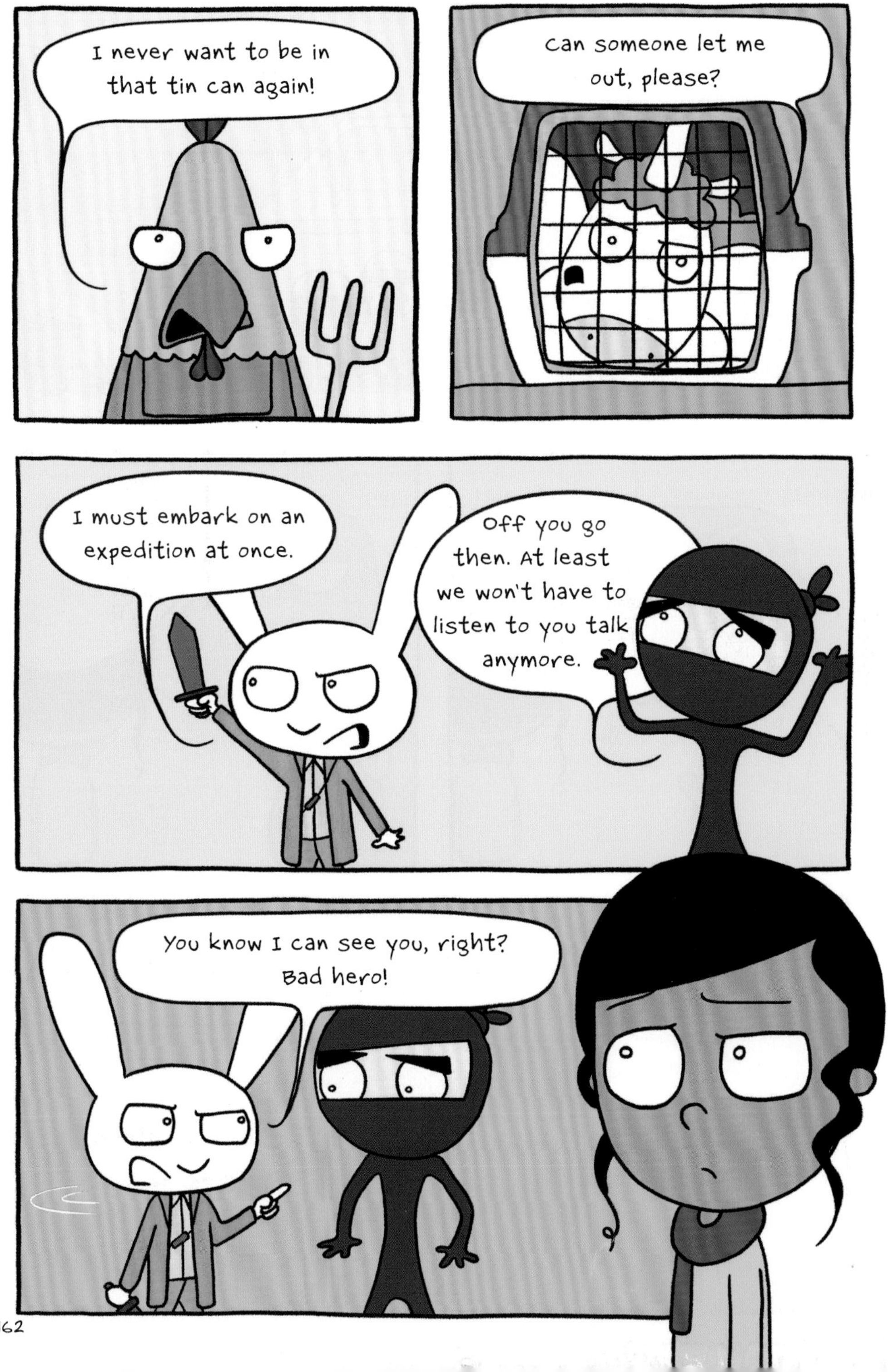
I never want to be in that tin can again!
Can someone let me out, please?
I must embark on an expedition at once.
Off you go then. At least we won't have to listen to you talk anymore.
You know I can see you, right? Bad hero!

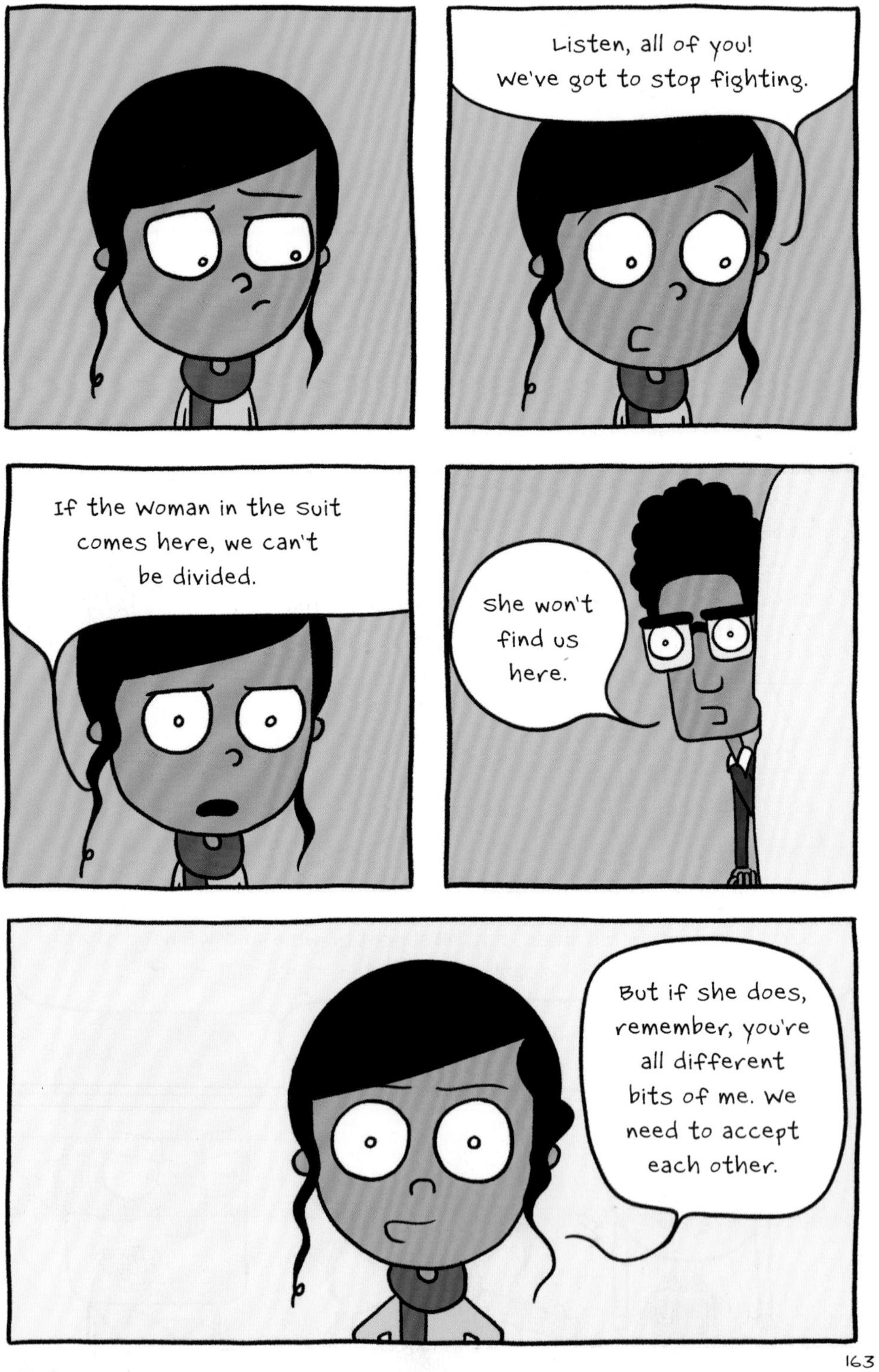

Listen, all of you! We've got to stop fighting.
If the woman in the suit comes here, we can't be divided.
she won't find us here.
But if she does, remember, you're all different bits of me. We need to accept each other.

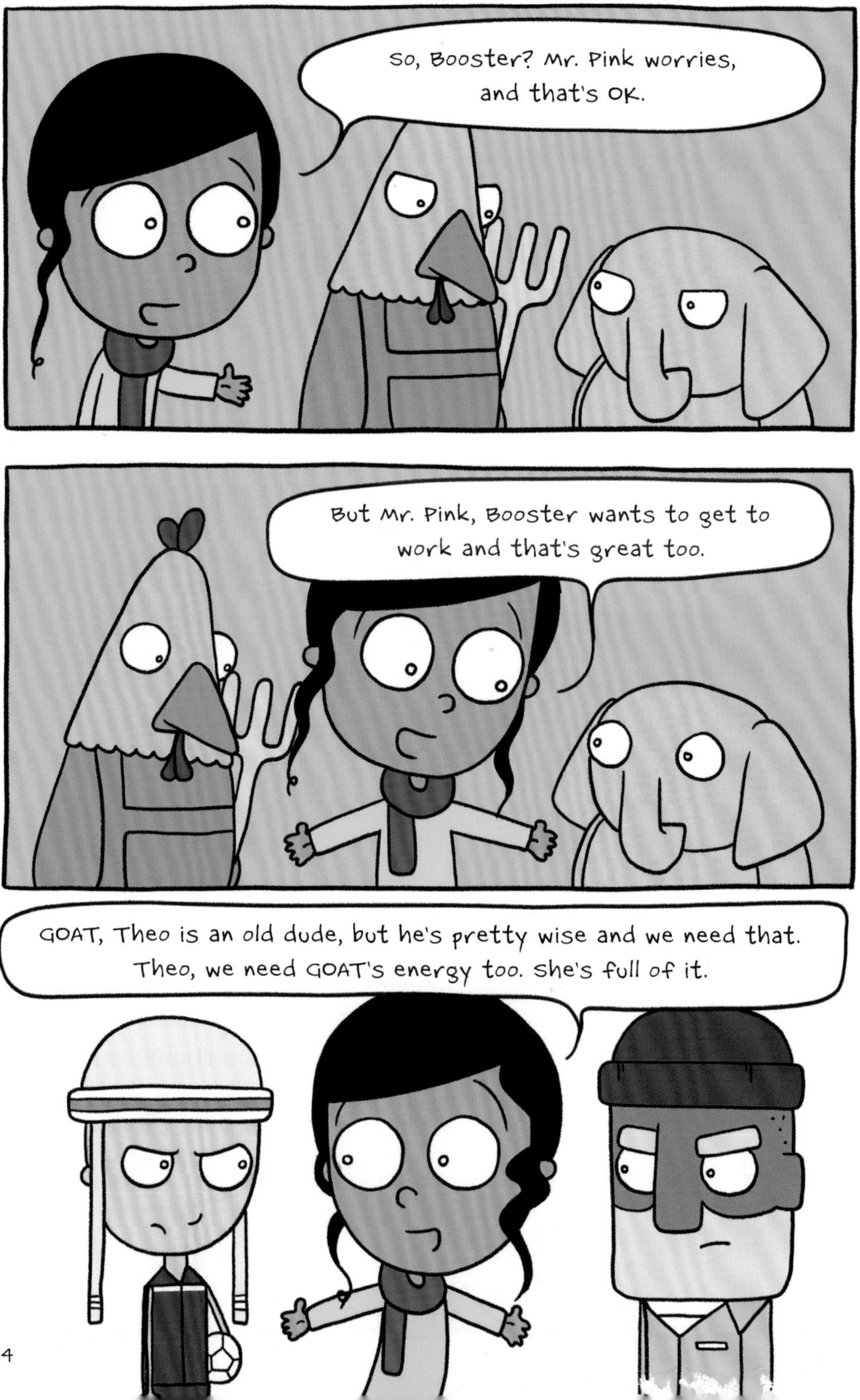
So, Booster? Mr. Pink worries, and that's OK.
But Mr. Pink, Booster wants to get to work and that's great too.
GOAT, Theo is an old dude, but he's pretty wise and we need that. Theo, we need GOAT's energy too. She's full of it.

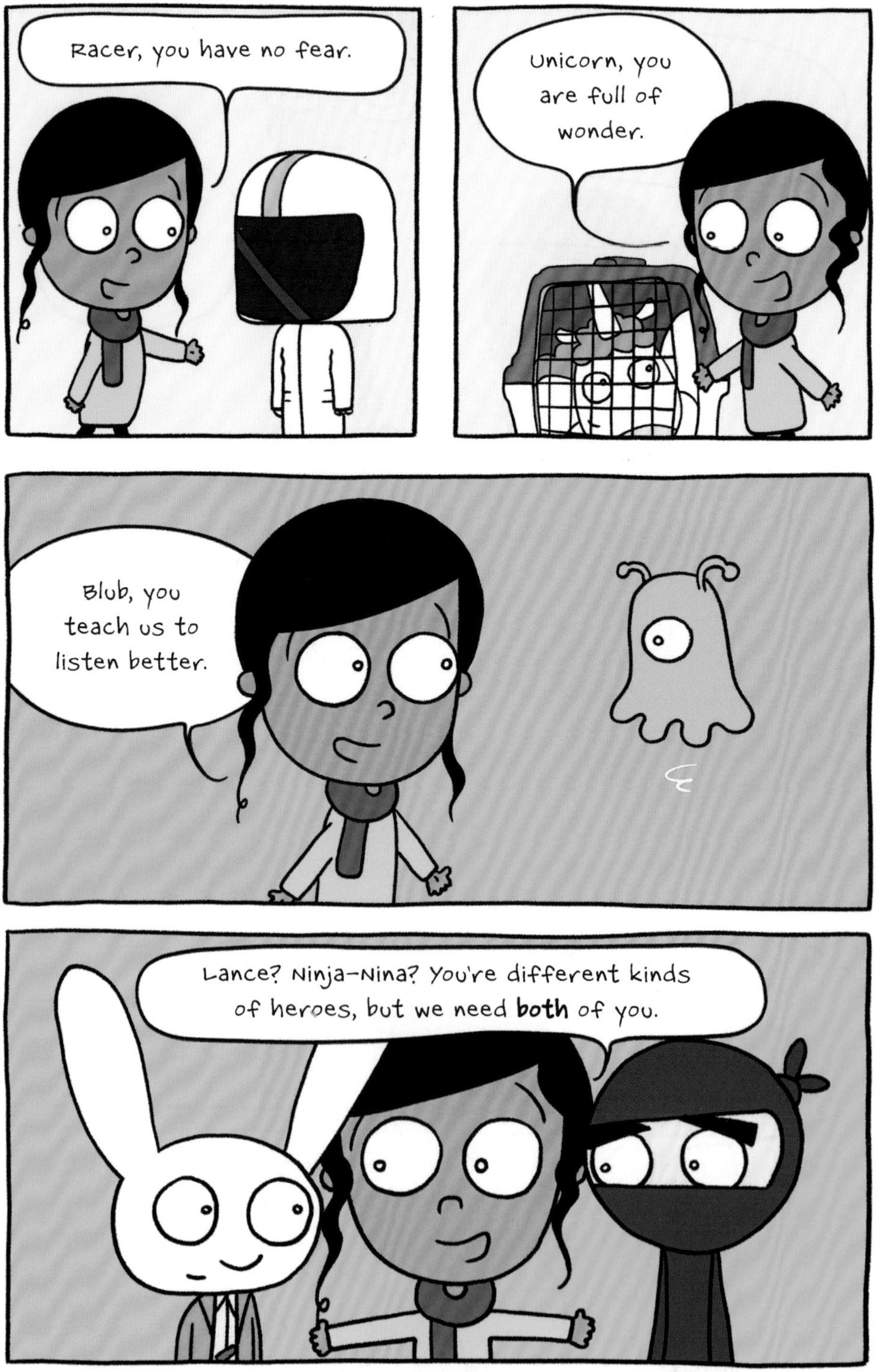
Racer, you have no fear.
Unicorn, you are full of wonder.
Blub, you teach us to listen better.
Lance? Ninja-Nina? You're different kinds of heroes, but we need **both** of you.

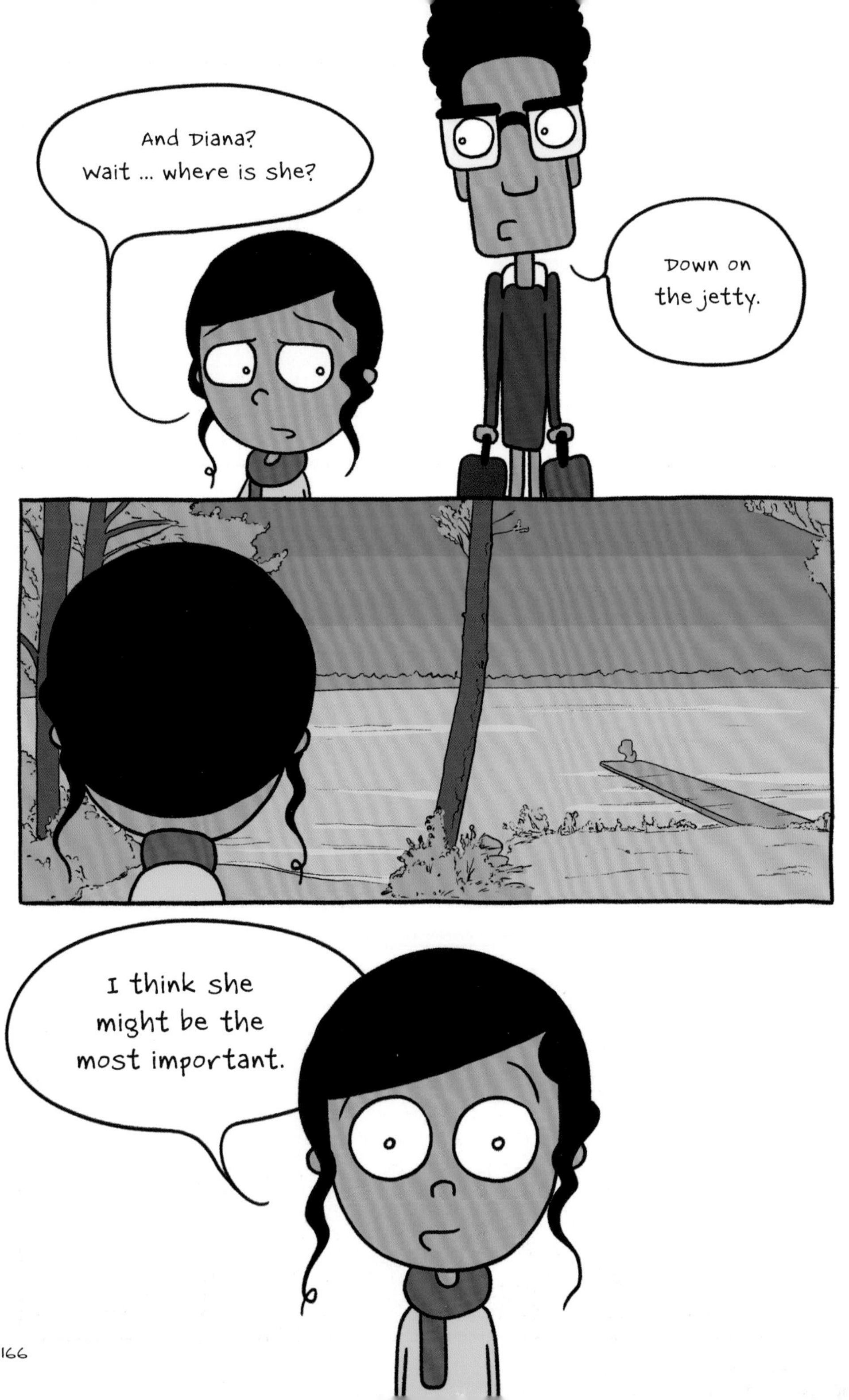
And Diana?
Wait ... where is she?
Down on
the jetty.
I think she
might be the
most important.

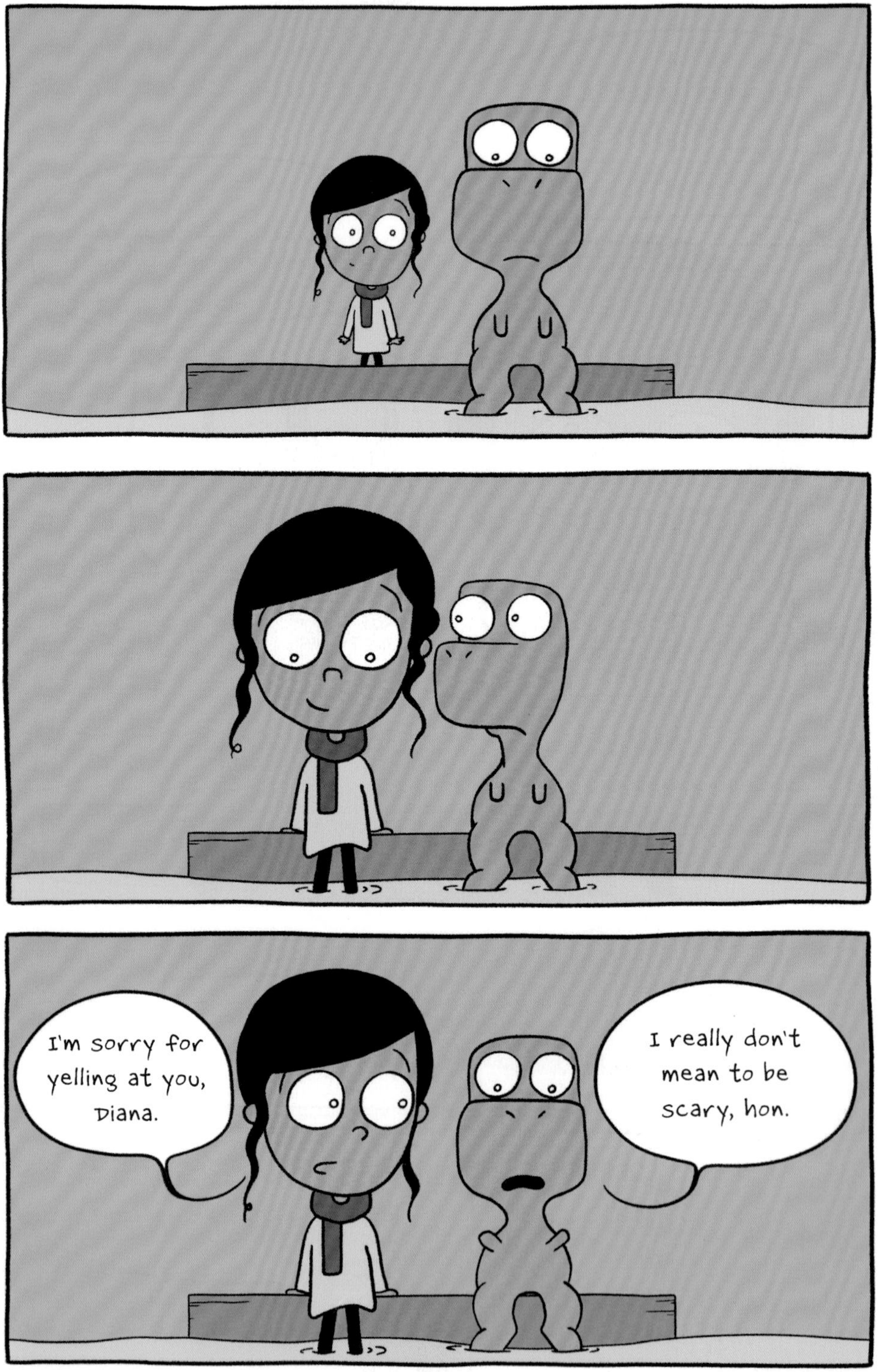
I'm sorry for yelling at you, Diana.
I really don't mean to be scary, hon.

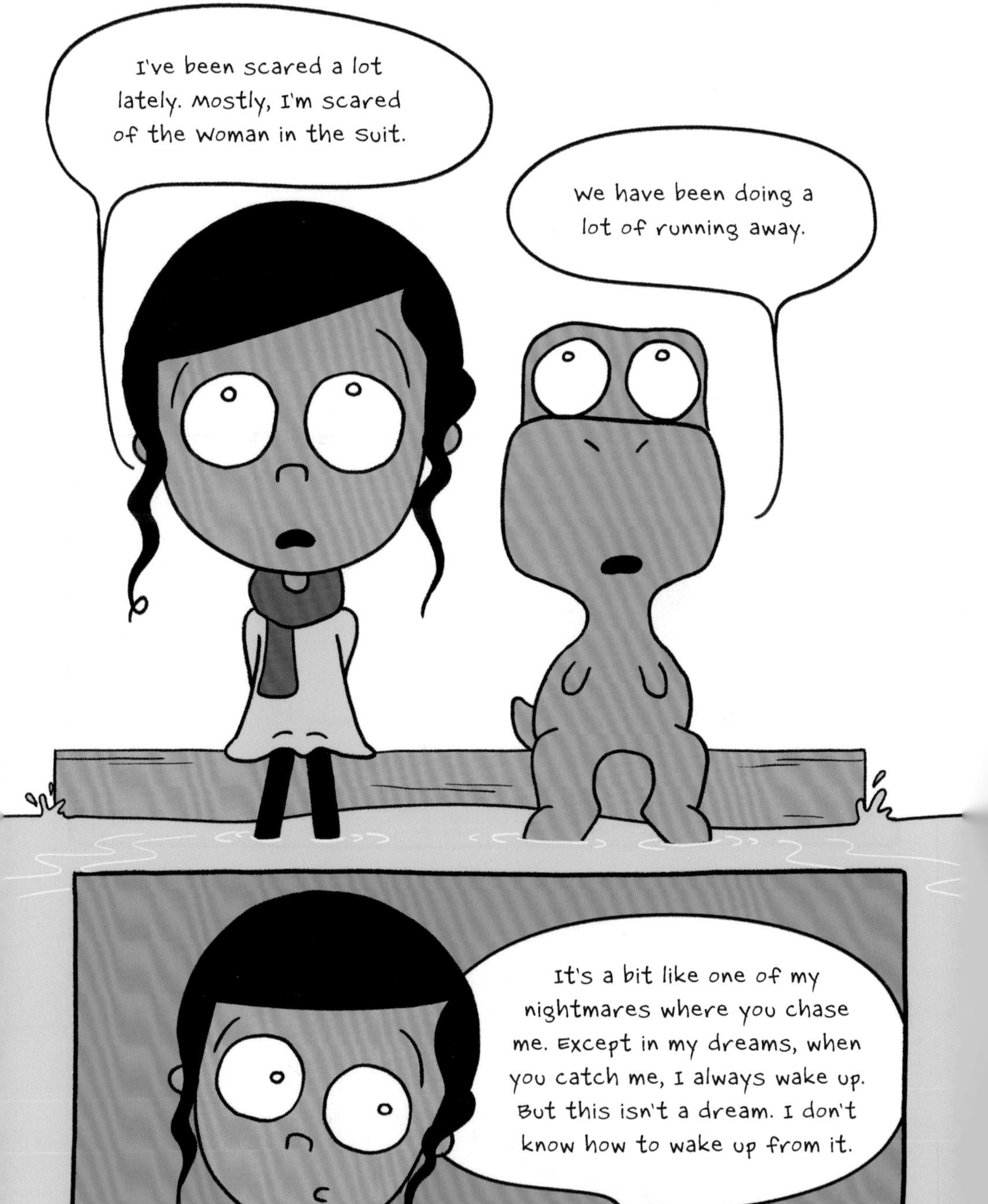
I've been scared a lot lately. Mostly, I'm scared of the woman in the suit.
We have been doing a lot of running away.
It's a bit like one of my nightmares where you chase me. Except in my dreams, when you catch me, I always wake up. But this isn't a dream. I don't know how to wake up from it.

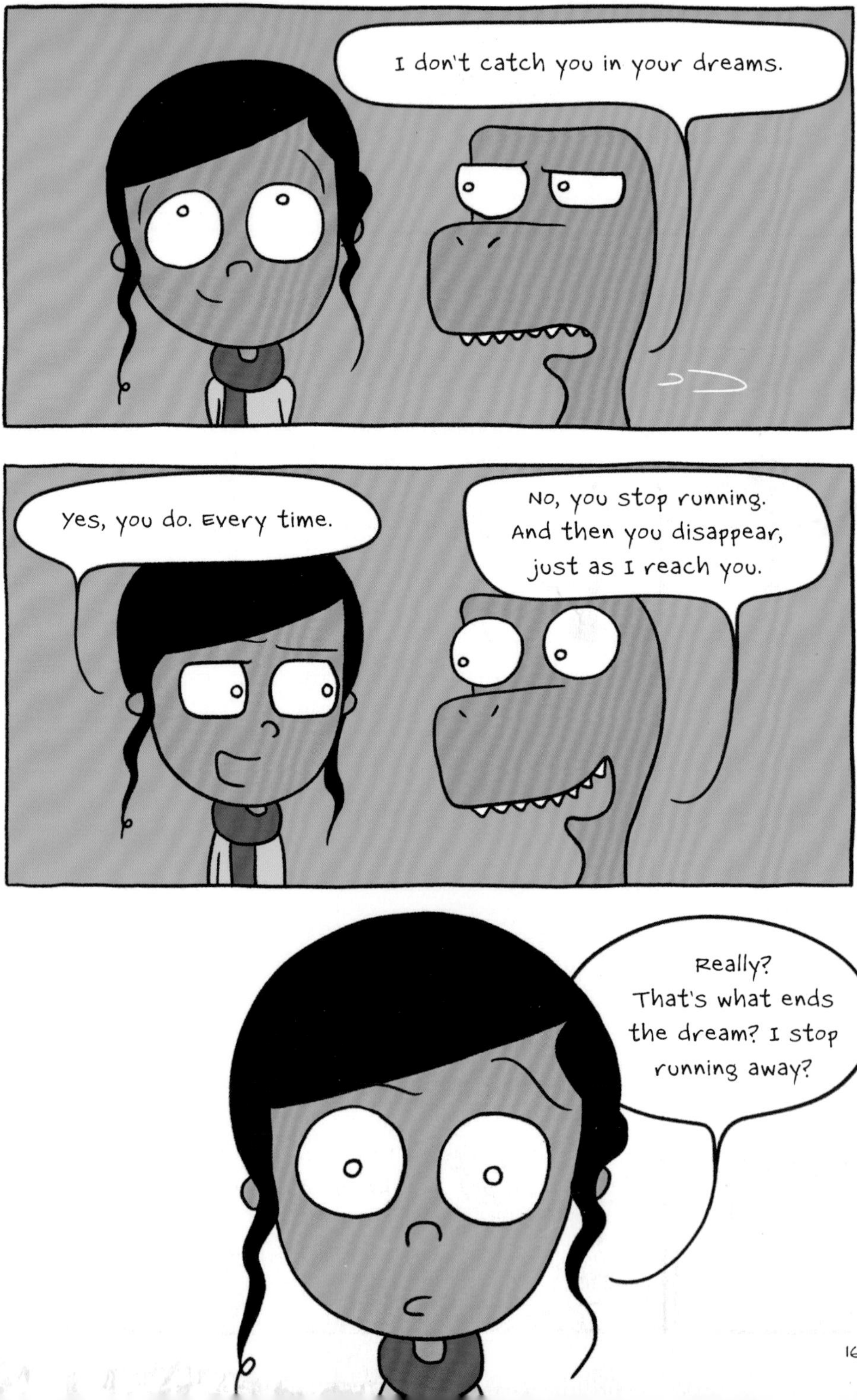
I don't catch you in your dreams.
Yes, you do. Every time.
No, you stop running. And then you disappear, just as I reach you.
Really? That's what ends the dream? I stop running away?

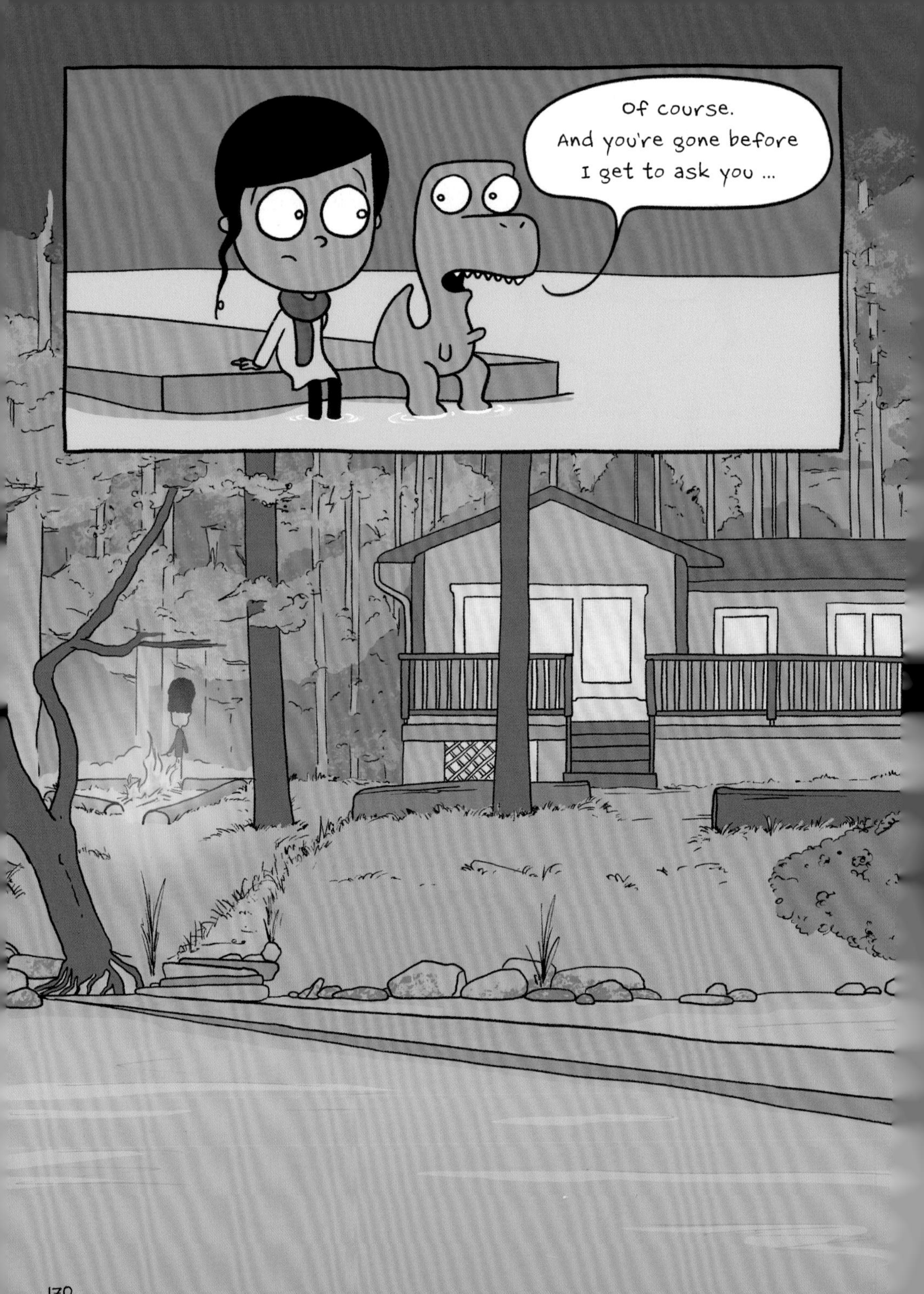
Of course.
And you're gone before
I get to ask you ...

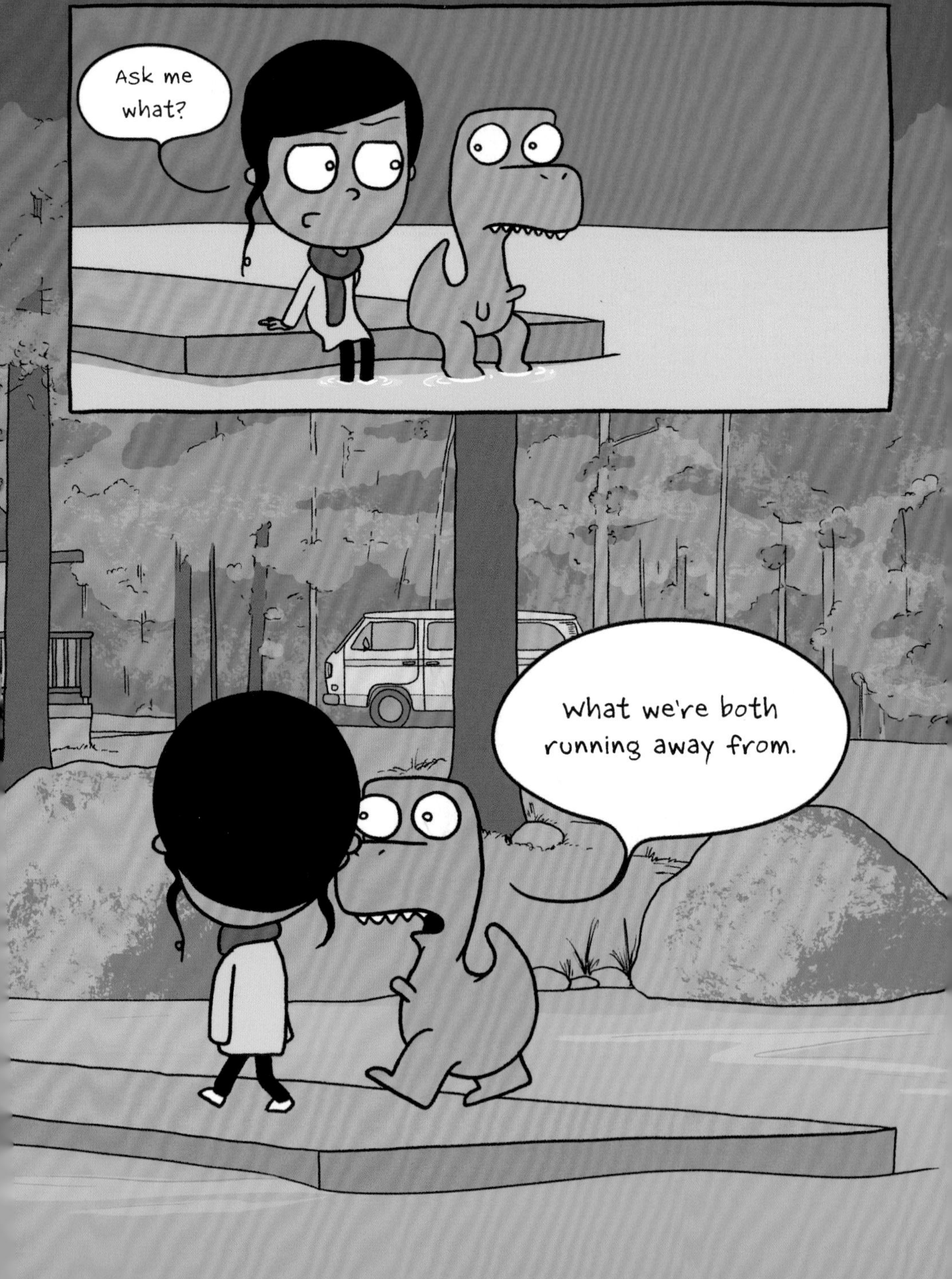
Ask me what?
What we're both running away from.

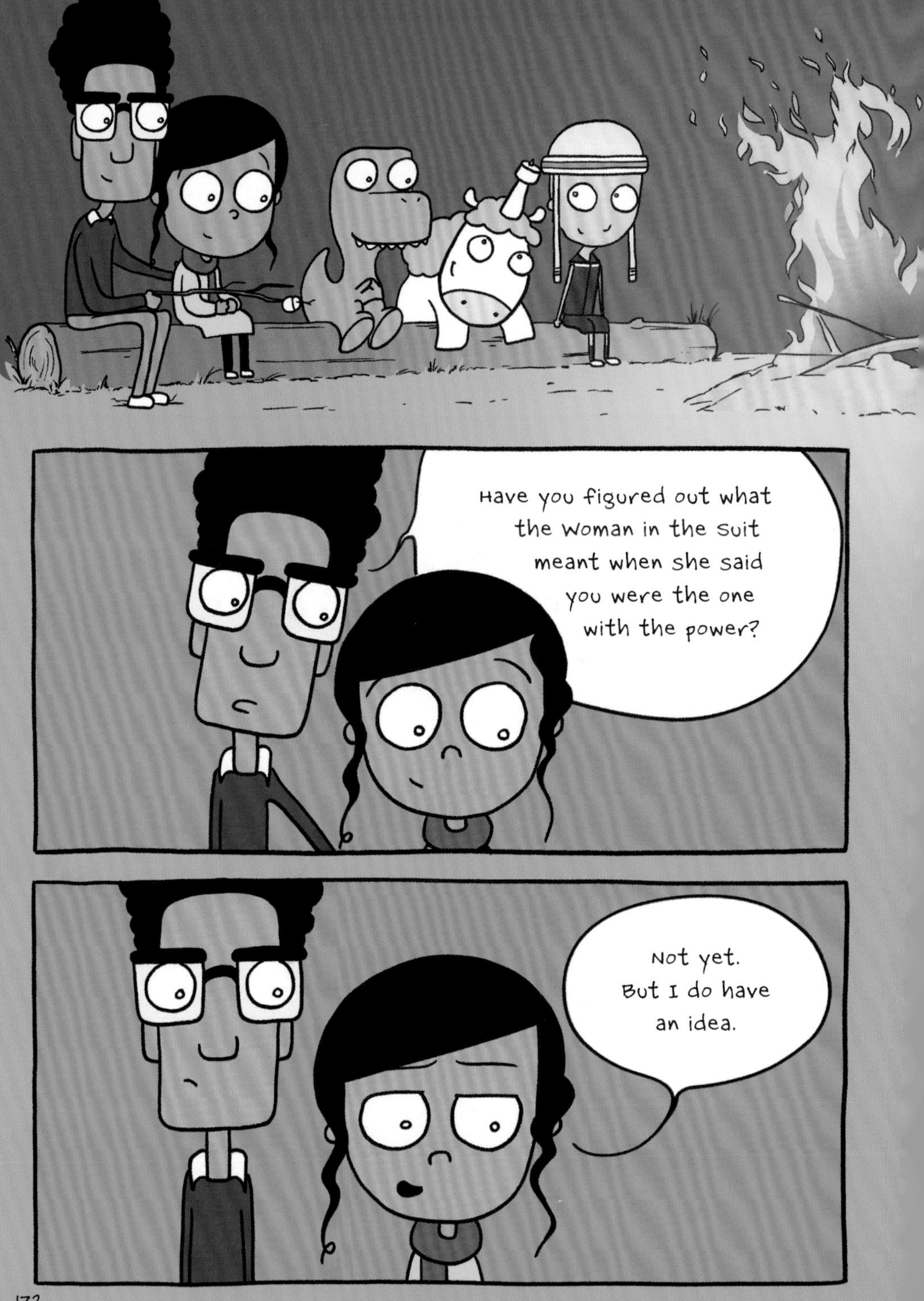
Have you figured out what the woman in the suit meant when she said you were the one with the power?
Not yet. But I do have an idea.

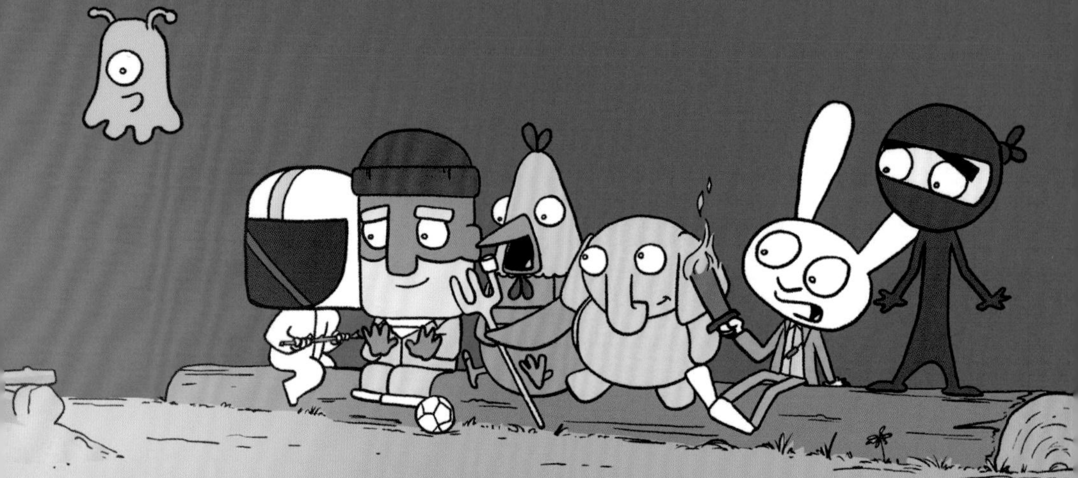

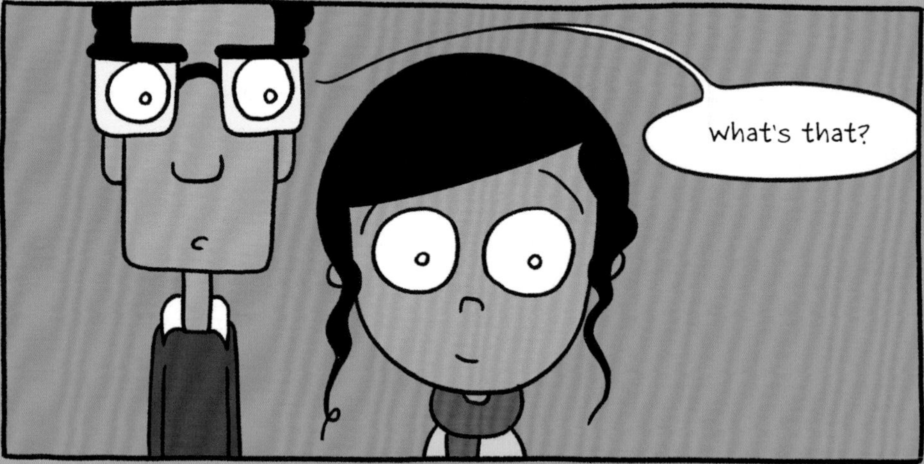
What's that?

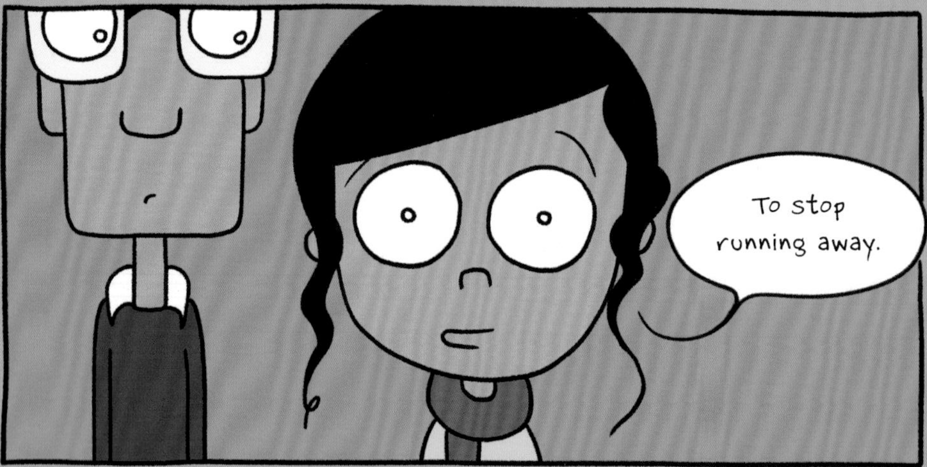
To stop running away.

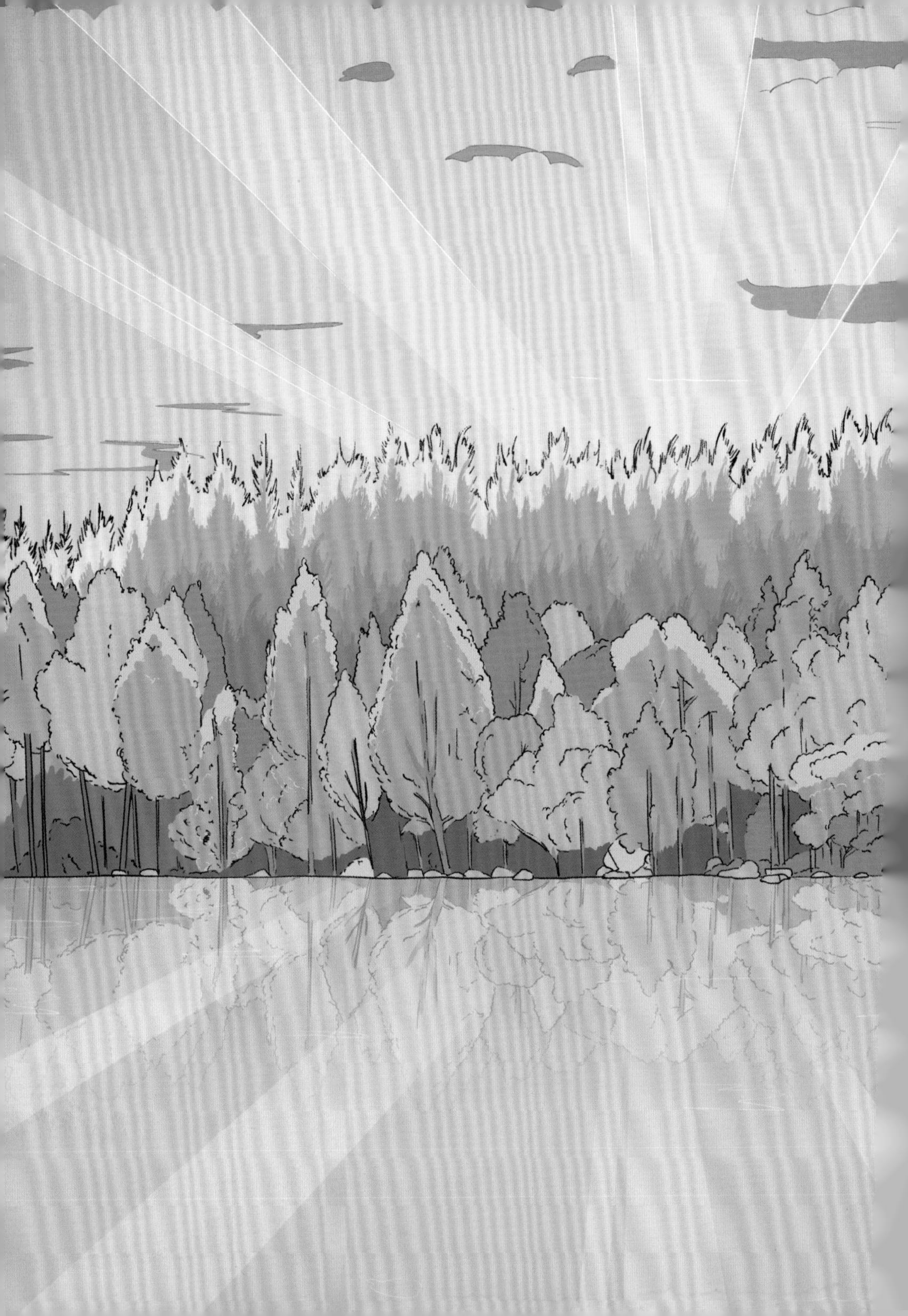

CHAPTER ELEVEN
An oddity of Odds

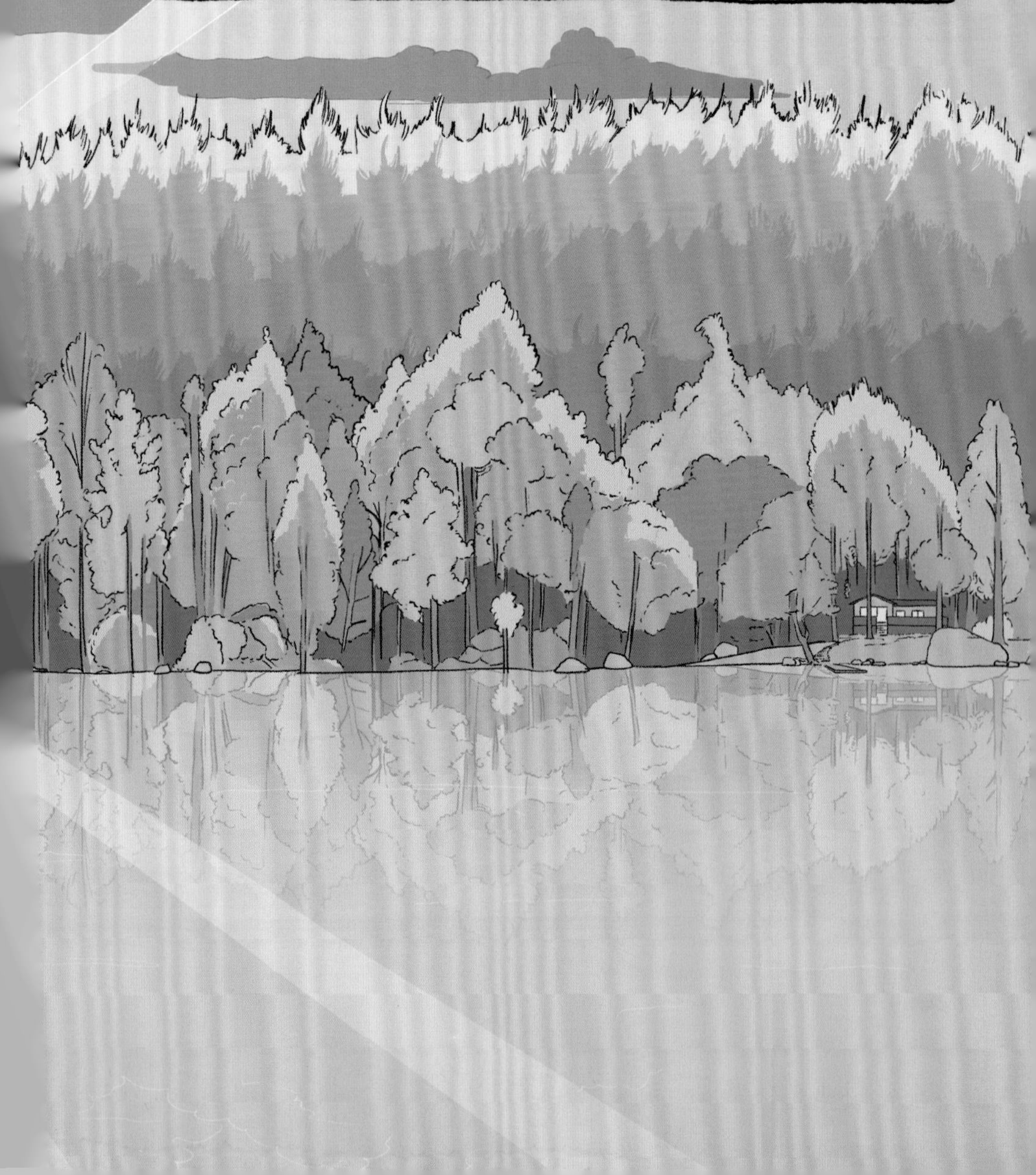

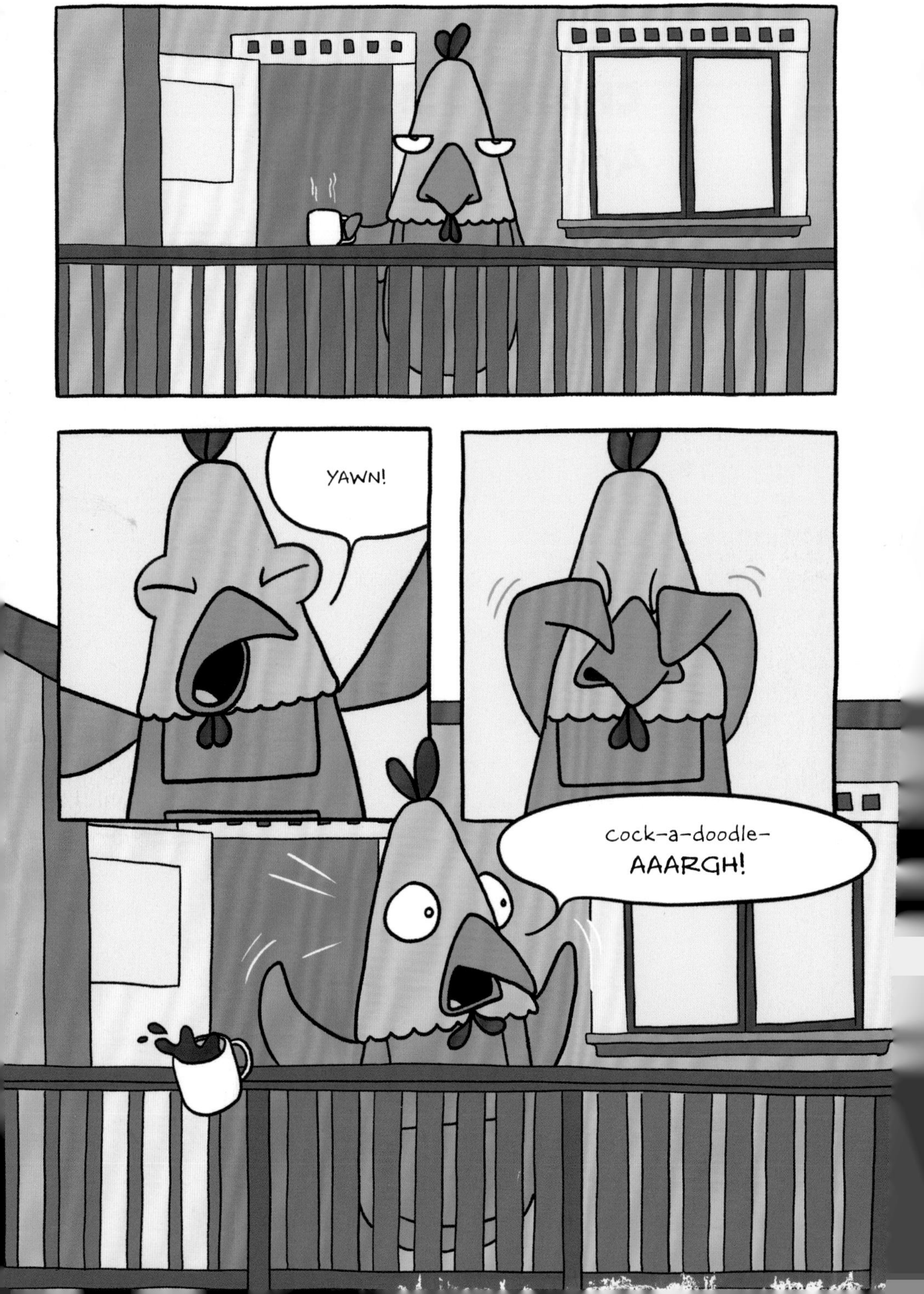
YAWN!
cock-a-doodle-
AAARGH!

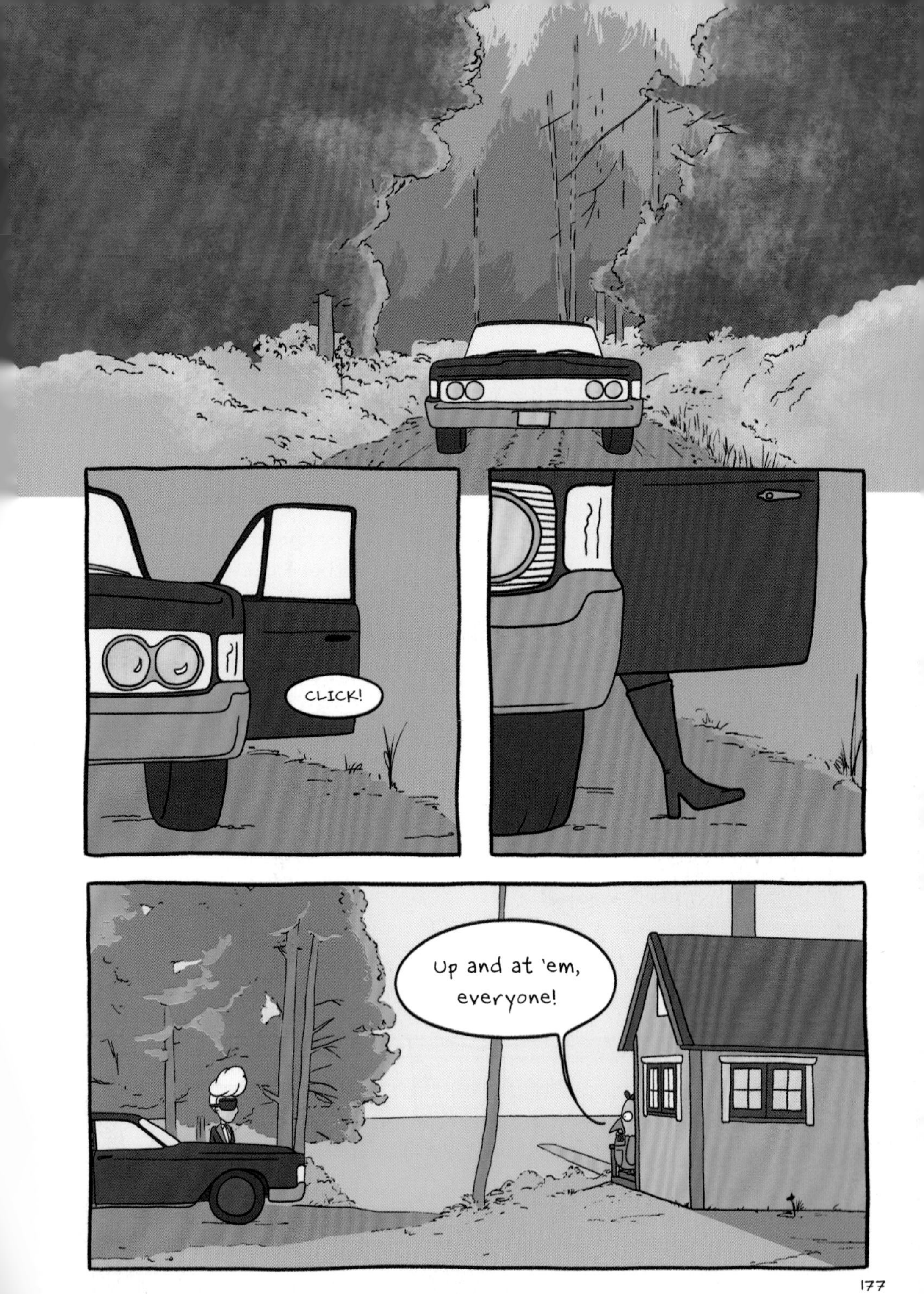
CLICK!
Up and at 'em, everyone!

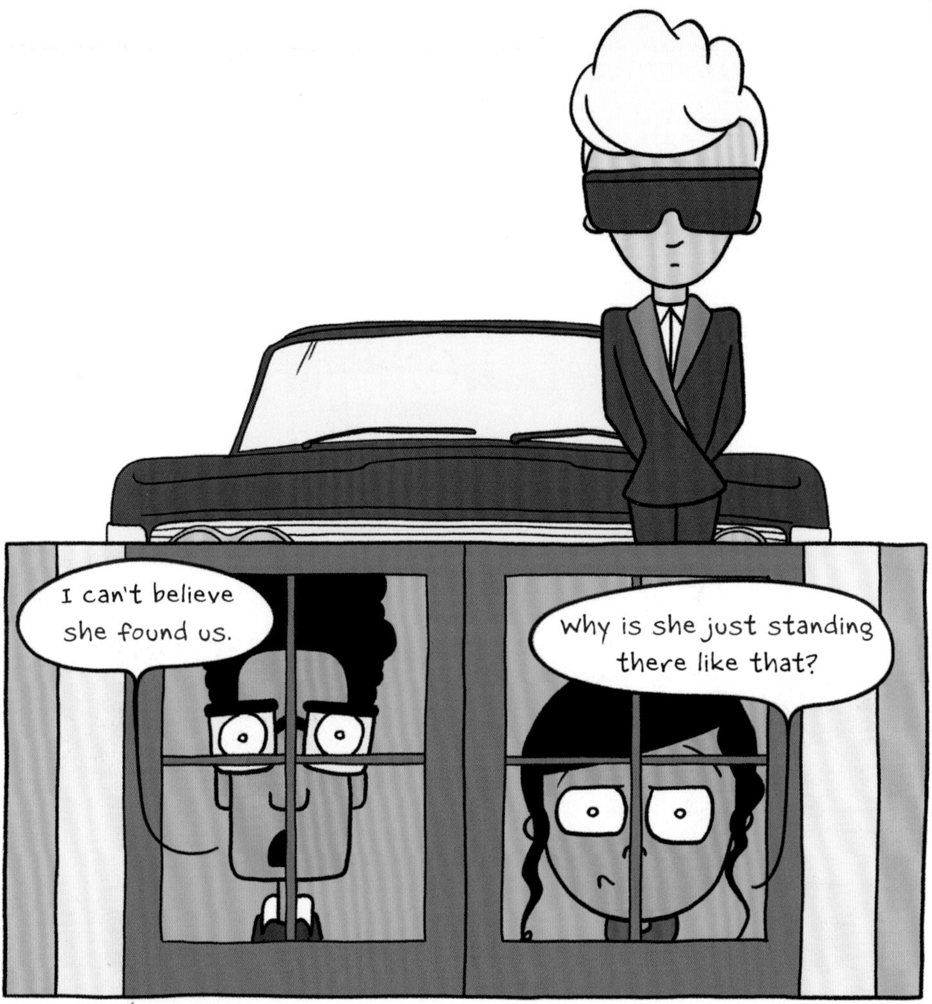
I can't believe she found us.
Why is she just standing there like that?
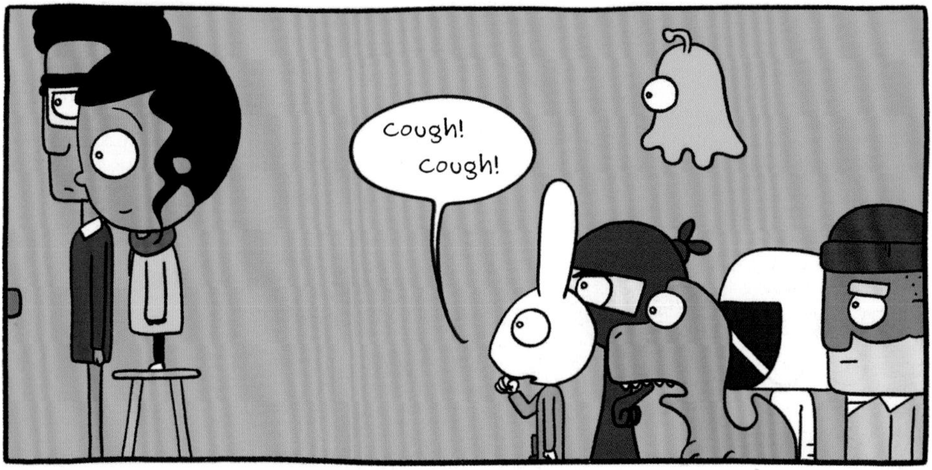
Cough! Cough!

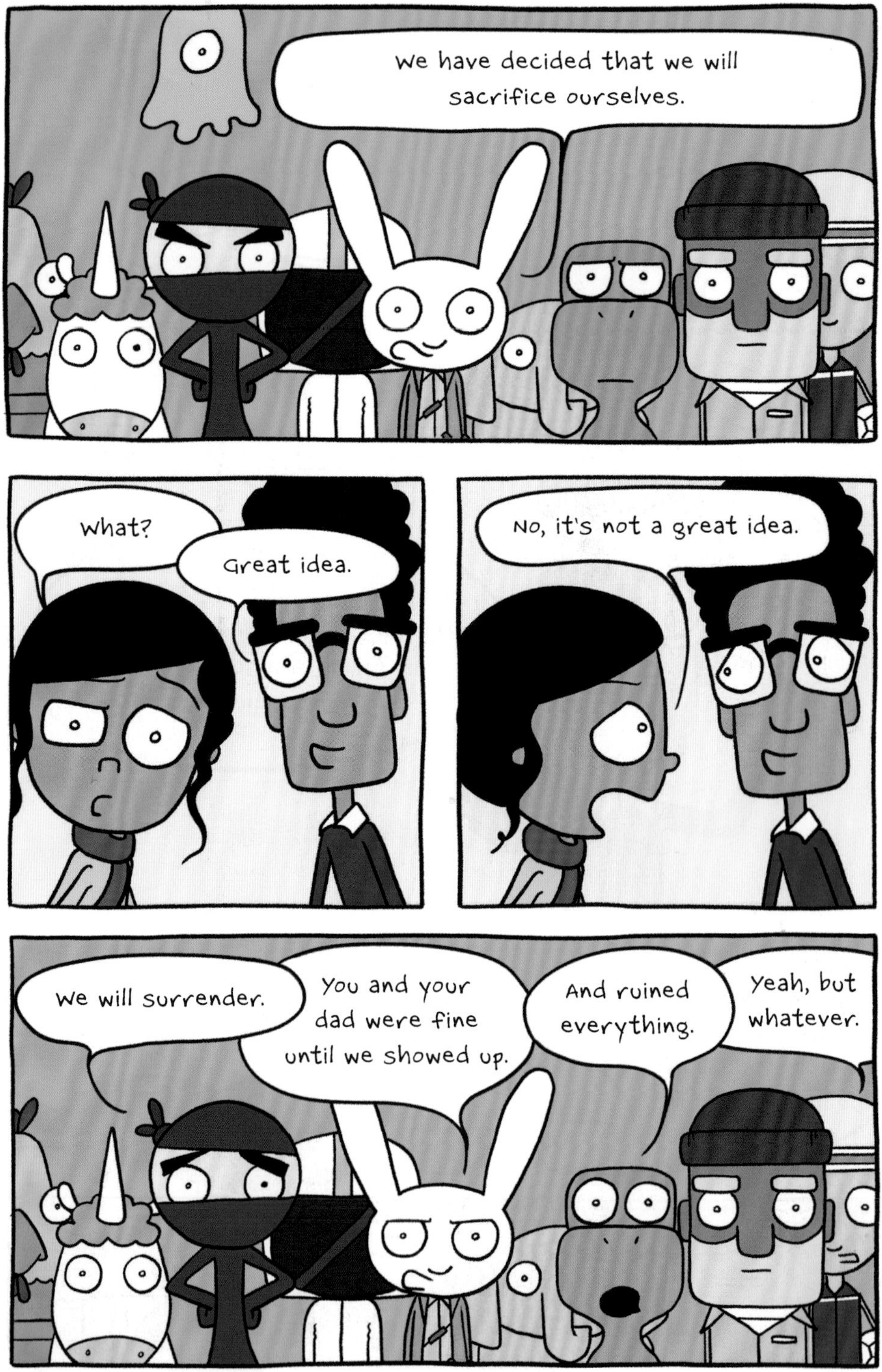
We have decided that we will sacrifice ourselves.
What?
Great idea.
No, it's not a great idea.
We will surrender.
You and your dad were fine until we showed up.
And ruined everything.
Yeah, but whatever.

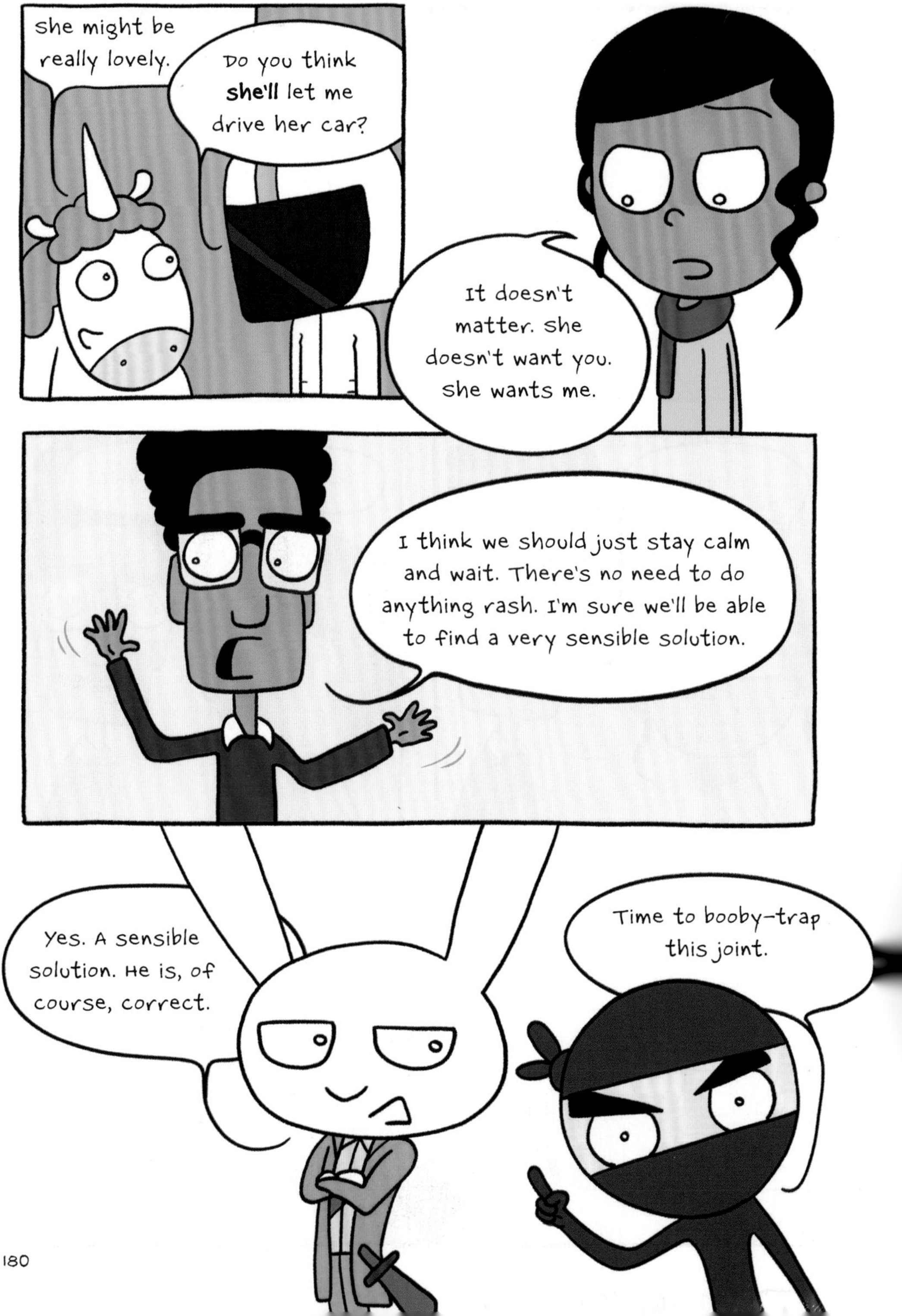
she might be really lovely.
Do you think **she'll** let me drive her car?
It doesn't matter. she doesn't want you. she wants me.
I think we should just stay calm and wait. There's no need to do anything rash. I'm sure we'll be able to find a very sensible solution.
Yes. A sensible solution. He is, of course, correct.
Time to booby-trap this joint.

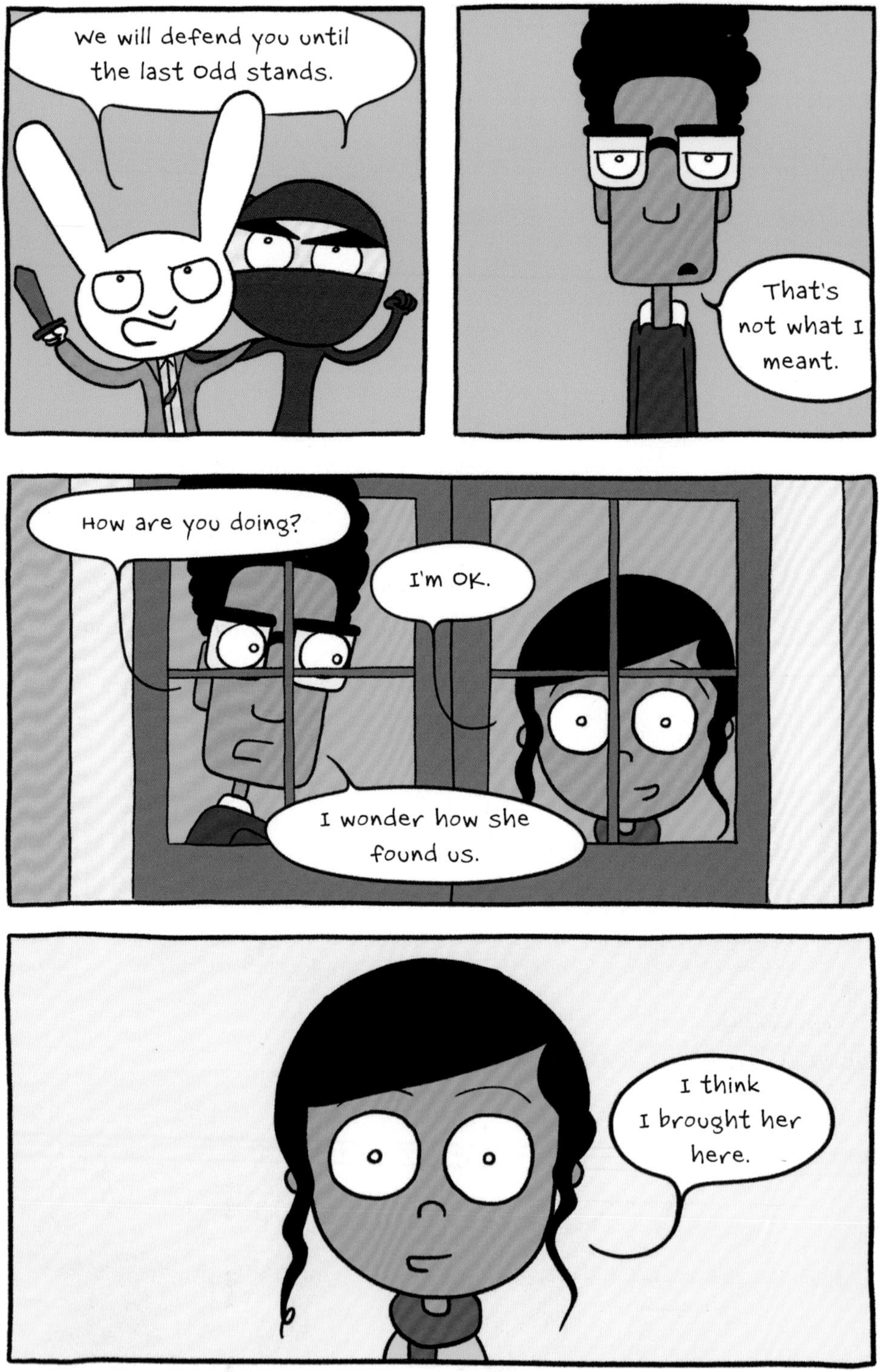
We will defend you until the last Odd stands.
That's not what I meant.
How are you doing?
I'm OK.
I wonder how she found us.
I think I brought her here.

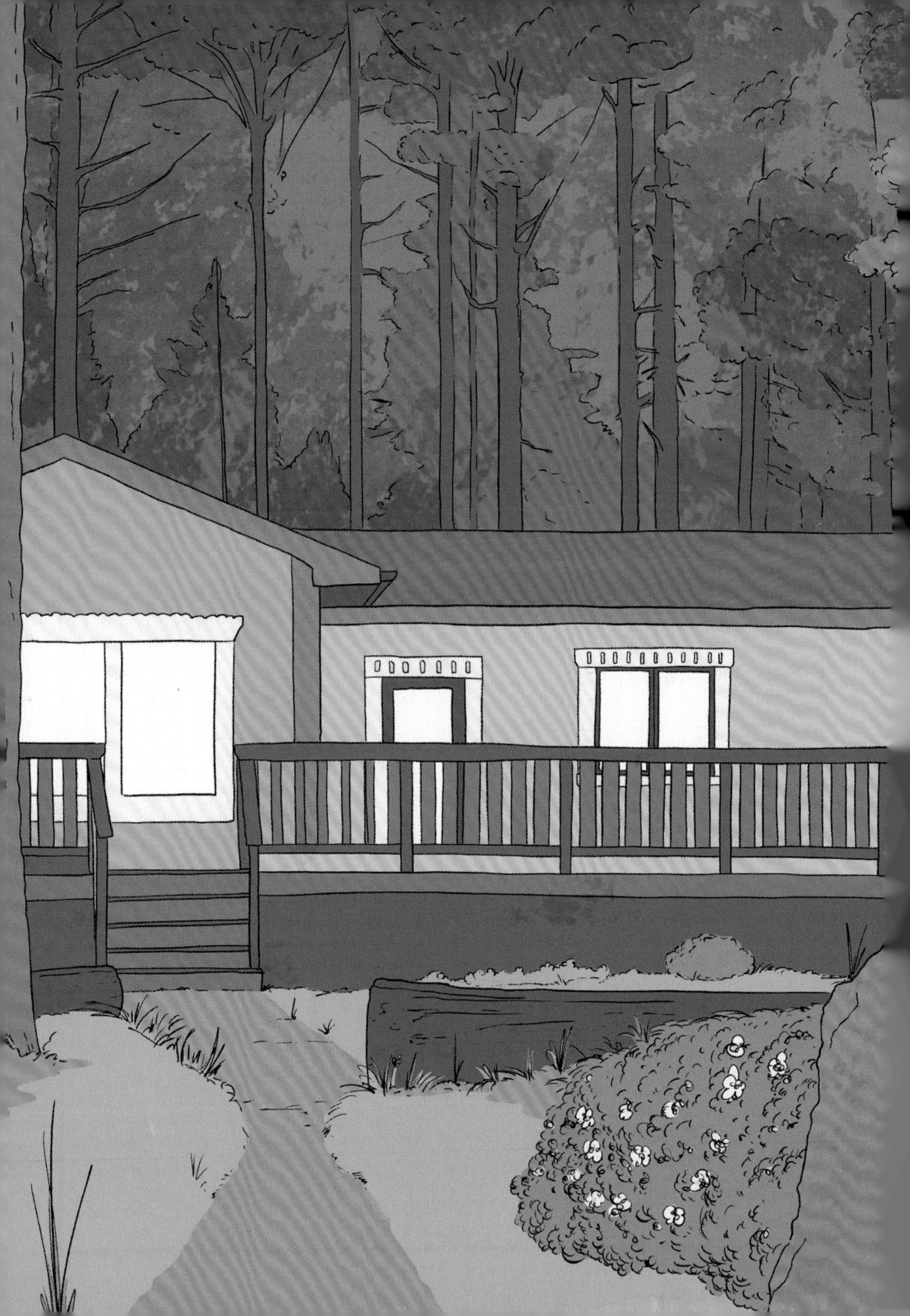

CHAPTER TWELVE
What are the odds?

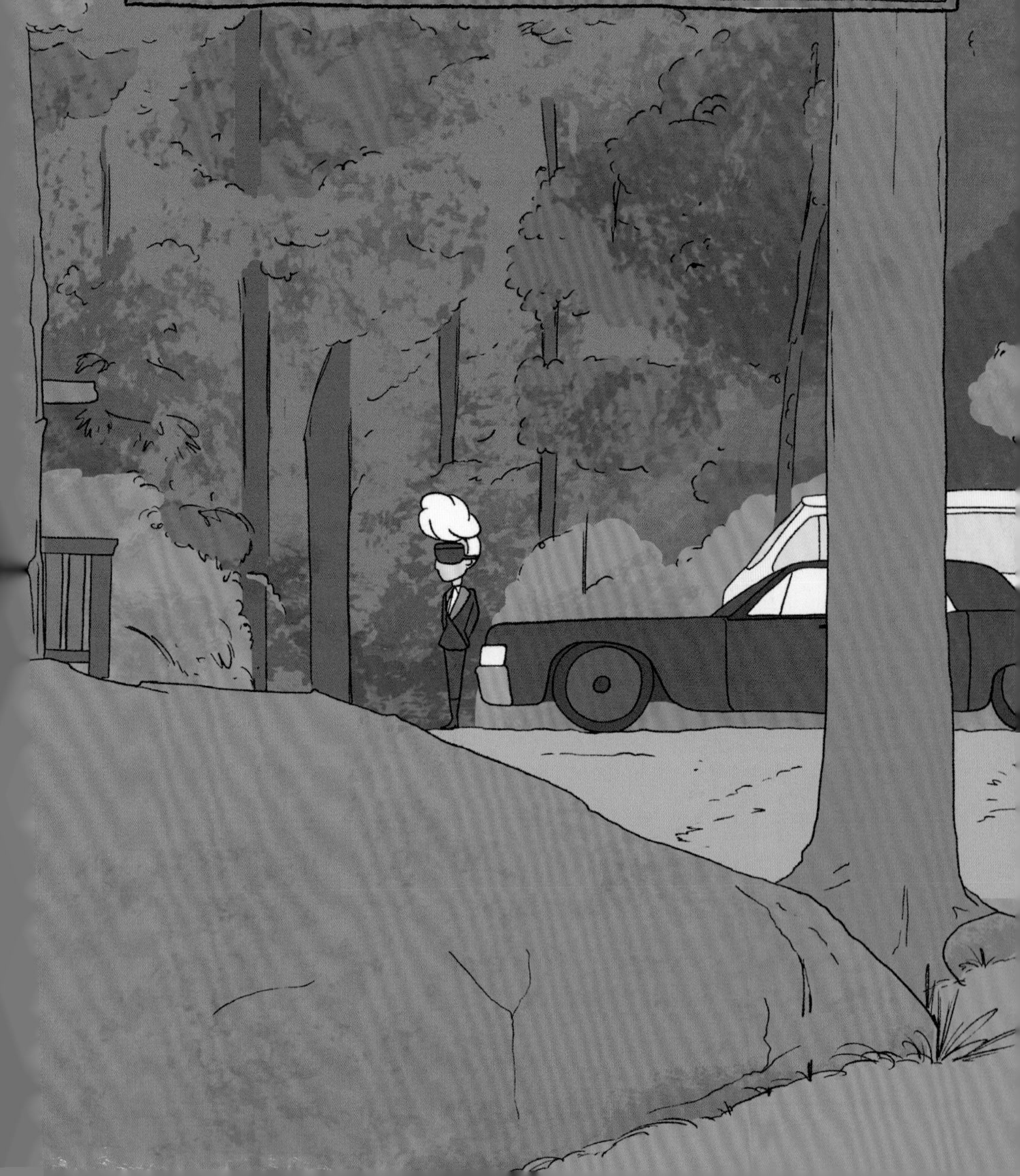

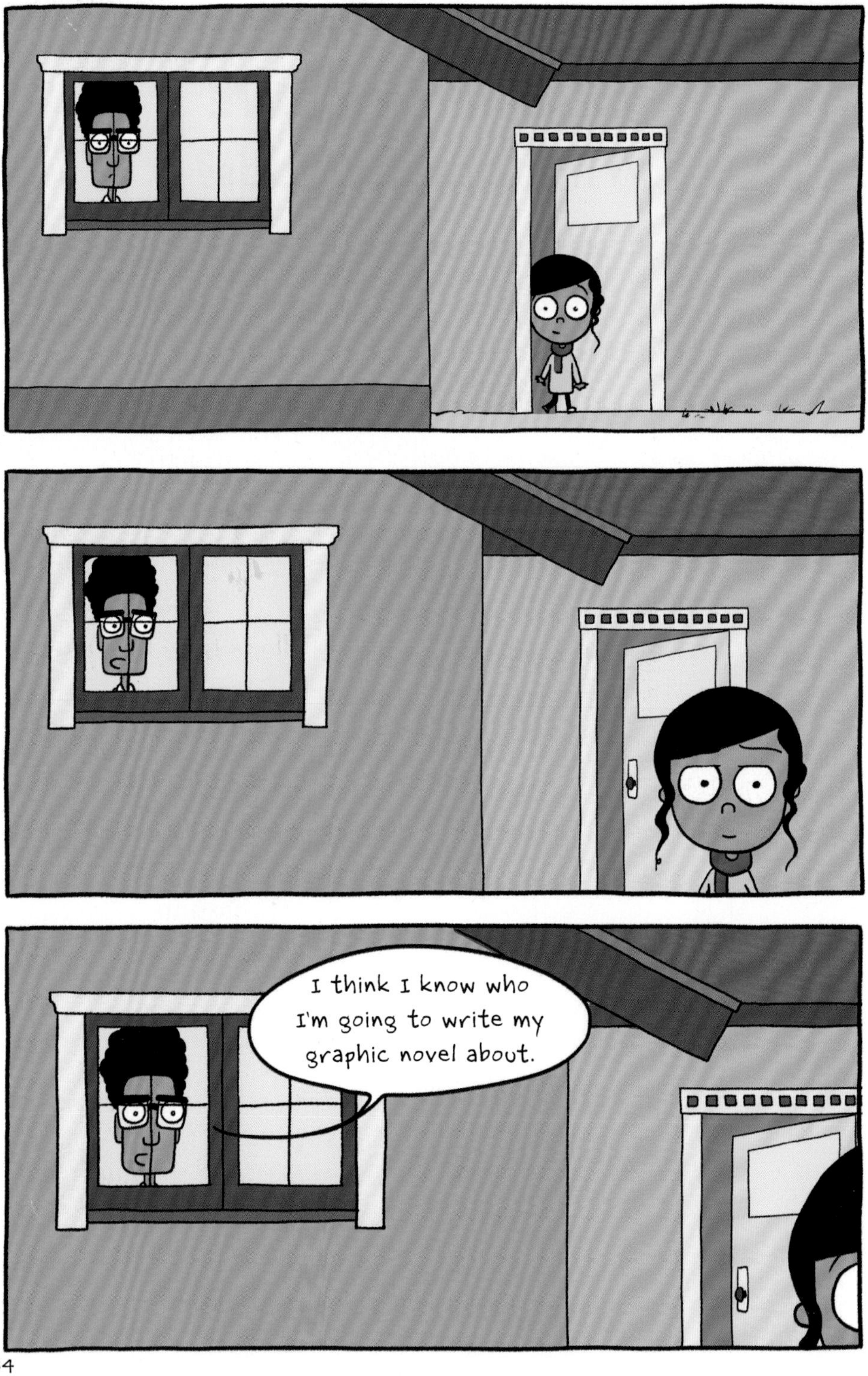
I think I know who I'm going to write my graphic novel about.

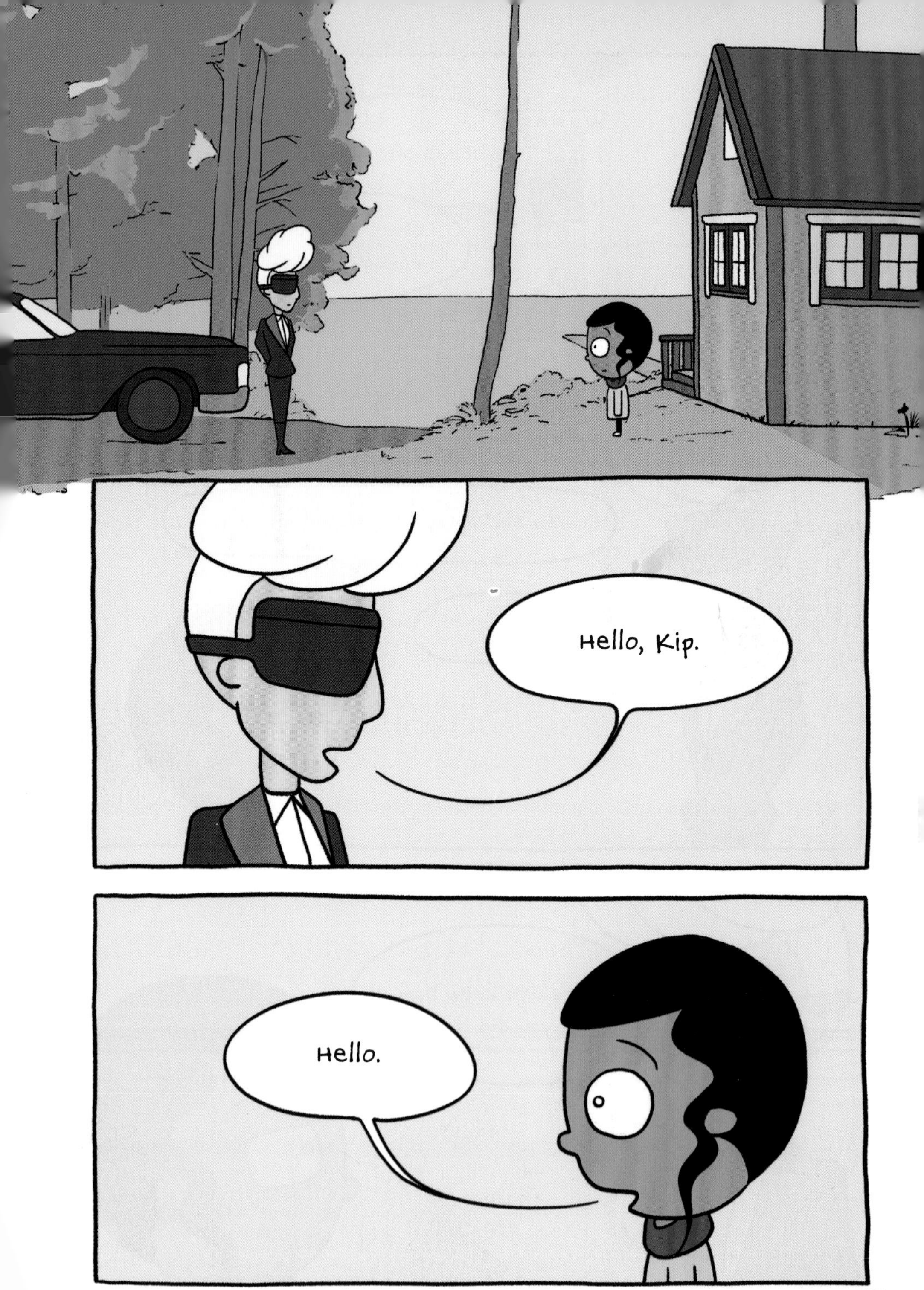
Hello, Kip.
Hello.

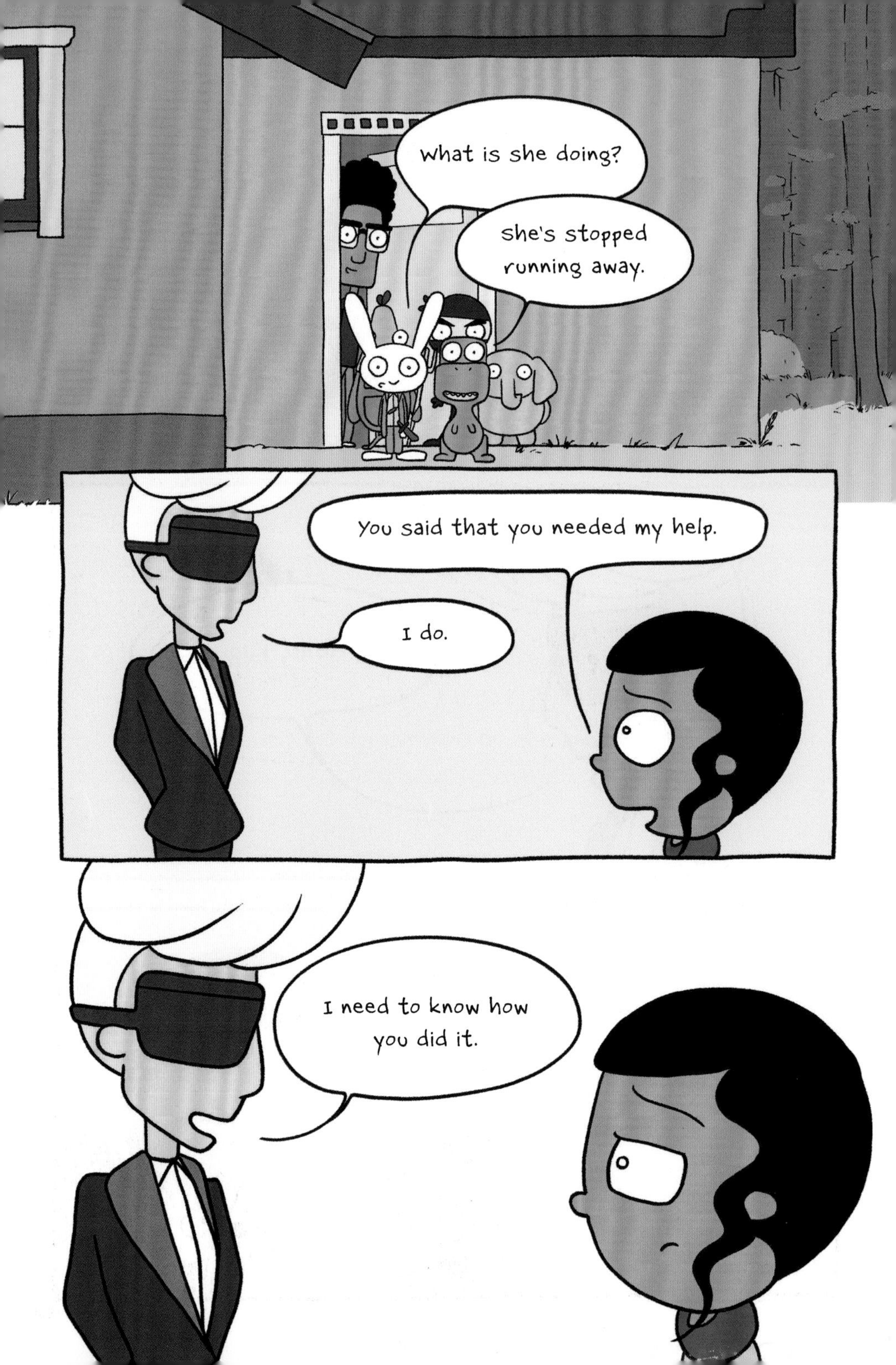
what is she doing?
she's stopped running away.
You said that you needed my help.
I do.
I need to know how you did it.

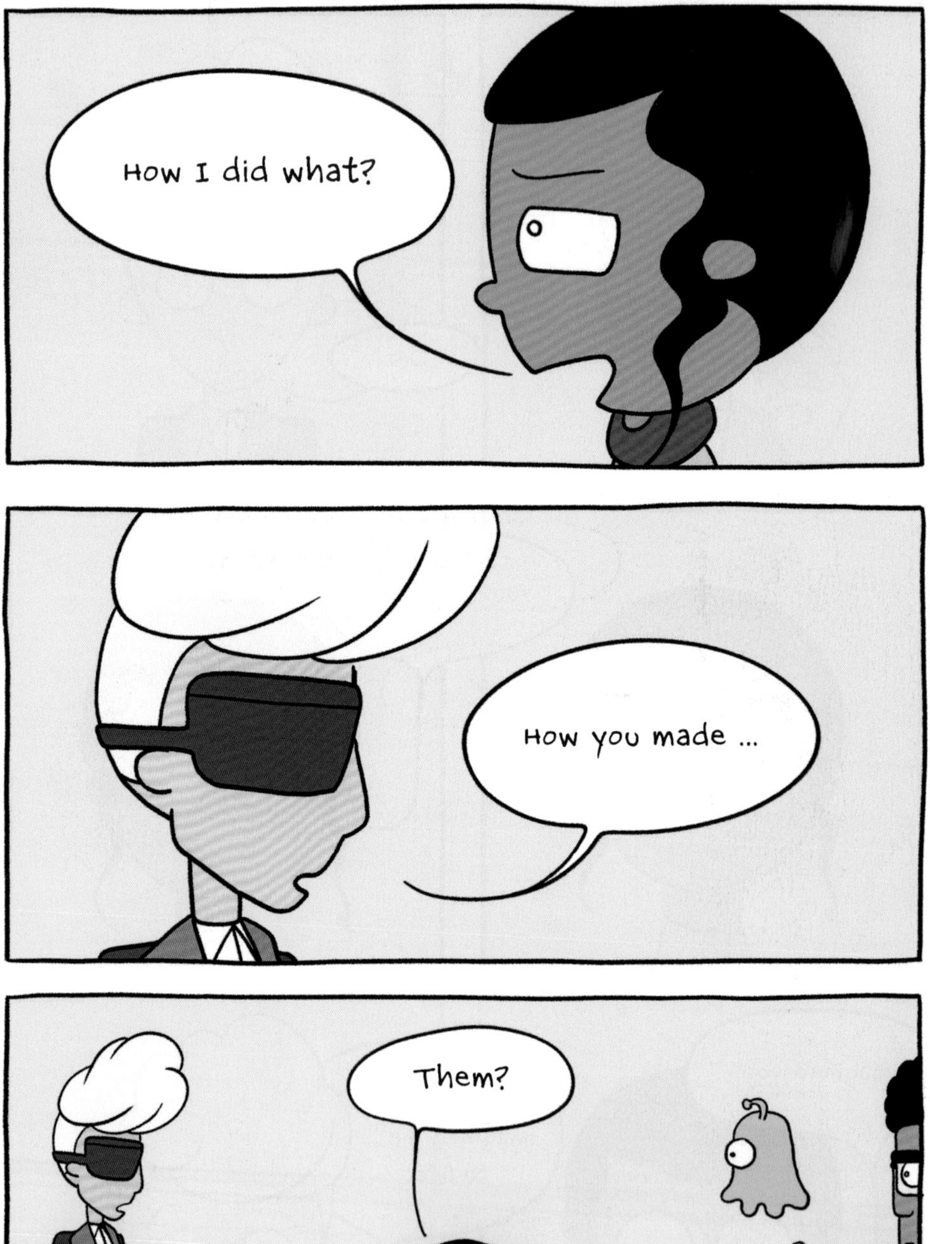
How I did what?
How you made ...
Them?

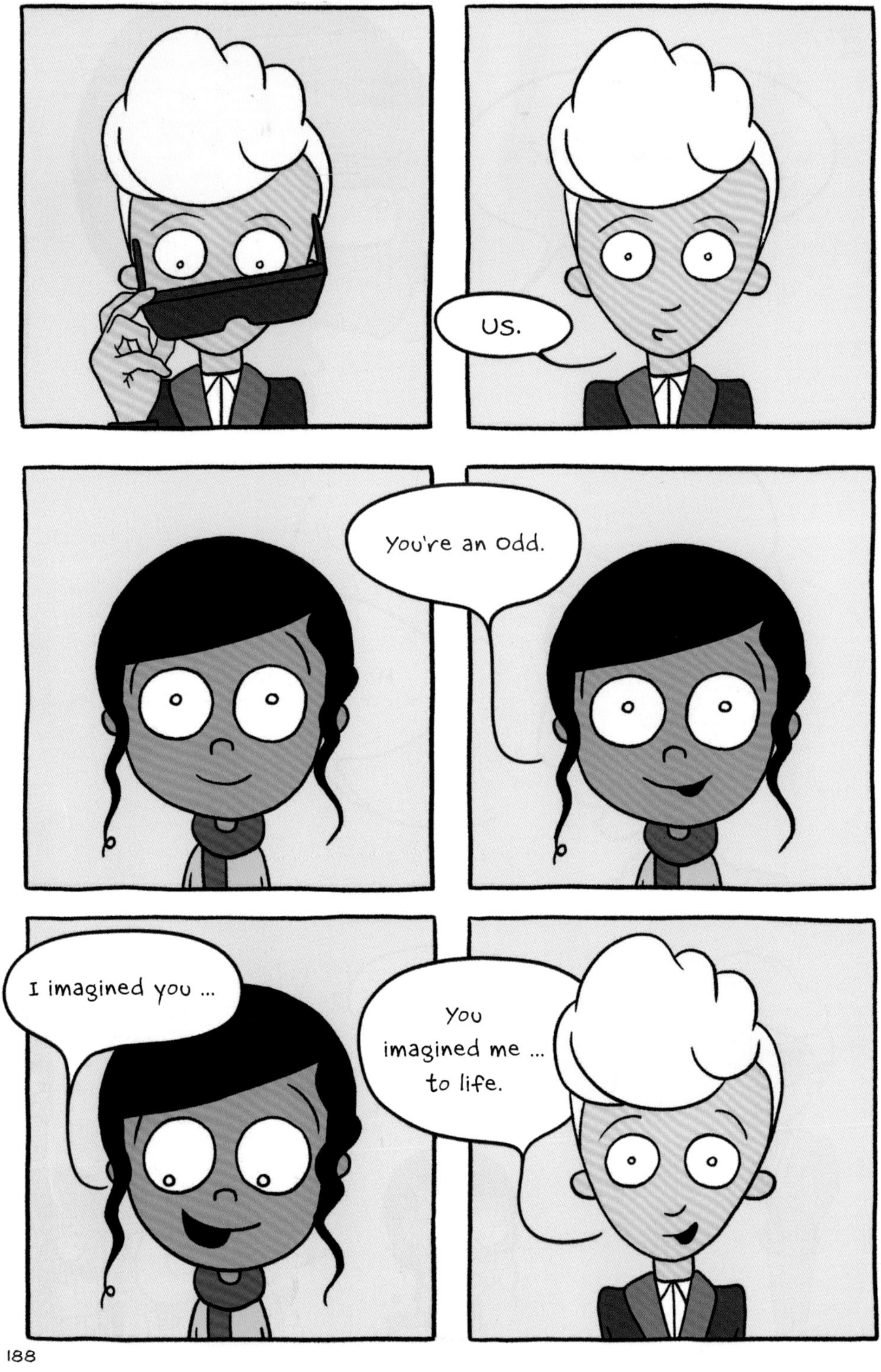
US.
You're an odd.
I imagined you ...
You imagined me ... to life.

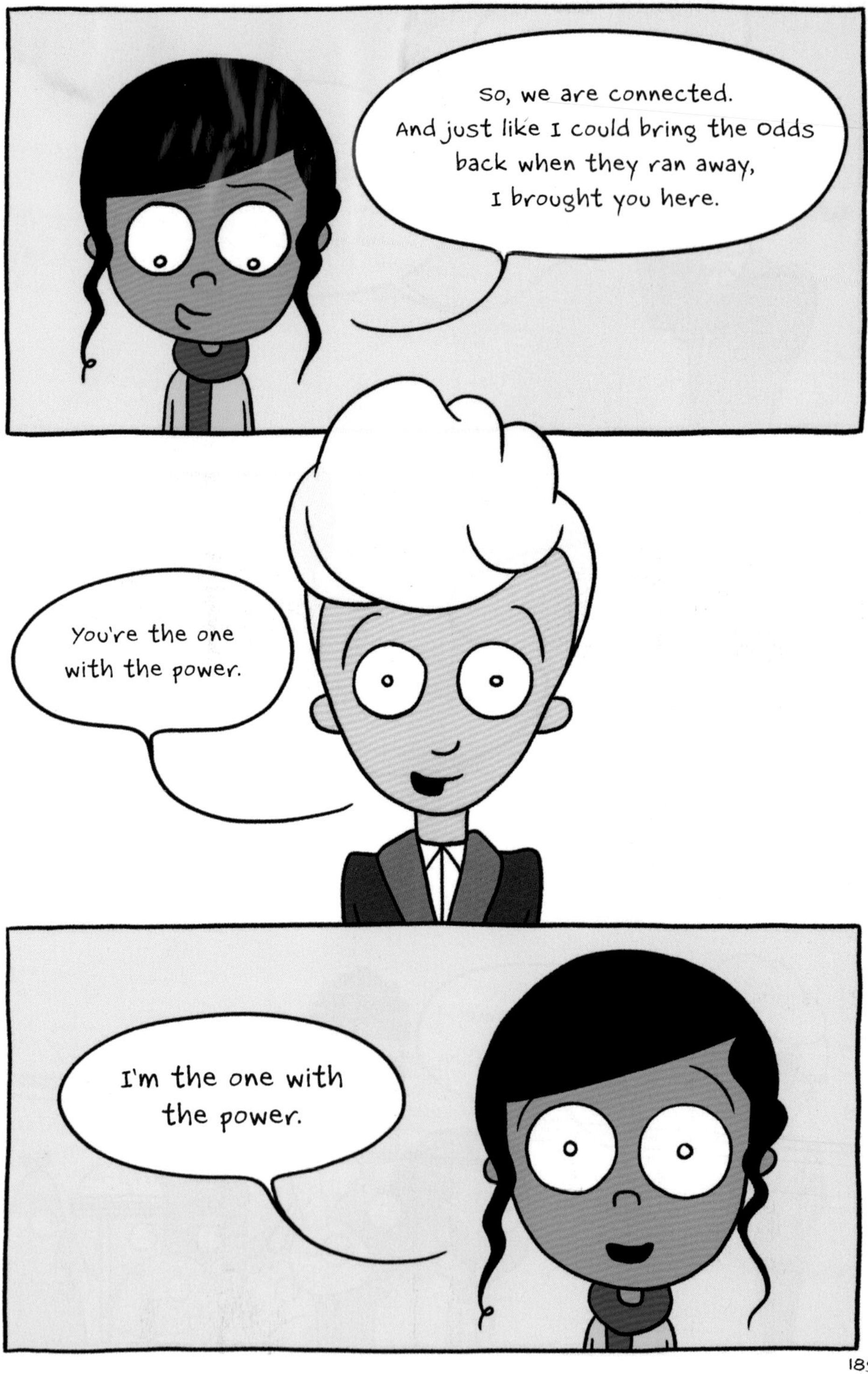
So, we are connected. And just like I could bring the odds back when they ran away, I brought you here.
You're the one with the power.
I'm the one with the power.

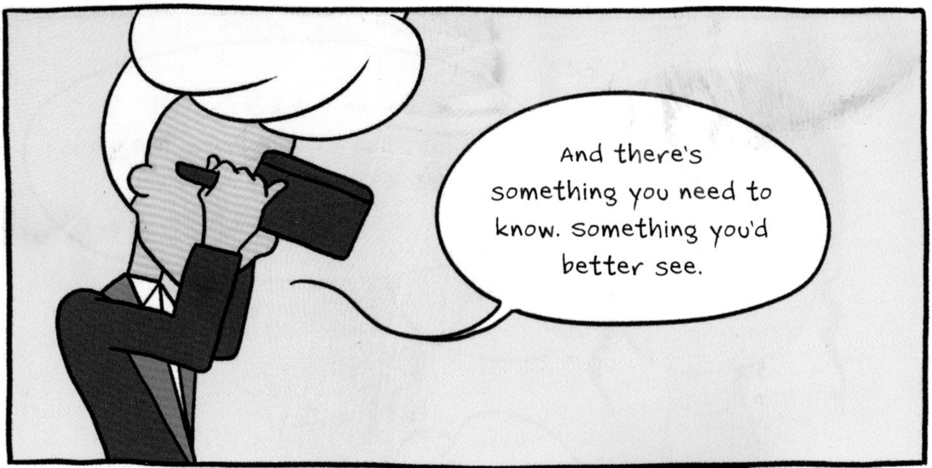
And there's something you need to know. Something you'd better see.

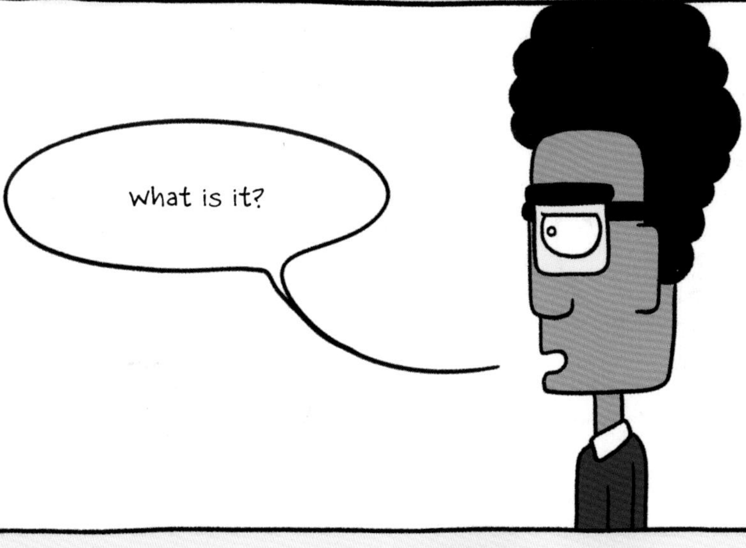
What is it?

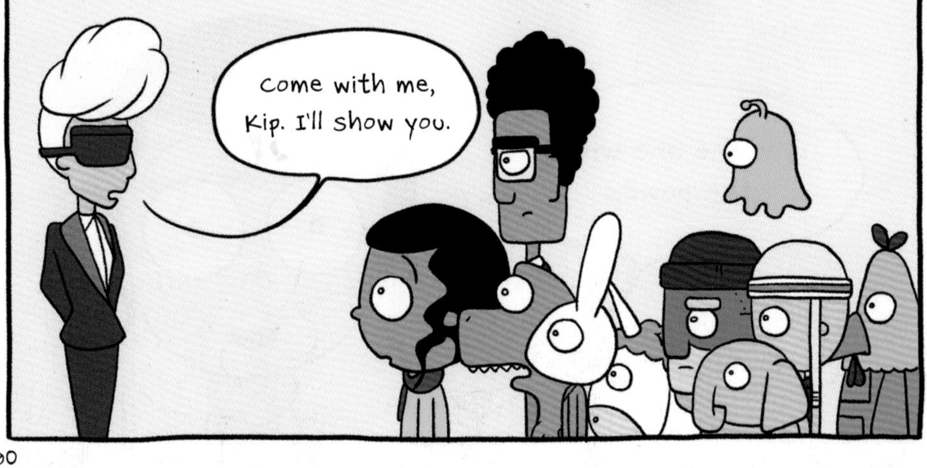
Come with me, Kip. I'll show you.

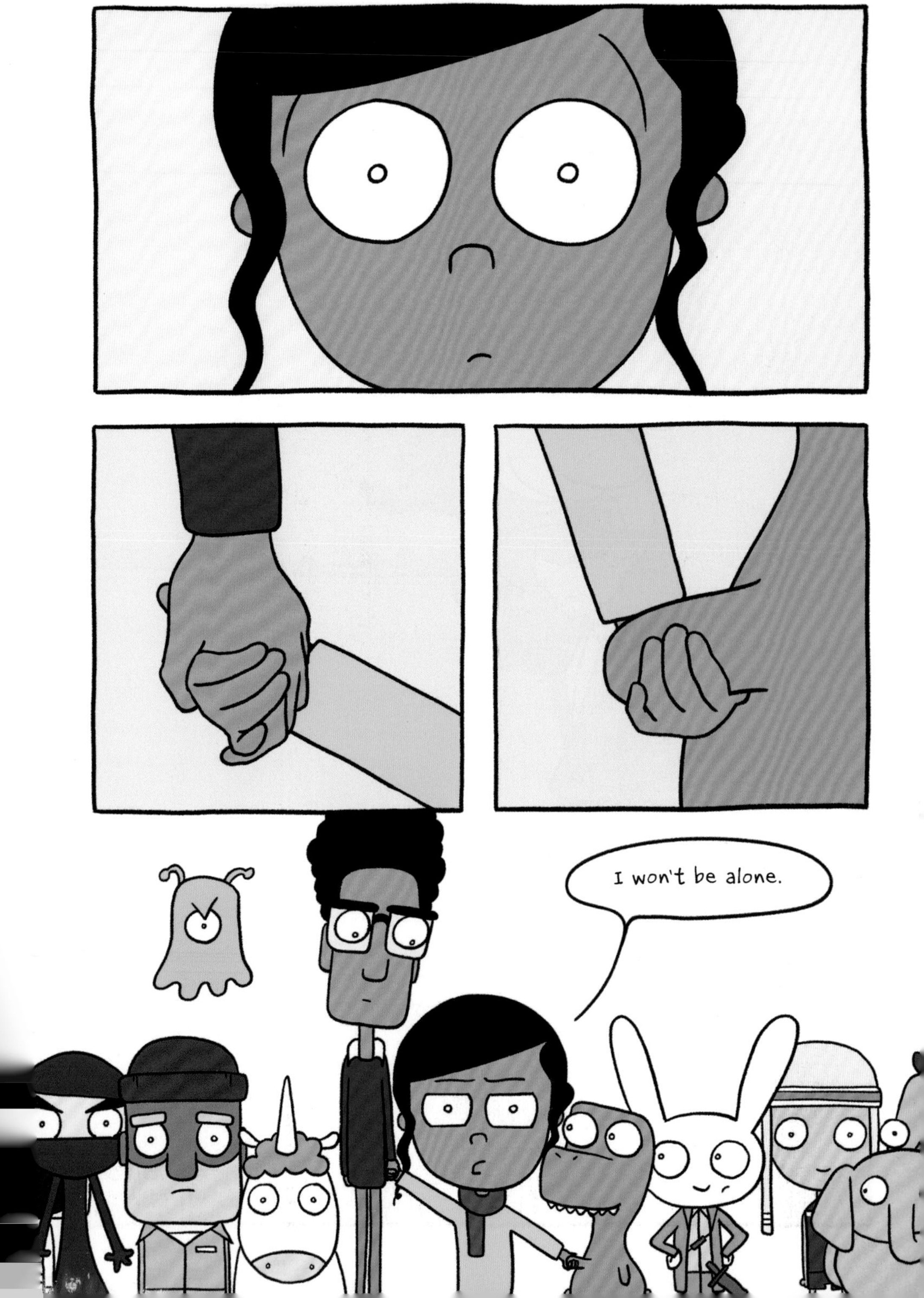
I won't be alone.

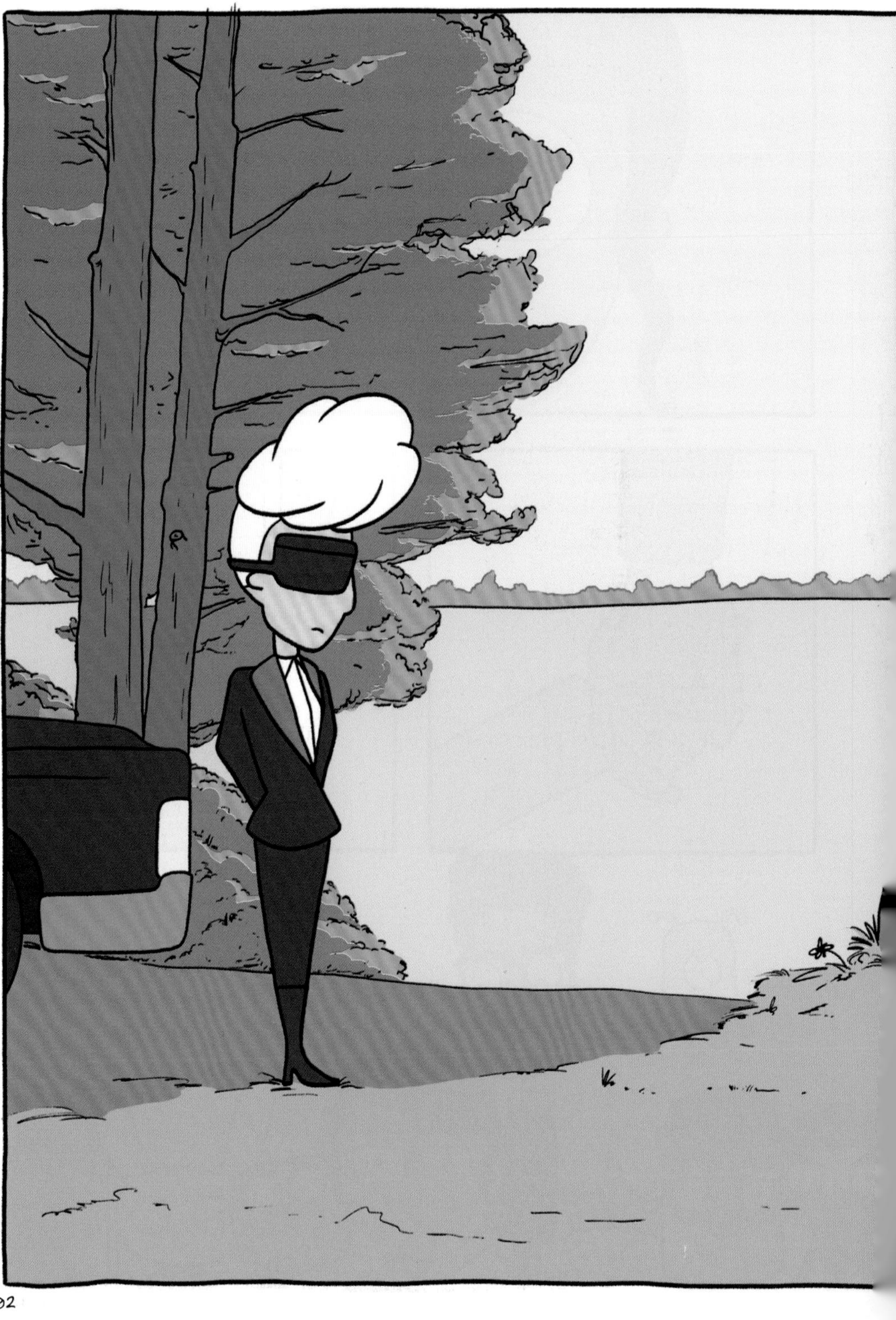

funny kid

You've read them all, right?

RUNNING FOR PRESIDENT
HAS NEVER BEEN FUNNIER
funny kid
for president
Matt Stanton

BEING A STAR
HAS NEVER BEEN THIS FUNNY
funny kid
stand up
Matt Stanton

PLAYING PRANKS
HAS NEVER BEEN FUNNIER
funny kid
prank wars
Matt Stanton

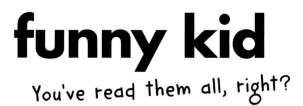

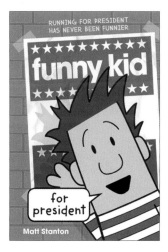

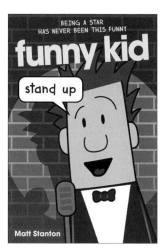

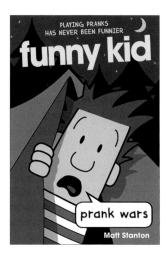

Books by Matt Stanton

Funny Kid series

Funny Kid for President

Funny Kid Stand Up

Funny Kid Prank Wars

The Odds series

The Odds

The Odds: Run, Odds, Run

Look out for the incredible conclusion
to **THE ODDS TRILOGY**

Also available ...

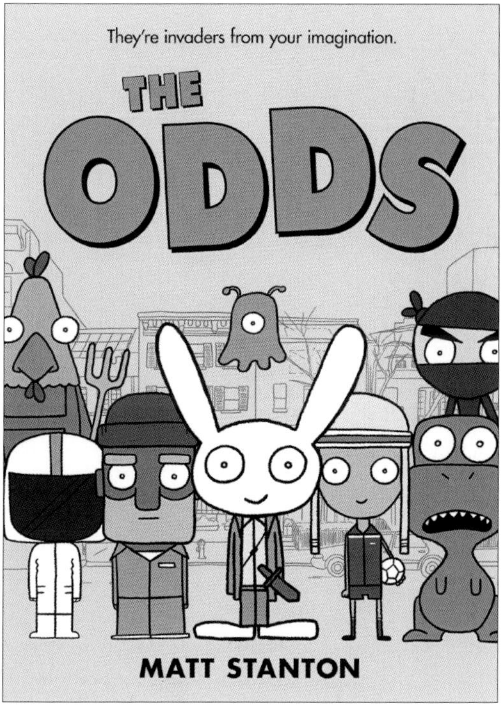
They're invaders from your imagination.
THE
ODDS
MATT STANTON

Kip is a quiet kid in a loud city. She's easy to miss and that's the way she likes it.

Then, one day, Kip's life is interrupted when ten of her favorite characters step out of their worlds and into hers.

Meet the Odds ... because fitting in is overrated.

**Kids all over the world
are emailing Matt!**

**Who's your favorite Odd?
Tell Matt!**

matt.stanton@gmail.com

the world – Bonnie, Boston, Miller, and Sully. This book is for you.

I still can't believe it, but in my Team of Wonderfuls I also have thousands and thousands of kids who take the time out of their busy lives to send me emails. These are children from all around the world, most of whom I will never get to actually meet. But still, you send me encouraging letters and tell me how these stories have traveled from my imagination, through a book, and into your imagination. That means we have connected and that's such an honor for me. You tell me that the stories mean something to you, and that is the most inspiring thing of all.

Thank you for being in my Team of Wonderfuls. I really couldn't do hard things without you all.

Matt Stanton

Sewankambo, Jemma Myors, Rachel Cramp, Kelli Lonergan, Fiona Luke, Janelle Garside, Amy Fox, Karen-Maree Griffiths, Pauline O'Carolan, Elizabeth O'Donnell, Brendon Redmond, Emily Mannon, Anna Bernard, Andrea Vandergrift, and Carolina Ortiz.

Thank you to all the people who work at the printers, drive the trucks, and unload the boxes. Thank you to those who work in bookshops and libraries, putting these books onto shelves and helping kids find them. Thank you to the teachers who read my stories in class and light a spark in young imaginations every day.

As always, a special thanks to Chren Byng. You have been with me every step and there's a part of you in each of my stories. I wouldn't want it any other way.

Thank you to Natalie Buckley-Cartwright for the hours you have poured into making *Run, Odds, Run* come to life.

Thank you to Beck Stanton – my love and all-of-life partner. I could write a hundred books marveling at who you are. Thank you to my favorite kids in all

ACKNOWLEDGMENTS

We very rarely do anything truly on our own. When we try and do something really hard we nearly always have partners, teammates, and supporters. These are the people who stand alongside us and will us forward. They tell us to keep going when we just want to stop. They know when to give us a hug, pat us on the back, or turn the music up really loud and start a dance party. Sometimes they even bring snacks.

I think these people are called our Team of Wonderfuls. Kip has her dad and the Odds. I'm curious about who is in your Team of Wonderfuls. This is the spot in the book where I get to say thank you to mine.

Thank you to the incredible book experts I get to work with – Chren Byng, David Linker, Kate Burnitt, Angie Masters, Cristina Cappelluto, Jim Demetriou, Michelle Weisz, Kady Gray, Yvonne

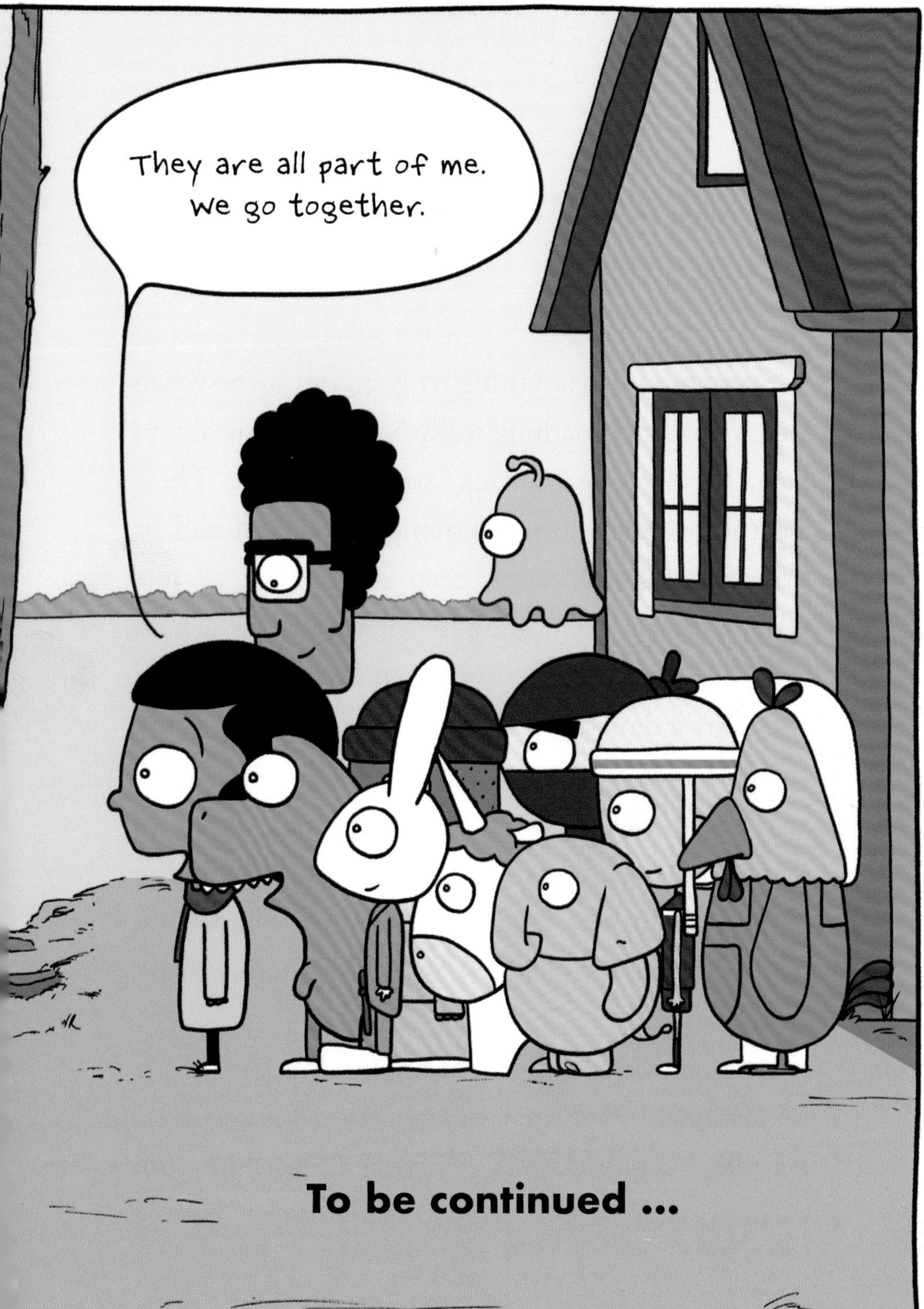
They are all part of me. We go together.
To be continued ...

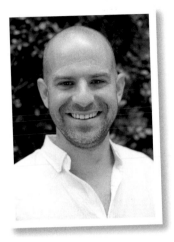

Matt Stanton is a bestselling children's author and illustrator who has sold more than one million books worldwide. His middle grade series Funny Kid debuted as the #1 Australian kids' book and has legions of fans across the globe. He has published such bestselling picture books as *There Is a Monster Under My Bed Who Farts*, *This Is a Ball*, and *Pea + Nut!*, and he produces a daily YouTube show for kids. He lives and works in Sydney, Australia, with his wife, bestselling author Beck Stanton, and their children.

mattstanton.net

Come and subscribe to Matt's YouTube Channel!

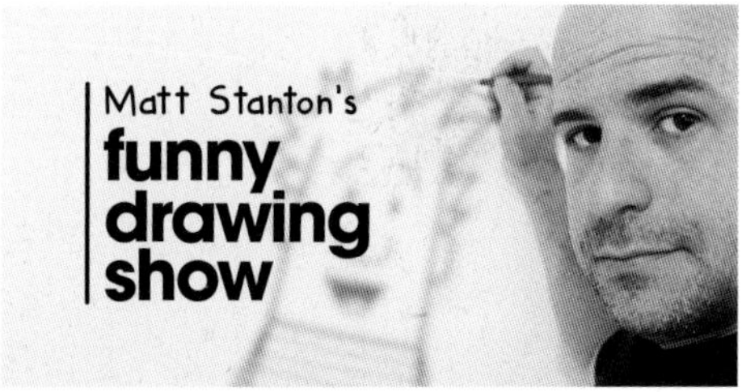
Matt Stanton's
funny drawing show

We learn to draw funny stuff!

Talk about how to write funny stories!

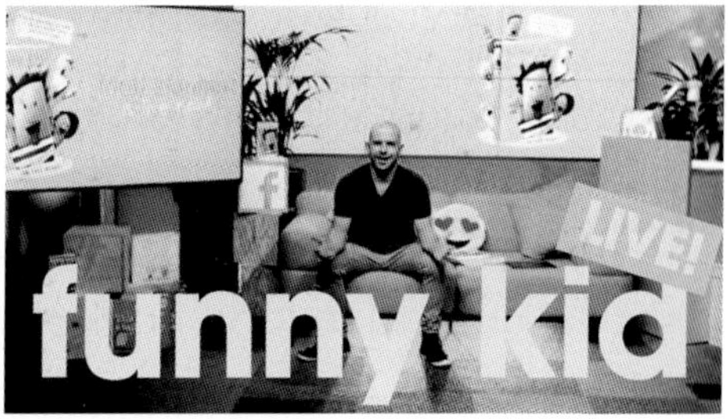
LIVE!
funny kid

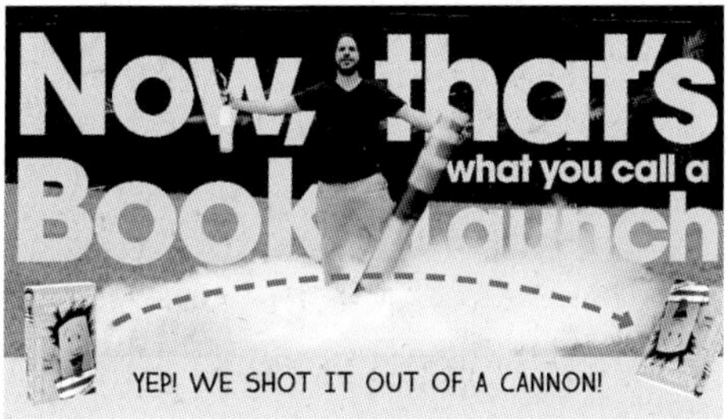
Now, that's
what you call a
Book Launch
YEP! WE SHOT IT OUT OF A CANNON!

And sometimes we launch a book out of a cannon!

MattStantonTV

youtube.com/mattstanton

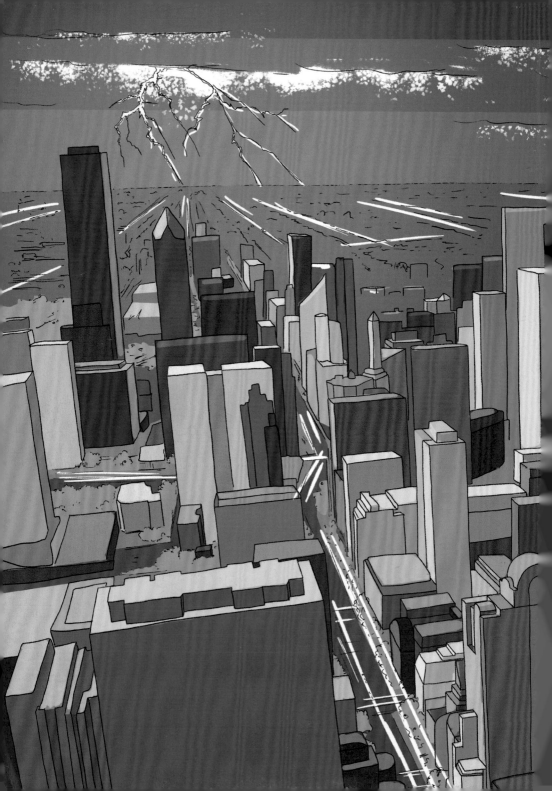

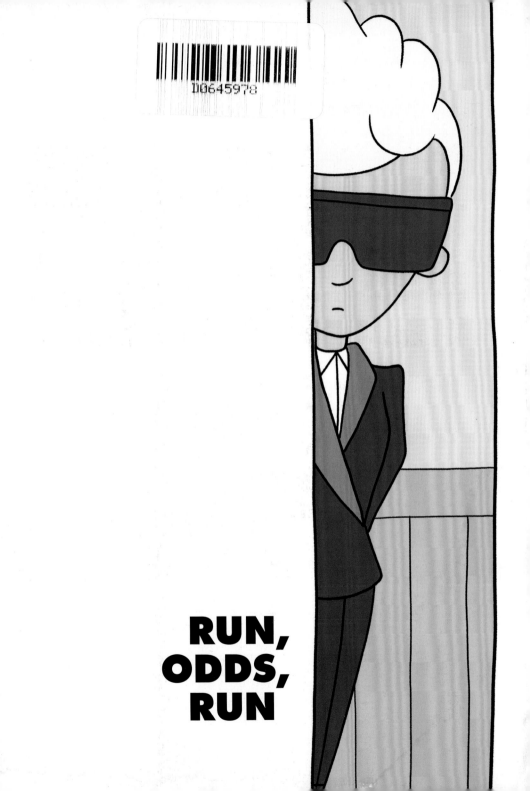

RUN,
ODDS,
RUN